The Other Hand

Other works by Deena Metzger:

Fiction

Skin Shadows / Silence
The Woman Who Slept With Men to Take the War Out of Them
What Dinah Thought

Non-fiction

Writing for Your Life
Tree Essays and Pieces
Intimate Nature The Bond Between Women and Animals
(with Brenda Peterson and Linda Hogan)

Poetry

Dark Milk
The Axis Mundi Poems
Looking for the Faces of God
A Sabbath Among the Ruins

Plays

The Book of Hags
Not As Sleepwalkers
Dreams Against The State

The Other Hand

✳

a novel

Deena Metzger

Red Hen Press | *Pasadena, CA*

This is a work of fiction, all the characters are imagined, even those who seem to have namesakes in the so called real world. It is often necessary to create an imaginal world in order to tell a true story; I have taken many liberties in the construction of this tale.

Book layout by Bryan Wong

ISBN: 978-1-59709-480-1 (Tradepaper)

The National Endowment for the Arts, the Los Angeles County Arts Commission, the Ahmanson Foundation, the Dwight Stuart Youth Fund, the Max Factor Family Foundation, the Pasadena Tournament of Roses Foundation, the Pasadena Arts & Culture Commission and the City of Pasadena Cultural Affairs Division, the City of Los Angeles Department of Cultural Affairs, the Audrey & Sydney Irmas Charitable Foundation, the Kinder Morgan Foundation, the Meta & George Rosenberg Foundation, the Albert and Elaine Borchard Foundation, the Adams Family Foundation, the Riordan Foundation, Amazon Literary Partnership, and the Mara W. Breech Foundation partially support Red Hen Press.

Second Edition
Published by Red Hen Press
www.redhen.org

Acknowledgements

A novel is a little world and so comes to be, like everything else, through mysterious circumstances, invisible agents and much human effort and assistance. Perhaps more than most, this novel arises from such a field and I am indebted first to what I cannot name but that the general term for such a companion or influence is Spirit. The circumstances of writing this book were such that I must acknowledge that Spirit assisted me and was alongside me, sustained me and informed me in the long years of study, the weeks of pilgrimage and the work of conceiving, researching, writing and rewriting this text; for this ineffable alliance I am humbled and grateful beyond words. Though I take full responsibility for the flaws and limitations, still I must say I could not have written this book alone and I didn't write it alone.

Assistance both for the pilgrimage and the writing came in many ways and forms from people known and unknown to me.

First I want to thank my husband, Michael Ortiz Hill, who heard with a shudder the first words with which Peter Schmidt entered my [our] life and knowing something of what was coming, what such a preoccupation might mean, still encouraged me even to insisting upon accompanying me to the Camps when I had the mad idea of going alone and who has stood by me through what were often hellish times in the thirteen years that I have been, one way or another, working on this book.

It is also my great fortune that I have married not only a loving and tender man but the best editor I ever hope to meet. Michael read the book in various versions and through countless days and nights of conversation and offered me his unerring eye, insight, heart and counsel which was, of course, informed by the fact that he had also been *there*.

I am grateful for the many evenings I have been privileged to spend with mathematician and hermeneuticist Ralph Abraham at his home at Santa Cruz, looking up at the stars with the perplexing and inexplicable sense that what we knew, sensed, intuited, somehow came from that direction, that we were being led to something, and were alongside so many others privileged and responsible, collectively, to enact or to speak or to be guardians of what might be given to us.

I am thankful to Reb Zalman Schacter-Shalomi whose spiritual guidance shaped the way I approached the Camps and what I brought back with me and how I've understood it. Thank you also to Bruria Finkel for the prayer she translated from the Spanish Jewish mystic Abulafia; it sustained me while I was there and continues to do so to this day.

I wish to thank Rakhel Kaplan for arranging an impossible trip and for introducing us to Klaus Weber who hosted us at his Inn in Mittersal; to Kristof Nowak who led us through Warsaw and Peter Schnitzler; Alexa Sekyra and Angela Roethe for being willing to walk with us through Dachau and comforting us during this bleak journey, and to Susan Tanner for introducing us to Peter and Maya Ulbrich who helped us feel welcome and even comfortable in East Berlin. At Auschwitz we were the guests of the Carmelite Nuns at Karmelitanki Bose and at Dachau we were the guest of the Nuns at Karmel Heililg Blut. In both Karmels we were treated with the utmost kindness and respect, and the spiritual presence and generosity of these women eased our pain. To Claire Ortiz Hill for her spiritual insights on matters Catholic, particularly regarding Edith Stein who became Sister Theresa Benedicta.

On my return, I was grateful to be able to consider, with Rabbi Arthur Waskow, Phyllis Waskow and with Gilda Franz, the nature of the journey and the vision/dream I had at Dachau; without their counsel and insight I might never have trusted the vision and so might not have committed to writing the book.

I thank Dr. John Seeley who led me with the utmost wisdom and caring through all the rings of hell in order to be able to see the wonders of paradise. Enormous thanks, also, to him for helping me decipher the Hebrew Letters I saw in the furnace and who, thereby, influenced the direction of the novel.

I thank Karen Gottlieb for insisting during one night that I do the assignment I had given to the writing class that I teach, for it was that night that Peter Schmidt appeared.

I appreciate the devoted and loving labor of Barbara Lipscomb who assisted me every step of the way, accompanying me through the horror as well as the wonder and who tirelessly and bravely researched a field that is painful and disorienting at its best. As my assistant at the time, I relied on her entirely and was gifted by her in countless ways. I also wish to thank my current assistant, Don Chin, whose devotion and dedication makes such writing possible.

When the book was underway and Daniella Stonebrook Blue and Peter Schmidt began to have lives of their own with particular birthdays, I asked the astrologer Geraldine Hannon to prepare their charts, which she did with terrifying accuracy and confirmed, thereby, the unfathomable mysteries and strange reality of the imagination.

Sometimes a single word, comment or gesture can make a great difference. I thank Connie Zweig for giving me Richard Grossinger's remarkable book, *The Night Sky;* and Irene Borger for her knowing the origin of champagne and for being a sister writer to me, providing the writerly company I longed for. To Brian Swimme, Rick Talbot, George B. Coyne S.J., Barrie Thorne, Kip Thorne, Sara Rajan, Hede von Nagel and Ralph Metzner appreciation for their counsel and assistance. And to all the writers whose extraordinary work is the intellectual foundation of this book, particularly, Charlotte Beradt, Richard Bessel, Robert Brawer, Fritjof Capra, John Mosley, Timothy Ferris, Martin Gillbert, Stephen W. Hawking, Raul Hilberg, David Hughes, Renya Kilkielko, Robert Jay Lifton, Alan Lightman, Joan Oates, Richard Preston, Denise Overbye, Ka-Tzetnik 135633, Klaus Theweleit, Steven W. Weinberg, Fred Alan Wolf, Mike Zwerin. Gratitude for the magic "brain pan" of Andra Akers who, knowing no boundaries between dimensions, assured me after reading the manuscript, that a unified field theory, encompassing the physical universe, the psychological realms and the spiritual is not only possible but necessary.

To my dear dear friends and writing companions who listened to me, encouraged me, restored me and also read and reread the manuscript in its various stages so that it could come to fruition: Marc Kaminsky, Ariel Dorfman, Naomi Newman, Peter Levitt, Pami Blue Hawk, Maia, Jonathan Omer-Man. And to Sara Blackburn who edited the final manuscript with such care, insight and intelligence, also, great thanks to Pami Blue Hawk, who made the medicine bundle that protected me at the camps.

To my sons and daughters and grand-daughters, to my family, kin and friends who are the ground, who create the little world in which I live and where this work is centered.

To Ron Eglash who as a scientist edited the manuscript for its scientific accuracy, I feel more grateful than I can say for the call to write this book took me into territories that were entirely new to me.

And to my agent, Muriel Nellis who has been so encouraging and who has stood behind me with this book. And to Kate Gale and Mark E. Cull of Red Hen Press who have brought this book into the world with such care, generosity and dedication.

And, finally, enormous gratitude to a man I have never met and do not know but who inspired this book and called it forth: Thank you Cardinal Lustiger, Your Eminence.

Again, then to return to the unknown dimensions from which this book emerges . . . my gratitude for the privilege of writing it and bringing it into the world.

For my father, Arnold Posy, who taught me the words for light and dark

And for the two who made the ordeal and challenge of this book possible:
John Seeley who offered me the guidance and blessings of the Father

and

Michael Ortiz Hill who provided both worldly and spiritual
companionship on the journey.

Mene Mene Tekel Upharsin
*We have been weighed in the balance
and found wanting*

I

Origins

Chapter 1

November 17, 1989
Dear Cardinal Lustiger, Your Eminence:

My name is Daniella Stonebrook Blue. I am—or was—by profession an astronomer. We are strangers to each other. Your name was given to me by a woman on a bus as we were traveling across New Mexico. Because of her insistence, I am writing to you about this dark period of my life. I need to speak to you about the matter of light.

Light is the alphabet of God. I knew this when I was born and then I forgot. This is the first time I have understood it as an adult woman. Even as I prepared to write these words, I didn't know what they implied until they appeared on the page.

Cardinal, this incident occurred at The Mountain Observatory where I have been Astronomer in Residence for many years.

School children are regularly invited to spend a few days living in tents in a nearby mountain campground. The highlight of the trip is an afternoon visit to Big Eye, the telescope, at the Observatory. A few years ago, one of the teachers told us that a little boy had peered up at the night sky from his sleeping bag and asked fearfully, "What are them things?" At the moment she said this, the teacher, the children and I were in a basement room among computers and monitors looking at data that had been gathered the night before by one of my colleagues who had been mapping an unexplored section of the deep sky. The images, if I didn't know how to read them, would not have looked like sky at all. The brilliant tones of blue, gold, magenta and black on the screens could well have been abstract patterns designed for dyeing silk and rayon.

"Can you show the children what you're doing here with these machines?" the teacher asked. "Can you explain the stars?"

Before I was twelve, I decided to study the stars because I loved them so much. Originally, science wasn't the language I wanted to speak, but I thought that when I mastered it, I would be among friends who were as taken by the wonder as I was. At some point, I hoped the mysteries would be revealed to me through or alongside science as they had been to Bruno and to Kepler and even to Einstein, but when he was an old man. I wanted this though Bruno was burned at the stake for his vision and Kepler and Einstein suffered their own forms of hell for what they saw. But I was never taken into the mysteries. Circumstances never required me to struggle to find exact language for what Kepler called the "harmony of the world." By the time I was in graduate school, I was completely absorbed in the ways and means of my chosen field. The memory of my early love of light, the child's knowledge that all light, all life comes from the stars, slowly diminished, then disappeared.

I don't know if I could have told you what a star is when I was young, but I had an idea that the light that came from it wrote secret words on my skin and these words were nutrients that I took in and they made me what I am. Only unlike food which nourished the body in its predetermined form, starlight invisibly inscribed its own image. Did this happen to everyone? I didn't think so. Why not? You had to want it. You had to call the light in. Light was a being, like Tinkerbell in Peter Pan, that you invited into your body and then she made magic.

Where did this idea come from? I think I dreamed it.

We were living back east when my parents, Aram and Rosa, asked me what I wanted for my tenth birthday; I could have anything I wanted.

"I want to go to the desert where I was born," I said, "to sleep under the stars." They didn't try to dissuade me even though they knew, and I didn't, that winter in the southwest meant snow. I had thought going west meant following the sun.

They rented a cabin in a desolate area. Just as it was turning dark, I was bundled up in stockings, wool socks, ski pants, jacket, cap and tucked into a blue down sleeping bag laid upon an air mattress on a double tarp overlaying the thin scattering of snow. They left me alone on the spot I had chosen where nothing obstructed my view of the sky or interfered with that tremulous, remote light.

It began to rain. It awakened me and I lay with it falling upon my skin without opening my eyes. If I opened my eyes, I would have to go inside, but if I kept them closed I was safe from the impact of the rain. The rain fell in distinct crystalline drops as if it were hail. I could feel each drop individually. Not only on my face but all over my body. I threw off the sleeping bag because I was afraid the dampened feathers would never dry out and then I undressed and folded the tarp about everything to keep it dry. I would dry off later and, anyway, the water wouldn't soak into me. But I was wrong. The rain did soak into me. It landed upon me and disappeared. It penetrated my skin. I kept my eyes closed but I couldn't keep the presence of the rain away from my eyes. The rain fell on my lids. It passed through them into my eyes. I was porous and thirsty as earth, dissolving in the rain, muddy with it.

Some hours later, I stretched my hand out, the surrounding earth was dry and cold while I, myself, was waterlogged. Finally, I opened my eyes almost to defend myself against the deluge.

It was raining stars.

When I really awakened from my dream, it was the middle of a cold clear night. A slight breeze ruffled the sleeping bag zipped up to my chin. There was not a cloud in the sky.

Another early memory is of a luminous woman shining at the foot of my bed. Fascinated and afraid, I watched—her body, long hair and white dress were composed of light—until she set with the stars in the sky. It wasn't only that she was shining, it was that in her presence, I was shining too, or so I thought, or so it felt. She seemed benevolent; I was not afraid. So only when the woman completely disappeared did I tiptoe into my parents' room and lie down on the bed on my father's side.

In the morning, I told him that the woman had been shining, I didn't tell him everything. "Shining like a nebula," I said, proud that I knew the word. "There was a nebula by my bed."

"It was a dream," Aram assured me the way adults dismiss children, but then he thought better of it: "Don't you think?"

"No." Then I had to say something that would seem credible. "I think it was your mother shining like a star."

He laughed but it seemed half-hearted. "When you die, you die," he answered me. "Why do you say that?"

"Because of what I have seen, Dani."

"What have you seen, Aram?"

Even though I had been calling him and my mother by their first names since I learned to talk, he wouldn't answer my question. When I pressed him, he said I was too young to know. It was a breach between us. Now I would say it was like a tear in space-time. He had never said such a thing to me before, and it impressed me as much as the apparition.

I turned to Rosa who, as usual, was looking away. I was a child who was piqued and so persisted. "Don't you think it was Dad's mother?" I asked her. Rosa remained stone-faced and adamant: "We don't talk about such things." It was not the last time my mother said those words, nor the first.

I never spoke about the woman again nor the rain of stars, nor any other experiences I might have had of a similar nature. Silence was a practice in my household and I quickly learned its nature and possibilities. When I was young, it allowed me to emulate Aram and Rosa, but it had other advantages: I heard things in the silence and they kept me company. As I grew older, these silent things faded away and I forgot.

Forgetting was painless; I didn't notice. I was content, satisfied, successful, I thought, or rather I didn't think about such things. I didn't realize I had fallen into or had been, unwittingly, dispatched to a world where what I had learned in silence went unacknowledged and finally disappeared.

How subtly a world configures about silence. I had learned, without realizing there was a lesson, that you may talk about certain forms of the invisible but not others. This information served me well. When I was in graduate school, and later at The Mountain, I was sensitive to the prohibitions.

You may talk about quarks though no one has ever seen one, but you may not talk about angels though they were seen with some frequency by several writers in my grandmother's library. The Babylonians made precise mathematical calculations of the movements of the stars, sun, moon and planets and these accomplishments are respected. They also charted thirty-six stars rising just before sunrise in the paths of the gods and accorded their lives to these divine stellar influences; these persuasions are considered absurd. Similarly, if you are interested in the star the Babylonian Magi followed, it may only be as a matter of archaeoastronomy but not as a matter of belief. You may speak about red shifts and blue shifts, about different wave lengths and their effect upon us, about the consequences of radiation but you must not speak, as Kepler did, of the individual soul bearing the imprint of the sky through angles of light.

Current scientific theory has it that the four forces—gravity, the strong nuclear force, the weak nuclear force and the electromagnetic fields—were divided from each other during the first seconds of the universe. Afterwards they were compatible with each other but operated differently. In the world into which I fell, there are two strong forces, the sacred and scientific, which were also split apart from each other in a series of cataclysmic events some as powerful as the Big Bang. Only these two realms are no longer governed by the same laws as they once were. They are no longer compatible.

My colleagues, Cardinal, are trying to go back to those first seconds in order to understand the way that everything emerged in a wild explosion out of a single point so dense that a universe such as ours might have been contained within it. I strike a match listening to the sizzle, watching the flare. A little mini demonstration; I like striking matches. Imagine if the flame expanded and kept going for billions of years and became a world. And then in order to know where they came from, and more importantly where they were going, some future cosmologists followed the fire back to the original spark. Will they find someone holding a match? I wouldn't have known how to entertain that question a few years ago. It was inconceivable that there might be something at the end of that trajectory that was not a mass of particles squished into a hot glowing point.

I'm going to make a cup of tea. In order to light a fire on the gas stove, I have to strike a match; it doesn't have an automatic pilot.

Here's the mystery, Cardinal. In order to find out where you're going, you have to go back to see where you come from to discover the nature of that point of origin. The theory is that everything developed as it did according to some simple and beautiful laws. If you know them, you have power. Some people think they can make their own worlds with this knowledge.

I didn't think about it this way when I was a kid. But I did have an idea that something was holding the match. And that's what I forgot.

I tell you what I forgot, Cardinal, and then I tell you what I remember, as if I hadn't forgotten at all. That's not how it is. I've been remembering these last years. But, frankly, remembering wasn't my choice. I was forced into it.

Now, I'm like an old woman who unravels a sweater she's knit in order to pick up a stitch here and there that she dropped. When she gets to the last pucker, she realizes the entire sweater is undone and she has to start again. She's at the beginning then and careful this time to include this thread of nettles here and that thread of nettles there with the hope that at the end of it all she will at least have a garment.

I didn't think of Bruno when I was a young girl. I mean I didn't think of his death. I was glad, actually, I was proud that he knew that Copernicus was right and the planets revolve around the sun. By then it also seemed so obvious that there were worlds beyond our little system. I gave no thought to the fact that the Church burned Bruno for thinking this. For this and saying that there were ways to know it that were beyond ecclesiastical revelation and beyond observation. Ways of knowing that came from inside. So they tied him to a little pyre of wood and struck a match. That part I didn't think about until recently. That and there being ways of knowing the stars that are unrelated to the telescope. Something besides Big Eye.

That's my sweater hanging on the hook. Next to it is Lance's. He's my lover and visits occasionally. You know I'm not working at The Mountain anymore. I like this old sweater. Forget the tea. I'm going to put the sweater on and go up the hill behind this cottage to look at the sky. No stars tonight, it's clouding over. It's cold outside.

This is what I'm thinking, Your Eminence. A sky where bits of knowledge and ways of knowing rotate in separate orbits about the same star. Maybe it's just debris. But maybe not. These orbits may actually constitute different dimensions, different ways of understanding. Sometimes these seemingly stable orbits shift as unprecedented and unexpected changes in mass or velocity occur. This, in turn, changes their gravitational relationships. Perhaps they intersect or smash into each other with unpredictable consequences.

What if we could reconcile these realms with their distinct epistemologies? What if we could find a theory containing the common principles underlying both synchronicity and space-time mathematics, a theory that spoke of the behavior of elementary particles as described by physics and the influence, let's say, of the zodiac. It would be one hell of a unified field theory that integrates metaphysics, science and ethics.

What a relief, Cardinal, I did it. I started the letter. I won't be gone long. Half an hour. And then I'll continue this letter until I've told you everything. I don't know how long it will take. Maybe months. Maybe years. To your health, Cardinal.

Chapter 2

This morning, Cardinal, before I sat down to the computer, I deliberately broke a glass. I wrapped it in a white table napkin and stomped on it. For a long time I sat outside in the cold, early winter light with the broken pieces in my hand. I could have made a fist around the broken glass or slit my wrist with that one triangular piece which is pointed and sharp. These are possibilities, not options. Instead I spilled the slivers across my desk like stars scattered through a galaxy.

As this winter sun, so low in the sky, hit the glass shards they glinted and led me to think that if I selected exactly the right piece, I would be able to reconstruct the entire glass. Then I picked up the pieces with an impatient sweep of the cloth and sat down at the computer once again.

Look at my lined palm. What do you think? Does it look like a map of the Perseid meteor shower, shooting stars streaking across the sky? Or traces of particles accelerating through a cloud chamber? After staring a few minutes, I don't recognize my own hand.

Your Eminence, I have started this letter so many times. Excuse me for . . . Oh, look, I have barely introduced myself or the subject of this letter and I am already apologizing. For what? For bringing you into this situation? By this audacious act, I contrive that our paths cross. Some minute invisible particles are said to pass through the earth without leaving a mark. But usually when two bodies collide there is an explosion or other serious consequences. Hydrogen meets oxygen, Pfft. Water. Is our meeting such a reconciliation? Will we continue together on a new road neither of us has walked? Or is this path the rack? I would never presume to lay this mystery at your feet, if I didn't believe that this matter of light and dark affects us both.

My father, Aram Stanebruch, is a forester, an environmental advocate of some international reputation. My mother, Rosa—Rosa Bluestein Stanebruch—Rosa B was her professional name—she doesn't perform anymore—is a jazz pianist. Three years before I was born, though separated from each other by thousands of miles, they both experienced the war in ways that silenced them. I was born out of, or into, their silence. I was also shaped by it and educated by it. It was a part of me as it had become a part of them. And then when I was forty, there was an explosion. . . .

They say that the Big Bang which may have initiated the universe lasted a hundredth of a second. Everything which was going to make the universe is said to have been in place within three minutes. 'Conceived in violence,' is a common phrase referring to the birth of the universe and the continual state of explosion in which the galaxies rush away from each other with speeds approaching the speed of light. That same explosion is ongoing some fifteen billion years later. We are living within the ocean of black-body radiation released in that instant, watching everything streaking away from everything else. Yet according to our perceptions, we are not in the eye of the blast, we are standing still and the explosion is long over. We have the habit of imagining that every explosion terminates in an instant. Even those who were at the Trinity site and maintained that the first flash of light from the bomb at Trinity lasted minutes, instead of its stunning two seconds, would agree that there comes a time when a bomb is no longer exploding. Not unless we think like my mother. My mother always said that once a bomb is set off it keeps exploding. She insists that the very first Bomb is still exploding and that every nuclear device detonated afterwards is still detonating. My parents speak in similar ways of the disasters that touched their own lives.

But my parents also say that history self-destructed, came to a dead end, in a singular explosion before I was born. Until this very moment, Cardinal, I didn't realize that what they had suffered is what I have been recently experiencing.

My parents insisted that I was born on the other side of history into an immaculate future that would never be transgressed because the universe on one side of that line was governed by laws fundamentally different from the laws on the other side. They willed it so, conceiving me as if they were wizards on the other side of a great divide. When I began to study astrophysics, I found language for their design. "You speak as if I appeared at the very edge of a singularity," I would tease them recognizing that, for them, singularities were not a danger—the end of the knowable world, the breakdown of all law—but an ultimate protection, the new world, the promised land. A tenacious idea, I realize as I set this down, which has its origins in the very tradition they were trying to escape. My parents pretended that I was a child of a people without a history or rather the child of a family which didn't have a people.

"Singularities are our deepest hope," my father maintained. "If we didn't think they existed, we would not have had a child."

In reality, I was born at dawn on Christmas Day, 1947. My mother did whatever she could, first to stop the labor, then to prolong it. From the very beginning their intentions were threatened. Sister Maria, the ecstatic nun-midwife attending my mother during the home birth, did not understand that her benedictions were unwelcome. When her instructions to my mother to "push and breathe, push, breathe," were intermixed with calls to 'Mary, Mother of God' and 'Sweet Jesus,' my father turned up the volume on the phonograph and drowned her out with Bessie Smith, "Caaaare-lessss Llloooovvve." Then I was born directly into his hands. Without thinking, he ripped his army knife from his pants pocket and cut the cord.

They had wanted a boy. A boy would have an easier life, would be safer. And they had chosen only a son's name, Daniel. So they gave me his name. And my mother added a particle of that little phrase she sings obsessively; la, la, la, la, la.

Aram insists he knew the moment of conception. My mother denies it. "I'm the one to have felt it. How can you feel something after it has left your body?"

"I felt it." The impact, his semen or the moment was, he insists, entirely elastic, always there, afterwards, tugging at him. He once confessed to me that he felt the tug in two directions, toward me, his little girl, who would, he had a premonition, be more of him than of Rosa, and toward the dead behind him from whom he expected I would free him and from whom he also insisted I would be free.

In order for me to be free, they tried to maintain a *cordon sanitaire* around my life while actually forbidding very little within. You might think that the prohibited would loom large as the forbidden often does, but it didn't feel forbidden. It had no intrigue to it, as if we were avoiding something shabby or exhausted, something which would make life uncomfortable—like ticks, poor manners or mud on the floor. The Bible, religion, spiritual matters, Judaism, all of these were avoided. Left behind in the old world, and good riddance. How much trouble they had caused! And one more thing incarcerated in the past; what my mother called the *H* word.

In other families, one could not say *fuck*. There were no such restrictions around language in my home. I could say, read, do anything. However, when the conversation hovered near World War II, my mother looking frightened would round her eyes and take on the expression of a little girl. It was almost charming then because I didn't know what I know now. Once or twice Rosa actually said, "Let's not talk about the *H* word." And the Holocaust being forbidden, the *G* word was likewise proscribed so that the possibility of God or the Holocaust were not ever contemplated on my side of the empty place where, my parents assured me, I would spend my life.

At six, in first grade in the Adirondacks, I encountered school and religion at the same time. Catholic children were released from grammar school an hour early every Wednesday for religious instruction. My teacher didn't know what to do with a girl whose parents refused to designate a religious authority.

"Turn her out to the woods. She won't come to any harm *there*." You couldn't miss my mother's meaning. The teacher was not amused so each week Rosa picked me up early and with much fanfare. Slamming doors, and swearing, we stomped across the road, across the still meadows and into the red maples and the yellow birches until the school was well out of sight. And then she'd look at me and we'd laugh. We were in Aram's temple and the school had been right to insist after all.

Maybe my father, being biologically inclined, was thinking of the physiology of the brain which is miraculously designed to allow the good to slip through to it but not evil. Even as my parents wrestled with the paradox of protecting my freedom on the one hand and protecting me on the other, knowledge they hoped to hold at bay seeped through. But not necessarily, as I have been discovering, from the outside but from within or from unknown dimensions I could hardly withstand.

My grandmother, Cardinal, was a stellar being. When I was eight, Shaena Bluestein was very much alive and my parents left me with her for a few weeks. Whenever I was with her, I felt as if she would teach me everything. My parents taught me by leaving me to my own devices but not Shaena; she made sure I wouldn't miss anything.

"Now, Dani, I am going to tell you a secret," she would say pointing her finger at me and fixing me with the light of her eyes. "Don't be bothered by anything I tell you, don't let it limit it you, Dani, but . . ." and the *but* made me tremble, "don't forget it either."

Earlier that weekend, I had removed a book from my grandmother's bookcase which had yellow stars on the cover and Rosa had promptly taken it from me with a look of alarm. Now I would be able to look at the book; there was nothing secret or forbidden in my grandmother's house. In the book, there were a photographs of people wearing little yellow stars.

"I'm going out," I said the next morning. The neighborhood was safe. I took Shaena's purse and put my allowance in it and went to the Five and Dime Store two blocks away where I bought yellow felt, a scissors, a package of safety pins. Then I sat down on the curb outside the store and made several stars because I wanted to surprise Shaena. After the stars were cut out, I fringed the edges of them until they radiated like the stars I already loved so much. Then I pinned them carefully on the underside of my sweater so that no one could see them or the small length of the metal pins that held them fast.

This was the heart of the star. I knew it needed to be small and dense; it was white hot, while the outer body of the star was yellow, cooler. I already knew all this from books Aram and Shaena had bought to encourage me to look away, outside, toward unexplored horizons.

"Don't look back," my grandmother always said to me. "But if you have to look back, look all the way back." I wore my stars back home secretly the way Shaena had told me wise men wore their knowledge.

It was Shaena whom I asked about the luminous woman. "There are thirty-six people," my grandmother began, "thirty-six people, Dani, darling, and they are the feet of the pillars which hold up the sky. Thirty-six people on one side, thirty-six stars on the other and the sky is held up between them. Every ten days another one of the thirty-six stars rises and you know that its double, down here, is especially alert. For the next ten days, the sky rests mostly on her head wherever she goes. Maybe you saw the star woman."

My grandmother lowered her voice so that I would know that she was passing on one of those secrets, my inheritance that Shaena had carefully garnered. Not for Rosa, who had never wanted it, but for me, her granddaughter. I was the little girl Shaena said she had expected to come along to receive the teachings and she was going to live just long enough to pass them on.

"How do you know it's me?" I asked.

"Because." Her irritation indicated I was asking more that I could understand. To appease me, she lowered her voice even deeper in what may have been a pretense of confidence, "Because you were born on the birthday of the sun. But," she cautioned, "don't tell anyone these secrets. You will have to learn to keep your own counsel."

The next day, Shaena said, "Those thirty-six people are different from anyone we know. No one must ever know who they are or that they're holding up the sky. If anyone becomes suspicious of what they're doing, they scuttle away just as quickly as they can. Like that blind beggar on the street who sells pencils and says 'God bless you' when you put your pennies in his cup."

I gasped. Shaena Baena had said the *G* word and in that moment I intuited that the *H* word related somehow to those little yellow stars.

There was so much more that I wanted to know, but by then Shaena had had enough and wanted a cup of tea. And to have a cup of tea, she had to bake cookies and I would have to push the dough through the tin cylinder with the star shaped nozzle at the end, which took time and concentration, and that was that.

The morning Rosa and Aram returned, the little yellow stars I had carefully hidden had disappeared and Shaena said nothing about them.

Chapter 3

My father says I was a love child. He means something more. He hoped that I would set the world in its proper motion again inasmuch as he believed the natural order of things had been reversed. By the time I was to be born, in my parent's eyes, the stockpile of things that mattered amounted to zero, and zero was the safe place to start. Beloved zero. A singularity extending away from what had been into infinity.

Obviously my parents failed. A past had already insinuated itself and was dragging history into this white space like a tire mark blackening ice. Perhaps because of curvatures in time or space, parallel, even contradictory, realities crossed each other.

And this past—so foreign it didn't feel like the past but like a collision with another universe likewise governed by its own inexplicable laws and insisting that nothing that was not it would survive within its domain—reached out to me. Pulled me into it, or enfolded itself within me as if into another dimension.

You understand, Cardinal, that though we are speeding into the future as if annihilating the past, every time we see a light, the past comes with it. Light, by its nature, is the past traveling in time. So when something that is not light slips through the walls and brings the past with it, what is occurring?

I want to say that darkness entered my life but astrophysics may forbid it in this instance. Certain kinds of darkness derive from density so intense they draw everything, even light, into themselves. What I thought was the past entering my life may have been myself drawn into its vortex. Without even realizing I had changed course, I was traveling in its direction, having come too close to escape its clutches.

This particular past had a name. A name, a history and a death. And then his history was mine. Peter Schmidt would have been eighty-one today, had he lived. It is not coincidental that I have begun writing this letter on his birthday. The reality of his existence still pulls me the way space is distorted by the pull of dense matter.

It was as if I, who have been alone and solitary my entire life, were suddenly two people in one body. At first, I wasn't taken aback because as a child I had the equivalent of an imaginary friend, the fantasy of a twin whose name I carried. But, it wasn't Daniel, my lost brother who mysteriously appeared to haunt me, it was this Peter Schmidt who was not related to me, or so I insisted at first.

Peter Schmidt—my nemesis, my dark star, my dark matter. You can already guess—can't you—what sort of man Peter Schmidt might be? I'll give you the particulars: A German officer dies at 4 AM September 4, 1946. In Nuremberg. Of lung disease. Not just a German soldier, a Nazi. A Nazi came into my life and claimed it as his own, said it was his. I had to believe him or else I would, once again, enact a betrayal, not of him, but of myself, or—I don't know—the future perhaps, the stars.

I was pulled into his life though it felt like an invasion to me as you must already feel that I am violating the boundaries between our formerly discrete lives. Whatever the real circumstances, I tried to follow his life back as best as I could. I had to see with my own eyes and, simultaneously, I had to see what he had seen. It's from this journey that I have just returned. I went almost everywhere Peter had been and more so, to the Concentration Camps of East Germany, West Germany, Austria and Poland. I went back across the line that my parents said couldn't be crossed and that had already been violated. "Don't pretend it isn't your life," Peter said.

This is the story which doesn't cohere. The unities have been violated, those blessed but arcane simplicities of beginning, middle and end, now and then, self and other. Like an astronomer turning a telescope toward the far light, I go backwards in time to see where things began. I look for the origins, but every time there is another path back composed of new possibilities organizing and reorganizing themselves.

If you travel for two and a half years at the speed of light, you won't leave the Milky Way, you will get only half way to Alpha Centauri, the third brightest star in our sky, but still you will have gone very far. These last two and a half years have been such a journey. I didn't take off in a space ship. I wasn't kidnapped by aliens, no such nonsense. But I went somewhere and fast enough or with enough spin to have entered what felt like other dimensions and to have encountered strange, unexpected, unpredictable particles—unprecedented dark matter. I don't know what the journey looked like to others, maybe it also looked to them as it felt to me; a woman being pulled apart by the forces which exist near the event horizon of a black hole.

I didn't keep records. I didn't realize what was happening. Chaos? I recognized it, but why record it? Things blowing up or falling apart? There is plenty of that in the sky and instruments and procedures with which to measure it. Madness? How even begin to understand that?

Here are the pieces. When we string them together in one pattern to make a life, we assume it is *the* life. But then the pieces break apart so we pick them up and in our confusion . . . yes . . . exactly . . . in our confusion, we begin to put them together in another way . . . and. . . .

We put them together in another way and find that there is another equally authentic pattern. Then we find that the third construction isn't random either. The first was organized, let's say chronologically, and the next pattern has another kind of organization, one of affiliation, let's say, or variation, as in a fugue . . . it doesn't matter. The point is one has to start with the elements, so one takes the smaller pieces . . . or. . . ! . . . Cardinal! . . . one willfully breaks everything down into smaller pieces . . . atomizes them . . . and then begins building. And, lo and behold, something else, entirely, emerges. A scatter of electrons, a haze of probabilities.

I get up from my desk and get a drink of water. I stop to break ice cubes from the tray. My fingers stick to the frosted metal. I would rather not write this letter to you and I can't refrain from writing. The sky is thickening. It can barely carry the heavy burden of gray that will have to be released soon. In a few days, I will be able to scoop snow into a cup to cool my tea. I get my sweater from the hook. It is misshapen, stretched out at the hips by all the years my mother wore it at the piano. When I moved here, I asked her for it. Something to keep me warm.

Never before have I been interested in myself, Cardinal. My parents taught me well. My life disappeared in the manner of my mother's music. A bit of ragtime and then silence.

I have to understand this. If I don't, there are serious consequences and I may not be the only one to suffer them. Perhaps I only need to write this to you and you will draw it together even without saying a word, even without ever reading it. Imagining you will read this may be enough.

Teilhard de Chardin speaks about an Omega Point. The entire universe heading toward a point that will contain it. All parallel lines meet. Maybe somewhat the way it was the nanosecond before the Big Bang, but not a point of annihilation, a point of supreme completion, everything contained and therefore present. Therefore understood. Therefore comprehensible. Even luminous. *N'est pas?*

You, Cardinal, are a kind of Omega Point for this story.

Chapter 4

Well, Cardinal, Peter's birthday is over. *Alles gut.* That little point in time isn't a thorn in my side this morning.

Six months ago, Cardinal, when I had just returned from the Camps, I was traveling by bus to the *Santuario de Chimayo* in New Mexico. I don't know why I was on that bus; I always drive, but I was very tired and had told myself a bus ride would be an adventure. In need of rest, I intended to spend a day at the simple chapel, built in the old holy style, whitewashed walls meeting a rough wood ceiling like two hands meeting in prayer, and set, according to the faithful, around a *posito* of red earth with healing properties. To honor a local custom, I was bringing a tiny pair of shoes to place before the shrine of the *Santo Niño* who, the local farmers say, wears out his shoes each night as he walks the fields blessing the crops.

As the bus pulled out of the terminal, I was compelled to offer the window to the plainly dressed woman seated next to me who, I assumed, was a visitor to the Southwest. She declined, laughing, saying that she had been born in New Mexico, in Los Alamos, as a matter of fact. But after she said this, her face expressed irritation which she brushed away with a stroke of her hand.

The woman described herself as a religious hermit living in Paris. She said she is devoted to another nun, Edith Stein, a Jewish woman who took on the name Sister Theresa Benedicta.

"I know Los Alamos," I told her, without adding that I had been born in Santa Fe, only a few miles away, just after the war. Without telling her that I was going to the *Santuario*, nor that I had been delivered by nuns. We might be the same age, we might have played in a park together or attended the same preschool. I was far too startled, unnerved really, wary, to tell her that I had just been to Auschwitz and had spent the night at convent, *Karmel Edith Stein*. I remained silent on the surface, though after awhile the same words coursed through us, spoken by her, unspoken by myself, that Sister Theresa Benedicta had been beatified on May 1, 1987, after having died in Auschwitz on August 9, 1942. Then I added, but under my breath, I think, that this was exactly three years before we dropped the second Bomb on Nagasaki, our scientific experiment to test the trickier plutonium 239 bomb, Fat Man, at a cost of 70,000 lives. It was all there between us, embedded in a single point Cardinal: Santa Fe, Los Alamos, Edith Stein, Auschwitz, the Bomb.

When I least expected it, she pounced on me with a barrage of questions and soon I admitted that I had been to Eastern Europe and to the Camps and then I said a few other things to her that I hadn't spoken about to anyone before. My confession exhausted me, for afterwards I dozed, awakening to find we were in Flagstaff far too soon. I was so awed by the snow, by banks of stars, brilliant white, against dark trees, that I didn't notice that the Sister had gathered her things together until she surprised me by whispering a rapid good-bye in my ear, the aftermath of her breath smelling something like roses. While pressing a piece of paper into my hand; she stepped down from the bus before I could say a word. Expecting that she was giving me her name and address in the event I came to Paris, I didn't open the paper immediately, then by the time I had read it and run after her, she had disappeared from the station.

The note said, "You may want to write to Jean-Marie Lustiger, the Cardinal of Paris. The Cardinal," she wrote, "like Edith Stein, like you, was born into the Jewish faith. I think you might petition him." The piece of paper had your address written on it.

I couldn't take her word for it so I did some research, then gave it up. I read two or three articles about you in the popular press. That's all. But the moment I saw your name, I thought of the Spanish, *lucés*, enlightenment, *lustrar*, to polish, shine, *luz*, light, and then lucid and inevitably, Lucifer and all the variations on the root of light. "The light." I thought over and over again. I have been thinking about your name for months now. A few days ago out of curiosity I called the reference desk at the University and they told me that your name means "cheerful" in Yiddish. Cheerful. What do you know about good cheer, Your Eminence? Something about faith: "Be of good cheer; It is I; be not afraid." [Matthew 14:27] In actuality, the librarian, herself, cheerfully hummed a phrase from a Yiddish song she had learned as a child "... *a freiliche, a lustig*...."

Dear Cardinal, I can't get you out of my mind.

With all due respect, I don't know a lot about you, Jean-Marie Cardinal Lustiger, even if I know too much. I'll tell you what I think we have in common. We come from desert people. And desert people have the stars imprinted on them. What desert people know, they learned from the sky. The stars are their night partners and teach them or lead them to what they need to know. When the Magi astronomers left Babylon on a pilgrimage to Bethlehem to pay homage to the new light, they were following a path of starlight foreseen by my name-sake, Daniel. And Christ, who was born under a star, must have been fortified by the starry night when he was in the desert preparing to wrestle with the Devil.

When I was a little girl, my grandmother awakened me one evening after my parents had gone out and sat with me on the porch looking out to the night sky. "Those are the stars, little one," she said.

"But what are stars?" I asked.

"We don't know," she answered. "So many people are trying to find out. But, to tell you the truth, Dani, the more we think we learn the less we know. We used to know a lot about the stars because we knew their names. Now we don't know their names. That's a tragedy because everything is in a name, Dani.

"The stars are their names, Dani. Everything is its name. A name isn't like a hat someone is wearing. A name is a part of what something is."

"What does my name mean, Shaena?"

"You'll find out, but not tonight." Shaena dismissed my question and went on. "Every letter of a name matters, Dani. Each letter is a different fire, Dani, and when they burn together to make a word, it is the same as the stars coming together, like so many eyes and hands and feet of light to make a constellation. Something happens, Dani, when they come together in that way, something different from what they are separately. Just as eyes and hands and feet make something different when they form a body. Do you see?"

"What do they make, Shaena?"

"Here is a secret, Dani. People say, 'It's all in a name.' They mean—the names are burning like stars. Only you can't see the fire in the letters the same way you can't see all the different fires from the stars. But that doesn't mean the fires aren't there. And all of it rains down upon us every night."

"I'll try to understand," I said reaching up to smooth her forehead which had a deep gash between her silver and auburn brows. I imagined that old stars looked like her pale freckles. Though I was very young, I could see that her heart was burdened by the uncertainty that I would ever understand.

"There's so much more to the stars than their fire, Daniella, you have to understand," she was holding my chin in her hand so that I would look up at her and be attentive. "Only we can't see what's there and since we don't like to be blind, we pretend there's nothing but what we see or measure. But if you watch the stars, night after night after night, the way the desert people did, you will know a lot more than the young men who think they see everything through their fancy telescopes."

Shortly after that I changed my name. My mother's name was Bluestein, my father's Stanebruch. I became Daniella Stonebrook Blue.

My grandmother, who had gone back home, wrote to me as soon as she heard of my name change:

"You come from a long line of people who have lost their names, again and again. In crossing the gangplank from the boat to Canada, I lost my name as surely as if it had fallen overboard into the harbor waters. What's in a name, Daniella? Everything is in a name so everything is lost over and over again. That is how it is. Better you should choose your own name then your own name should be taken from you or distorted by some little, uniformed tyrant of a man with red spider lines on his face. The little insect stood before our shaking queue of ragged immigrants and said, 'You, you Shaena, you're Sharon.'"

"*Merci*," I said. I knew he wouldn't understand Russian or Polish.

"'And you, Rifka,' he said to the woman standing behind me who was so frightened the bone handles of her purse were knocking together, 'You're Rosa.' And so on. Since he's the angel, and you don't know if he's the angel of life or death, you say, 'Thank you. *Merci, monsieur, est très bien, très jolie*,' hoping you sound Christian. And then,

I named my daughter, Rosa. Your mother, I always say, is the Rose of Sharon, a rose without a thorn."

Here's another point of connection. Of course I am aware that the Vatican is involved in scientific explorations of the universe, that Pope Leo formally founded the Vatican Observatory in Rome and one hundred years later, in 1981, it expanded to Tucson, Arizona. Also that, the Vatican, in collaboration with the University of Arizona, is constructing a small advanced optical telescope alongside what may become the most powerful telescope in the world and that these projects have the go-ahead even though the site, Mt. Graham, is seriously contested by environmentalists and the local Apaches who argue that the telescope is displacing the gods who teach them healing.

Originally, Cardinal, I intended to outline professional concerns we might share; I now give this up. I don't think they are relevant. But I'll tell you what is germane so there is no subterfuge here. I know that you were born Aaron Lustiger, that you converted to Catholicism when you were a young boy, and that you don't deny your Jewish heritage. As a young boy, your parents sent you to Germany to study; I don't know how you survived the war.

A woman named Giselle Lustiger, who was born on August 14, 1903, left for Auschwitz on convoy Number 48 and probably died on February 15, 1943. I'm sorry to tell you that I know this. It is public information, but perhaps it was rude to search it out. My training as a scientist hasn't prepared me to distinguish between investigation and intrusion. And this further imprudence: My intuition tells you may be Pope before you get this letter.

What history, Cardinal, inveigles itself across the border of our supposedly inviolable self with the giving or taking of a name? What did that angel with the ugly face guarding the boundaries between one world and another want for my dear Shaena? Maybe he wanted her to have a name that would carry her across a boundary into a new world, a name that would save her from the angel of death.

I look like someone who was born across a line. I'm red headed with broad bones, strong hands, square fingers, powerful calves shaped like a dancer's, white skin with summer freckles. In the U.S. you might guess I was born in Minnesota or Wisconsin. Nordic stock. Eric the Red could have been my kin. If I had been living in Poland, I could have passed as a Catholic peasant girl, the kind the Nazis liked to send back to Germany to breed soldiers.

I never thought about passing. I never used the word until one day last year I heard a voice inside of me sneer: "No one passed. Don't you know that? No one passed. We were precise, meticulous and accurate."

When I went to Europe, I was looking for that voice. I was moving very fast. On the one hand, Cardinal, the past is by nature or, rather, by law, separated from the future and, on the other hand, if you go very, very fast, approaching the speed of light, you can go back into time becoming the hot blue light of the future approaching the cold red fires of the past. Just so, Peter Schmidt turns up. It's not unlike someone's Jewish, long dead, grandmother showing up in his or her present life in Germany, the Nazi version of the past appearing in the telescopes of the present. It was an abomination to be Jewish when you were born, even to be the grandchild of a Jew. For the Nazis this "first light" was a contagion. The Nazis also wanted to live in a pristine universe.

How odd it is to write this letter. As odd as it must be to receive it. A letter written in the American desert arrives in Paris. A Jewish woman asks a boon of a Cardinal. I bring myself to my own tribunal and I need a witness to my own interrogation. . . .

I can't get my bearings. The story swirls and whirls; I can't account for all the variables. Clouds of stars in the heavens seethe and boil like turbulent gases, as above so below. Another analysis not derived from the scientific method is suggesting itself. I have virtually abandoned chronology, which means cause and effect and the Newtonian universe, to follow clues which I know can not be verified or reproduced in the usual ways. All of this is as personally disturbing as was the discovery of quantum mechanics. Even a few years ago, I would not have recognized this method, because my experiences had not yet thrown me against the limitations of materialist investigations, a stone wall I had not known existed.

Cardinal, my father kept a war journal but it turned out to be a letter to my mother. My father says that every word he wrote down diminished a memory, but I don't believe it. I think every word made the memory transportable so that he could bring it home in a manageable form. Also Aram claims that if he had not had my mother to write to, he would not have survived the war.

I want to ask you what all this means. But then I hear Einstein cautioning me in my mind: "This persistent search for the answer," he says, "may be a constant flight from wonder."

What is the proper etiquette, Cardinal? May I offer you that cup of tea on this gray and cold afternoon, the sky quivering with just a hint of pink as the sun disappears from view?

Chapter 5

In order to understand what happened, you will have to know a few things about my life. We moved all the time. Because of my father's work and temperament, we almost never spent more than one year in the same place. We did spend one year in a city and after that we were always escaping to somewhere more remote and less accessible. Not very much in our lives spoke to continuity, but what there was came directly or indirectly from my grandmother even though she had been the one to advise me: "Live your life knowing Death is standing in every doorway you pass." That was when my dog died. She had been visiting us, and it was she that had taken me out to the back yard where he lay under a tree and insisted I sit down and put his head in my lap until he was gone. I was about eight at the time and afraid. But she was adamant, fixing me with a beam of light from her eyes so intense, I didn't know if Shaena transmitted it to protect me or to burn me up on the spot. Then she left me alone with him and I sat there dutifully until my love for him softened my fear and I could stroke him. Immediately he shuddered as if an electric current were passing through him and he died.

"He's gone," I announced as I came into the house crying.

"Maybe," Shaena murmured, reaching for me and folding me into her arms. Rosa's anger flared, but Shaena was impervious. "What was that piece you were playing?" she asked as if deflecting the fiery surge back to the piano. Rosa bent gracefully into the curve of Shaena's intention and sat down, not so much obediently as with relief, and began playing again.

My mother's piano was another stable element. It was a Steinway. Shaena Bluestein believed in Steinways the way others believe in a deity and so she had bought this one for Rosa. It was the best piano she could find at the time and most of her savings went into it.

As soon as we arrived at a new house, Rosa would find the carefully labeled box with her music wrapped in a fringed shawl that Shaena had brought with her from Poland. Rosa would open the piano carefully, dust the keyboard, throw the blue and purple silk over the back of the piano with a flourish, securing it with two heavy old world silver candlesticks, our other heirloom, and sit down to play the first chords: La, la, la, la, la. After that, we would unpack.

I know my mother's straight back best. Dark hair falling down to her shoulders, covering the collar of her white blouse, a dark sweater, the careful fold of a skirt—gray wool, camel's hair, herringbone tweed—under tight buttocks on the polished ebony bench. She looked like a metronome, but at the piano she could be wild.

There were two things my mother taught me. The first was, "Life devours." The second was: "Learn to survive in solitude." I wasn't the blessing to my mother that I was to my father. There was a hole in my mother's heart and I didn't fill it. Whatever emptiness she felt, she filled with music. Not just the piano but a constant, abstracted song or hum issued from her. She could sing any part of any piece of music she'd ever studied from beginning to end without faltering and she practiced this on all occasions, while attending to household tasks, or putting me to sleep, or walking through her constant insomnia. The body makes a little sound, issues a frequency, a hum and series of overtones. When people get tinnitus, their sound has gotten out of hand; you can sometimes hear it if you stand next to them. That's how it was with my mother, only it was a deliberate hum.

I don't think my mother is silent by nature. Something happened to her and her words fell away. Initially my mother's voice is always tentative. It is not the kind of voice you would imagine knows the name of real things. But then it breaks away, becomes resonant and graceful, wraps around the words musically, embellishes with crescendos or tumbling descents, even bursting playfully into an occasional folk holler, so that I always want Rosa to keep speaking, no matter what it is she is saying, for the beauty of it. That's why it is such a loss when Rosa is terse or subdued, or worse, humming in that abstracted way of hers.

In his spare time, my father nursed seedlings. There were always flats of little trees that he would care for whenever he had a chance. I didn't know that he was unhappy, or let's say unsteady, because he was so tender with these small plants. When I saw him bent over them, from a distance, I felt protected though he was talking to them about things he never discussed with me.

When my father turned forty, Rosa thought a party was *de rigueur*. People flew in from everywhere. There was no shortage of acquaintances or colleagues who loved him or were grateful to him for good reasons. That night, I found my father huddled on the floor of the back porch staring out across the hills above the darkening Wisconsin meadow, his arms crossed about his bony knees looking like a frightened fruit bat enfolded in its angular wings. I sat with him without saying anything and finally someone found us and pulled him back into the house.

Rosa was not any more gregarious than my father. About women friends, I asked her mother what to do. "It is lonely sometimes," I said. "I would like someone to confide in."

"What would you confide?" my mother replied.

I shrugged.

"I didn't have friends either," Rosa continued.

"Why?"

"Its better without. Whatever you can do without, it's better."

Silence. It was true, I had never known her to have friends. And yet, before I had been born, before the end of the war, there had been friends. I was familiar with the photographs of the four women, a jazz quartet, playing, posing, clowning.

"Where are the women you used to play with? The 'B' girls."

"We never played after the war." Rosa's voice slammed shut.

"You had friends in Santa Fe. Aram talked about them. Before he came home from Germany. He was always glad you weren't alone."

My mother disappeared. She was elsewhere. At a far point in our concentric orbit.

Then Rosa answered deliberately, "I made the wrong alliances. I didn't know it then. But they were wrong. It was like playing a scale, one note following the other and I was caught in it. Like we were a chord and each note was played with the others. We were all fixed in it. There was no way out. Do you see? Do you understand?"

I watched my mother's face pale, the subtle draining of skin tone until all the planes were flat and there was only a mask of a face covering exhaustion.

"It's better without if you can do without. It's a matter of temperament. Or character. Character can be formed. You can work at it. You have a lot of strength, Daniella. We saw to that."

Chapter 6

I look out the window and watch the storm. Snow following the angle of wind. Heavily laden bushes and trees occasionally shake themselves, branches careening into the air, limbs suddenly freed or electrified in an explosion of white, nebulae of white powder, thuds and crackles.

During the war, my mother drifted to Santa Fe following a music teacher who had developed asthma and wanted the desert air. Aram joined Rosa there. It was the ideal place for him to forget World War II. The landscape couldn't have been more different from Germany. Also the Southwest is as far from New York, from everything he had known, and as far from European Judaica as he could imagine.

I never have understood why they didn't stay, when for the rest of his life my father has longed for it, but he says he would rather preserve its pristine beauty in his mind. Or, he says, we would have gotten lost in the Southwest. People get lost in it, disappear there all the time, he insists. The Anasazi disappeared hundreds of years ago. Left no trace.

When he started out, my father—not the first forester to come out of Central Park—felt safe studying trees because they were so abundant. He maintained he was never going to run out of woods. A few years in the profession taught him otherwise. He had expected a decline but it had never occurred to him that trees might disappear altogether. In my opinion, our life was directed by panic. Aram was like a man putting out forest fires. Sometimes, this was literally true and then he was sometimes called in order to supervise reforestation projects. One way or another, we almost never spent more than a year in the same place. Aram assembled a maverick life combining teaching, research and consultation, moving from one state, federal or private agency to another, or from one university wilderness position to another. He was always on the move and so were we.

Given my background, how much we moved, it's no surprise I've had two educations—the formal education at school and my own idiosyncratic regime. At eleven, in Idaho, miles from the sea, I taught myself stellar navigation when Aram was called down for a few weeks in late spring to work at a wild life refuge. The desert expanse offered a view to the horizon almost equal to the extent of sea—I jumped for it. As soon as night fell, I would walk far enough away from our dimly lit encampment and dig my stake into the ground to serve as a helm, then I would memorize the sky in all directions. "I'll never get lost at sea," I assured Aram afterwards, "at least not in spring. Do you want to test me, Aram? Do you want to blindfold me and take me somewhere I haven't been and leave me there with only the coordinates to get me home?" Pride – his eyes were teary with it.

What I discovered about Aram that he would never admit was he had taken to following me at night when I went out to watch the sky. Not especially there because the landscape was so empty, but at home where the tree tops circumscribed my view and I had to learn the configurations as they moved over a small space, studying progressions without the advantage of their relationship to the entire field. Sometimes he hid behind shrubs or trees, sometimes he watched me from the various blinds he had set up to watch wildlife, marveling—he would use that word, Cardinal—marveling that my interests took me so far from him, and yet, clearly, I had learned this discipline from him. I was *his* daughter; my mother was inside the house playing with the vibrations of sound.

From watching him—we all watched each other—we were so introverted a family, we only had these observations to keep us on a course of being human I can imagine what he was thinking while he watched me. He was fascinated with the fact that I was alive. Motion, warm motion, drew him, his attention drifting to the calls of the night birds or the small rustles in the grasses all of which he would automatically identify. He was far more attuned to the padded race of a mountain lion looking for prey then he would ever be to the constellation Leo that I showed him several times.

I can move inside him and see out of his eyes; I know I'm right. I must be because he taught me so well, the way he moves inside the little animal he's watching. We would check my perceptions, and his, by what the bird or mouse would do next. He was infallible. So only in this was he in error; I knew he was there—and he thought I didn't.

He taught me to be so still and honorable that many small animals would pass close by our hiding place without ever knowing we were there. This small animal thought she knew each time he was there, but maybe I didn't. He was skilled enough to fool me; maybe I simply thought I caught him each time. I never let on because he was so careful never to respond to me later on the basis of what he may have secretly observed except I sensed his growing confidence in me as our relationship changed and we became, not friends, not colleagues quite, but comrades, wordless comrades. He never gave himself away; it was just that he had taught me well to hear the imperceptible, to sense the hidden.

Oh, Cardinal! I understand now. He always gave himself away. He *always* let me know that he was there. He wouldn't spy on me; that was not in his nature.

Aram was called west immediately after a particularly devastating fire in the Sierras; I was thirteen and went with him. It was that one terrible year when we lived in a city. I was happy to escape from school and both Rosa and Aram agreed I would learn more in the field than I would in a classroom.

At the fire site, the scorched earth was still smoldering in places. The two of us walked among the ashes, burned trees standing like blackened sentinels, the air acrid with remnants of smoke. Walking gingerly in this desolation, my father was not consoled by the theory that fire, a natural occurrence, provoked new growth. This particular forest had already been seriously debilitated by logging and human habitation so each such fire was catastrophic.

The undergrowth was gone. Trees had fallen, or in some cases, had been cut down. The familiar forests sounds—whistles, calls, chirps, cracks, rustles were strikingly absent. A soughing of wings over head, the solitary flight of a black crow streaking across the gray sky and disappearing. Quiet again. Within a star, this debris would have vaporized into heat and light.

What was on my mind, as we walked over burned earth heated almost to the point of glass, was the mystery of light. There were the stars. And then this heat in my body and other bodies. A dog's body. A sunflower. And now this fire. The external heat of the fire leaping onto the internal heat of the tree and the tree exploding as if rushing to meet it, a frantic rush of one fire to another, sometimes putting each other out. It was more than I could understand, and it didn't seem to me that Aram understood it either.

Before us was a sequoia that had once been struck by lightning, a long narrow scar down its trunk opening into a charred wedge at the roots. The new fire had lodged in the blackened cave of the old, but the tree had survived twice. "It can burn a very long time and survive," Aram said.

I rubbed my hands along its trunk. The more recent carbon dust lodged in the thick furrows of its bark acted like a light pumice eating its way into the skin of my fingers. Such black ashes were not the products of the night sky. In the night sky vast swirling eternal storms ultimately produce the gentle light that penetrates and informs all things.

We began walking again, trekking across the worst of the devastation. Finally, I asked Aram, "What can you do?"

He only shook his head. "When you go on to college, study something that will last."

Accordingly, my father applauded me when I formally announced my decision to study astronomy. "A good profession," he said with a little more heart than was trustworthy. I knew he was disappointed that we wouldn't be buddies and go out into the field together. But hadn't I learned from him the wisdom of choosing a field that would outlive me?

He led me to a stand of pussy willows where pulling one of the furry ears from the stalk, he placed it in the palm of my hand.

"Out of such violence, this," he said, or asked, I couldn't tell. What did he mean? Instead of answering me, he walked further until he dropped a green bud into my hand alongside the gray one.

"Dani, if you want to duplicate the processes through which an assembly of sub-atomic particles—under great heat and pressure—were fused into something green, watch out. Would you like to create this green from scratch? In the star, Dani, life and death, creation and annihilation, coincide. You want to bring the stars down here and begin again? Be careful."

"Be careful?"

"After the Bomb dropped in Japan, Dani, giant flowers blazed near the site and the land bloomed suddenly with a terrible green."

"But Aram...," I protested, insulted and confused.

"Just be careful, Dani. Beware the glories of the scientific method."

The pussy willow on his palm gleamed like a star on a photograph shining with silver light. And the green bud, well, he was trying to tell me that the green bud may have come out of what we call violence, but it was the bud and not the violence which required my focus.

In a few minutes, he recovered. "It's fortunate to study something which can never be confined to a museum, a park or a zoo. Soon," he added revealing more bitterness than he normally allowed, "the stars will be all that will be left of the natural world."

There was a book he loved, *The Last Lords of Palenque*, written by Victor Perera on the Lacondon Indians. He had always liked to read to me from it. "The roots of all living things," he read, "are tied together. When a mighty tree is felled, a star falls from the sky; before you cut down a mahogany you should ask permission of the keeper of the forest, and you should ask permission of the keeper of the star."

Just before I left for The Mountain, we took another long hike together in the redwoods. As usual, he was cautioning me to step more lightly, to place my feet flat so that I walked silently, leaving less of an imprint. Sometimes I would be speaking and he would silence me or interrupt to point out a nest or a burrow I certainly would have missed.

But I was really going away now, so this time I stopped him and made him look me in the eye while I told him I knew enough about walking on earth.

"It is different," I said, "in my world." I'd never told him before in so many words how it was for me. Words were insufficient even for that kind of exchange. I said, " I want the stars to see me," meaning I wanted the experience of light entering or passing through me.

He looked so perplexed and he knew we were parting. "You have taught me," I was as deliberate as I have ever been with him, "that if I come upon a bear, I'm to lower my eyes while retreating carefully, so she won't think I'm challenging her. You have taught me that and I have learned it. But, Aram, I have also learned myself that one never need avert her eyes from the stars."

Chapter 7

My father has the face of someone who had been in a war. His is no longer the smiling face of the young man in uniform in the gold tooled leather frame on the piano. His is not the face of that young man in that hand tinted photograph, his eyes hazel, his lips and cheeks russet. And not the face of the young groom, also in uniform, the medals and brass polished, standing with his arm around his bride, her parted lips, rosy, her white crepe silk skirt in a graceful flounce about her knees. I never knew that young man who looked so innocent and carefree. That young man had been wounded in the leg, and though he claimed not seriously, had managed to get sent home to be treated. That's when he married my mother.

I like his limp, the irregularity of it, the slight hesitation before he takes a step. It makes him odd and I like odd ducks. After he healed, Aram went back to the war. When he was discharged a year after the war, his face had changed. From then on he had the face I know; he was not a young boy anymore.

When I was young, my father never spoke about the war to me. He never told war stories. Only Rosa, my mother, knew what he had seen.

After I moved to Devil's Peak, my father came to see me without my mother, asking whether it would be possible for us to spend the evening without Lance.

When I opened the door he was holding little black and white composition books, the kind I had used in grammar school and that, as a youngster, I had seen in his study. I had felt important because we both used the same books even though I couldn't decipher his. When I finally asked him what they were, Aram shrugged saying I would have to learn the art of decoding if I wanted to be a scientist. If I were to understand what was written there, it was up to me. I tried and I failed.

Now here he was, a frailer man, leaning ever more slightly toward his game leg, holding his notebooks in front of him as if we were handing over a gun. "Here is the war, Daniella," he said.

His journal had been written in code, using the names of flowers, trees, animals to speak of what was forbidden to record. That night my father translated what he had witnessed reference by reference.

Deadly nightshade . . . meant . . . night bombings. Fuchsia in full bloom meant paratroopers, purple by night and white by day. Dogwood meant a search party; white birch, medics; Venus flytrap, tanks; porcupine, machine gun fire. When he was lost in awe and despair during an all out night battle that illuminated the skies he spoke of it as *fregata magnificens*, the Magnificent Frigate, the Man-o-War bird.

Seeds exploding from impatiens meant artillery fire. Snapdragons were bullets. Fungus meant booby traps everywhere. Hemlock was loss. Mistletoe meant they had taken prisoners. He hadn't known if his subterfuge would be successful. Sometimes he thought that everything he wrote down was obvious and would get him and his men into trouble; other times he enjoyed the danger and his own cleverness. He had been pretending to be writing stories:

> "I was a young boy. We were hiking in the woods. We came upon a grove of hemlocks and I thought of Socrates and refrained from leaning against their trunks, unlike my poor four companions."

By that he meant they had lost the battle and he would have lost more, his own life, more of his men than the four, if he had obeyed the orders. And yes, it also meant that he was not saved, he had simply not yet run into his death.

His favorite little wood was his squad. The forest, depending on the size, indicated a platoon or a division. The redwoods were the five star generals; the Kellog oaks with the bitter acorns, the colonels; the eucalyptus, the majors; the pine, the captains. And so on to the infantry, the orchards. To each of the men he knew well, he attributed a particular sweetness through a variety of fruit trees. He identified himself as one of the lowly pine, but of the furrowed, bristlecone variety, tenacious, and bent by the wind, prickly, irritable. He had planted box hedge and thorn bush so many feet apart: he had ordered his men to dig fox holes and set up their bayonets. Many broken twigs and branches indicated the wounded. He had neglected to water the young trees, they had died and the ground was covered with fallen timber: his men had died, he had not protected them sufficiently. The relentless creaking of the timber in the high wind, the trampled, muddied seeds meant pain, pain.

"I fear for the time which seems imminent," he wrote, "when all species of trees are gone. And then what? A world without trees will not endure."

We sat next to each other on the couch as he read carefully translating each line. Deciphering his secret code. After all this time.

In tiny script, he had filled in the details of each day. Each day had a page. He covered it completely. Each day was discrete. I marveled at his tiny, orderly handwriting. No entry for one day ran over onto the other day and no page was left empty. His writing was precise, as careful as any of his botanical observations had ever been. Around the margins of the pages, he carefully drew the plants that were the foundation of his code.

He read to me into the night as I imagined he had read to my mother, intent, lost in the pages, irritated by any offering of food or drink, unwilling to accept any respite. He didn't even take a piss, Cardinal. It went on for hours until I understood he was building a wall between us.

He was in the war. I knew that by the way his body jerked, his teeth clenched, his fists clenched and unclenched, his trigger finger twitched. He was also in its aftermath. His face had become unbearably young and sorrowful. He was in that room, wherever it was, in which he had first read these pages to my mother.

The last pages were different from the others. They were scrawled, agitated. The script and the words were indecipherable. As if they were written by someone who was mad in a language he had created himself. Sometimes there were just dark lines smearing across the page or almost etched onto the paper. Interspersed within the gibberish were other words, repeated over and over, quite distinct from the original code, words that had not appeared in the journal before: wild cries, cackles, sputtering, poison oak, nettles, locusts, red ants, vipers, plague, scorpions, vultures, quicksand.

May 1945 was written across the top of the page in block letters in different ink. He must have written it later.

A tangle of poison oak around the perimeter. And within several smoking pismires of red ants. A hideous smell of ugh ugh ugh of urine which is common to these rank mounds. The compost heap will take years to decay. #+######!!##^# Soil rejects the foliage—ne-ne-ne-net-nettles le-le-leprosy locusts—which is planted, pla-pla-plague planted there. This occurs when the foliage is not indigenous to the area. It has been discovered, for example, no, no, no examples, please, no examples, not that, no, that when a forest is cleared, the earth will not accept the new crop which is planted instead of the trees. That's it. That's it, man, breathe. Sometimes there is an earthquake or a flood and what does not belong is vomited—vomited, vomited—vipers, vipers, vultures,————————————————————————————vomited up followed by a hideous hiiddeeoouss sulfuric stink.

Coming upon this garbage heap, Rosa, I found myself . . . vomiting upon this pismire. . . . Coming upon these incinerators. I am lost. Rosa. Rosa. I have, I have, I have, I am n o t h i n g ======================= ====== =========================== I have no thing, I have, am no thing, no thing, no thing, nothing, have, had have no idea of how to get back to my pla-platoo . . . Pluto. Get your bearings, man. Get your bearings. Get your fuckin' bearings, man.

Take a break. Start again. Right, right, right, hup . . . ! ! ! ! ! ! !

When I was a little boy, I had a re-re-rep-reptile reptile re-repetitive dream. I was finally walking in the forest of my favorite trees after searching for it for days and suddenly something exploded it. Momma. Momma! I was in a shambles of broken sticks, Momma, Rosa, help me please, help someone, of sp-sp-spit slit split splin splintered trunks and twigs. I had loved these trees best. They were rare, so rare, so rare, odd species, exotic, fragile, Rosa, so rare. . . . Mommaaaaaaa! Groans of phantom trees in the air where branches ought to be. Wind wailing through burned holes in the air. Unbearable silence. Screams [mustn't mustn't] which become saws. Rosa. The fabric is ripped to pieces. . . . I can't go on. I

am afraid I will forget. I am afraid I will remember. Rosa . . . Rosa, Rosa, Rosa
ROSA ROSA **PLEASE**.

Then, Cardinal, my father began to tell me things. He confessed that he had not been
well when he was finally discharged. He was not well for a long time and he let no
one know it. Afterwards he told himself he had cured himself by reading the journal
to my mother. There were pages he hadn't wanted to decipher for Rosa, pages he had
started to read and then he had faltered, wouldn't, couldn't. As for the very last pages,
he had read her some of them, in the middle of the night, when he awakened, as he
often did afterwards, heaving.

"That's the story," he said. It was after midnight. "I came home, Daniella. The war
did end and I did come home. And your mother was there. Her presence was a great
comfort to me. Actually it was necessity."

We were sitting on the couch together as we had when I was child. He could have
been reading me a fairy tale. I wanted to take his hand and play "This little piggy." I
wanted to tuck his unruly brown hair behind his ears or run my fingers through his
hair. I wanted to put my head in his lap, to do all the things a three year old would
do, but we just sat there immobilized. Then he recognized me and, as if there had
been no interlude, began speaking once more.

"Then, we wanted a child, Daniella. But as I'd been conceived and born during
World War I, I wanted to wait for you until the second one was behind me. Maybe
the time of my conception jinxed me. Maybe it jinxed all of us who were born in that
time. I wanted you to be free of taint."

"You were conceived on the Equinox." He was beginning that story again that I
knew so well, so I tried to deflect him.

"In three minutes, the universe came to be." Immediately I knew I had been unkind.

He lost his train of thought and looked embarrassed. He was so willing to speak
about himself, I didn't dare stop him. The first time Lance and I had stayed up all
night talking, I knew we would never stop talking to each other. But after all these
years I hadn't expected this with Aram. Finally, I was getting a glimmering of a past
from the one person who had insisted that it didn't or mustn't exist.

"You were a new light for us." He was hesitant, not knowing whether he should
continue.

"We stayed in Santa Fe. Your mother seemed happy to apply herself to the piano.
I became known in my field even though I was young. People said I had a certain
fervor they liked. I had a certain reputation. After the war, I was called in when blight
struck the Austrian oaks. It wasn't anything miraculous I managed over there. I was
just the right person at the right time."

We went to sleep. In the morning, I suggested a walk. The snow had melted. When the sun is out, it is very warm during the day. I wanted the relief of bathing in the whiteness of the air. Aram, seated woodenly, drinking coffee, was not at all inclined to move. A walk was not something I had ever known him to refuse. My father looked at me for such a long time it felt like a first time. Not as if I were his daughter and he wanted to know whom I had become but as if he had been carrying a burden for so long time, he wanted to know if he could set it down before me, if I could be trusted.

I have seen him evaluate the health of a tree or a grove. I have watched him use his eyes and his fingertips to examine individual leaves, inspect the bark, the mulch around the roots, the soil, touching, rubbing, smelling. And I knew that if I invited him to run his fingers across my face and shoulders and arms, he would know whether I was solid or not, and whether he should speak. As it was, he had to trust his eyes. We had come to a crossroads.

The infant he had held in his arms just after he had cut the cord, my mother's ruddy blood staining the shirt which afterwards he would never throw away, was now a woman, much the woman his Rosa had been when he had first come to love her. I saw that he saw that; it was in his eyes.

"You're even beautiful," he said.

"Why do you say that?" I asked.

"It's a fact. As with a deer or an elk in the wild. Something we depend on."

"We?"

"I don't know. We. Men, maybe. Me and Lance. Only me. I am depending on you, Daniella."

I said two sentences to him I had not expected to say. I said, "You know, Aram, I am forty-two years old. And sometimes I think I'm mad."

"Because you've left The Mountain?"

"That and other things."

That's all it took to confirm him in what he had seen. He looked proud of me and then his face changed as his eyes filled with grief. "Then, Daniella, I haven't protected you from anything, have I?"

Again I wanted to put my hand on the back of his hand where it lay on the table by his half-empty cup, but I didn't. He had to trust his eyes.

"Shall we walk outside?" I asked pouring more coffee into his cup and pushing the rolls he had brought and the local sage honey just a bit closer to him.

"I think I need the walls around me," he tossed his head bewildered by everything that was transpiring.

"Do you want to talk more?"

"I want to talk about your mother." His eyes which were never any single color searched mine to be certain that it would be all right and he began.

"Some months after you left for college, it occurred to me that something was wrong and I began to wonder if things had just gone wrong or if they had been askew for a long time and I hadn't noticed. It wasn't Rosa, I didn't think, she seemed exactly the same. I didn't dwell on it. Your mother's life seemed to continue in quite the way it had been before. Maybe that should have alerted me. She's never needed friends. If I was home, we were together, in the ways we had found. She was, as always, devoted to the piano. The way Lance is devoted to the flute, only, of course, she never plays for anyone except for us.

"But for me it's difficult to say this to you Daniella—after you left home, I found I lost momentum. I became bored, dissatisfied with my work, irritated. Boredom is different from anger, frustration or despair. When I am angry, it is because I really care about things. But now little crevices opened up under my feet when I didn't care, and I fell in. It was an unusual time not to care because things were heating up in my field. Finally others were caring and occasionally listening to some of the things I had to say. Possibilities presented themselves to stop a little logging here, to save a little habitat there, to recover some of what had been devastated. I was relieved that I had never thrown in my lot with any particular interest. That remove which had always been an impediment had become an asset. People trusted me because I had kept my distance. They began asking what I thought was wrong and what we might still do about it.

"Maybe I was hoping that what had always eluded me in Rosa would emerge now that you were gone. No longer preoccupied with caring for you, Rosa might be willing to expose herself to me. I was wanting her to communicate in words. It wasn't that the music or silence was insufficient, in itself, but that it left so much unsaid and that ate at me. I became unbearably aware of a vacuum, a hole, emptiness, the erosion of what had disappeared. As I myself was wanting to begin to speak, I thought there might be something inside of her, something she hadn't shown me or given me that I could plant in the center of myself, something within me that was vital and would attract new life to itself.

"Had she ever spoken of herself? I wondered. Before you had arrived? Before our dear Daniella, Dan-iel-la-la-la-la had come?"

He drew the sound of my name out so that I heard it again exactly as I had heard it as a child, heard all the music they had put into it, all the longing, heard all the diminishing tones of the bell. Then it was as if I wasn't there again; he was speaking aloud, once more, to the air.

He continued, "I began to ask myself questions. When I'd met Rosa, had she been more outspoken? Before the war? Maybe. Maybe then. Yes, I thought so. And during the war, her letters, yes, those had been open, fresh. I began to remember. She had been playing in a little Jazz band. The 'B' girls had been thinking about going to Europe, playing for 'the boys.' Had she given this up for me? Why? I was overseas. There were four of them, all women, all classically trained and crazy for Dizzy Gillespie, Louis Armstrong, Bessie Smith, Leadbelly, Blind Willie McTell, Blind Willie Johnson, Blind Boy Fuller . . . they really liked those blind boys, I don't know why. Remember—you must—when we first heard George Shearing? Your mother went nuts; she bought every record he made. She said she heard something in the music that wasn't there when people kept their eyes open.

"She had been so bright. The physicists' darling in college where we met. Math, physics and music, they all seemed to go together and I was amazed I'd won her when I was just a modest natural scientist. I didn't even play chess very well. She does. So do you, Dani.

"It was great seeing you playing together. I would look at the board and kibbitz and even you would laugh at the advice I gave you. Once when we were in Wisconsin, you said, 'Aram, please, I'm having a hard enough time beating Rosa without you helping her so much.'

"I was embarrassed. I just liked the castle and was looking out for its welfare."

"I always knew that, Dad," I said. "I like the rook myself. It moves like a particle in a Richard Feynman diagram. But I don't let that spoil my game."

It was like we were pals, Cardinal. He was on a roll.

"When I was in the war, your mother's letters to me had been like little jazz riffs. They'd go off on a theme and embellish it, move in here and there, then they'd build. She'd turn herself inside out, pull out a long note, press down a minor cord, sweet and surprising, she'd just unzip, no holds barred, tell me everything she was thinking and feeling in a wild crescendo up and down the scale, naked. I tell you, Daniella, her letters were as good as her music. She used to be good with words." He was drumming on the table as if to prove his point and snow was melting off the roof in a regular rhythm—and Rosa was there with us, making music, like she always did.

"And then?"

"It was over."

"When?"

"I don't know. I don't know."

There was a long silence and I moved my chair closer to him out of the winter sun which was low enough to make its warm way into the room. He took my hand, turned it over, and he traced the lines in my palm with his index finger as if he were tracing his life.

"By the end of the war. Yes, by the time I was home, it was over. As if she'd lost her breath.

"I do know when it changed. It came back to me after you left and then I forgot and remembered again and forgot. But now, Dani, I remember.

"The last time we, Rosa and I, spoke, really spoke, the last time she was present, not only to listen to me, but for herself, Rosa was recounting a party. Was that it? Some gathering in the desert. Perhaps I hadn't really understood what she was saying. Perhaps, I wasn't listening attentively. Here it is. It occurs to me now, now, for the first time, that she didn't leave me. I left her."

He walked to the window and put his hands on the sill and leaned out into the winter morning, opened the window and breathed in draughts of icy air, swaying back and forth in the light so that sometimes I could see his back clearly and sometimes the light was in my eyes.

Without turning around, he asked: "You and Lance?"

"We're fine, Dad."

Turning and positioning himself carefully so that he knew by the shadow on my face that he was blocking the sun sufficiently for me to see him, he spoke very deliberately. "I left her the evening when she was trying to explain exactly how hard it had been to be here in New Mexico, not a hundred miles from where the two of us are now ..."

"Closer than that, Aram."

"How hard it had been to be here, here at the end of the war, to be so alone."

He walked around the room and then we went out the door so he could look south toward Los Alamos, but he turned northwest as if he were looking for Rosa. "Can you hear her, Dani? Can you hear what she's saying? I can hear her so loudly, it sounds like a bomb going off in my head. Amazing to be able to hear so well when I wasn't able to hear it then. I couldn't listen then. That's the truth. I couldn't.

"It's as if she's in the next room, isn't it, Dani? I can hear her fingers running up and down the black and white keys, swift as water falling over rocks, becoming a waterfall. Endless. Day after day, the same, that music, note for note, the same." It was, Cardinal, as if, he, we, were talking about the dead.

He closed his eyes as I had seen him do when he was trying to remember statistics. I knew he was going to repeat her words exactly as she had said them.

"'Alice asked me to spend the weekend with her.'" I could hear my mother's voice speaking through his.

He continued. "She said, 'The war was almost over. We knew it. We could tell. It was that time, you know, when you know something because no one is saying anything. You know what I mean, Aram? Nobody was saying anything about anything and so it was certain that the war was going to be over but first something terrible was going to happen. Suddenly certain ideas weren't talked about. If anyone was speculating it was only to themselves'. 'The women on the Hill,'—you know, Dani."

He interrupted the story, Cardinal, to remind me that the "Hill" was what they called the top secret place at Los Alamos where they were trying to build a bomb.

"'The women,' your mother said, 'weren't even coming into town to go shopping. Every day there were dead spaces in conversations. The rhythms of things made me nuts. Everything was very jumpy and it didn't stop. Like a boogie-woogie that went on interminably. Change the chord, I would scream, but the chord didn't change; it was such an ugly chord.'

"I remember what she said, word for word, Dani."

And I remember what he said, word for word, Cardinal.

"'I'd gotten used to certain things' she said. 'I knew that friends from college had come here to do important things. We all knew they weren't slighting us. We all knew they weren't allowed to talk to us and that we couldn't visit them. Still, when they crossed the street as they saw me coming, it gave me the jitters. I knew the people on the "Hill" had given up their lives and research to do what ever they were doing. We all knew there was a war on. It wasn't that we didn't know that.

"'It was pretty lonely. After awhile, we got stopped talking among ourselves, afraid we might inadvertently guess something. It was if we were living on the "Hill."

"'Maybe it was just how long it had all gone on and how futile it seemed. Everyone was increasingly edgy. We were afraid. You know how it gets. We'd survived so long. We saw it was going to be over, and we were afraid we were going to lose it all in the last moment. I was sure I was going to lose something. Something that was everything.

"'I thought it was going to be you, Aram. I began to think you were going to die just as the war ended. It seemed unbearably tragic. I was afraid to answer the doorbell because it might be someone in uniform with a message ... "Hello, Mrs. Stanebruch...."'

"'I began imagining it, you see. It was unimaginable. I mean unbearable. But also there was something else. Something in the air. Frenzied. Nothing said. Nothing! So we knew something.

"'Alice said, if I didn't come there would be no music. She insisted. I just think she couldn't bear being alone in her house out there anymore. She said she'd had the piano tuned just for me. She wasn't kidding. It had needed a tuning, it was so dry that summer. I was always complaining about what the heat did to their grand. What else did I have to do? I offered to drive out for the day. Alice had something else in mind. An overnight in the country. She said it as if everything was hunky dory. Well, it was summer. She had an adobe house in the Jemez range. I wasn't studying or teaching. What else did I have to do? There were just going to be a few of us. I knew she was lonely. She was lonely in her marriage and I was supposedly one of her best friends.'"

"I feel like I'm drowning, Daniella," Aram said. "I feel like I'm drowning in ice while the sun coming through your window is burning my back. It must have been hot as hell then. It was summer. If it is this hot now when there is snow on the ground. ... How hot was it there where your mother was? It was summer. It was too hot for humans to survive. It was too hot to stay sane."

We walked outside. I leaned against the wall of the house but he stood in the center of a snow field with the sun beating down on him.

"Your mother was telling me all of this. It isn't only that I didn't say anything. It is that I didn't hear it. I didn't hear her. The words imprinted themselves in my memory and still I didn't hear them."

"'I went,' she said. 'I don't know why. Because. Because I didn't want to be alone in my apartment waiting for you to die. I went out there, waited for the others to gather. I skimmed through a few magazines. *Good Housekeeping*. I don't know where the other 'B' Girls were. The B Minor Band. No one showed up at first. I got impatient. I felt Alice wanted to sit down and have a heart to heart. I couldn't bear the thought; I would just fall apart. Rather than risk it, I was getting ready to leave but Alice insisted, "The gang is coming." Then she offered to take out her recorders so we could play together. Anything. She was acting as if it were a state occasion and also, admitting for the first time, that it was all too much for her. We were all friends. Not intimates but good friends. You know what I mean? We played music together. You have to be friends. Then everyone arrived. The 'B' girls: Sue on coronet, Josie on sax, Karen on drums. Alice's husband, Jeff who played violin. Craig and his guitar. We jammed till late.'

"This is where it gets hard, Daniella. I remember every word."

"You should have been an actor, Aram. Do you want to quit for awhile? Shall we take a walk now?"

"No, I think I need to stand here. Remember that song we used to sing each summer, Dani? Only mad dogs and Englishmen go out in the noonday sun."

"That was in summer, Aram. It's winter now."

"Maybe, but it's still hell."

He wiped sweat from his forehead with a handkerchief and folded it carefully into the back pocket of his chinos.

"Rosa said she couldn't sleep that night. 'I don't know why,' she said. "You know, Dani, it's like remembering a piece of music that you haven't heard before. You listen to it and then a few days later it comes back. Has that ever happened to you?"

"I don't have that kind of ear, Dad."

"Well, it doesn't matter. It's just that I am remembering it exactly as it was. And it's been how long? How old are you?"

"I'm forty-two, Dad."

"Then it's forty-four years. Forty-four years it's been lying around in my brain, untouched.

"She said they'd started to improvise quite late and she'd finally gotten high on it. So when she couldn't sleep she got out of bed and took a walk. 'It was dawn,' she said. 'Gray. It was about 5 AM. I don't know what possessed me,' she said.

"'It had been Alice's idea that I come to her house,' she repeated. I should have had a clue when she started repeating things over and over again. Things that didn't matter, like why she'd gone to the house. As if she shouldn't have gone. Why not?

"'I don't think Alice had anything in mind but some way to relieve the tension that everyone was feeling. Everyone. Even those who weren't even remotely connected with the "Hill." Alice had insisted. It was all so odd. I didn't see her after that time. I didn't want to.

"'I saw it.' your mother said. I could hear her voice puncture, the air rushed out of it."

I could hear my mother's voice saying the words, Your Eminence. I knew how Rosa would say such a thing. Flatly. With a dull evenness that pressed all the natural music out of her voice. I heard what he had heard. Sweat was running down his face again and the air was out of him too.

"'I saw it,' your mother said.

"What had I said to her when I'd come home after I'd entered Dachau? Maybe I also had only said, 'I saw it.' Maybe that was all I'd said to her in the beginning. But then I had read to her. Not poetry in the middle of the night, or mysteries, I read from this book. I read her everything. Just like I read it to you, Dani. I would wake up in the middle of the night and when she woke up too, I'd read it to her. Just like I read to you.

"But your mother. She only said, 'I saw it.'

"She saw it, she told me, Dani. She had seen it in the distance.

"This is more than I want to remember, Dani. Do you know what I said then?

"I said, 'Maybe you only imagined you saw it.' That may have been the only thing I said."

Both of us were drowning in the music in the next room that was two states away in California. My father began again. "How often does she play the same pieces of music over and over again. Why haven't I ever noticed before that she repeats something hour after hour, again and again?

"I said, 'Rosa, maybe you only imagined you saw it.'

"'No,' she answered, very deliberately and slowly, looking directly into my eyes. But also no longer looking at me. In the moment her eyes seemed to meet mine but they were glazed. And then they turned back inside herself as if she were seeing it again. 'You'd have to be blind not to see it,' she murmured.

"She stood up and put her hands on the back of the wooden chair, and looking at me, nodding slowly as if checking things out inside she said 'A man and a blind woman were in a car heading toward Albuquerque when it went off. She saw it.'"

We were both silent. I walked inside to the living room because part of me was afraid Rosa was playing there. Aram followed me. He sank heavily onto the couch, made a huge dent in space and pulled it around him. I didn't dare sit next to him or I'd fall in too.

"She left the room. She left. She left me then.

"Now, Daniella, I know everything, but too late. Your mother saw what I saw. She saw it too. Your mother. Rosa saw that enormous white light and it burned out her mind."

That's it Cardinal. I got it just the way it happened. My father, Cardinal, was one of the soldiers who liberated the Camps. Yes, let's start there. He never spoke about it to me or anyone except my mother, until the night he came to read to me. My mother, Cardinal, was in the Southwest when they tested the first atomic bomb and she saw the mushroom cloud. She never spoke about it.

I took a sabbatical from The Mountain in January 1988. I met Peter Schmidt for the second time that November. Why was I surprised? The war, the camps and the bomb. The war, the camps and the bomb. I got it all in one night. Why not? Isn't that the way it happened to everyone. The War. Isn't that the way we talk about it? The War! *The* War! *The* Camps! *The* Bomb! But now I know something, Cardinal, don't I? Despite my father's insistence, I wasn't born into a safe place; I was born into the heart of it, just like everyone else.

I waited awhile. Then I said, "I think I need a little time alone, Aram."

"I know," he said. "We've all relied on being alone. Don't we, Daniella? It's not so bad, is it?"

"It's not so bad, Aram."

"Tell Rosa I know," I said. He wasn't certain but I nodded to reassure him, both of us knowing that he would have to tell her that he finally knows. I didn't know, Cardinal, what other kindness I could extend to him in the moment. I went outside and filled a pewter bowl with snow and brought it to him insisting he wash his face with it.

"Shaena taught me to wash my face in snow. 'For a beautiful complexion,' she would say."

"You too," he said and took the snow in his hands and washed my face as gently as if I were still his baby.

II

The Mountain

Chapter 8

Dear Cardinal:

In my imagination, we have become familiars. When earlier I approached writing to you with hesitation, now I find myself unable to resist the page. When I awaken late during this winter season because it is dark so much longer and I stay awake longer—I make a cup of coffee and sit at this desk facing the slope of the hills, and continue this letter.

Just before I was born, a two hundred inch mirror, which had been in the works for twenty years, ground and hand polished on two separate occasions for the preceding two years, and had been traveling across the country, greeted by crowds all along the railroad lines and unseasonable thunder and lightning storms, was finally set up at Mt. Palomar in California above the Pala Indian reservation. Three days before Christmas 1947 and three days before I was born, the Hale Telescope saw first light. This is how my father explains my career.

Accordingly, I committed myself to learning everything I could in my field and earned a B.S. degree with highest honors and entered graduate school. It was not easy for women, but I was relentless in my studies. By the time, I received my Ph.D, I had gained begrudging acknowledgment from most of the faculty. What Rosa had been calling "the dirty little war," Vietnam, was over.

I become a colleague though the progression of girl to woman to colleague in my field is not accepted as part of the natural order. Still, I was awarded a prestigious post doctoral appointment and then, to my surprise, I was offered, that is, I was allowed to create, my position at The Mountain.

Until two years ago, Cardinal, my career was assured. I have, or rather had, I suppose, claimed an infinitesimally small part of the night sky. I know something about the whirling community of stars we call the Great Andromeda Galaxy M31 or NGC 224. But Kepler might say that despite rigorous research, I have not learned its music. Andromeda, fortunately, was not the basis of my career, I always knew I couldn't just be a researcher, not the way science is practiced now. It wasn't that I wanted to know the stars or harness their power, I wanted to be with them. As it never mattered to me which part of the sky I was observing nor whose name is on the research paper, nor if I made a great discovery; I was able to construct a unique position for myself on The Mountain, guardian to that telescope, you might say.

Prior to taking my leave, I was resident adviser to a myriad of astronomers, astrophysicists and cosmologists who came up to scan and photograph the sky. Because of the nature of the profession—funding demands, teaching schedules, competition— astronomers focus exclusively on their own research and rarely accept administrative duties in order to assist others or supervise public exhibitions. And it never happens that a telescope as powerful as ours is not in use. Researchers reserve time on it years in advance and they only get a few days. It would be reserved far into the next century if we allowed it. Researchers only hope that the nights they take their turn will be clear and they'll return to home base with enough data to last a year. There is so little time on the telescope, astronomers waste very little of it trying to see the stars directly with our relatively blind little human eyes. In any case the night sky is rapidly disappearing everywhere in the wake of city lights that threaten it the way the lights of Rome threatened the Vatican Observatory and then the Observatory at Castel Gandolfo. One kind of light is always putting out another.

Astronomy has become a matter of data and analysis. In that sense, much of it can be done almost anywhere. Princeton, New Jersey, Los Angeles. But, I didn't want another home base. I wanted to be on The Mountain all the time. Not any mountain, Your Eminence, *The Mountain,* our own Ziggurat, our Mt. Sinai, the sacred place from which we receive the Tablets of the Law, from which for so long we have seen farther into the universe than anyone could have imagined. The place where first light touched us. That breath, exhalation or exaltation of all beginnings, reaching us finally after billions of years and gathered into the eye of the telescope to be preserved for all time. You understand, Your Eminence, I went into the field to see; I wanted to be the telescope. It was always with me, even in my dreams.

I was looking directly through Big Eye at a star that was brilliant and also very far away. The star was aligned precisely in the center of the telescope. Somehow it did not blind me. It shimmered like a crystal doorknob and then I looked through the star to yet another telescope, another lens; it was the star, itself. I was looking through the telescope at a star which was at the end of the universe on a curve of shell, pink and smooth as the inside of a nautilus, and the star was itself a telescope looking back at me. The star was gathering light from the other side of the universe where I was. It was drawing the light into itself. And I could feel the light leaving me and flowing into the star.

Then a black spot appeared in the middle of the diamond light. It became so dark that I could not see my own hand. The light of the star had gone out.

No, Your Eminence, I didn't ask the purpose of the investigations I was facilitating. Astronomy is a neutral science. It's nothing more than having a good set of eyes, better than the previous generation. It's information. We see what we see. That's what we do, we see.

Chapter 9

I found a profession which suited my rhythms. I have always been a night person. If I wasn't ambitious like my colleagues, I was a fanatic about what I loved. I managed the administrative work with relative ease, reserving the dark for solitary pursuits, trying to maintain the old ways of gazing directly at the stars though it is no longer practical, alongside the ways of professional astronomers seated in a warm, well lit, clean, swept, carefully organized rooms hovering over instruments and computer screens gathering data from outside the earth's atmosphere far into the deep sky. As I went about making a place for myself in this world, I had to overcome my reluctance to being indoors and my reluctance to being outdoors, each carrying their own anxieties.

After my appointment to The Mountain, Lance and I rented cottages on a nearby ranch that was no longer being worked. Lance took over what had long ago been a barn at the far far side of the property and transformed the loft into a sound studio. My quarters had been the stable. They were set in a meadow far back from the road, all the rooms facing a far stand of trees. There were peacocks on the roof. The stalls were gone, of course, and the owners had white washed the adobe and then built a verandah along the eastern wall. Still thinking horses, they had kept a semblance of the original construction so that the rooms did not connect to each other but each opened onto the verandah. The way I thought about it, I was living in a block of row houses each of which contained only one of my lives so I had a bedroom life, a kitchen life and a reading life, a star life and a sun life, a night life and a day life. A single life and a partnered life. An indoor life and an outdoor life.

Most days, I was able to hike to my office on The Mountain and suffered the very long ride into the city for meetings, classes and occasional lectures because I knew I'd soon be back in the woods and when I was among the trees, I longed for the unobstructed sky and the unimpeded vision of Big Eye.

As if I were living alone, I got a cat but she liked to wander. "Your days are numbered," I explained to her. "You will not survive the owls and coyotes," I scolded. I was particularly concerned because the Abyssinian creature was white, blue-eyed, unearthly. I kept the name that she had been given as a kitten: Ishtar, Queen of Heaven.

Despite Ishtar, the mice multiplied in the house; I allowed them to be. I left food for the raccoon and the opossums. I left morsels near the manzanita for the coyotes. I fed the birds and the squirrels. I placed salt licks for the deer. I felt a shudder of excitement and aversion when I heard the peacock screaming above me on the roof of the long house. His cry piercing as the iridescent blue of his feathers, the two waves, one of sound, one of color, following each other as thunder follows lightning in a storm.

I invited the woods in and Lance as well and then I began to feel crowded, intruded upon. Between one animal and another there was the crush of scent, urine, fur, saliva, dander, musk. Everything was seething; I increasingly searched for places where emptiness maintained the perfect distance that was called eternity. Between the stars, people once believed there was ether, but now most scientists believe there is nothing, nothing, no thing, *nada*. I went there. Lightly. Light is a motion, a no thing, a miraculous *nada*. I was happy when I found that *nada* within myself, the invisible "no thing" which drew together exactly as it held apart.

"*Nada*," as Hemingway had written. "A Clean Well Lighted Place" was one of my favorite stories. I had always liked the *nada,* longed for it because it was clean, because it was well-lighted, because the floor, I imagined, had been swept. It opened punctually, it closed on the hour. It didn't demand that one left until it was time. The glass was shining, or the bartender polished it with his soft red striped cloth before he poured the dark wine. And when I went home from that place, I went home alone.

Sometimes I imagined how it would have been had I been in that place, in that time. If I had actually sat there, reading, night after night, or writing figures with a fountain pen in black ink straight across unruled white rag paper. They would have called me *La Americana*, whispering about my red hair, my fine hand. I would not have asked about the wine, the kind of grape, the kind of soil and weather which created it. I would not have asked about the anchovies, the nets they used, the dyes for the hemp, the details of the life of a fisherman. I would have withdrawn into my book; they would not have known what to do with me and so they would have left me alone. I liked thinking about the *nada*. I wanted the *nada* to prevail.

The Mountain is connected to a University where I also used to teach. During one afternoon lecture I was entranced by a young, heavy set woman who sat as the blind often do with her eyes shut. Deprived of an image of itself, her shapeless body ran muddy down the seat back and arm rests as if it might slide away. I directed my focus toward the diffuse woman, searching for language precise enough to bring the young sightless woman into focused understanding of the nature of light. At the end of the lecture, she opened her eyes and scrutinized everyone, as if startled by their presence or her own corporeality. My heart sank. I had offered an entire talk to a sleeping person. The young woman sauntered toward me with lazy confidence and I was certain that this impudent undergraduate was going to push one of those ugly little tape recorders into my face, with the demand that I summarize my talk so she could get credit for attending. I looked for someone else to speak to, but the young woman held me, undaunted, with her eyes.

"Thank you," the young woman said. "The stars. Poetry. The same, 'The forms of deformed animals are beautiful in heaven.'" She was quoting Giordano Bruno who was burned at the stake for believing in infinity. Lowering her gray eyes, the student walked away quite steadily and without a cane.

My eyes filled with tears. I quickly wiped them and turned to face the next student.

But that night, at home, I couldn't set the interaction aside and opened Bruno at random, "Some men," Bruno wrote, "resembling the dim-eyed mole, who the moment he feels upon the open air of heaven, rushes to dig himself back again into the ground, desire to remain in their native darkness . . ."

Chapter 10

I expected to live like a monk isolated from everything and everyone, a life that needed nothing, the life for which my parents had implicitly prepared me. I didn't manage it. I have a partner and I had a brief remarkable friendship with a woman, Amanda Cartwright. Amanda and Lance Decan appeared in my life in the very same moment.

My colleagues are, as my mother predicted, unusually jovial, shaping an uncommon symmetry with work, obsession, music and clowning. Eccentrics all of them; I felt almost comfortable among them. As Roger Quidney, the Chair of my department, found it difficult to balance his professional life with his cultural interests, he had the habit of scheduling meetings in uncommon places. One evening, some of us, including Amanda convened at a small jazz supper club where the food was acceptable and the music exceptional.

"I told Roger he was to seat us next to each other, or I wasn't coming." Then without taking a breath, she continued, "What are you thinking?"

I became alert, and tried to distill the last observations I'd made of Andromeda into a few cogent sentences.

"Not that. I have some idea of your research—it's my job. I mean, what are you thinking now, this minute?" she continued as if this were not an intimate question.

"I don't know. I mean, I'm thinking, I've never met anyone like you before."

Amanda grinned. "It's about time they hired a woman. Not that it will make a difference. Nothing stops them but it's nice to have a counter force. Know what I mean?"

Rosa had assured me on one of the rare occasions when she tolerated my choice of vocation, that I would meet women like this in my field. "At the very least," she had said, "you will meet some people who speak their minds, and quite a few will be women."

On the surface, Amanda was cool and crisp, a stylish woman usually dressing carefully in elegant natural fabrics, pressed and tailored linen suits, pale, smooth silks, hand loomed sweaters, nothing like my work uniforms—casual skirts and shirts. She was smart, quick and efficient. "Formidable," was the word used in the Department. She had a brilliant mind, capable of assimilating complex research ideas and translating them into compelling language. It was her responsibility to get money for our various projects. She gathered up impressions of people, personal anecdotes along with their ideas and made good use of everything. "Ruthless," was the adjective I had privately used for Amanda but, chagrined by my judgment, I had tried to think "dedicated."

When Amanda came up to The Mountain, she never seemed quite at home. Her Mountain demeanor was a bit self-conscious; new jeans too well ironed; sweat shirt too carefully chosen; hair too carefully placed. It wasn't as if I were comfortable there either so I watched her more than I wanted to, wondering if there was something intrinsically misplaced about women altogether.

The evening we met, Amanda's blond hair, this time slightly disarrayed, fell in loose abandoned waves over her shoulders. She wore long earrings, silver stars suspended from delicate chains and gleaming against the bronze silk of her blouse, a heavy necklace on which an amber eye and silver rays formed a glowing sun between her breasts; the jewelry was a tease. She was the last person I expected to appear at a meeting, no matter its site, in wild jewelry, well worn western boots and a suede jacket, clothing commonplace enough in Idaho but not the costume of a grant writer on the town. In the mirror on the opposite wall of the restaurant, I glimpsed my own untamed red hair blowing into Amanda's blond hair, two storm fronts colliding, violating the code that we should be invisible and thereby undermining the conversations between my male colleagues, mostly bearded, dressed exactly as expected in jeans and sweaters, a uniform that had come to signify a partnership between maverick intelligence and methodical investigation.

That night, in Amanda's presence, I felt myself getting a little giddy: "I thought grant writers were supposed to be tactful. . . ."

"Politic, my dear, not tactful. My task is to get the money—by any means necessary, as they say.

"This flautist who's coming up soon is quite a number. If you can do with the telescope what he can do with the flute, I won't have any trouble supporting you."

"How do you come to this work?" I asked. It had seemed like a neutral question.

"I was one of those graduate students that makes everyone uneasy because I couldn't stay in one field. But as my grades were perfect and I didn't ask for student aid and I didn't want to be someone's TA, they couldn't throw me out.

"I studied a little astronomy, a little physics, cosmology, advanced math, topology, that sort of thing, mixed in with literature, religion, anthropology. All very interesting but not enough of any of it to make a career or get the degree. I drove my adviser crazy. 'We finally admit a woman to our department and she's all over the place. What are you doing?'"

"'I'm getting an education,' I said to him, 'is that still an honorable ambition? At least I haven't gotten pregnant on you and fulfilled all your worst prejudices.' Somehow I got them to let me do it my way. When I was organizing a dissertation committee—with everyone but my advisor from outside the department—and refining the topic, I realized I still hated math, I'd rather read a novel, and I didn't want to read any physics that didn't have *meta* in front of it. Well, the first grant I wrote, I got my advisor a lot of money; he forgave me.

"I don't mind the work. I like the people. I like their ideas. Some of them. And every night I drop my papers on my desk and close the door on *that* life."

"I can't imagine," I said.

"I never wanted to get to the place where I couldn't imagine. Anyway, some of the stuff some of you guys are into—it's pretty, but it's incomprehensible. Maybe, Daniella, I'm like that post-doc who everyone thought was a genius until he quit after he tried to *understand* quantum mechanics."

This was Steven Weinberg's story. It had been making the rounds.

"But, I'll teach you the art of grant writing. If you want half as much, your grant will have to be twice as good. That's simple arithmetic for women."

She touched my arm ever so gently and then stared up at the ceiling not removing herself from the conversation, but as if she were making a serious assessment of my character.

"I just don't think the astronomers and physicists really speak God's language yet and if I'm going into the unknown, I'd rather go in a big way. Sorry for the heresy." She wasn't sorry. "Sometimes I think we've made a god out of ignorance. Sometimes . . . yes, sometimes I'm grateful for penicillin, lasers *and* a paycheck. But . . . Oh hell, that's my life story, what about you, Daniella?"

I didn't get to respond. Roger called us to order. We disposed of department business. A trio came on, the warm up for a flautist who was the featured performer. Percussion like the sea coming in, chush chush chush. There weren't many local venues where a classical flautist devoted to Mozart got to play jazz; the trio set up was for Lance Decan.

Lance approached our table after the first set. Roger casually moved his chair and placed an empty chair between us. With so simple a gesture of chairs, my life was sealed.

"How could a shy and retiring person like myself, meet both of you in one evening?" I asked Amanda later.

"You drew us in," she insisted.

"*I* drew *you* in," I protested,

"*You* drew *us* in," she repeated.

By the time I left The Mountain, I was no longer baffled by such events. I had become familiar with the sudden force with which one reality might enter another and how impossible it is to maintain a shield against it. I began to fear that the *nada* would no longer be in my life.

Chapter 11

Perhaps I begin the confession here. How else justify speaking to you about Lance? The interlude of the body or a little bit of eros to liven things up? I don't believe in this, but Lance assures me I don't know what real life is. He's the teacher. I hadn't expected to partner. He wanted to partner. With me. It seemed straightforward.

I love him, if I understand the meaning of the word, if it means anything anymore on this side of history. Melody and harmony is the best I can do to explain our relationship. A melody proposed, then elaborated, first by his instrument, then mine, or vice-versa.

Several months after we met, I was lying with my eyes closed on the day bed while Lance was playing sounds that, for him, approached the stars.

"What did you see when we met?" I asked him.

"What did I see? Your wild red hair. A body that could belong to a dancer. Your eyes that might have been lapis, or emerald or moonstone."

"They would have to be moonstones," I said surprised at my willingness to play.

"But, it wasn't what I saw, it's what I heard, Daniella."

"What did you hear?"

"I heard the silence in you," he whispered, "and I hoped to fall in love."

That afternoon as I lay back on the bank of soft pillows alongside his day bed listening the room filled with long, blue shadows, the notes falling down like so many tendrils of flame. "Moonstones," Lance whispered between movements, "fire opals. Who are you?"

"A changeling," I answered pulling on his hair as I like to do. "Play Brahms."

"What is a changeling?"

"Someone the Fairy people leave when they steal your child. My grandmother, Shaena, said the fairies would come into her village in Poland in the winter playing little violins, and then before you turned around, they disappeared."

"I wouldn't mind, Daniella, if you were the child of the wee people. We could go around together making music. It wouldn't be a bad life."

"In my next life, Lance, I'll make music with you. For this one, I've been given a steel trap mind instead. Play Brahms, my love."

"What do you love best?" he asked me hopefully.

"Your mouth on the flute," I answered trying to please him.

"And then?"

"Your breath in the flute, my love."

"And then?"

"Stars."

"And then?" He was not going to be defeated even though I couldn't and wouldn't lie.

"Silence, I suppose. Or trees, like my father."

"And . . ."

I interrupted him, put my broad, flat square hand on his mouth. "They say, that to love another person, one must love oneself."

"That's what they say."

"Why? Why, do they say that?"

I can understand becoming a priest, Cardinal, and partnering with eternity. Were you watching everything going to hell in a basket and wanting to make an alliance with something that would last? Infinity is a damned complication in math and science but it must be a blessed relief in religion. There's a moment when the endless combination and recombination, chaos, transforms into its other face—perpetuity.

Lance is due here in a few hours and I want to tell you about him before he comes. The holiday season is a busy time for him. He plays a lot of churches and cathedrals. Now he's coming here. I almost wrote home. But I'm not used to saying it yet. He's coming here and I need to introduce you to him first. Otherwise you will be on the page and he will be on the couch and the arrangement will seem rude to me even though he knows nothing about you. This tête-a-tête is strictly between us, Cardinal. Would you like a cup of tea?

When Lance and I had been together two years, I bought him a rare platinum flute for his birthday because of the symmetry between our two instruments, the flute and the telescope. I wanted him to have the best, the ability to hit that high note, to hold it sweet and clear, like my ability to see a star which no one had seen before Big Eye appeared on the scene. Through the telescope, with just a little bit of focus, a star sometimes broke before my eyes into a galaxy the way his note broke into trembling arpeggios of light.

The flute came from the estate of a venerable musician I had known, actually, an old acquaintance of my mother's and someone Lance considered a mentor, though they'd never met. This flautist had become my friend when I entered the sciences. "One of the cadre," he had labeled himself before he died; he believed that physical scientists and musicians developed from a common mother language of vibrations.

This is how we enacted commitment: Lance moved to The Mountain with me and I bought him the most beautiful flute in the world.

Despite the times, Lance wanted to settle down, meaning, I assumed, that he wanted to be with me and wanted to be with me permanently. Time and space, forever and infinity. But every note ends. Lance lives in the vanishing. Music is ephemeral. How then did Lance come to such desire for constancy? It is as if Lance can still hear every note he's ever played, as if it passes from the visible to the invisible and remains engraved there.

"What do you want?" I would ask him.

"Exactly what we have," he answered, amused that I was always perplexed by our connection.

"Well then...?"

"But not the moment, not the single note or chord. By itself, it is not music."

"I don't understand," I would say, meaning it. When I tried to question Rosa or Aram about their marriage, they both retreated from my inquiry insisting that no standards from the past persisted into my world. I think, Cardinal, my father wanted to say what fathers had said in the past: "He's a good man. Settle down. Let him protect you." I would have laughed and my laughter would have wounded Aram who had tried and failed to protect what he loved.

"What shall I do?" I asked Rosa then but my mother only shrugged. However, Shaena believed that Lance and I were made for each other. Knowing that neither Rosa nor Aram would ever venture an opinion, she told me exactly what she was thinking.

"Our people have a tradition of hearing revelation and Lance's people see visions. So, Daniella, it's exactly right that Lance plays for you and you show him the stars." Shaena was visiting Rosa and Lance and I had driven up north to spend the weekend. Her mischievous grin lit up her face as it always did when she said what no one in the family would say. I knew my grandmother's strategy. Though Shaena was speaking quite loudly, no one else but I could hear her because Rosa had just flung herself down at the piano and was playing the first chords of a mean boogie-woogie daring Lance to follow her with a laugh both wicked and delighted, and he taking his flute in hand had met her glance with one equally challenging and audacious. His first musical slide was like a goat leaping up the mountain or a waterfall reversing itself and vaulting toward the peak. Rosa, undaunted, was laughing and playing ever more energetically as Lance sometimes kept up with her and sometimes leaped ahead daring her to follow. It was over in an instant with a clap of thunder, a flash of lightning. Then they looked over at Shaena and I huddled together and began again, in a pace that was more sustainable. "They've had an attack of life," Shaena whispered in my ear, "It's good. It's good for you, Dani."

I remained uncertain. "Not even the stars are permanent, Lance," I said. "They may last billions of years, but that's only a blink. They could go out in a cosmic second. A flash. A supernova, whoosh, and gone. You think you're looking at new light, a star being born, but actually it's a star going out." Nevertheless we stayed together. We'll probably stay together forever and live happily ever after. Who would have thought?

There are a few Czerny sonatinas Rosa plays each morning because she learned them as a child and they force her to practice her skills before she launches into a more demanding or expressive piece of music. They are her version of scales or the dancer's warm up at the barre. Lance looks at our daily life as if it is that kind of composition.

Lance awakens long before dawn. When the sky is overcast, he telephones me, and I put the phone down on my pillow or turn the speaker phone up at my desk. He puts his phone down on the night table alongside magazines, books, sheet music and practices his flute. Eventually I pick up the phone and hum into it, acknowledging that I hear the flute, the piccolo and that the endless orbits of his music have been entering my thoughts and dreams.

Even when he is on tour, he calls. When I answer the phone, I hear only the sweet notes, waves lapping in a rehearsal hall or a hotel room thousands of miles away. I am used to this language of sound; my mother raised me on it.

What would Lance say, Cardinal, if I were to read this to him? All of this which I have never said, have never admitted that I have noticed or that it matters to me.

Lance was a city boy from New York raised alongside the Central Park "wilderness," like my dad, but he moved to California because he found the music less restricted and he adapted quickly to the west. The culture which he described as raw, energetic and open, backed up by deserts and mountains equally raw, energetic and open influenced his music. He had always wanted to open it up, to find the notes between the notes, to find the exact and only coordinates for his eccentric maybe even rude variations, unexpected juxtaposition and interpenetrations, impromptu and improper leaps and declarations.

He says he's learned to play geography now, earth and sky. No surprise, he knows the land almost as well as I do. We go off road to nowhere, throw sleeping bags onto the earth behind some chaparral to protect us from intermittent automobile lights on the far away I-15 and watch the sky until dawn. Sometimes I ask him to play the stars and he does; I always recognize them in his music, can trace the orbit of the planets in his notes.

Once we found a motel where I slept while he played to me all morning, or as he said, played me the way one plays a cobra, penetrating its skin with the notes, finding the resonance that is the equivalent of its own inner motions, the exact rhythm, pitch and timbre. Every body has its dance, he says, and it is his task to find it. He does that when he improvises before an audience, he plays them, Cardinal.

That morning, he said, he turned the air conditioner off when I was asleep, let the light filter softly through the white shades behind the opened drapes to watch the sweat begin to accumulate on my body sprawled face down in a diagonal across the bed like an animal, he said, until he saw sweat, metallic and luminous, beginning to run along the cavities, settling along the musculature like a mist of aluminum descending on a mirror. These are his words; I memorized them. He insists he always knows when I'm dreaming and composes deliberately to send me further into the dream.

"Do you see me now?" I ask when I awaken, falling into our ritual conversation, raising the shades immediately to look out the window watching the shadows disappearing as the sun rises to mid-heaven.

"Yes, I see you now."

"And what do you see?"

"When I look at you, I see a body of music," he says quietly and deliberately. Every time, the same, Cardinal, and I never tire of it.

This woman, Cardinal, never expected to have a woman friend or a lover. Those relationships were over there on the other side. Over here was the company of my own mind and the secret and then suppressed hope that the stars would speak to me in their language the way bones speak or birds; and it would be sufficient.

Here are two primal mysteries, Cardinal. In one, with enough fire and force, inner resistance is overcome and essentially distinct or alien particles bond to each other. Enough fire and heat can do anything, can form helium from hydrogen and from that with enough insistence can create other elements through fusing what does not naturally move toward unification.

In the other mystery, things—again under enough force—break down into more and more essential particles. What are these essences which seem to have essences themselves—the breakdown may go on forever. What if behind every understanding, is there still something else to be understood?

This is what Lance says when he gets irritated with my preoccupation with stars. "Don't you get it? The universe is one big cock tease and she's not ever ever ever going to open her legs to your big fat telescopes, no matter how much you guys probe."

Then he laughs because I invariably cross my legs when he says this and I answer, "We're not all guys trying to find the answers, you know."

And then he says, "Show me." And sometimes I open my legs and sometimes I don't.

And you, Cardinal? Did you give up the expectation of romance, family, all of those entanglements? Do you think I'm rude? Really I have no lurid plans, no seductions in mind. Why am I speaking like this? To break the light barrier that separates us so that I can speak to you about Peter Schmidt without running into a stone wall, without running up against an absolute prohibition. "You must not!" the voice says. "You must not!"

But I will, Your Eminence. Bear with me. I must sneak up on him, the way he sneaked up on me.

Chapter 12

"Do you still love the stars?" I asked Amanda after we had come to know each other.

"I love getting things done. And I love helping the unknown become known. That's one part of me."

"Is there another part?"

"I love leaving things as they are. I love leaving the mysteries mysterious. That part of me doesn't come to work." Then she looked at me quizzically. "That's the part that wants to know you."

"I don't understand," I stammered.

"Nevertheless, it's true."

Because ultimately I didn't have enough time with her, each moment we did have has become a little world that serves as a retreat, perfectly preserved through the miracle of space time. In one sense it is an exact artifact of what was, except that it bears the shadow of my regret and is altered accordingly.

One evening we walked out of The Mountain dining room into a cold wind whipping through the brush. Tiny, brittle leaves scraped across the dry ground, metal twanged as loose ropes sounded a flag pole or shivering chain link. Above, the stars glowed icily in the winter sky. How long since I had really been starry eyed? The stars were so brilliant, one could almost forget that we weren't seeing all of it, that so much even of this sky was erased in the city glow.

"There's Procyon. Ten and a half light years away. And coming closer by one hundred and fifty miles a minute. That's how many miles a year? Oh, forget it." I was embarrassed.

"I know," Amanda said. "Whatever the current explanations, it's still mysterious."

Confession poured out unexpectedly. "There used to be some magic in this field. . . ." A repeating childish nightmare had hold of me: Their essential light being obscured, the stars would all go out and disappear.

"It isn't," I persisted, "that we no longer perceive their magic, it is as if we have taken the light out of them, as if it has disappeared from the stars as well. It isn't in our perception alone."

When I saw that Amanda was really listening, a forgotten memory broke through so forcefully I didn't have time to stop it before it left my mouth.

"My grandmother used to like to talk about the stars. But she didn't talk about them they way anyone here talks about them. She didn't read the horoscope to me from the Sunday paper. But . . . well, one night she pointed out Cappella, in Auriga. Said the Charioteer was really a goatherd. Said I was a Capricorn, and . . . well, it doesn't matter. It was a silly moment, we had, that's all."

"I actually know a great deal about astrology. I just don't talk about it here," Amanda said.

"Do you see Auriga's little hat and his three faint stars. . . ?" my grandmother had been teaching me how to see with her binoculars, Cardinal. "They are his nose. Those stars stay together making a shape, making a word in the sky, only we don't understand the language. This goat, Capella, is the very bright eye of the man who drives his chariot around and around the sky. You were born in Capricorn and that's why your mother likes to play music *capriccioso*.

"Did you know that all of Jacob's sons are said to live in the sky and when you were born they rained down gifts. Capricorn is probably Asher, which is what my father thought, but my uncle Vladie argued that it is Naphtali. We can't be sure which is which and without knowing the true name we can't understand the light. But if Asher was there when you were born, darling, you will be wealthy your entire life, if not in money, then in something else."

"What else?"

"Oh, you'll find out. That's what growing up is. It's finding out the answer to that question."

"And if it was Naphtali?"

"Then you'll live on the sea or in the desert and will always see the stars."

"I'll tell you another secret." As I grew older, my grandmother's secret confidences made me uneasy, but I always listened Cardinal. She was convincing; It felt as if her knowledge did have currency but in another world.

"Capella really isn't a goat," she continued, "or he isn't only a goat. He has another secret name and that makes him something else entirely. Now, I will tell you his secret name it is "the messenger of light.""

"But Shaena," I burst out, "it's all silly."

"Don't be so sure." She chided me and her face wrinkled with frustration. I had never seen her so dismayed.

"Would you like me to read your chart sometime?" Amanda asked.

"Oh, I don't think so," I said quickly, but looking for something to say that would not create a wall between us. I didn't want her to think she'd made a terrible mistake talking to me when in actuality, I had started the conversation. I didn't want her to think I was untrustworthy.

I was flustered and we embraced each other perfunctorily but not without my awareness of the unusual tenderness of the event. It had been so sweet, that evening with my grandmother. As sweet, really, as this evening with Amanda. The wind whipped around again, blowing Amanda's scarf onto my cheek and, shivering, we walked away from each other, Amanda to her car and I toward the road.

I tell you about this friendship. So that you will understand what follows? Yes. As I will tell you about Lance so you will understand what follows? Yes. What Amanda taught me? That Lance accompanied me to the Camps? Yes, all of that. I pace up and down repeatedly asking myself a question: "Why, Daniella, are you telling the Cardinal all this? What does it matter?"

A journalist named Richard Preston once said that we astronomers believe that "Five billion people concern themselves with the surface of the earth and ten thousand with everything else." So we are both concerned with the heavens. Is this sufficient?

Hardly sufficient to justify imposing upon the time and energy of someone whose life is already dedicated elsewhere. But still, something, Cardinal.

Amanda stopped her car alongside me. I had already told her I didn't want a ride even though it was cold. The clarity of the night demanded that I walk home the few miles.

"There's something else I want to say to you," she said, then paused, not unsure of herself, but of me. "There's something else. I mean, Daniella, there really is something else beside the stars."

"My father tries to explain that to me too." They would like each other, I was thinking.

"No, not what he means. A sky inside us as well as outside. I want to tell you about it. Not now, of course." Amanda wasn't forthcoming with the details.

For the next weeks or months Amanda would run into my office, allude to other worlds and then dart away. When I pressed her, Amanda wouldn't say anything more but it sounded to me as if she were speaking in mathematics and multiple dimensions. I was intrigued and I had reservations. Then Amanda gave me some books. "About the spirit," she said. "Contemplation. Meditation."

After I perused the books, Amanda was more open: "One practices," she said, "dissolving the physical world and psychological worlds, moving air or breath in between the molecules of self and thing so that enormous distance is created between them."

The image played in my head. Consequently, I ruminated, the parts move more slowly, no longer subject to the same intense attraction, they spin away, fall apart. Amanda was postulating a place where there could be that no thing, nothing I craved, but of another order. I was interested. I took one of the books home and studied it carefully before slipping it under the pile of scientific papers that never seemed to diminish. Some days later, I, who had been relatively silent my entire life, began to practice silence formally.

I sympathize with my colleagues who are concerned about my condition and avoid me. They think I've gone down the wrong road, that I've done it voluntarily; that it's catching. Lance understood that I was wary of this path and though he is not a man to jeer at someone else, he questions what he calls the tyranny of the scientific mind. "The truth is, your sometimes too self-important buddies in the Department are like people who are afraid of the blues note," he once said. Then he played a theme in a classical mode and transformed the same theme into a blues piece. "It's the same," he said, "only one is respectable and this other is still thought to be dangerous, a *patois* white folks are not supposed to understand. Or more precisely, the first is considered high class and this one," and then he really got down, Cardinal, when he played it, "this one is a baaaad note. This one is loooooow class, loooow, grief stricken and truth tellin'." These notes are just a wee bit closer together than the other notes and sounds slide in between that no self respecting person wants to hear. And if you add the devil's cord, baby . . ." It was lewd, Cardinal, more than a bit leeuuuuwwd, if the truth be told.

Ok. So I won't pretend to be innocent. I will not say I didn't have any idea what was coming. In fact, I said the words to myself: "There is a danger here," I said and began to meditate anyway.

I sat still regularly, following my breath. Then something came into that space, something numinous and indefinable. Compelling. It was not a thing but it was something nevertheless. In my world, the equivalent was called gravity but in the world of the contemplative, it had no name, was taken in and in silence was given back. And something else. Equally ineffable. Not compelling but unavoidable. Fearsome. Ominous. A dark force. Darker than dark. This I put out of my mind.

I continued to follow Amanda's first suggestions. I sat on a round black pillow simply breathing. On occasion when I came to an empty place without emptiness and felt joy which frightened me, I returned to my breath which was good until I went through my breath, until I followed it without following it, until it also dissolved. Something different then. Something. No thing. I entered all things. I was frightened. I persisted. The emptiness drew me. It was like spacetime. I could not resist it. Sometimes it was the *nada*. Sometimes I heard a voice, like encountering a galaxy in the midst of nothingness after having traveled millions of light years. Sometimes it was an image, or an intuition. Sometimes it was a story or an equation, equally elegant.

My colleagues spoke matter-of-factly of such events and scoffed at the popularizers who made religion out of intuitions, dreams and synchronicities. "If I hear the story of the discovery of the structure of benzene rings in a dream once more," Roger would moan, covering his ears. His confidence in the face of the inexplicable reassured me. "We just don't understand it," Roger said. "What else is new? That's our business, pushing into what we don't understand. When we understand everything, we're finished as a profession. It was predicted that physics would be dead by the end of the century, and look it's only just begun. So let's be thankful for the unknown and not give it over to the misty eyed."

I began to think I could do both at the same time. I could sit on my zafu, and I could do astronomy. I could read Nature and I could read Zen. Maybe I was becoming ambidextrous. Sometimes when I sat I felt a rush of kindness, like a flare erupting out of the sun, a plume of light. Sometimes (very rarely) a blaze of generosity, or gratitude, in the form of a spiral, again like a galaxy. Compassion. Then I was frightened again. I didn't know where to turn for understanding.

I went back to my stars. As Amanda had suggested, I found the night sky inside myself as well and they were similar but also they were different. Between the external stars, to the best of my knowledge, there was nothing, nothing, no thing, except the invisible which drew together exactly as it held apart. When there was something entering the external sky's darkness and emptiness, I knew what to call it, could imagine how it would behave, could calculate it. It did not leap up on to my shoulder, mewing, it did not telephone me, it did not drop its leaves at my feet, it did not want to embrace me and it was not ineffable.

There were bodies out there, massive and fiery, or cold, clusters of iron, but all minuscule compared to the extension of space; there were wild and brilliant explosions, but they were negligible compared to the pervasiveness of the silence.

There was something. I could feel it even if I couldn't name it or trace it or calculate it. Something between the in between. Something present and not present. Gravity? Was that it? Or was it something else not yet named, mostly unmanifested and so not quite existent, but also somehow existent, sometimes leaving inexplicable, intangible traces, a hint of a substance which you must not call substance but which might be filling the entire infinite universe, which was the invisible mass, or ether—that a few scientists are claiming once more should be put back into our equations—between the lights, between the fires of fire, between the whirling ice clouds of hydrogen, something that was the galactic space between one electron and another.

There were other forces I did not understand that sent everything fleeing away from everything else and other forces equally incomprehensible that drew them back ineluctably toward each other. A universe of longing and resistance of contraction and expansion. I could not decide which prevailed, whether it was a universal fear which caused everything to recede, pull away, run from the other, or eros, the longing that each body had for other bodies, no matter how distant that calling.

I persisted, read Kepler again for reassurance. Bruno. Pythagoras. They unnerved me and I preferred them. They were in my lineage. I went back further. My horizon expanded or perhaps it came to a point. The point from which it had emerged. There was a mystery. I wanted to wrap it about myself. It was something like the way my father sat under a tree when he wasn't studying it. It was the music in the music that my mother played. It was inexplicable. I went back to the mathematics, the calculations, the photographs. It was all more than I could undertake. Origins. Something in the beginning which had been lost. And I, they, it, were bereft without it.

First my colleagues' rationality reassured me and then it unnerved me. We were probing mysteries, but something in the methodology, in the focus, began to make me uneasy. It was insufficient. I didn't abandon it. But I wanted something else. Whatever I did, I found myself going in two directions, both forward and backwards. It was like the search itself. It would take a long time, an infinitely long time to get to the end of the universe, but then one would be at the beginning. Similarly, I thought, if I studied these old books an infinitely long time I might get to the beginning, to the first knowledge, which like the first light might contain all the secrets and all the mysteries, everything which had since been obscured, distorted, or disdained. "Where do I come from? Where do we come from?" I asked and shuddered.

Chapter 13

Shaena Bluestein was eighty when she died unexpectedly on the operating table during minor surgery. She had been what hospitals call *no code*; a woman who had determined that she didn't want anyone employing exceptional methods to revive her when she died. But since her first death occurred during surgery, the physician did not hesitate to try to revive her with a needle into her heart. I flew to her bedside immediately, beating my mother and father who were out of the country by a few days. My grandmother died again just hours after my mother arrived, having waited only to say good-bye.

Shaena Bluestein, as her name implied, had always been a beautiful woman. Exhausted, pale, wrinkled, she was still beautiful after her first wrestle with death. When I entered her private room, Shaena was gazing down at the journal which she started when I was born. Surprisingly, she had learned journal keeping from my father who had not kept much of a journal since the war, nor before it, but who had indicated to my grandmother many times how profoundly it had sustained him during his ordeal. Rosa, who one might have expected to keep a journal, never wrote anything down. Shaena's journal is a random record, sometimes intimate, more often impersonal, composed of personal events and family history, of musings, thoughts and feelings interspersed with news clippings, editorial commentary, historic citations, and pointed references to arcane magical and mystical texts as if there had been some collusion between her and Amanda, whom she never met, to guide me after their deaths. The only one who acknowledged my birthday and tried to visit our family every December, she invited me to wander through the journal, if she was there on my birthday day, but when it was over, she took the book away. She never said anything about this ritual and neither did I.

Shaena had been writing when I entered her hospital room and took the time to finish the sentence before she looked up, expecting a nurse or attendant, certainly not her granddaughter, the heir apparent, to whom she would finally entrust this remarkable, if eccentric, manuscript. I was standing at the foot of her bed when she raised her head. She greeted me; her eyes lit up. Two green fires sparked and ignited. A light, which I had never seen before, blazed from them, Shaena's lids pulled back not to widen her eyes but, it seemed to me, to protect themselves from their own fire.

As soon as she saw me and I had planted a kiss on her cheek which was softer and smoother as she aged, I hung a star map and a photograph of the Andromeda galaxy across from her hospital bed. Shaena smiled in appreciation, making a wry comment on its resemblance to female anatomy but she seemed equally thankful for the quieter photographs of trees I had placed alongside in order to honor my father's passions.

"All those charts, all those diagrams, all those photographs, what can you really see in them?" Then my grandmother whispered conspiratorially, "Those aren't the real stars, you know," as if her intent was, for the last time, to instruct her granddaughter who was still too young to understand what mattered.

"No, Shaena, it's a photograph of what is there, an image. Still, if you look up at night, through a telescope, this is close to what you'll see. It was taken on The Mountain. From such images, we have been learning everything." Without meaning to be rude, I had answered my grandmother's teaching with condescension. But it was my confusion in the face of death, not Shaena's.

"I don't think so, Daniella, dear," Shaena said very gently but so that I would know that Shaena would never, so close to death, risk unkindness. She said nothing more on the subject. I had quite forgotten that it was my grandmother who had first told me about Andromeda. Pointing to a place in the sky where, because of the city lights, I could see nothing, Shaena had said there was a tiny hazy point of light within the constellation, which was mistakenly called the Andromeda nebula, and it was the farthest stellar object to be seen with the naked eye. My grandmother said it was a galaxy like ours.

"Andromeda was chained to a rock and a whale was sent to devour her," Shaena had informed her little granddaughter.

"And how did she get in the sky, Shaena?"

"She flew away on a winged horse."

"Is that true?" I had asked conscious of being motivated by both hope and challenge.

"Probably," my grandmother had answered, "but it is very difficult to understand."

I reached out to stroke Shaena's thin legs under the hospital sheets. Shaena began speaking again. "When I was a girl," but before she could finish I interrupted her.

"What has that to do with what we're talking about?"

"Well, it's not a direct line."

"I don't see any connection."

"I guess you don't. But maybe its not anything you can see directly, Daniella. You have to wander back, winding into concentric circles. Then . . ."

"Why do you always talk about what it was like when you were a girl?"

"Because it started there."

"Not for me. I don't remember what happened when I was a girl. I don't remember anything."

"Nothing."

"Yes, nothing. One story."

"That's sufficient."

"How could it be?"

"Because everything comes from that one story. That's what you'll find out when you circle back."

"How can I circle back when there is no path, nothing but that one story?"

"I know which story, Dani. About the stars raining . . . "

"Don't!" The sharpness of my retort startled me far more than my grandmother. Shaena was crossing a line. I felt a little vertigo. "The swirl of the astronaut," I started thinking to steady myself in information, "at the lip of a black hole."

"Would you like me to tell you how everything comes. . . ?"

"No." It was an ugly "no," Cardinal. In it I can still hear the arrogant clang of my profession: "I argue that . . .'"

Naturally I didn't intimidate Shaena. She was transforming before my eyes, not without some annoyance at the effort involved, into Mrs. Sharon Bluestein.

"Your mother has a story and your father has a story, *Professor*. Everyone does. Ask them."

"Aram doesn't think he has a story."

"Not true. Aram won't talk about it. He has a story. He certainly does have a story."

"Well then, Rosa doesn't think she has a story, *grandmother*."

"Rosa doesn't think she has a story, *grandmother*," Sharon was able to mimic my petulant inflection exactly, "but it's not true *granddaughter*."

"Listen, Shaena,"—I initiated a slight movement toward accord—but not a complete recapitulation—"whenever we were driving in the car and I would say, 'Rosa, look at that we just passed,' she would refuse to look back saying, it's not important. She always says if she turns around she'll miss what's coming."

"Well, yes, that's your mother. And she is often blinded. She doesn't know you can't see what's in front of you if you don't know what's behind you."

"Ok. So tell me what happened to you as a child."

"No. The moment has past. I don't know what I was going to say."

"Well, just look back."

"No. I can't."

"You won't. And you're . . ." I caught myself, I thought.

"That's true. I won't and I'm dying. That's what you were afraid to say. I'm dying and you're afraid you'll never know." Shaena didn't ever lie.

"Why won't you tell me?"

"Because you don't know how to listen now. You'll listen for information. And that isn't it."

"Information isn't it? What is it then?"

"If we weren't in the hospital now, Shaena, if we were home and I was younger, this is the moment when you would say, 'Let's have a cup of tea.' Or 'let's bake cookies.' That's right isn't it?"

"Yes, that's right. I'm glad you remember."

Then I did remember, first the set of my grandmother's face, then a far away look—I saw it coming over her face even as I remembered it—as if she were thinking of what else she might do or say that she had never done or said before and then resignation—yes, there it was—as she realized she was coming up against her own fatigue. Shaena slid down toward the foot of the bed, pulling over her breasts the rough sheets that were so stiffly pressed the light bounced off them creating a sterile shimmer of white in the room.

"Shaena. Shaena Baena," I had gone far beyond relenting and was hoping to cajole her into speaking.

"Daniella, dear, you're on one side and you won't come here, and I'm on this side and I can't come over to where you are. Anyway I am quite certain I shouldn't even if I could. Anyway, they're pulling me backwards. You go so far and then there is no pull in that direction anymore, which you once thought was the only direction there could be. And you start to slip back. First slowly. And then more quickly. I can't explain it," her voice was less than a whisper, the aftermath of an echo.

"You've explained it exactly," I took her hand to see if my grandmother was indeed slipping out of my grasp. "Only you explained it in astrophysics. So maybe I should tell my colleagues that the universe is not expanding infinitely and it's not a steady state universe. Maybe I should tell them that it will begin, eventually, to wind back."

"I wouldn't bother, dear," Shaena smiled. "They'll find out. They will also have to die. Now, Daniella . . ."

"'Now leave me because I want to sleep a little.' Is that the right ending, grandmother, to your sentence? But will you be here when I return?"

"I'll be somewhere. I won't be here, of course." Despite the light bouncing onto the ceiling and back to her eyes, it was getting dark. The dusk entering the window quickly muted the flat whiteness gathering in dusty shadows in the folds of the cloth. "But you won't be *here* either. So it won't matter."

"But you and I will be together somewhere in space-time, promise me that, Shaena."

"As together as we can be at that moment." She saw my fear which made her even more tired. "Don't worry. I'll be here." I saw how exhausting it was to speak the truth and assure me she would remain alive a little longer; I was becoming tiresome.

The next morning I was back at her bedside. Her first words were in French. "Tout est vrais, Daniel*la*. *Très vrais.*"

"*Non, Français, non,* grandmother." I was hardly as fluent in French as Shaena who had lived so many years in Canada and wanted to understand every word my grandmother would say.

"*Pourquoi?*" Shaena asked. "Do you want me to speak Yiddish? Do you want me to die in a dying language?"

"Not Yiddish either, English, please."

"Dani, you don't have to die in a dead language and you don't have to die in the government's language. You don't have to die in anyone else's language, if you don't want to, Daniella. What do you want me to die in? In Quebecóis? In Polish? In American? When it comes to dying, you can die in whichever language you choose.

And whatever language you choose for your most intimate moment, for your dying, remember this, Daniella, whatever language you choose, it determines everything. Everything. *N'est pas?*"

"What do you mean? *Je ne comprends pas.*"

"The language you die in enlivens it; when you die in a language you give it life, you even bring it back to life."

"You're not dying, Bubie."

"I'm not? What do you call this in your language, *kleine maidele*, my darling? What's the matter with you? Are you like the rest of your friends without a word for dying?"

"Bubie . . . I only meant you're not dying this moment. Are you?"

"Don't be so afraid, Dani. You're a grown-up; dying won't hurt you. Listen, little one, *kleininke*, I have something to tell you, so don't interrupt me. You study the stars, right? Do you know what the stars are?"

"What are the stars, Bubie?"

"The stars are a large sea of remembering. That's all they are. They are the light of remembering coming here. The light of so many memories rushing here as fast as they can. Do you know why? Why are they rushing here? Because everyone here is trying to forget. So don't forget, little one."

She was already tired. She lay back on her pillow and put her journal over her face. End of conversation. I pulled a chair up to the foot of her bed so I could take her feet into my hands and rub them. They were very cold. I remembered the times my grandmother would dress me in the winter, reaching under the covers, pulling out a foot, blowing on it to warm it, putting on the sock then putting it back under the covers while warming the other one.

"Don't forget what, Bubie?"

"Don't forget to say *Kaddish* for me."

"What's *Kaddish*?" I was surprised and got irritable again. "You've never wanted anything religious, why *Kaddish*?"

"What's *Kaddish*? *Kaddish*, little one, is the prayer for the dead. It is praise. *Kaddish* is gratitude. Is 'thank you.' Is 'thank you very much for. . . .' Every day for a year you'll say *Kaddish*, which means you'll look up at those stars of yours and you'll say, 'In the name of my grandmother, I say Thank You. Thank You for remembering everything.'"

"Is that it? Should I say it in Hebrew? Should I learn the Hebrew for you, Bubie? Would you like that?"

"Why? You can't say thanks in English? If you say it in Hebrew you won't really know what it means. You can say thank you in silence. You can say it in mathematics. You can say it in Chaldean, in Esperanto.

"Just before I left Poland, Daniella, when I was a young woman," she studied me to see if she could continue. I behaved myself and she went on. "I went to the grave, in Warsaw, of the man who invented Esperanto. Every other grave was like all graves, gray, dark, unhappy, even though the sun was shining. But his grave was a mosaic covered with colored stones with a great star in the center, a great blue, five-pointed star. You'll see, darling. He thought he'd found a way for everyone to speak to everyone else and it made him happy even when he died. So then you'll have to stop, look up, and say it: Thank you. And then also: I remember."

"What should I remember, Bubie? I'll never forget you Bubie."

"Me, I'm easy to remember. I made you cookies, so how could you forget? Remember difficult things. Remember everything we've all forgotten."

The journal returned to her face. She'd found a technique of closing a door between herself and everyone else by putting the journal on her face. I thought she had fallen asleep. It was winter. The light which had just risen was falling. I had placed a candle on the window sill that cast a halo on the rectangle of cobalt blue, a perfection of sky incising the white walls of the hospital room. I had only been able to find Catholic votive candles, the kind one lit in churches, but decided they were better than *Yartseit* candles; the Jewish candles in water glasses which are lit for the dead. *Yartseit*. Year time means death time. I didn't think the nurses would let me get away with a regular candlestick but this might pass. My grandmother liked candles and also always liked to look at the night sky with me and tell me the names of the constellations as she had known them, always emphasizing that my sign wasn't certain though it was most probably Asher.

"Who was Asher?" I always asked.

"A trouble maker, like they all were," Shaena had answered. "And a rich man. You'll never have to worry. I am seeing to that." She left me a little inheritance. Just enough so I would never have to worry and not enough so that I wouldn't have to work.

"Asher people work hard," she would say. "They're lucky. They *have* to work hard. Others may not be so lucky."

Shaena moved the journal down to her chest and continued talking. "Daniella are you here?"

"I'm here Bubie."

"When did you come?"

"Several hours ago. In the morning."

"Have we been talking?"

"A little."

"Why are you calling me Bubie?"

"What shall I call you? *Grandmère?*"

"Call me Shaena Baena like you used to when you were a little girl. Didn't I tell you already that everything that transpires at the last moment matters?" It was difficult for her to breathe. I pulled the chair up closer to her face and leaned forward.

"Do you know what Shaena Baena means, Daniella?"

"I didn't know it meant something."

"All these years, you didn't know it meant something. *Shaena* means beautiful. *Baena* means bones. It means beautiful bones."

"You have beautiful bones. You always did, Bubie."

"Wait darling, you haven't seen anything yet. Wait a few decades. She fell back, then roused herself again and murmured as if she were a little girl jumping rope, "*Shaena baena, kleina tzaina.*" Her eyes were closed. "*Vaint nisht, maine aintziker . . .*"

"How do you know I'm crying, grandmother, you're eyes are closed and you're sleeping?" It didn't occur to me then to marvel that I had understood her.

"Don't cry, your mascara will run."

"I don't wear mascara. I never have."

"That's the trouble. If you did, you'd know not to cry. So listen to me now about what I said before. From the last moment comes the beginning. You see? And so whatever you do at the last moment starts everything. So, Dani, you see, on the one hand you just live and on the other hand each moment should be a last moment so something good can come from it. After a while, Dani, it's easy."

"It's easy?"

"Yes, it's easy. So now don't make it hard for me. You sit still and I'll take a nap."

The nurses came and went. Shaena fell in and out of awareness. I was reaching for her journal which was about to fall off the bed when she opened her eyes, "Read these pages I have marked with a paper clip and no more," she instructed me and closed her eyes again. I picked up the book happy to have those pages with the small, very orderly yet curling script in her hand. The pages contained a story:

A very pious and very poor Rabbi living in the village of Z in Poland had a dream that told him to go to the Castle in Krakow and dig under the bridge where he would find a pot of gold. Walking day and night, he made the long journey to Krakow where he came upon the bridge and began digging. But soon a Castle Guard interrupted him, gruffly de-manding to know what he was doing.

Not knowing what else to say, the frightened Rabbi told the guard his dream. The guard laughed. Only a peasant, only such a foolish man would believe in dreams. "Why," the guard sneered, "just the other night, I had had a dream that there was pot of gold buried under the bed of a very poor Rabbi who came from the village of Z. But, at least, I have the good sense not to go searching for this pot of gold." At which point, Rab Yankel thanked the Guard for his wisdom and went back to the village where he found the pot of gold under his own bed.

After the story, Shaena had written: "This is your inheritance. When you go to Poland, you will see the castle." I had no intention whatsoever of going to Poland, Cardinal, but of course I said nothing as I didn't want to agitate her; I was still hoping Shaena would live a long time.

Shaena did sleep for almost an hour when suddenly her eyes flashed, really suddenly, the way a star suddenly explodes flaring wildly and then retreats into itself, but smaller, that is more intense, all the energy contained and directed toward the core.

"You can even die in a dead language. You can resurrect a language in your dying, you can bring back worlds with your dying. Dead worlds don't die, Daniella, they simply recede from us, but, little one, *kleininke,* they wait for us, they wait for us at the edges of our eyes, of our life, so that when we step into them again, we bring them back to life."

"What are you talking about?"

"I am going to do something useful with my dying," she said. "My life didn't mean anything. Except for my family. And, for myself, of course. And, if not for me, there wouldn't be you. But outside that . . . my life, it means nothing. But my death, that can have meaning."

"What do you mean, grandmother?"

"On my stone, Daniella, I want you to write the following. And I want you to do it, even though your mother will be annoyed. I don't want any prayers or anything that says, Shaena Bluestein wife of—may she rest in peace—or mother of or grandmother of. . . . Whose business is it? Those that know, know and those that don't, it's only names. And don't put a "Woman of Valor" either. One psalm for the women and so every Jewish female who is dead in the cemetery is a woman of valor. If you want to know who was born Jewish, you go through the cemetery looking for valor. Please. . . . So this is what you will say: "SHAENA BAENA, AT THE LAST MINUTE, SHE REMEMBERED."

"What do you mean, Bubie?"

She wouldn't say, Cardinal, but as I write to you it is obvious—isn't it?—that she was teaching me something which I absorbed without knowing its details or its meaning.

The next morning, Shaena was still alert. "You slept all night like a baby, Dani," she said.

"And you?"

"And I? When you're dying, it's no time to be asleep."

I got up from the cot that had been wheeled in for me after some complex negotiations with the hospital staff the night before which had been won, ultimately, by Shaena when she got off the bed in protest and without saying a word put her suit skirt over her night gown, then combed her thin white hair, put rouge and powder on her cheeks from the little gold case which Shaena called a compact and had had since she'd been what she had called a *kalla,* a young woman who was engaged to be married. When she almost fell on the way to the closet to get her shoes, the nurses brought the bed.

"This afternoon," Shaena said with comic seriousness, "I want you to do my nails. Please go to the five and dime and get some nail polish. A dusty rose. Not a pink little girl color and not a bright red, please, not a whore color either. Something pretty and dignified. And undercoat. And final coat. The works. And a nail file, a good one, and an orange stick, some oil for my cuticles, everything. You hear darling? Everything. If you don't know about such things, and I don't think you do, and I can't wait for your mother to come, stop into a beauty shop and buy it there. Tell them it's for your grandmother, a lady with taste, she's dying and she wants everything. She doesn't care if it's wasted. Afterwards you will go down the hall and give it to some poor woman.

Tell them you want the best. And then I want you to do my nails. A good job. Because I'm going to die soon and after I die my nails are still going to grow a little and I don't want them to look ragged. You'll do my nails with the moons showing. Okay?"

A manicure was not on my mind, Cardinal. I was thinking of other things, of what she had said the day before. "How do you know about the Chaldeans, Bubie?"

"A Bubie may not know about the Chaldeans but Shaena Bluestein, my darling, she knows about a lot of things. Do you know Abraham, Daniella?

"No. Your mother didn't want you to know anything, did she? Maybe she was right. Well, Abraham came from Ur. And Ur, is Ur of the Chaldeans. Everyone knows that. And Daniel, do you know about Daniel yet? He hobnobbed with the Chaldeans. How do I know such things? You know about the stars. How do you know about them? Well, I also know about the stars. You Americans think you know everything. You think you invented the stars because you invented the telescope."

"We didn't invent the telescope."

"You see. That's not the only thing you didn't invent. The Chaldeans, Daniella, they knew about the stars. But what, Daniella did they know? Aha! You see! You don't know. But your Bubie, Mrs. Shaena Bluestein, a little old lady from America, Quebec, Poland and Europe, from everywhere, she knows."

"What do you know?"

"What do I know? I remember it all."

"Since when?"

"Since when? Since infinity darling. Do you know infinity? Since infinity, I remember."

"Bubie . . ."

"Please Daniella. I'm tired. You're mother's not here yet nor your father. They're always late. And I'm trying to die. I met infinity. You could say he's a nice man. So let me sleep a little because the language is calling me and it's hard to remember. It's hard to practice dying, to die right. First you have to remember everything, everything, even what you didn't know you ever knew and then you have to forget this and then that, one little thing at a time, but not everything, until what is left is the essence, the essential, what they call the truth and then you have to take it across with you. I'm glad I have the chance to do it. My cousins over there didn't have the opportunity before they died, so I have to do it for them."

"Bubie . . . Shaena Baena . . . I want to know everything." I was reeling. The old woman had become someone else, or so completely herself, a hybrid of a mad woman and a sage, that she was unrecognizable. "You want me to teach you how to die? Darling Daniella, *kleininke*, you will have to learn by yourself. And do you know what, darling? I think you should start learning now because you have so much more to remember than I do, because what your people think they know and fill your head with is increasing like an escalator. Now please, get a cup of something and drink it while you sit hear quietly reading a good book and then go to the store, please. But before you go, darling, put on a little Mozart in the tape recorder. Or the tape I have of your mother playing like what's his name, George Shearing, that blind man she likes so much. And let me do my work."

"Bubie ..."

"Daniella, I know you are a grown woman, but behave yourself. Go get breakfast and nail polish."

"Bubie, but please ..."

"I'm not going to die till your mother comes and your father too. So don't worry, you have plenty of time not to bother me. Right now I'm fine. Ask the nurse. She'll tell you all my vitals, they're terrific. I feel fine except where he put that needle in my heart."

My parents arrived within a few hours with an expression on their faces of those who had seen death too often and hadn't learned to befriend it. Death was a contagion. Once released into the world through Shaena's demise, it would spread like wild fire. Nothing would be safe.

"Don't cry, Rosa," Shaena instructed her daughter who looked far too stunned to cry. "I'm already on the other side and it's very nice here. Don't call me back.

"I gave Daniella my notebooks. She will need them. Don't keep anything of mine unless it came from the old country; everything else is junk. And Aram, plant a little grove of sugar maples for me somewhere they won't be cut down. A grove, you hear, not a single tree. A bunch of trees, a proper memorial, but no sign, you hear, the birds can't read."

She closed her eyes and settled into her pillows with satisfaction. Then something must have overcome her because she called my mother to her, not me this time, and took her hand saying, "You're my Rosa, poor thing. My little Rosa, my little Rose of Sharon."

She turned to Aram as if she were lucid and instructed him to take care of Rosa, to make a magic ring around her, to protect her from harm, and fell into a whispered reverie, "Ring around a rosy, ring around a rosy, ring around a rosy." Her voice was getting weaker and weaker and her eyes, which opened occasionally and were not dull, were looking elsewhere. "We all fall down, Rosa dear. We all fall down." Then she closed her eyes so forcefully it was clear they would not open again, said something totally incomprehensible, took a few very slow breaths, uttered a long rasping sound and was gone.

When Shaena died, Cardinal, I lost a link to something which I hadn't noticed existed. I might have hoped that once Shaena was on the other side, she would connect me to those mysteries, but it was the opposite. Immediately after she died, I lost sight of the other side. I forgot that it existed. Actually, I'd never really acknowledged it though I had relied on it—or on my grandmother.

Shaena Bluestein died and a world was lost to me. I won't compare it to the loss my father felt when he returned from World War II; he still maintained he had returned from no place, that nothing was left. Nor to the loss and shock my father's parents felt right after the war when they read the material which had been released about the Concentration Camps. The articles, images and newspapers were dropped by the side of their bed when my grandparents had lain down to sleep, as if they had been gassed themselves. Naturally an autopsy was ordered but the coroner's conclusion was decisive; they had both died of natural causes within minutes of each other, improbable as that might seem. Age was the condition given because heartbreak is not a diagnosis. These grandparents had worried about what meaning their lives had if their people, not just a village or a city, were going to die out. That question killed them right away.

Now, Your Eminence, everything is threatened, our individual lives, languages, cultures, nations, not only human beings and their artifacts, but animals, trees, the planet, the entire shebang. Just because you think the entire universe may reduce itself to a point again doesn't mean you accept it. But it makes a difference doesn't it, if the reduction to a point is natural and inevitable or whether we hasten the process by disappearing ourselves and the planet altogether?

Until my grandmother died, I didn't think about any of this. Maybe my grandmother was thinking about it and that was sufficient for my family. Shaena had an elegant way of thinking about things without imposing her thoughts upon anyone. It was as if Shaena's thinking expanded the universe just enough for my family to be able to live in the world. But, in retrospect, I see that my grandmother's death and the disruption in my own life seemed to coincide. It is as if my grandmother's little asides about the nature of reality did not puncture my world view as I have sometimes maintained, but are, rather, the lynch pins that held everything together.

Chapter 14

At my insistence, Lance picked me up at the airport in Los Angeles. The thought of descending into San Diego, an adamantly cheerful city, set my teeth on edge.

"You hate Los Angeles," he had objected, "wrong stars."

"No one can see the sky in L. A. Lance, so I won't be in danger of seeing a new star and imagining it's Shaena Baena."

Of the three places he had found by adhering to what he said were my maddening instructions—The Gold Star Motel, The New Moon Hotel, the Star Dust Motor Inn—I chose the one which, it turned out was more than a decent room and bed. Despite my inclinations, I was to be afforded creature comforts. I was bested at my own game. I put my head on Lance's shoulder. He gathered me up the way one gathers beloved broken things and before he had hung my garment bag in the mirrored closet, I had thrown myself across the bed and fallen asleep.

Lance was used to hotels, had learned through years of touring to make himself at home in them, otherwise, he would not have been able to perform. So it was he who opened the windows and tied back the drapes so I, who relied on light to rest, could sleep deeply. It was he who ordered narcissus, daffodils and lilies, who pulled off my boots without disturbing me and arranged our toiletries in the bathroom. He unpacked both my suitcases, the one I'd taken to Canada and the one he had packed hurriedly. It contained a few books, select music tapes—Kohachiro Miyata playing the shakuhachi with a koto in the background—Lance's own preference which he likened to wind playing on water.

At first glance, you might think our things were strewn around but everything was carefully placed here and there, a pale silk nightgown like sea foam that he had bought for me—or for himself as I accused him when accepting it—next to it, my green silk robe, nearby my best, that is to say, my most worn jeans, a silk and mohair, indigo and silver *rewana* covered the television and a green silk shawl that he draped over the desk chair. From his own suitcase, he extracted my beloved blue porcelain platter—a gift from Shaena Baena, 'one of the few *heirlooms*' as she had liked to say as an underhanded way of insuring that we would keep and use the object—on which he arranged wedges and wheels of cheese, winter pears, tangerines like small suns, mangos and champagne grapes. Pouring himself brandy in one of the glasses he had also brought, he sat down beside me to read. He did everything he could to make me comfortable and so we were at odds. Fortunately, I had my dreams.

A blue wall. Lapis Lazuli. It opened like a gate. Tiles and bricks slid aside or dissolved. I was dissolving. First I was the wall, then the gate. There was a star over the gate. The Gate star. And I went through the gate with Auriga the Charioteer. He was a fiery man. There were goats about, or perhaps they were part goat and part fish and then one was sacrificed. I heard it bleat. It was a terrible sound.

I saw a lion, erect like a man with a diamond in his eye, walking toward me wearing a seal ring of dark blue chalcedony. Heat waves shimmered on his shoulders, fell down in folds of cloth puffy with yellow dust and pollen. I wanted to look the lion in the eye. I wanted to look through his eye as if it were a star.

"This star is the gate," I repeated several times and then lost the thought or the meaning. The lion's eyes whirled like kaleidoscopes; diamond gears clicked as its eyes turned. Light came through them, which was not their light but the light they were transmitting. I was pierced by the light which fell upon me.

"*Verboten*," a voice said. "*Verboten*." It came from the sky.

"No," I called. "No. Why?"

"*Verboten*!" The eye closed, like the shutter of a German Leica. I felt a hot wind come up and dropped the camera as my eyes closed involuntarily.

I awakened with a start and sat bolt upright. It was dark now. A few dull stars were barely visible through the window.

"What did you dream?" Lance asked me as he brought me coffee. I set down the cup and ran my hands through my hair in a gesture he says he loves more than all the others. "You're playing with fire again," he said.

In the background, Jean-Pierre Rampal and Ravi Shankar were playfully chasing each other up and down the octaves. A candle was flickering in a glass star next to Lance's music stand alongside the open flute case lined in old blue velvet that, like his flute, reflected the rhythms of light. We weren't home but we weren't in alien territory; he had seen to that.

"Is it okay?" he asked watching me look around.

"I hate it," I said.

"I must have done a great job then, objectively speaking." He sighed, "Tell me the dream."

I faltered. "It was awful and beautiful. There was a lion in it. He looked like a man. Amanda says, you're a Leo. So I think it was pointing to you. Then something was prohibited. A voice said *Verboten*."

"What does that mean?"

"I don't know. I'll ask Amanda."

Leaning forward he handed me a square of sand colored vellum on which Amanda had carefully written, "It's a terrible loss, but she is still with you."

Before I knew what I was doing, I tore it up.

"Why did you tell her, Lance?"

"What do you mean?"

"Why do you keep asking what I mean?" A shock wave of fear or recognition went through me.

"Perhaps your dream was about your grandmother," he started again.

"Everything had come to an end." I began. "Everything is coming to an end."

"Don't be silly. It was only a dream," he said without intending to be dismissive. I was startled.

"Everything is coming to an end."

"Don't say that." He was off balance and his voice was harsh.

"Why not?"

"Ok. Let's not talk about it."

"What do you mean, Lance?" Things *were* coming to an end.

"Maybe I mean, there are some things we can't talk about."

"Like what?"

"Daniella, I only mean there are clearly some things we shouldn't talk about now." He only wanted to start again, but he was exasperated. When he hit the wrong note in rehearsal, he always stopped, often going back to the very beginning of the piece so it would be right.

He had done that in a concert, had stopped playing, paused, closed his eyes, bowed his head, remained silent for a moment and then, looking the concert master in the eye, nodded courteously to indicate they would start again. The audience was stunned, but then the music soared. Afterwards the audience jumped to their feet roaring with appreciation.

Now he wanted to start again but he couldn't find the beginning.

"Some things are just not discussible. You know, like music." He was aware that he had hurt me, but he didn't know how or why he would hurt me at this time. I had flinched, then blanched and then flushed, almost as if he had struck me. He *had* struck me, though not with his hand.

"I don't understand," I said.

"Let's not talk about this." He was defensive. A bad habit. It was dragging us down further. "Don't you see? We can't talk about it. There are things one can't talk about."

"How do you know, Lance, that there are things one can't talk about? How do you know that?" I began crying.

I looked around the room and saw all the efforts he had made. There was too much of me in this room, my things, what I liked, my lover. I hated him for being there too. I must have been insufferable, Cardinal.

Lance improvised a little tune, a tricky one, the breath and fingering were very difficult. He was trying to be a bird. The task of playing it perfectly, absolutely perfectly, diverted us both.

"Whip-poor-will," I whispered, putting the silk shawl on my head, scuttling down into it. "The infamous nightjar, or goatsucker."

It had taken so little to restore me. "I'll tell you, Lance, what you were trying to say about music. David Bohm, the physicist, warned that we are mistaking the content of our thought for a description of the world as it is.

I liked remembering the quotation. I liked the comfort of knowing that someone quite eminent and respectable knew that neither I nor anyone of my colleagues knew the hell where we were going. I liked disappearing into the shawl.

"Whip-poor-will?"

"From the family *Caprimulgidae*, meaning, goat milker," I said smugly. He saw the little girl who had first learned these words.

"Did your father teach you that?"

"He did after Shaena Baena told me they were witches' birds."

"And did that explain it?"

Latin didn't explain anything. Shaena's mythology didn't explain anything. Latin and mythology were just other languages one could master. Mathematics, physics, and astronomy were essentially languages. Amanda had been hinting that there were other languages I might learn. Languages which had once been a *lingua franca* and now were disdained. Animal languages. Spirit languages. Astrology was one of those Amanda spoke.

"Lance, you're a Lion, Greek from *leon* and I'm a goat, of the genus *Capra*, of the zodiacal sign *Capricorn*, the star *Capella*." I was lost in my head, "'madly ruminating, the goat was one of the *Ruminantia*. . . .'" I couldn't stop myself.

Languages have always interested me. I could have responded to Lance in Greek. I laughed after I spoke the Latin words and hid more deeply in the shawl.

"Is it Shaena Baena you are thinking about?" Lance asked tentatively.

"Don't call her that. Call her Shaena, or Mrs. Bluestein or 'your grandmother.' I can't bear to think of her bones. I can't think about anything, Lance. Everything I knew is gone and I don't know a thing." I was beside myself. "I think she knew it all in Polish and she didn't tell me *bubkis*." The shawl was over my head now in what my grandmother might have called a *babushka*.

"What's *bubkis*?"

"Goat shit, Lance, everyone knows what goat shit is."

"Maybe she couldn't tell what she knew in language."

"She could have told me and she didn't. She wasn't *only* wonderful you know, she was also a bitch like everyone else."

He gave another desperate trill on the wooden flute. It was rather remarkable for such a simple instrument. Then he took a chance. He put down the flute and pulled me to him, easing the two of us down onto the rumpled bed, holding me as I put the shawl over my face and burrowed into the covers, sobbing.

When Lance awakened from his nap, there was a woman staring out the window with a shawl over her head. Now I can say many things about her that I couldn't have known then. I can say she resembled an old man hidden in the sanctuary of his prayer shawl. I can say she was like an old woman overcome with grief. But how can

I say such things about myself? Lance stood behind me and ran his fingers under it and through my hair.

"Don't touch me," I said in a voice which must have been terribly flat because I remember that the sound disturbed me like an untuned instrument. I didn't stir, that is, I couldn't move; I remember a voice inside saying "Your lover is awake. It is time to move." But I couldn't stop looking directly in front of me though I could see nothing of the gardens below.

"Don't touch me," I repeated in exactly the same tone as if I hadn't said it before. "Don't touch me," I repeated once more. He hadn't touched me again after he'd heard me the first time. "Don't touch me," I repeated.

"I'm not touching you," he said carefully.

"Don't touch me, you'll catch it." The cadence of the second phrase was exactly like the first. The meaning was in the sound, in the dull repetition.

"What will I catch?" he asked, pulling my head back against his chest and holding my forehead firmly without removing the shawl that covered my face.

"Don't touch me, you'll catch it." I repeated without pulling away. He stopped touching me but the phrase continued out of my control.

"What will I catch?" "What will I catch?" He began to play with the phrase, trying to syncopate with my phrase, trying to make music with me. He varied his voice, the tempo, speaking under and over my phrase, trying to dislodge me but I played the phrase like a percussionist. "Don't touch me. You'll catch it."

He passed his fingers gently down from the crown of my head to my forehead and then over my eyes. The rhythm continued. I was undaunted. When he removed his hands I was blindly staring as before as if through the fabric into the darkness of the garden.

"What will I catch?" He placed his fingers and then his palms over my ears and held them firmly, whispering his phrase barely audibly over my head. I heard the rush of his breath, its rhythm, but I could not hear the words. "What will I catch?" I think he began to enjoy the repetition himself because he was dancing with it.

"Death," I said. "Death. You will catch your death."

"What will I catch?"

"You will catch your death."

I opened the folds of the shawl to cover my face even more fully as well as my hair, so that it draped about me, over my shoulders, on all sides while I continued to sit still staring straight before me.

There had been a simple funeral. My grandmother had been buried in the ground. As no stone would be placed on the grave for a year, I was afraid Shaena might fly around the room.

"Before she died, Shaena said you must cover all the mirrors so that the dead don't get caught. I must call The Mountain and warn them." I remember giving him the shawl then and keeping my eyes closed until he covered the mirror over the bureau with it. If our roles had been reversed, Cardinal, I would have called an ambulance instead.

After a long while, eyes still closed, it seems I reiterated it all again. "Don't touch me. You'll catch it. You'll catch your death." Then I paused. "The universe is dead," I continued. "The universe is dead. You'll catch it. It's a chain reaction.

"The sky is dead. The sky is dead and all the stars have gone bye-bye. The sky is dead," I said again. This was the phrase Lance found unbearable, but I remember only the incantatory pleasure of repeating over and over again, "The sky is dead. All the stars have gone. Bye. Bye."

I stayed motionless until dawn. Lance pulled up a chair and sat by my side also staring into the dark. But dawn does come, Cardinal. And sleep is inevitable. And then one awakens. I couldn't bear the hotel and wanted to go the desert and Lance, bless him, having anticipated this had packed our gear.

"My down jacket?"

"Yes, your down jacket."

"We're all set?"

"Yes, we're all set."

"Let's go on," I said, when we got close to Joshua Tree and then when we crossed Arizona, I wanted to go even further. "Chaco Canyon," I said. "Shaena Baena is as disappeared as the Anasazi."

"Are you sure you want to go to Chaco canyon?" Lance was uncertain and a little spooked about what had already transpired. But I was insistent. It was the loneliest place I knew and sometimes when the light was right, Lance would arch his back and bend over into the music as he played so that his shadow on the wall resembled pictographs of Kokopelli, the hunchback flute player who calls the dead.

The Anasazi disappeared from that area so mysteriously that a variety of malefic influences, some even extraterrestrial, are rumored. But Cardinal, I think it is the terrible loss of the knowledge they only barely recorded on the monumental stone walls which alarms visitors to that awesome deserted site. How could a people who constructed observatories, painted solar calendars upon the rock to mark the solstices and equinoxes, calculated the complex cycles of Venus, recorded the appearance of a supernova, the Crab nebula in the constellation Taurus, in 1054, vanish so completely? Why hadn't knowledge protected them, I wanted to know.

As we approached the Canyon, it was raining toward the southeast. The storm was coming closer quickly while the sun's rays were still behind us. The light was on my back as we moved toward the dark clouds so it seemed as if we were transporting one light zone to another. Rough black macadam road yielded to packed earth covered with gravel as we edged north, snaking through narrow canyons of red clay. Then, just to the northeast as if it were an entryway, a perfect rainbow arched against the black sky.

"Do you believe," I asked Lance, a bit restored by the landscape, lowering my voice, half seductress, half child, "that there is a pot of gold at the end of the rainbow?"

"If you can find the end, then . . ." he chuckled.

"Then. . . ? Then what? What if there *is* an end to the rainbow?"

I was beginning to cry again. Lance reached over and took my hand gently.

Then we were in it. We were driving away from the sun toward the rain and the sky before us was black while the sun was burning the backs of our necks. We couldn't brake in time. We couldn't turn back. We were in it. We were in the rainbow that plummeted first through the front grille, then the hood, then through the roof of the car above our heads. Moments after pretending like children that there could be an end to the rainbow, we had fallen into a stream of radiant colors; red, orange, yellow, green, blue, violet. This was *the* place, the absolute line where sun was shining on one side while rain poured down on the other, and nothing but rainbow, broken radiant light, was in between. We had come upon the crack between the worlds.

Chapter 15

Except for the creek, Cardinal, Chaco Canyon looks like the moon. Its lunar landscape was enhanced by winter. Narrow patches of snow, pock marked by the recent rain then frozen by dropping evening temperatures, lay about like mineral deposits, the veins exposed. I didn't mind; I rather liked the difficulty of camping at the water's edge in bitter weather. If I had preferred, we could have stayed with the staff. . . . Why do I fabricate in this manner? I was in no shape to stay with anyone. I couldn't have been civil. Whenever we took a hike, I had Lance check out the trail to be certain it was empty and then I wrapped my shawl about me so that I was unrecognizable.

The flute is a cold instrument and the weather was so very cold, the metal almost froze to Lance's lips when I made him play laments, but transposed to the highest registers. The sound went through me like a knife of ice and then I wanted the piccolo, something even higher, colder. Sharp, white, white, piercing ice blade; that's what I wanted.

As soon as the light came up, we hiked up the canyon to the wall where the Anasazi had recorded the Crab Nebula, the supernova of 1054. I don't know what the Anasazi thought, but when Tycho's nova and then Kepler's appeared within thirty-two years of each other, they forced the likes of us to consider the forbidden idea that the universe was in a constant state of creation, decay and recreation. The doctrine of genesis teetered and everything has been atilt since. Stars, they learned, were still being born *and* outside the immediate vicinity of earth, outside the galaxy, in that distant eighth sphere that doctrine asserted was immutable from the day of creation to eternity. Only it wasn't even a star being born as Tycho de Brahe assumed; it was a star dying, as Simon Marius irrefutably confirmed forty years later in 1612. *My* Simon Marius who published the first sightings of the Great Nebula in Andromeda. Kepler's nova following upon Tycho's star of 1572, an even more brilliant supernova—which, try as everyone might, could not be identified as a meteor, comet or planet undermined the already shaky foundations of Aristotelian and Platonic thought and—Cardinal, you know this as well as you know the back of your hand— undermined Christian theology as well.

I want to say: "Don't you remember, Cardinal?"

Images of light painted on rock almost a thousand years ago. That human need to record light. There in the canyon of the dead or disappeared. Chaco Canyon was the right place to mourn. I didn't know if I was in the past or the future. Unlike Canyon lands or Monte Verde or Canyon de Chelly which are so vibrant, Chaco Canyon warns of desertion and desolation. There is a mystery here far greater than the mystery of why the Anasazi left and where they went. The land itself is a mystery. Comparatively, it's easy to decode the pictographs.

I was drawn to that site and we stayed there as long as I could bear the cold. Then we hiked a little to get warm and I was drawn back to it. Most people assume those images mark the winter solstice but there's enough evidence to believe they represent the Crab nebula. It must have been an astonishing sight, a star in the sky by the waning crescent moon so bright it could be seen in the daylight. Despite the display, one way or another, the images refer to a light going out. The death of a sun before its rebirth or a star flaring up before it darkens forever.

Okay. Cardinal, maybe I wasn't simply mourning my grandmother's death. There was a new light in our sky. A supernova in the process of explosion had been discovered in the Large Magellanic Cloud, as brilliant as the supernova of 1604. I didn't know that until I got home. While we were looking at old images on stone walls, a similar light was flaring again in the southern hemisphere. Welcome SN1987A. Was it a coincidence, Cardinal, or was it, as Amanda would say, a *co*incidence? She held that events in different dimensions influence each other, intersect. Maybe Amanda thought there is a master plan. The supernova wasn't my grandmother. It wasn't her style to flare up and go out. It was just happenstance.

But there was something else on my mind I hadn't acknowledged, something the Anasazi couldn't have seen with the naked eye. There was a new old light appearing in our telescopes. First light, we called it. Six months earlier, quasars had been sighted with a red shift of 4.0 to 4.73 indicating their light had been traveling toward earth for twelve billion years from the very beginning of the universe.

When I got home things were different. If I were used to speaking a psychological language, I would have simply said, "I'm depressed." I didn't know I was undone. Not so much by this damned supernova that was thrilling everyone, confirming the theory that supernovae produce neutrinos. Not that, I swear, though it put me over the edge, I admit that. But, because without realizing it, I had been shaken by the discovery of quasars, of first light.

When the sun was rising the last day we spent in Chaco, Lance walked over to where I was lying on the ground and pointed out black storm clouds crisscrossed by lightning, coming in. Fire and its chariots. I wanted to hike up the cliffs and look for rainbows, but he said the creek would be rising soon. The way he said it, it sounded like a movie: "Creek risin'," a taciturn warning before the deluge. And that's just what it was, no joke. It started to pour within minutes and we had quite a struggle getting everything into the van quickly and taking off. When we reached the wash, I looked at the swollen water and knew we had no more than twenty seconds, asked him to gun it and he did. We made it—barely—by the distance we were pushed west just crossing those few feet of water.

Or we didn't make it. Not that we drowned, but that I was left behind. Or was lifted up and landed somewhere else far away from myself. Isn't that what they say

94 ✳ The Other Hand

about that group of Anasazi? Extraterrestrials came and got them. Or they were the extraterrestrials and they got disgusted with life here and took off.

I'm not really steady yet, Cardinal.

I'll tell you what I think happened in Chaco Canyon. I tasted the invisible. It was bitter and poisonous. Chaco Canyon leached my spirit from me.

Chapter 16

"I've learned a new word," I said to Lance one evening on my return from The Mountain.

"What is it?"

"Disillusion."

"Did you learn it from your father?"

"Maybe I did," I said, wondering why everyone knew things I didn't know.

"And what would your grandmother say to you if the two of you were having this conversation?"

"She would ask, 'What are you doing with your life, darling?'"

Before I had had time to consider how preposterous his question had been, I had answered it. As if my grandmother were there with us and, like Simon Marius, I was making the terrible discovery that a supernova could be resurrected from the dead.

"She's trying to follow her grandmother." Amanda suggested to Lance who, equally perplexed by my behavior, related their conversation to prod me toward my old self.

"And what did you say?" I asked him.

"I speculated that you're emotionally exhausted and so you're cutting down on your social life."

"Did she buy it?"

"Of course not, Daniella. She said, 'You could explain it that way, Lance, but you would be foolish to believe it.' Amanda understands that she is being dismissed. What she really wanted to know, Daniella, is what is wrong and how can she help?"

"And what did you say, Lance?"

"What do you think I said? I said, 'Something is definitely off and I certainly don't know what it is.'"

When he said that my lips pressed together the way Rosa's did; it was curious to feel my mother's body instead of my own. I still didn't think I missed my grandmother. I didn't think the death of a grandmother could or should be a trauma, could or should affect anyone else, so maintaining it would pass like an influenza or a bad cold, I turned back to the book I was reading, hoping Lance wasn't too perturbed.

There were other things on my mind. Maybe Shaena was finally getting through to me. I was acknowledging that my chosen field had not, for fifty years, been what I had imagined when I began studying. I had had the fantasy of reliving the life of William Herschel, a life defined by music and stars. He had played the violin and cello as a child, then as a young man had migrated to England where he became an organist at the chapel at Bath. But the stars had called him and he learned how to fashion more precise telescopes so he could penetrate and memorize the sky. His own mind became as accurate a star map as existed in 1781 when he discovered Uranus, or later when he was able to describe the Orion nebula and the red heart of the great nebula of Andromeda. How had he done it? By fashioning, with his sister Caroline, a precise instrument and then by staying out each and every clear night and learning the sky. I had foolishly planned on such a simple life.

I had come to science because I wanted to enter a passageway from the unknown to the known. It was to be like focusing a telescope. First, everything is fuzzy and indeterminate, then the precise shape of light comes into view. But obviously, Cardinal, that wasn't how it was turning out. Certain problems in astronomy, the most interesting, actually, were becoming more mysterious the deeper they were probed. If there is a single consistent pattern in my field, it is that any discovery of great moment—of quasars let's say, or of dark matter, or the existence of a great attractor that seems to be drawing everything toward it at the same time that everything is also flying away—all these bring us more deeply into the mire of the unexpected, contradictory and unknown. I imagine that faith, also, Your Eminence, was once far simpler.

Before Shaena died, like everyone else, I relegated mundane tasks to a graduate student. Now I entered them with enthusiasm. I relished the time required to sort, order, observe, identify. It reminded me of Henrietta Swan Leavitt pouring over photographic plates of the sky day after day in a painstaking effort to identify variable stars. This allowed me time to think. Then when my thoughts collided and recollided in wild disorder, I returned quickly to this fastidious work, in the hope of forgetting the swirl.

But the swirl nabbed me. There are men dreaming of building a super collider particle accelerator in Texas with the power of a star through which physicists hope to duplicate the original processes of the universe, not only to learn the laws of the universe but to observe them in action. It's a way of going back in time to the Big Bang and the simplest and most fundamental processes from which the universe developed. They're looking for six quarks and a final theory, a "mathematical" final solution to the problem of origins and beginnings. A solution, beautiful, simple and orderly as a pointless point, that would re-establish a more predictable universe governed, at least at its essence, by consistent and inviolable laws.

They frighten me. They frightened me then as much as it frightened my father, that an Illinois team is restoring the ecological prairie system above the Fermi National Accelerator Laboratory. "Four miles of elemental violence," Aram insisted, "can't coexist with herds of bison living among six foot tall blue-stem and Indian prairie grasses. Have they asked the meadow larks, falcons, bobolinks, coyotes and foxes if they like what's going on underfoot?"

Aram is usually soft spoken even when he's mad. Tree people, in general, don't talk a lot.

"Sure," he continued, "the native plants and grasses exude an atmosphere of bucolic nostalgia but underneath Faust is living dangerously."

His colleagues badly wanted my father's support for their restoration. "One hundred and twenty-five native plants! You would think this would fulfill every one of your desires and conditions. Species which we haven't seen for decades and which we didn't plant but which old diaries indicate were actually once here, have transplanted themselves and now the animals are following. Have returned themselves, by themselves, Aram. Why don't you approve?" They were clearly exasperated, Cardinal and I understood why, but my father maintained, "It's not where *I* would want to put down *roots*. Forget the accelerators, restore the prairies and see what comes from that."

My equivalent of Aram's dilemma was the banter in the observation room at The Mountain. Of course we got a little goofy when working on projects in the middle of the night. On occasion, the teams play an engaging game which can inspire research projects. Someone asks a question about something currently unfathomable which he or she—he, mostly for there were very few she's about—wants to know: Are there white holes? How many parallel universes exist (on the head of a pin)? What happened before the Big Bang? That kind of thing.

Then it was our task to address the questions. Those questions for which none of us could develop any plausible research approach, would, we agreed, *temporarily* belong to God. Sometimes we split the area, for example, we allowed that conceiving a universe both finite and without boundary lay in the territory of the Unknown, but the task of deciding whether our universe could be described in this way belonged to us. The idea was to wrest as much territory as possible from the Unknown; to relinquish an arena altogether was to lose the game. Of course, we never used the word, "God." We spoke about the Unknown as if it were an entity but one that was always getting smaller, like an evaporating black hole that may over billions of years disappear.

After a while, I began to like losing, coming up against something that was not only unanswerable but unapproachable. I liked shaving off everything we could handle ourselves, and being left dumb struck with the Ineffable even if I didn't have the faintest idea of what It might be.

One night, we were roaming around a familiar field of questions. We were playing with the mysteriousness of boundaries, trying to fathom the liminal space-time between a particle and a wave or the event when inanimate becomes animate, when inorganic becomes organic or vice versa, when life and death appear and are distinguishable. And so we were arguing about the wonder or happenstance of the sun being 93 million miles away and shining 1.99 calories per minute per square centimeter on earth which happens to be the exact and only condition under which we can survive—the anthropic principle. We were contemplating the precise soup of atoms and molecules cooked at exactly the right temperature under the only possible conditions, to form those first molecules and amino acids which, we understand, were the beginning of life.

At one point, the conversation which had been quite engaging, fell into familiar territory and we began taking positions we had each taken before like the neoDarwinians insisting that the universe was only a complex physical reaction based upon certain fundamental laws and, accordingly, life was a consequence of a chemical mix and was no special condition. Then, regular as the clockwork universe, Wilbert the computer whiz brought the discussion to an instant halt by reaching into his pocket and pulling out a handful of bubble gum jawbreakers and we were silenced by the formidable task of rolling them in our mouth as if it were the cosmos itself we were chewing down to size in advance of blowing it up again to an expanding universe. Wilbert himself could blow one bubble inside another, modeling his own Venusian fantasies, translucent pink spheres, with his breath.

We didn't stay with the bubble gum too long. Wilbert, the champ, got to choose the next subjects. We went through the origin or meaning of intelligence, our expectations of the consequences or possibilities of genetic splicing, the causes of depression or mental illness, until we landed directly on Wilbert's favorite; the secrets which would be revealed by a microscopic analysis of Einstein's brain. I, myself, had always thought Einstein had bequeathed it to science as his last joke, while Wilbert maintained the secret of his intelligence and his remarkable intuition was still there in the gray matter. I found myself arguing adamantly against this with a passion which surprised me. There was a moment when I was afraid I would burst into tears. And as I realized that I was putting the wonders of Einstein's brain in God's corner, rather than in physiology, I also realized that as far as my colleagues were concerned, the universe was strictly mechanistic. According to them, everything in it—everything—was attributable to the, albeit wondrous, interplay of one elementary particle or field with another. And if God or the Unknown existed at all, *He* was absolutely bound by the laws of the physical universe as we have discovered them to be and, therefore, *He* would not interact with, could have no more effect upon it than we would eventually: *"Anything God can do, we will do better."*

That room with all its screens, charts, dials, graphs, is like the inside of the collective brain, everyone's mind added on to everyone else's mind and then boosted to the nth by powerful computers. Soon we would know it all and then we would get to play with it. Open season on imagining the future: Black holes would be harnessed for energy; stars linked together to serve our technological purposes; baby universes birthed in baby universe nurseries; the twenty-two missing dimensions discovered and colonized; we would flit in and out of worm holes showing up here and there helter skelter to make mischief in the past and the future; and finally the entire universe, not just the solar system or the galaxy, would be colonized in relatively short order through reconstituting the DNA of anyone who ever lived so we could work with the problem of mass and prevent the big crunch. Immortality, here we come.

... Ay lai lai lai lai lai lai my baby
Do you want a star to play with?
The moon to run away with?
They'll come if you don't cry,
So ay lai lai lai lai lai lai my baby ...

How, Cardinal, could I say "No!" Who doesn't want her own star?

Some want to know more than the secrets of the universe. Want more than to identify the fundamental particles. Maybe they don't want to know how things are but how the world might be if everything were in their hands. A few are quite willing to contemplate how they can create a world, duplicating the processes, combining and recombining fundamental particles until they chance remaking the universe or burrowing into a next one of their own making. When I'd studied Greek drama in college, I had not thought that I would be applying the term *hubris* to myself.

I'm making a speech, Your Eminence. I don't mean to. I want to know what light is, Cardinal, to take it into my body and my mind, and to be ruled by it accordingly.

"Don't take it so much to heart," Amanda cautioned. "Live your own life."

In the past I hadn't taken it to heart, but then I did. Amanda's attempt to soothe me raised anger. I wasn't coming across anyone worried about the negative consequences of his work, obsessing as Einstein did afterwards about what he had dared, what he had unleashed. I didn't want to be accused at some future time of being complicit in . . . in something I couldn't imagine yet. Meanwhile around me nothing was constraining research—except funding, of course; there were no serious discussions among peers pondering the consequences of our fundamental right to know.

My grandmother died. Amanda said I was grieving. Studies in my field were progressing as they always did. Did I want to stop progress? Was I against knowledge? I began to notice my investigations were all predicated upon violence as the nature of the universe; stellar events occurring in violent eruption supported this view. This time round, I understood my father. Quite a drastic change from the world of my now beloved Kepler and his harmony of the spheres.

Chapter 17

"Why does it unnerve me that we've spotted a supernova? A supernova *and* a new quasar?" I would ask Lance again and again. "Imagine a star that, falling in itself after having used up all its fuel, bursts into unparalleled light. Imagine a body of light that becomes brilliant from the energy of a black hole in its center."

The rhythm of my sentences changed, a sign that I was becoming more and more agitated; even I could hear my fingers drumming on the table as if I were some Keith Jarrett but without his skill, just a thunderous rush of feeling overwhelming each individual note.

"What does it *mean* that great light follows immediately upon the possibility of extinction, or that extraordinary light manifests from the direction of darkening? What does it mean?"

"Strange questions, Daniella."

"Strange questions? Out of character? Unprofessional? Naive? Foolish? Boring? Childish? Stupid? What do you mean, Lance?"

"No, what do *you* mean, Daniella, by these questions" he said gently.

I didn't want Lance to answer any of my questions, Cardinal, but I was relying on his knowledge of what it was to teeter on the edge of discovery or chaos, what it was to find a new set of relationships or a sound that made every tonal relationship obsolete, a breath, sometimes harsh, that erased all the nice little chords that had contained him until that moment.

"Am I simply losing my mind or am I moving from one mind to another, like Tycho and Kepler when they saw those new stars?"

"About these sightings," Lance ventured, "why don't you talk to Amanda? I don't know what Amanda will think, except sometimes she sees some marvelous dance . . .'"

I didn't want to hear about any dances. And I especially didn't want to hear about anything marvelous. "Amanda thinks . . ." It annoyed the hell out of me.

Then I called Amanda confessing I didn't know what was happening to me. When she tried to make a date with me, I hung up. When we met in the hallway afterwards, I'd tried to dodge her, but she didn't allow it.

She followed me to my office and sat down in the almost comfortable armchair designated for visitors alongside my oak desk.

"I understand you don't want to see me anymore."

"Did Lance tell you this?"

"Why ask if I spoke with Lance? It's obvious isn't it? I can see what you're thinking."

"I don't want anyone to see what I am thinking."

"No, you want to be in a world apart. It's not possible, Daniella."

Her voice softened. "You look thin."

"You're jealous," I wanted desperately to make everything light.

"You're not that thin."

"Look Amanda," I said, hoping to break free of her, "work has piled up, my desk is covered with papers, and . . ."

"And your grandmother died and you need a friend." Her audacity smarted.

"That's not it."

"What is it then?"

"There are questions I can't answer. I don't understand any of it anymore."

"It's not that you don't understand it anymore it's that there is more to understand."

How annoying she could be, Cardinal, with her clandestine allusions to mysteries to which she always wanted me to surrender. "What do you mean, Amanda?"

"Well, maybe there are more than ten dimensions. Ten or twenty-six that mathematics accounts for and who knows how many others that will always be invisible to the mathematical eye."

I picked up the images that had been on my desk with the accompanying spectrum analyses and brought them close to my eyes. Then I gave them to Amanda. "Are these or are these not stars, Amanda?"

Had Shaena Baena been right when she had said they weren't? I didn't dare ask Amanda that.

"'Is you is or is you ain't . . . ?'"

Was she deliberately taunting me? "Amanda, I wouldn't be asking this question, if I hadn't met you. I met you and so I ask questions. Now get out of here."

Amanda stood up and hesitated in the doorway. "Truth? I don't know if they is stars or they ain't stars, but why *did* you meet me?"

"You're impossible, Amanda."

"No. Nothing is impossible. That's the problem isn't it? Do you want to tell me what is on your mind or not?"

"Not," I said and closed the door. But then I opened it immediately and called after her down the hall.

"It's not you, Amanda," was my best attempt at reconciliation.

"Of course not. I know that." She came tripping back toward me but this time paused outside my office, not intending to come in. "That's why I've brought you a gift." She reached into her purse and drew out a package wrapped in blue paper with ancient drawings of the sun, stars and moon, rendered in gold and silver. "It's not that I didn't want to give it to you before, it's that I wasn't sure you would receive it." She paused, "It's a going away present."

"I don't plan to go away."

"You didn't plan to go away from me either. She paused and then acting as if she hadn't paused to catch her breath, continued, "A friend of Roger's has a little place for rent in the desert. Near Devil's Peak. It's a shack really, but there's hardly a better place in North America from which to watch the stars; you'll like it.

"And you'll like this book. It's the I Ching, an ancient Chinese text of divination. One asks it questions and it answers them, maybe even the kind of questions your strange mind is asking. Don't be afraid to ask."

She was turning the corner by the time I unwrapped the package and found a little yellow book.

At home, I put the book on my library shelf near the books on mathematics. Amanda had once described the I Ching as a very mathematical book, based on a binary system deriving sixty-four hexagrams that had been arranged in a magic square by Fu-hsi. Meanings and images were attributed to each line and hexagram so that it, like some other auguries, was said to contain the universe and all its wisdom within itself. But certainly I did not think that the kind of wisdom it contained resembled in any way the fields of knowledge to which I had devoted my life.

Still, that afternoon, I turned to Lance, and asked, "Why *did* she and I meet each other?"

"And why did you and I, why did *we* meet and on that same day?" he countered.

Chapter 18

Four months passed. The light of SN1987A began to diminish. My grief subsided with it. I initiated a few cautious evenings with Amanda and found I was enjoying them. My life seemed to have returned to what it had been.

One morning, two peregrine falcons skated overhead in tandem and tight formation, wings almost touching, down the wind in a perfect parabola of descent and swept up again so seamlessly they took me with them. Just the previous evening, Lance and I, ice skating together on the frozen neighboring pond, had become a single body. A stream of air molded around the sides of the birds' heads, their outstretched wings, their tail feathers, became a body with the bodies of the birds, in animation. Or the birds were within the body of air. An invisible order, implicit, as David Bohm was saying, out of which the birds streaked, shaped perfectly to it and attempting with each other what was implicit within air: the thrill of the speed, of the perfectly coordinated plunge, the long glide—just—through the narrow passage between the branches of the two trees and then swooping up, in precise formation, in an aerial display, Bells theorem, the corps de ballet, Escher in motion, a doppleganger or two lovers. All accomplished without a single word spoken in any language whatsoever. The Janus line between will and necessity.

The mystery presented itself, or all mysteries presented themselves, fleetingly and so much greater than I had ever conceived, and still perfectly contained as well in that singular form, so that I was stunned to realize I wanted to know everything and in all its forms.

Plummeting in that same avian arc, I also wanted to know what the fundamental particles were and what the original interactions had been, or whether the world had emerged from a pointless point, and I discovered that I might be willing to advocate the supercollider and other research projects I had formerly questioned in order to find out…In other words, I saw I might do anything to know. And notwithstanding my deep concerns, I still felt safer with investigations within the academy than I did addressing the same questions through Amanda's night time methods.

Lance and I had skated so perfectly together long into the night, moonlight glinting off the ice. One long curve after another, hour after hour, alone. And now it was as if the birds were tracing those same circles in the sky. Paradise, I thought, then corrected it—perfection—as the falcons plunged down behind the knoll and disappeared.

And just in time, I thought, Cardinal because it would take me two hours to drive to the University. If I left immediately, I would have time to prepare a lecture in my mind, do a little research and make some notes for the lecture I had offered to give in lieu of another speaker who was too ill to come. I could have changed his subject, but I didn't, even though The Great Attractor was rather far from my own interests because I had simply never been interested in what I couldn't see.

But there it was; a series of circumstances had made it irresistible. A meta-interest because I was literally being pulled toward *it*, The Great Attractor, not unlike the stellar bodies which were also, as unexpected observations indicated, apparently falling in toward *it* even though they were supposed to be moving evenly away in other directions.

I had been speaking of the seeming decline in the velocities of galaxies within 130 million light-years of this speculative realm of overdense matter, when it seemed to me I heard a squawk which, at first, I dismissed as a chair scraping while someone shifted position, but then I heard it again and it was not possible to attribute it to the scrape of metal against wood. It had to be a voice but that was impossible; there were only a few dozen people gathered in the small lecture room. I heard it again; a guffaw and definitely disrespectful. I couldn't locate the source nor imagine the motivation.

When I heard it again, I heard more. Words in a voice not so unlike my voice, only the speaker had an accent and was probably a man. Then I couldn't quite ascertain where the voice came from. No one else seemed to have heard it. The audience was focused on what I was saying; they didn't seem distracted or startled. At first, I couldn't accept the decided possibility that it came not from the audience but from within myself.

If I were asked to repeat exactly what the first words were, I would have been incapable of doing it. They were clear in the instant and then the clarity vanished. I had learned early on with amateur telescopes that to see certain faint stars you sometimes have to look slightly away first as they seem to disappear in the direct focus because it is the aura that is really visible. The voice was like that. I could hear it echoing in the air after the direct communication was over, or it echoed in me when I myself was speaking.

I had just started a sentence, "What dark matter . . ." when I heard the voice again, clearer this time. Exceptionally clear.

You're in the dark about the dark.

Well of course I was. Everyone was. First quasars and now this "Great Attractor." It was turning all our ideas about everything—the beginning and the end—upside down or inside out or whatever the new direction might be.

"We'll soon see . . ."

You won't see anything. You can't see it or into it. The dark is completely dark. And if you pursue it, you will always be in the dark.

Just a whisper of ridicule in the voice. Yes, perhaps I had chosen the wrong word but I was using 'see' in its is most general understanding, as a way of knowing.

Tell them. Tell them what you know about the dark. Tell them about its attraction. You pretend to like the light, but you're drifting toward the dark. Tell them how it feels. That irresistible circling toward the lip of it. Tell them how deeply you feel that you must get inside of it. Tell them that you want to bring them into it. Tell them how it turns you on.

Sometimes a crisp voice and sometimes slurred.

There was no sign that anyone I was addressing had interrupted my talk. I was beginning to tremble. Was it the voice fading or my reception which was faulty? Fortunately I had notes and decided to stay very close to the text for the rest of my talk, ignoring any interruptions, if there would be any, pushing through desperately as if there were a heckler in the house who had to be overcome even if he couldn't be silenced.

No heckler. No heckler would say these things. The voice was at the nape of my neck, at my ear, at my breast. A man's voice, definitely. Germanic. Icy and insinuating.

At the heart of every light is a dark place. A very, very dark place. You can feel it. A stinking place. Here it is. My fingers are on it.

I spoke louder.

"You can't see it, but you can smell it. Everyone here can feel its presence. Here.

My voice became efficient, professorial. I had not decided when I made my notes whether I would lay out some of the formulas. I launched into the math.

"I warn you. It is forbidden. You have no right to talk about this. Not you. It's not your material. It's not your field. You don't know anything. You're falling into a hole and pulling the world in with you. Bitch.

I didn't know how to continue.

Jew dog scientist.

I didn't know if I had ever used that word in my life.

Bloody hausfrau. Your black holes have a stink to them. You know the stink. Sniff between your legs.

I could hear the words gaining volume under all my own words. My voice was faltering, of course. Whenever it was appropriate, I tried to look as if I were thinking about things. I lingered over the formulas. I allowed time for the implications of the hypotheses to sink in. A dark area of dense matter perhaps 300 million light-years across, drawing everything toward it, perhaps even over its edge. The audience stirred uncomfortably as audiences always do under the impact of that primary fear incited by the inevitability of extinction whether through the inevitable demise of the sun after another five billion years or the expansion or contraction of the universe, the presence of a black hole in the center of the Milky Way, or the shadow of the Great Attractor pulling on them.

The great attractor. You are making it up. It didn't exist until you and yours started showing it to everyone. Opening your stinking cunts to everyone. Pulling everyone into your smelly juden holes so you can eat them up.

I was distraught from speaking while also hearing the voice which filled every space it found between my words.

Be quiet. You.

Another tone, quiet, conciliatory, if slightly paternal.

You. You. You mustn't speak. Don't speak about this. Don't speak, darling. Keep the dark matter our secret.

I couldn't make out the slurs. Why was it after me? Because I was a woman? Because I was Jewish? Or both? In order to finish the lecture, I had to eradicate the voice from my mind.

Like a little girl, I pleaded, "Bubie help me," as I continued to stride toward the end of the talk. And perhaps Shaena did help me because after I felt an initial wave of hopelessness as I realized people like Shaena had been helpless against such voices, I did feel relief as if Shaena was there in the room as well. That was also startling. That shook me as much as the voice had. And balanced me. And *that* was startling. Then in this new confusion, the voice disappeared.

Giving a public lecture of this nature was routine and I was pleased to discover how very reliable my professional skills were. Speeding up to drive my final points home—emphasizing wonder, the intrigue and possibility of what they didn't know yet—I told a final anecdote with more dramatic flourish than I normally indulged that synthesized the progression within the last decades of assumptions and disenchantments of theories postulated and rescinded and then, pleading another appointment, got myself quickly out of the lecture room.

Chapter 19

Two more hours driving home did not so much calm me as give me enough time to distill particular—if irrational—questions from the swirl of confusion and these I tried to arrange in categories—absurd as they were—and the process distracted me from the event itself. My mind bruised as it fell down the stairs from stars to ethics, from physics to metaphysics, as I tried to relate the subject of my talk to the incident of the voice, wondering what I had attracted to me, and how physics might explain it all.

How would Lance respond if he were with me? Would he suggest that the last place a sensible person would look to discover the secrets of my mind and emotions would be deep space and quantum mechanics? Would he think they were less likely to be found there than oranges in Antarctica? He had said this before.

And what would Amanda say? Amanda secretly thought the sky was exactly the place to look. She would say the ancient world had known this and nothing in modern science refuted what they had known.

And what would Aram and Rosa say? They would say . . . nothing . . . and how bewildered they would look.

I started climbing up one way of thinking and found myself collapsed and aching at the bottom of another.

Were Black Holes not only threatening but . . . dangerous? . . . destructive? . . . therefore bad? . . . therefore evil? Was the expanding universe a sign of good and was dark matter a sign of the devil? What then about the possibility of a steady state universe? Bad as things were, was the status quo the only salvation?

Were the forces of light and the forces of darkness as carefully balanced as matter and anti-matter? Was a small portion of anti-matter . . . of negativity . . . of evil . . . sufficient to undermine a much greater preponderance of good? And had the balance shifted just before I was born and in which direction was it going now? What did it mean that ninety percent of the universe is dark matter and unaccounted for? Was the Great Attractor that might devour everything a sign that evil existed in the universe? Was there an instructive corollary between the physical structure of the universe and the moral afflictions which beset the century?

Evil was now in my mind and the thought of it hurt. I had never considered it and somehow, therefore, it hadn't existed. But now the word—evil—was on my tongue and so it did exist. And I wondered if I, therefore, was having a hand in its genesis.

As above so below. As above so below. As above so below. It was as if the tires whirring down the freeway were speaking to me: as above so below.

Until that moment, Cardinal, from my point of view, everything had been light. Stars, dust, bodies, leaves, thought, everything had been light, for the universe had been known through the eye that was designed to perceive light. And just when the light could be followed almost to the inception of time, either to the time when light was beginning or to the time before it went out, darkness deeper than any darkness that had ever been anticipated or imagined showed itself. Darkness in the physical world that even terrified my colleagues; dark holes, dense dark matter, anti-matter, were discovered at the same time that a never before known, predicted or imagined darkness spread over history and time.

I wouldn't call the voice, *the devil*; I never used such language. I wouldn't say these times were the work of the devil, but others did. I wouldn't call it evil either; I never used that word, but others did. I had never really spoken about the state of world affairs or allowed myself to think about them very much; I had been up there, far away, with my beloved and most distant stars. But it wasn't as if I didn't read the newspapers: wars, torture, terrorism, all this was being enacted among individuals as much as between populations and nations. The world had been on a downward spiral since just before World War I. And concurrent with all this, matter and particles were seemingly being drawn, ineluctably, toward a dark oblivion.

When I got back to our home on The Mountain, Lance was practicing. I could hear his flute rustling the leaves as I stepped so very carefully through the crackle of twigs and pine cones. The flute stopped. He turned his lights out. Dark descended another decibel into darker. I sat still through the night without turning on my light. A single image repeated itself in my mind and I could not free myself from it: The sun was setting, not at the horizon, but in the center of unending dark waters. It burned there until everything disappeared.

Dawn came too soon. I heard the wind and the flute come up together in the same moment so I knew Lance's windows had been left open and it would not be long before the breeze would enter Lance's studio and blow so many papers around the floor that he would have to stop and make some order. The window slammed shut just as I had expected. I had until two in the afternoon to be alone.

I was wishing for an old fashioned well on this ranch land, bricked down the shaft and a metal scaffolding going down to the bottom. Looking at stars from a well had been a rudimentary way of studying the sky—the light collecting on the water as in a telescope, water calling the darkness in. The ancients had descended into deep dry wells in order to see the stars in the daytime, the narrow passage sufficiently blocking out the light of day for some stars to appear above.

I'd often thought of the telescope as stars gathering in the bottom of a well. Sometimes at night when I went out on the platform and looked down into the mirror it was as if I was looking into the waters which held all the stars. I had once heard a very young boy say to his father, "Let's go to the place where the stars pour into the night," I'd wanted to see it as he saw it, all the stars streaming out of the well of Big Eye, flowing across the sky.

The sun came up like it was an ordinary day. You must have been really tired, I said to myself. Staying up nights, sometimes lecturing during the days may no longer be feasible. You're getting older, you need more rest. I found this lecture comforting and sensible. Hadn't Rosa been saying similar things? Hadn't I heard that people deprived of sleep or dreaming—which was it?—sometimes hallucinated.

Clearly I was stressed. Everyone in my field was stressed; I had been arrogant, thinking I could handle it better because I lived in the woods. Lighten up, I said to myself.

When the sun was shining directly into my window, I exited my night room and walked into the library, two rooms down the verandah and went directly to the little yellow book Amanda had given to me. In almost a year, I had not looked at it.

There were, I suspected, intrinsic relationships between the meanings attributed to the hexagrams of the I Ching and the meanings attributed to numbers themselves, but I had no idea what they might be. Shaena had once told me that in Hebrew each number had a specific meaning. Eighteen, for example, was *Chai* and that meant life. "Eighteen," I would call out in lieu of *l'chaim*, clicking the tea glasses in silver holders that Shaena had brought from Poland.

If each letter had a specific number and each number a specific meaning, then words were numbers too, and one could read documents by translating them into the numbers then reading that secret text, finding the secret mathematical meaning, the hidden code of the universe. Sometimes my mathematically inclined colleagues sounded like the Kabbalists Shaena had mentioned in hushed tones and to which Amanda had recently referred telling me that she was fascinated by their mathematics.

As I glanced through the book, I became interested in the trigrams and the progression of images and decided to take the plunge. But I was so wary of handling these elements, I wouldn't throw the coins as instructed, but devised another way to speak to the augury.

For a few hours, I scrutinized the images in the book that were purported to contain all things, to be a shorthand for the structure of the universe. There were eight images and it was claimed that the entire world was composed of these in their sixty-four possible combinations. Sixty-four essential elements. Not unlike the periodic table of elements.

Finally, in the last hexagram, I found the image of the sun falling into the sea. Sixty-four. "The Clinging, Flame above; The Abysmal, Water below."

"This hexagram indicates a time when the transition from disorder to order is not yet completed. The conditions are difficult. The task is great and full of responsibility."

Maybe the I Ching understood my nightmare. I closed the book and opened it again and closed it and went next door to make a glass of tea with lots of sugar just as Shaena Baena had liked to drink it, and still in my robe, took the steaming glass wrapped in a green linen napkin to a scrub oak and sat down against it.

Cardinal, I was used to thinking about ideas, solving problems. I had no experience with thinking about myself. How did one do it? In the past, I would have asked why would one do it but now I knew: It was to keep oneself from interrupting one's own lectures.

I began to formulate simple questions in what I thought was a rational progression. Was I stressed? How long had this been going on? Why hadn't I noticed? Had others noticed without communicating it to me? Had Amanda been on to something when she had suggested that I was affected by my grandmother's death? Was I kidding myself by thinking I had resolved all my differences with my colleagues? Was I disappointed with my work? Was it more than disappointment?

The night image I had found in the I Ching returned to hover in the background of my mind. Without warning, everything I had been devoted to had sizzled out. What my colleagues liked to call the great light of science seemed to me to be imitating the supernova that had been firing off in the Large Magellanic Cloud. The great light of science exploding intensely, becoming so bright everything was blinded, and then falling into the dark and going out. Was that what the Church feared in the days of the enlightenment, Cardinal, that the great light of science would blind everyone to other more essential lights?

Rosa had never really wanted me to be an astronomer. "The company you'll keep," she'd said when my decision to pursue the Ph.D. had become final. Her voice had been clipped. Enigmatic.

She had been improvising at the piano. Two or three chords. And then a long silence. As if she were testing the piano. Or had forgotten where she was going. A long silence, but then, not too long. The chords again. The silence. A variation. A silence. Aram and I had both started listening to the silence between the notes. And then she'd begin again, so quietly picking up on the chords.

Who could be better company than astronomers, astrophysicists, cosmologists? Weren't they exactly whom you were supposed to bring home for Mom to meet?

Rosa had gotten up from the piano and walked into the kitchen as if she were going to prepare a meal and then, just as suddenly, she laid the pan down on the counter and returned to the piano, improvising on Twinkle, Twinkle, Little Star. We were spellbound.

"Twinkle, twinkle, little star. How I wonder what you are? Up above the earth so high . . ." It took a long time to get to the fourth line but when Rosa was there, I had chimed in as I had always done as a child, "Like a skymond in the die."

"What's a star, Dani?" Rosa had asked without stopping.

"What's a star, Dani?" She hit an insistent dissonant chord in the middle of a scale and then returned to her variations on the simple melody again. Without waiting for my answer, "A star, Dani, is a time bomb. Do you know what I mean?" A few bars of music. "What's a bomb, Dani?" Again, without waiting for an answer, "A bomb, Dani, is a container with a star inside it, ready to go off, taking the whole world with it." That plaintive singing. I could still hear it clearly. My mother's terrible, even demented, singing, "Twinkle, twinkle, little star . . ."

I didn't know where my nightmare sun had disappeared, but I was sitting at the bottom of a well. I dared myself to look further into the yellow book to see what I should now do—or not do—with my life.

Stubbornly, I followed my own methodology, looking once more for an image in the book to match the image in my mind. It took only an instant to find The Well. It was the name of a hexagram, number forty-eight:

"The well from which water is drawn conveys the further idea of an inexhaustible dispensing of nourishment."

That was a surprise. I had expected to drown in it.
   But . . .

   ". . . If one gets down almost to the water
   And the rope does not go all the way
   Or the jug breaks, it brings misfortune."

I was afraid to read further and I was afraid not to read further. Propelled by my newly acknowledged desire to know, and by the realization that though I was in completely unknown territory, I still had to follow its procedures.

   "We must go down to the very foundations of life. For any merely superficial ordering of life that leaves its deepest needs unsatisfied is as ineffectual as if no attempt at order had ever been made."

I was reeling, Cardinal. I didn't know what any of these words meant and yet they seemed exceedingly pertinent. Someone or something was speaking most precisely to me in a foreign language.

What could I lose by asking the augury a question, a single question of all those questions that were setting my mind spinning? Ultimately it seemed there was only one question. It was the question I would have liked to ask Shaena if we had really been speaking.

"What are you doing with your life?" Shaena had asked. If only I had been able to turn to my grandmother with the next question: "What shall I do with my life?"

This question, I now admitted, had entered my mind as the voice had assaulted me during the lecture.

I threw the coins and was returned to the first hexagram, Before Completion. A few lines stopped me:

"Perseverance brings good fortune.
Remorse disappears.
Shock, thus to discipline the Devil's Country.
For three years, great realms are awarded."

What the devil, I thought. And then I heard a sound and looked up to see that it was two o'clock and Lance had just opened the door to the library. I said, without thinking, "I've decided to take Jack's cabin at Devil's Peak."

He said, "I think it's a good idea. How did you decide?"

"Well," I hesitated, "I consulted an augury." He did not blanch, actually the little smile on his face was kindly. As I spoke, I realized I was grateful to Amanda who was, indeed, my friend, grateful for the friendship and for the I Ching, for the augury, actually, which I would not have come upon by myself.

Cardinal, I had lived my life in the known. In what I thought could be known. In a world of whirling ever changing certainties and assertions. This was another world, one of shadows and innuendoes. Like my mother's music. Both there and vanishing.

I imagined a scene and described it to Lance: I would stride into the dining room at The Mountain, looking like a million dollars, a little eye shadow, a magenta silk blouse shocking against my copper hair, my favorite black cashmere skirt, my black suede boots, Shaena Baena's tasteful diamond stud earrings flashing as I threw down a stack of journals and say, "Listen, fellas, it's clear. We're going about this the wrong way. We're barking up the wrong tree. . . . We've got to turn the big eye inward. . . ."

I had to laugh at myself. What would they do? Ask me, if I was pre-menstrual or had I been in California too long, and did I need a sabbatical, a little R and R in London, or Moscow? Should they send me to the next international conference? Did I want to cool out by teaching a few weeks on the east coast? A colleague was very anxious to work on the west coast—we could spell each other. The students there would bring me back to earth as quickly as anything would. . . .

I was laughing and then crying and looked up at Lance expecting the same skeptical look on his face, but it wasn't there. He was simply waiting to hear what I had to say. He was listening the way he listened to music.

"I wanted to know what to do with my life. To answer my grandmother's question."

He fumbled for the little wooden flute he always carried in his pocket, reassured himself by finding it and then returned it to its place. "Finally, you're beginning to consider that you have a life. Now that you have a life you may be willing to have other things which begin with the letter L."

"Like what, Lance?"

"Like lively, Lance, love. Like love, Daniella."

"Like lemon trees, like locust trees, livestock," I quibbled.

"Like lust," he said, holding my forearms firmly so that I was positioned directly in front of him and could not easily avoid his gaze.

"I have lust," I said. "Lust is something that has been given to me as a great gift."

"Yes, you have been known to lust. And it delights me," he admitted releasing one arm and running his index finger down the center of my body, between my breasts and across my navel to where my emerald green silk kimono fell open softly just at the soft division at the base of the mound of Venus.

"The delta which divides the Euphrates and Tigris was once the most fertile land in the world," he said as I knew he would.

"Unknown to most," Lance whispered, "that fertile crescent remains. Not in its ancient form, but remains nevertheless. It's imprint can be found in many mysterious places if you know how to look for them. There is a mystery school of adepts who have devoted their lives to following all traces of the fertile crescent and when they come across it, in whatever guise or disguise it has assumed, they worship there. Devotedly. Even for their entire lifetimes." His finger had opened the robe.

"What was it we were discussing, Daniella? Something about what you should do with your life?" He was looking directly into my eyes, watching for my response, insisting upon it, speaking one language with his mind, one with his eyes and another, altogether, with his hand.

I thought I knew what he was hoping for, that I would let go in the stretch between the forces which were acting upon me and fall toward him. That the pull of the passion he was invoking on the one hand would over come the gravity of the questions I was asking pulling me in the other direction. Not to mention, the spin, the whirl I was in ever since I had looked in the book.

"I'm tired," I said. "I have to be alone. And I have to live someplace more lonely. I saw a neighbor jogging this morning. I waved. She waved back. It seemed so friendly . . . and disconcerting. Sometimes I don't want to see anyone for days. Do you understand?"

He took the flute from his pocket, fingered it, put it to his lips and played a short passage in his mind. I didn't hear a sound but assuming that he was playing a composition he was writing, I imagined the opening measures in a minor key, a long, slow lament.

"I understand," he said when he was finished. And so I did fall upon him.

Almost two years ago, I exiled myself from The Mountain to the foothills beneath

Devil's Peak, a similar terrain to the one where, when I was a little girl, I stared, for the first time, at the stars all night. The peak itself looks accessible through a long hike up a winding trail but half way up one always get lost. The residents laugh at the visitors who expect to make a day hike of it, up and back. It isn't so far in miles, but they never make it somehow. There are barriers we can't cross as easily as we expect.

Now from this study window, I stare at an invisible line where the desert approaches the mountain. Pine trees descend to the rising manzanita and junipers weave between. No houses are visible in any direction. To the north, a little pass leads to the nearest town more than ten miles away.

Behind this cottage, I have created my version of a ziggurat, a few stairs to a platform that is higher than anything in the area and unimpeded in its access to the stars. Here on the boundary of the high desert, so far from other houses and little towns, the night is the night and the starlight freely enters the dark.

Here I call it down—the white light and the blue light, the yellow and the red, the dark light and the golden, the old weary light that comes from the farthest edge we can imagine of a universe which has no edge and the new light that burst into the sky two years ago, in 1987, from a supernova some 160,000 light years away. Those invisible rays which spill like a silver pool into my palm and also those elusive particles that are streaming through our bodies and the earth, maybe even stars, without being altered or leaving a trace. I call all the light down, Cardinal, onto my naked body hoping to remember something I once knew.

III

Descent

Chapter 20

Dear Cardinal:

When I called my parents to say I was leaving The Mountain, Aram was alarmed, but, of course, he would say nothing. He had liked thinking about me living by The Mountain, a peak that was often above the clouds. It had made him feel safe. That is, if I were safe, he was safe. He had not been able to protect Rosa nor himself. I had been his second chance. Maybe he didn't think about me as a person anymore, but as a probability, a calculated bet, a long shot.

Lance did not know about land or habitat the way Aram did, so before committing myself, I explored the territory with my father, coming on the cabin the way he had taught me so many times, circling on to it, investigating the environs first, so I wouldn't be fooled into thinking it was something it wasn't. A house could look like it was in the woods when, in fact, the suburbs were bumping up against it. We drove by the large fruit market in the nearby town, Pears, which was closed because tourists came only in the summer; not far from it was a small open stand for the locals where we bought sage honey, jalapeño jelly, green chile salsa and blackberry preserves. There was no snow on the ground in Pears, but closer in toward the hills to the south, there were patches of snow and Devil's Peak, though no where nearly as high as The Mountain, had a heavy mantle of snow and the sun was bouncing off it in Morse code.

The snow reassured Aram. It had remained white. There was little traffic, little smoke or ash even from wood fires. We stopped at the Pears post office while Aram chatted with the lone postmaster. Small town talk; weather and water. He was good at it.

We drove closer. At the end of the day, we went to Devil's Peak itself. Though it was bitter cold, we hiked quite far. We both slipped on the icy path, lost our footing, laughed. Nothing had changed between us. Aram looked for signs: hawks, rabbits, squirrels, deer, bobcat, coyote tracks and scat. There was life; he was heartened. Then we trailed down the steep slope, drove past the cottage that was almost at its feet, and circled down further to the high desert and the town.

Pears had a few motels, the one open during the winter season was clean and pleasant. The next day we visited a local monastery. Your territory, Cardinal. Aram liked the monks' orchard. It was well taken care of, the trees carefully spaced, carefully pruned. He guessed they didn't spray with insecticide; later he discovered he was right. They were relying on the health of the individual tree to protect itself and were experimenting with a new approach to agriculture called permaculture which considers all parts of the econiche so that the plants, trees, birds, animals, microbes, wind, water literally take care of each other. Aram became more and more enthusiastic about my move.

The gift store clerk didn't try to sell us anything, asked only once if he could be of help. A priest in black robes walked swiftly between the small buildings through the bare trees. His eyes were warm and quiet. He did not avert his gaze but he did not pry either. Aram was reminded of his early days in New Mexico where the Church was part of the village life. You could see Devil's Peak in the distance; the monastery and the mountain looked like they were in harmonic relationship, one guarding the valley and the other guarding the heights. From the very beginning, Cardinal, I seem to have been under the protection of your people.

Reassured, we went to the cabin. It was small and modest. It was set into the hillside rather than being placed on it. No more earth than was necessary had been dug away when it was constructed. There were enough hills between it and Pears to provide shelter from the village lights so I could see the stars. There was a raised flat area behind the cabin suitable for a viewing platform and a few small telescopes and where I could lie at night somewhat secure and sheltered from the elements. To the east and south I had an unimpeded view of the sky.

We threw sleeping bags down and lay next to each other shivering while we watched the stars come out. As is my habit, I also showed him Capella, my favorite constellation, though I'm not certain I have ever seen what the Babylonians saw, the Goatfish, a mythic beast with scales instead of fleece. Because I was looking in the wrong direction, I admonished myself. To see the goat fish, as Amanda always reminded me, you have to look inside. Inside was a new dimension. It has been speculated that time didn't exist at the big bang, that there were only spatial dimensions, then time came into being. I was discovering new aspects of time and space: the past and inside.

Aram listened as I recited the names, then we both entered into reverie until Aram leaped up to continue surveying the territory on his own. Like a wolf intending to mark his territory, Aram walked along the perimeters looking back to see if I would be exposed from any angle. The knoll behind the house was secure, he decided. I could see the sky, but no one could really see me because of the scrub. The house protected the knoll from the north. There were a few small trees all set back far enough from the house and knoll not to obscure the view.

The land itself was beautiful, almost untouched. Aram walked gingerly, disturbing little. I could see his pleasure increase as he inspected it. As is characteristic of this part of the country, the terrain changed quickly and dramatically. A short drive south from this mixture of pine, oak, juniper and manzanita took me to cottonwoods and large sycamores alongside a creek whose roots gathered boulders and rounded stones into small caves while a sharp left east led to sentinels of yucca in the high desert.

"You'll be okay," he said when we were drinking Irish Coffee to get warm. "I'll tell, Rosa, you'll be okay." Once again, I could feel his satisfaction as if he was finally thinking, "We have done well. Better than we had expected." Rosa had been so afraid.

When he came home, he might not know how to reassure my mother about some things for he did not ask me any of the questions Rosa had posed: Why was I taking a sabbatical? Why was I relocating? And why were I and Lance intending to live apart for good portions of the month? But he could reassure about others—the location, the land. He had always believed—or hoped—that place healed circumstances, and he trusted me, as much as he had ever trusted himself, to take charge of my own life.

Aram gave me directions to fields of delicate orange poppies that would emerge in the spring and spread like flames in the wind over the hillsides. He had satisfied himself. As far as civilization went, there was very little of it here; momentarily I was secure.

By April 1, 1988 I had moved. April Fool's. I had deliberately chosen that date as if I could change my mind: "I'm moving to Devil's Peak." Pause. "April Fool's!"

Leaving my car at the road, I walked up the drive, Ishtar, Queen of Heaven, following my footsteps. It was a long uphill approach past the dormant garden on one level and the well house that protected the electric pump on the next. Though I would never view the stars from this well, for it was the kind one dug in the desert after a dowser carrying a forked willow branch had located a most favorable site then covered up so the water could be drawn and piped directly into the house, I was not surprised that there was a well on the property. Not surprised that the original owner had had to dig very deep to reach this reliable source of water. Not surprised that it guaranteed to be sweet and uncontaminated. Even before I drove up and completely unpacked my car, I filled a large jar from an outside spigot and stored the water in the refrigerator. And then I went for a long walk. The area was almost completely silent. Only the sound of wind, insects, other creatures. When I came home, the water was cold and quenched my thirst.

Chapter 21

My dear Cardinal:

What lies did I write last week when I described finding this place? The sound only of wind and other creatures? How sweet the water was? How uncontaminated? How cold? My father inspected the cabin and its surroundings and was happy. I would be happy here. It was safe. Who am I kidding?

What was it I was thinking when I left The Mountain? Not about my toothbrush, nail polish, pillows and rugs for the cabin, nor about disagreements with my colleagues, retirement funds, PMS, nor whether my flight in tears was a hormonal response to stress, the female equivalent of the male's fight or flight, not about Lance's response, nor about my loneliness.

One story I told myself was that I had run down from The Mountain as soon as I could after my grandmother died and Marteen Schmidt, Jim Gunn and Don Schneider and others started photographing quasars which were further away in time than anyone of us, even Marteen Schmidt had ever expected. They had added a few billion years to the age of the universe and I needed to get away. The beginning of time was being pushed so far away by the discovery of older and older quasars that I suffered inexplicable molecular panic. The future that I had expected to extend indefinitely into limitless space was impinging upon me, the ineluctable approach of a horrible and unavoidable thickening, a gross, vulgar and ever increasing density was descending upon us without recourse or remedy. A gathering of forces not predicted to occur at this time neither by mathematical models, nor the most advanced calculations, but implicit nevertheless in the approach of an unspeakable reality. After the first instance of the voice, I could feel it before I thought of it in words. We were elsewhere in the speed of time and the trajectory of universe than I had thought.

Additionally, it was increasingly apparent to me that exploring the beginning of time through a telescope—even the planned Hubble Space Telescope—wasn't going to address any of the questions that were forming in my mind because everything which we are learning and, accordingly, everything we do, is determined and limited by the languages we are using. I would never understand anything unless I could get out of myself and my world view—out of or maybe into history—out of science, out of the only languages I had ever learned.

Western science analyzes, makes distinctions, says here and there, this and that, before and after, past and future, self and other. But since I've come here, I can't separate the direction of the universe from the direction of human life. I can't unequivocally distinguish the universe from the mind. Outside and inside are blurred. Some say that despite the extraordinary precision and development of our instruments, we are always looking inside. When we believe we are training our telescopes outwards to the distant stars, we're not doing much more than exploring the particular configurations of our own intelligence.

After a few weeks, everything that had been outside was inside as time and relativity and space were all inside me too. The night sky, the stars and the points of light, they were all inside me and took on new aspects for what I had seen as finite, bounded, limited, defined, absolute, I now perceived as incalculable, immeasurable, unceasing, timeless and boundless, infinite. And as it had been with first sightings through telescopes and microscopes, I didn't understand what I was seeing; it would take a long time to decipher these strange and unexpected configurations.

I was a huge space, which somehow kept its shape, moving among other similarly huge mysteriously defined spaces. Within this space, motes of dust, specks, particles, waves, so small themselves the space between them was proportional to the space between stars, whirled about each other. And, if I were able to see it, myself, Lance, anyone, anything as it, I, he, they, it, really were, I would know I was seeing the equivalent of the night sky. What I called myself, what I fed and bathed and combed, was not substantive at all but was intermittent flashes of light or color which were neither light nor color and whose internal pattern could be predicted but not observed and certainly not guaranteed.

Had anyone known how to ask me what was happening in such a manner that provoked me to answer precisely in words, I might have said that I was experiencing atomic theory as a reality—in my own body—now that I had time, infinite time, I thought, to consider the implications that I as someone who had been born after the discovery of the atom, had taken for granted.

The reality of the atom was more of a shock to the nervous system than the Copernican revolution ever could have been, and that had been traumatic enough. Once having entered this abyss, I knew the terror that had gripped the Inquisitors as they scurried desperately to ferret out any carrier of the contagious idea that earth and humans were not the center of the universe. Inevitably, I began seeing myself as succumbing to delusion, not unlike those who had been accused of fleeing the Church for science, order for witchcraft, law for sorcery, or fleeing reason for the madness of alchemy. But it was not "the other" who was to be purified of the heretical thought, it was the Inquisitor who needed to protect himself from the infection of the other's knowledge, from the thousands of odd ones, like Kepler or Bruno, who devoted their lives to looking for the mysteries despite being persecuted for falling into a morass.

But now this: Atomic theory had not even begun to enter consciousness when subatomic quantum theory was upon the century. These nascent understandings of the nature of matter were also its undoing. Space, infinite space opened up within me and I felt the vast almost incalculable distances between one whirling, sometimes disintegrating or transforming speck of—what was it—matter or energy?—and another. The entire damned masquerade of substance became clear—a flash of light, no more and no less, than the flashes of light that composed me and all bodies. Yet when I tried to see myself for what I really was, it was also clear I was no more dust, specks, particles, waves, flashes of light, no more the combination and recombination of quanta, atoms and molecules than the stars in the sky were only those same particles and flashes, were merely the stars in the sky.

Increasingly, my colleagues maintain that I, we, humans, are chemical patterns, electrical impulses, that body and mind are no more than these material combinations and recombinations. But everywhere I looked, either within me or without, either in the patterns of the smallest or the patterns of the largest, I faced the insistence of something that was carried by, manifested through these flashes of light but was not of the flashes of light.

I didn't know what was happening. I didn't know why a star was no longer just a star. But it wasn't. The flashes of light, the dust clouds, the appearing and disappearing muons, pions, kaons, protons, neutrons, were the letters of an alphabet that formed itself now into one language and now into another. They weren't, however, the-thing-itself, "thethingsinthemselves." This essence was there, somewhere, in, around, above, within, about, both with and without those very different languages created with the very same strange letters of light. Language wasn't the right word for it either, nor was light the exact word, except in the way the kabbalists had understood language centuries before me—as Shaena Baena had once secretly imparted to me—that the letters of the Torah, the letters of flame, were light, were divine, that the Torah was not only the word of God, it was the Name of God, that is, it was creation itself.

When that word, *the* word, "God," appeared, after I first arrived at Devil's Peak, I laughed aloud. I put down the paper where I had been scribbling notes and laughed and laughed. God!

It had not been difficult at all for Copernicus, Galileo, Kepler, and even Darwin, later, to find God in the universe after the sun became the center of the smaller world. In fact, it was almost impossible for them not to find the Divine. "This most beautiful system of the sun, planets and comets, could only proceed from the counsel and dominion of an intelligent and powerful being." Thus wrote Newton, at the conclusion of the *Principia*, this same Isaac Newton had also been born on December 25, which given Rosa's antipathy to physics and astronomy, would not have consoled her. The Church Fathers were not reassured of the existence of the Divine Presence when it was discovered that the earth was no longer the center of the solar system. Now there wasn't even a center anywhere, space-time was no longer a lovely round globe and I was thinking the forbidden word.

What did it mean? That I was losing my mind. That's what it means, I thought, I'm losing my mind. I should have lost my mind in drugs, I reasoned, and had a good time on the way, but I had always been too timid and serious, too preoccupied with my studies to follow those trends among my acquaintances, so I had simply lost it anyway, without any effort on my part.

About this, Lance teased me mercilessly. I had not only missed the entire cultural exploration and preoccupation with psychology, I had, as far as he was concerned, missed the sixties altogether. "Astronomy," he said once, "is a poor psyche's compensation for real space travel." And then, as if he had known where I would be going he added, "Peering into a long black tube with the best lens in the world is never going to compete with what everyone your age saw when they looked inside their own minds. You are pointing in the wrong direction."

I had pretended I was going to Devil's Peak for R and R. I hadn't expected to be thrust far and fast out of the gravitational field that had kept my mind in its orbit. I hadn't expected—ever—to be thrust into a different dimension altogether. I hadn't believed, with all my mathematical training, that these mathematically postulated dimensions actually existed.

There are accounts of how it happened to others and as these others discovered, each experience was completely different and also similar. Science fiction primed me for exploration by proposing the existence of other worlds. But I had never considered that the writers themselves actually believed in these worlds. I had always assumed they only believed in their imaginations.

I began to search out memoirs to counter my growing fears for my sanity and to help me explore the new territory. Had I simply been left on a desert island, I would have known how to proceed for Aram had read Robinson Crusoe and Swiss Family Robinson to me when, as a child, I had dreamed longingly of the advantages of shipwreck. Now desperation drew me to testimonies and biographies that I had previously disdained. For some, I read, the entry into similar awareness or dislocation had been antedated by calamity: catastrophic illness, inconsolable grief, devastating loss. For some it was gradual, for others it was as if they were struck by lightning. Many people who had had intimations of disaster (or rescue) confessed they had tried to escape being struck, consumed by fire, parched in the desert, starved in the forest, swallowed by whales, imprisoned in the labyrinth, buried alive, leveled by cancer, paralysis or heart disease, eaten by ants, reduced to bones, driven mad, drowned in the great mother sea, humiliated, broken, pulverized, tortured, flayed, ruined, and annihilated—to no avail; these are the recurring means of initiation and transformation. The writers often alleged that the wall of the body or mind was shattered at the behest of a something greater—spirit, they called it—that then entered through each new opening. Invasion through a rain of stars. And such a rain, like radiation, further shattered or dissolved whatever it rained upon before the ultimate reconstitution in a new form.

"How can you know anything if you don't know shit about yourself?" Lance was trying to be helpful but his voice revealed uncharacteristic irritation. And why shouldn't he be annoyed when his partner had disappeared herself from his side.

"What do you mean?"

"Don't get us involved in a theoretical argument. You know what I mean. We've had this conversation before. What you don't know about the sky is peanuts compared to what you don't know about yourself. Why don't you do a little post doctoral study on Daniella and the mystery of the human character?"

"I think I will," I said, not knowing what it entailed, not knowing how to proceed, nor suspecting the consequences.

When I was young, Shaena had given me a journal—not a silly little book with a fake lock and key which most of my school mates received, but a blank book of fine white unlined paper, nicely bound—but it never occurred to me to use it to discover who I am. "What do I do with this?" I asked her.

"Write the truth so that you will remember it," she said as if she expected me to understand.

Now I was pursuing my history and the present, keeping records even of the dreams which had followed me to Devil's Peak as if they were my true companions.

The room was composed of mud bricks. Not far away there was another wall, glazed blue and topped with a similarly blue dome. The moment just before the sun was beginning to rise and just before it set, the dome and the sky were the very same shade of blue. This was such a moment. But I couldn't see it because I was concealed in a room of sun dried mud bricks. Outside these walls, were other surrounding walls of baked bricks. The floor on which I was standing was also mud brick with a copper tub set into in one of the corners, straight on one side and curved on the other as if the tub were a cross section of the blue dome laid out horizontally. The side of the tub was engraved with animals and plants. I examined a lion minutely and found it perfect, then I went on to a bull. Without being told, I understood that I was looking at a coffin. As always, I could not look at anything directly. It had been legislated that everyone must look through lenses and I was complying with the protocol by gazing through a narrow tube. Because of this, my focus was narrow and a long time passed before I noticed that there was someone else in the room. This was impossible, I knew, because I had been brought here secretly, had been admitted through a break in the wall that had, afterwards, been sealed. I was having to trust that my patrons would return for me, would open the door and let me back into the light. Because I could see, I realized that some light was entering the room, perhaps the bricks themselves were glowing, but I couldn't see the source.

The man was gathering bricks, numbering them carefully and placing them in boxes. Each time he packed up a box of bricks, the room seemed to get larger. On the other hand, though, he was dismantling the walls of the room, the room remained sealed. The lens I was looking through slipped out of my hands and felt to the floor with a clatter. The man looked up. He had white skin and eyes of blue ice, the color of the winter sky. He was not startled by the noise, only curious to see where it had come from. When he saw me, he was undaunted. He came toward me carrying a box. He reached his hand out to me in the way he had approached the wall. First my thumb went into the box, then my second finger. As I watched, he placed all the dusty parts of my body neatly into the box. The box was now large enough to contain the disparate parts in the same relationship they had to each other in my body. I could see myself laid out in the box as if I was gazing at a box of bricks. Then he, himself, climbed into the center of box. Once he was inside, I couldn't see him anymore. Perhaps he was fitting himself exactly into my body. There was a copper glow about the box. It smelled like swamp gas.

The phone rang but no one was on the other end. It happened several times within one day and then it didn't happen again for a week and then it happened again. Sometimes, I thought I heard someone walking up the drive in the day time, but when I went to look, no one was there. At night, when it was even more quiet, I could detect the stealthy padding of coyotes and rabbits across the dry earth, I sometimes thought I heard a man's footsteps on the road or the presence of a shadow, a slight thickening in the region of a parabola of air.

The books I read of others who had undergone my ordeal, spoke of the advent of such terror, springing out of nothing, challenging the mind to dethrone it, but these recountings didn't loosen me from the shackles of fear. And anyway, there was a central dilemma I hadn't solved. Had I been destabilized and thought I had heard a voice? Or had I heard a voice and its appearance had rendered me distraught, unstable? What if I wasn't merely losing my mind?

Sirius. The dog star. Until recently we thought it was a single star. In 1844 Bessel suggested that only a dark companion could account for its wobble. By 1915 we knew that the wobble was caused by a white dwarf alongside it that was perceptible only with instruments, a star in a state of extreme density and degeneracy collapsed to twice the radius of the earth but with the mass of the sun. The dog star, Sirius, wobbles from the force Sirius B exerts on what comes into its reach.

The wobble. That's what happened: I was wobbling. I was no longer in my own orbit. Nothing as prosaic as not knowing where I was going or not having control of my own life. Nothing as banal and contemporary. I was wobbly because something invisible, massive and dense was pulling at me. In the beginning, I didn't know any-thing about it, only suspected it was there and so pretended it wasn't. No, that isn't quite accurate. Ignored it by looking away, by pretending I had other things to do. Like discovering who I was when I should have been investigating *it*. But if I didn't know who I was how could I possibly know that *it* was a part of me.

When I called Lance, he was kind.

"I'm afraid."

"Of what?"

"I don't know. I can't imagine."

"Put on a light."

"How can that help when it extinguishes the stars?"

"Did you hear something? Maybe it was an animal."

"I'm not afraid of animals."

"A prowler?"

"Don't be so sensible. It's worse than that."

"Do you want me to come out?"

"I don't think so."

"Do you want to come back home?"

"I don't think so."

"I think I need the fear. I think fear is a radar showing me things I can't see with the naked eye."

Singularity, Cardinal, means that what happens on the other side of the line is a world unto itself, completely distinct, unknowable and incomprehensible. Singularity means that what happens on other side, in that other time or in that other world, can't affect us on this side. Singularity also means that we can't travel from one universe to the other.

But if universes and dimensions are not bounded by singularities, if they are, in effect, continuums of each other—if the other side is a continuum of what was and if this side is a continuum of the other side, an infinite extension into the past and the future, well, then—how can we bear it? It means it's us. It means that side over there and this side are the same, that light from one area reaches another and influences it, affects it. It means we're part of each other, one and the same.

When I could no longer contain my fear, I would telephone Lance asking him to play his own music for me. I allowed myself to miss his music when I couldn't, didn't allow myself to miss him, the comfort of his body, the intimate chatter that connects one day to another. There was something to be done even if I didn't know what it was and I could only do it if I were alone. Desperately alone. It took the edge off my terror when I could hear Lance's breath shaping the notes or filling the silences between the notes. Because the distances I regularly considered were so vast, it was as if Lance, though actually hundreds of miles away, was playing in the next room. Sometimes I played one of his recordings, but it was not the same. I needed to know he was playing the music in the moment that I was listening to it and accordingly I was always more at ease when we were in the same longitude so I could call him at high noon and it would be exactly high noon where he was: "Look at the sun, Lance, and we will both see it almost exactly the same way. Look for the dipper, now. Our eyes are meeting in the light. Do you see?"

"I love you, Daniella," Lance reminded me.
"I forget."
"I don't."

Chapter 22

Dear Cardinal:

The first few months, I lived at Devil's Peak exactly the way I might have lived at home with my parents. I became an observer again. In the night, the stars, as usual, but during the day, I walked a great deal or sat still against a tree or in a meadow watching. I quickly gave up trying to learn the names of things which Aram would have done first. Rather I noticed little eddies of energy that united different beings into small communities—wind, branch, jay—as a rock in a creek might create a whirl of activity around it. I was at home in these niches and found myself trying to formulate simple, definitive statements: "I am a woman who is at home here," or, "I am a woman who walks at dawn and at dusk," and, of course: "I am a woman who watches the stars."

I secured a shape through these observations and acknowledgment; this cheered me. When I tried saying: "I am an expert on Andromeda," I was not cheered. This statement, though true, was not essential; it did not tell me who I was. I tried this technique with Lance: "Lance is a man who plays the flute." It was accurate. "Lance is a soloist;" this wasn't false but it was not pertinent. "Aram is a man who loves trees. Rosa plays the piano." Bull's eye. "Rosa has a daughter." Irrelevant. "Aram has a daughter." Not quite. "Aram is a father." Better. "Lance is a man who loves a woman, Daniella." Accurate. "Daniella loves Lance." What was wrong? I do love Lance. But at that moment, it wasn't part of my identity. After a while I understood what I was doing: I was setting down basic principles. "Amanda...."

It took me a long time to be able to frame a fundamental statement about Amanda. "Amanda is a woman who has tried to befriend Daniella." It was all I really knew about her. Fortunately, I discovered this principle just in time.

When Amanda arrived at my cabin at Devil's Peak, I realized that I had the capacity to hurt someone. The singularity that divided my parent's world from my world had seemed a boundary between cause and effect so that I had assumed that I and everyone else were confined in immaculate worlds independent of each other. On the one hand, physics asserted that even the neutral observer of an event affected its outcome and, on the other hand, there could be dimensions so tiny they were tucked away within the fabric of reality without, seemingly, any visibility or impact.

Then, one afternoon in summer several months after I had begun my "sabbatical," Amanda was walking very slowly up the unpaved drive to my cabin. I had been standing before the window and had seen a car drive back and forth several times and then disappear from view behind the little knoll where I parked my car. Amanda stood at the unhinged gate gazing up for quite a few minutes before she began the climb. Maybe the heat that slowed people's activity also slowed perception, because it seemed to me that it was taking Amanda hours to reach my door and yet despite this luxury of time, I was unprepared for the knock and opened the door in a flurry of confusion to meet Amanda's steady if weary gaze.

"I didn't know if I had a right to come," Amanda said simply.

"How like you to hide your car behind the hill so it won't spoil our view," I responded awkwardly, not expecting that the sight of my friend that had so agitated me from a distance would calm me once we were face to face. "Come in."

I went into the kitchen to prepare two glasses of ice tea while Amanda settled herself in a chair on the patio. I set the glasses down on a small table. It seemed that simple except that Amanda was weeping.

"I've thrown everything away. I've distracted myself. What have I been doing with my time?" Now I realized that Amanda had been crying for a long time and that I had not understood the flush of her face and the reddened eyes.

"It is as if I have died and . . ." she stammered. "It is as if I am dying and can see everything in this last flash . . ." she continued.

"What is it, Amanda?"

"Can't you see? Can't you see how thin I am? Flesh is falling off my bones. Everything that insulated me is sliding down into an oily heap. Soon only the bones will remain. I hope they will be nice and white.

"I'm sorry, Daniella, for coming to you in such a state. But where else would I go? And don't be alarmed, I'm not too distressed, just upset that I waited this long. I hope you were smart. I hope you left in time."

"What is it, Amanda?" I repeated in bewilderment. I had been so far away for so long, it was as if I had forgotten the relationship between sound and meaning and I had to pay strict attention until the babble sorted itself out in words. I was not used to having people in my house. Lance came often, of course, and my father came sometimes and a colleague every now and then when there was work that could not be discussed on the telephone, and the astronomer landlord who used the excuse of checking on the cabin to have a day in the mountains away from the University, but other than these, a friend had never come to see me. I didn't think I had a friend who might have come. Except Amanda. And she had clearly not been invited.

"Don't worry," Amanda was saying. "I'm not going back either. I've bought my last business suit. I thought there was some good reason to live the life I was living. I thought I was making a contribution. I thought the work you guys are doing was important. But is it worth my life?"

She continued the rush of words as if afraid I would cut her off. "I just wasn't living the right way. You know, sometimes it doesn't matter, but if you know it isn't right, and then you continue . . ."

"I didn't know, Amanda."

"No. You didn't. I didn't tell you. How could I? You weren't speaking to anyone, certainly not to me. I did talk with Lance and then asked him not to speak to you about me." Scrutinizing my face, Amanda saw that Lance had not said anything. "Your partner is a good man. He kept his word," she paused long enough to assimilate this. I had been not, as she might have thought, wantonly neglectful. "I could see how distressed you were. And also, I didn't know if you would understand. And if you did understand? I couldn't completely blow my cover, could I?

"I'll tell you, it was a shock when you actually moved here. It occurred to me, Daniella, I didn't know who you are at all."

"It was your idea, Amanda."

"Yes, you're right. It was. But I didn't know you well enough to realize you would accept it. I didn't know the meaning of my own advice. I might have taken it myself."

"Are you angry with me for running away, Amanda?"

"No. I was glad you came here. At first, though, I was so preoccupied with your move, I didn't think about myself at all. As if you were doing it for all of us. And then one day, I spent a day, all twenty-four hours of it as a matter of fact, thinking only of myself. It was as if you gave me permission to think this way, because you had left. But it is probably too late."

I brought a bowl of ice cubes to the table. The clink of the ice against the blue porcelain was very soothing. We sat quietly listening to the summer sounds of bees and the tinkle of ice rearranging itself as it melted.

"My heart is breaking," Amanda said.

"Maybe that's a good thing," I answered in the way my grandmother would have answered. We sat quietly together, the sun burning our hands.

Amanda wanted to walk, now, in the heat because she said she couldn't ever get warm enough these days. We took my car and drove a few miles down from the foothills to a path that forked through the desert scrub. Though it was high noon, I didn't object. I didn't have confidence in any thoughts I might have in this situation. Along the way, we passed the graying husks of yucca that lie about like the long-limbed dead. Braids of coyote scat had turned hard and silvery in the brutal sun.

"When are you coming back to The Mountain?" Amanda's voice was metallic with provocation. "What are you going to do?"

"I don't know." I knew full well that Amanda wasn't urging me back soon, quite the contrary, but I was wary of seeming to know anything I didn't know. Then unexpectedly I heard myself hypothesizing new possibilities: I would not study galaxies, would not study those larger configurations. Would not study anything in the plural. I would find one star. A star I could also see, however faintly, with my eyes. And I would study it until I or it was exhausted. It was an absurd idea. This meant my professional life was virtually over. So be it. I could keep my administrative position at The Mountain. I could always teach. I liked that idea. I wanted something modest to pursue. The decision had sweetness to it. It was almost as if I had come to it while munching on cookies which Shaena Baena had just taken from the oven.

"I don't think I'm going back," Amanda said.

"No," I began, "I don't think you're going back. And today I can't imagine going back myself, though I don't know what I'm going to do with my life.

"I'm glad you came." I paused this time so I could be aware that I was choosing to speak so openly to Amanda. "I wouldn't be here, if not for you. It wasn't only that you told me about the cabin. That little yellow book you gave me brought me here."

"Well, you can have all my books when I die. But not before. Until then, I will need them." Her grin was wholehearted; she was calling the shots, legislating my responses. "When we get back from this walk, let's get an elegant dinner and champagne on the last of the big paychecks I will ever receive."

I sometimes came down to the desert by myself in the early mornings or late afternoons, but I had never walked here with anyone but Lance and certainly not in such ominous and funereal heat. It was difficult even for me to walk under the sun's hell fires, but particularly hard for Amanda who was insisting that we continue. She was pale, despite the flush from the effort and it was clear she was unused to these conditions but what I couldn't grasp yet was that Amanda was very ill. The sweat was running down her face from the contact of sunglasses upon her prominent cheekbones, and her owl brown hair having returned to its natural color was trailing limply out of a visored hat.

"It's like an oven," Amanda commented but without complaint. She threw her face back into the sun calling out, "Bake me like bread."

There wasn't any shade, so we sat down against a boulder and drank some water from the thermos in my pack while I carefully trimmed the spines from a prickly pear. "We call them *tunas* in the Southwest," I said, cutting one in half. I scooped out the fruit and gave it to Amanda. It was an odd lunar red, a harvest moon, dusty and ruddy like the flesh on the inside of one's mouth. The wetness was startling and we were grateful for its sweetness.

Then Amanda couldn't support herself against the stone and lay down on the ground with a sigh of resignation, and hoping aloud that it would not be misunderstood, she put her head in my lap, reproaching me at the same time: "You didn't even ask how I found you. I didn't ask Lance for your address. I didn't want to implicate him." Then she looked up at me, her eyes steady and said, "You know, I'm dying."

When it was obvious that I did not know what to say, Amanda went off on a rant to allow me enough time to assimilate what I had heard: "Death and dying seem to be the new path for Americans. It's our spiritual path. It's our psychological path. It's our national anthem. We're hungry," Amanda said, "for dying. Death and dying have become a fine commercial venture—just add enough violence. Ask the book publishers and the television moguls. Maybe I should write a grant . . ."

She stopped short. Both of us knew then that the conversation wasn't about *a* woman dying—*this* woman *was* dying. This was different. *Amanda* was dying. I put my hand on Amanda's forehead, stroked her gently, took her hat off and fanned her with it, adjusted her visor and position so the sun wouldn't be in her eyes.

Amanda was staring at fallen yuccas in the distance. "They look like corpses, don't they?" I knew exactly what she was thinking. The heat, or our exertion, or this news had toppled the wall that had always been between us, that barrier, I had thought, was nature's way of insuring the autonomy of different species. Raising herself slightly, she saw that she was crossing me exactly the way the one yucca crossed the other, the two trees lying together as if by design. "Did they make a suicide pact? Let's not do that," she said in a voice that was quiet and sober.

For a moment, I was afraid Amanda would die then and there in my arms, but when Amanda was rested, we walked back though even more slowly than before. I allowed myself to put my arm around Amanda's waist, something I had never dreamed I'd ever do, but Amanda needed to be steadied, and when we reached a stride Amanda took my arm and then, as unexpectedly as she had placed her head in my lap, she took my hand and the two of us walked as two good friends might walk with the pleasure of hands clasped. Saying nothing.

I never remembered feeling such comfort except when I had explored the woods with my father as a little girl. Then at the age of twelve, he inexplicably stopped holding my hand and even pulled away slightly but enough for me to notice when I reached up to him. It would have been a reflex to pull away from Amanda in a similar way, but I didn't. Instead I thought of Aram and clasped Amanda's hands even tighter so Amanda would know that I was acknowledging our bond.

When we reached the cabin, Amanda didn't want to stay any longer. "I'm not wriggling out of our dinner date. If it's all right with you, I am going to return within a few days. I would like to spend my last days nearby, closer to the desert and the warmth. I don't want anything between me and the sun."

"It's all right with me," I said. "It's right," I continued, not understanding anything that was going on.

She was standing at the front door, propping open the screen, about to leave.

"Don't die." What else was I to say?

"Not today. I'm not going to die today, Daniella."

"No one told me, Amanda, not even Roger."

"I swore everyone to secrecy."

"Can you tell me...?" There was a pause at the end of the sentence. I didn't know what I wanted to know.

"I'll tell you the worst. One assumes the presence of a black hole next to a star by the luminescent sheen of the x-rays passing across into that vortex. I couldn't see the x-rays, of course, when I underwent radiation but still I thought about the black hole in me that was pulling the radiation into it."

"No black holes in you, Amanda. I know something about this. You're just shining on your own." I hoped she hadn't seen me shudder. Black holes aren't contagious,

Cardinal. Amanda hadn't caught one from me. Cancer wasn't contagious either. My decline had nothing to do with Amanda. We were just both afflicted. Only I wasn't dying and she was.

"I don't know if I am good for you, Amanda."

"You're good for me. The best, Daniella."

"You don't know."

"No, you don't understand. I do know. You're good for me. That's why I am coming here to live next to you until I die. Is that okay?"

"Of course it's okay. I will like the company," I said meaning it. "I want to be alongside you this time."

Cardinal, before Amanda died, something in her died. She died and something else, someone else was born. Then she died again. You would understand this, but I didn't at the time. She did throw away her old clothes and her old job. She rented a cottage near me for awhile. We met as often as she wished. Sometimes we walked, mostly without speaking. That was her choice. I was available for whatever she proposed and mostly she proposed silence. Sometimes she left a note in my mailbox suggesting that we eat a meal together, specifying the time and the setting, assuming, correctly, that I would be willing to cook if she desired or to visit her—whatever. I discovered that I like being with the dying as I was finding her so very much alive.

At the end she liked to say that she had first died while she was working as a grant officer and then she came to life again or that she died again when she discovered she had cancer, and then she really came to life. In any event, she had the habit of speaking of her present condition as her next life. Maybe everyone dies twice, not only those two people whom I know to have died twice.

"Do you understand yet why I moved here?" Amanda was arranging objects on what she called her altar which resembled the end table on which my father's mother had collected knickknacks, except the objects Amanda treasured were not porcelain nor silver, but talismen she found on her walks, feathers, leaves, dried bones, a few rocks, a fossil—her prized possessions.

"It's hard to know what you're really aware of, Daniella. But it doesn't matter. I didn't come here to be with you, exactly. You were just a light and I followed it."

"Maybe you were the light and I followed," I said to her. "After all, you did contribute to this, you know, giving me funny books, making odd remarks I didn't understand when we were both at The Mountain, and finding this cabin for me."

I wanted to tell her about the darkness then. About what was pulling me in, but when I saw how much pain she was suffering in the moment, I couldn't say anything.

"Maybe, Daniella, maybe we were the light at the same time."

"How are you feeling now that you're here, Amanda?" I asked her with more tenderness than I usually expressed.

"Can't you tell? I've never been happier. Dying is a great gift. If I'd known that, I'd have started sooner."

"I'm on a pilgrimage, Dani." I must have looked at her peculiarly because she managed to pull herself together as if she were going to instruct the members of the board.

She took a paper from her pocket. She must have been writing notes when I entered:

A pilgrimage, the rigorous retracing of a prescribed journey, following steps or walking in the footsteps of others who create or follow a four dimensional map in order to live out a mythic story.

"I think I'm on a pilgrimage, Dani. Who would think dying would be a pilgrimage, but I think it is. I am trying to die so very carefully. I am doing it alone so that no one will interfere or influence the process. I wish I had studied the process earlier, but I didn't think in time. I thought years. I hadn't even begun living my life, I was so busy trying to earn a living by helping others earn their living. So here I am and very unprepared. I will do this as well as I can. It is the only thing I have ever wanted to do for myself."

She gave me the paper. Then she took it back, folded it in four, and put it in my pocket saying, "Read this afterwards. Not now."

I know there is a map for this. And I must most carefully repeat the series of movements from place A to place B, from my life to my death. I must include everything essential and eliminate everything tangential to this odyssey.

I am thinking of death as a temple to be approached after enacting the proper rituals of purification and dedication. I want to get to that temple and I want to do it in the right way and at the proper time.

Dying is a process. I must do it by myself. No one who is alive can help me. But the dead help. I am searching out the ones who died well in order to follow them. Maybe they will meet me on the other side. That is irrelevant. What is important is that they have left traces of their dying and I can try to follow those. I will gather their dying into myself and my dying will be deepened. I understand that I will only make this pilgrimage once.

I have entered into a diligent review of my life and now, with equal fanaticism, attend every detail of my current life, hoping to achieve a focus which will transform the daily, mundane activities into a proper ritual capable of transporting me from the mundane into another world.

I'm in a dilemma here. I'm trying to die. I'm trying to leave the physical world. And I am trying to "do it well." But, I can't leave the physical world before the time is right or by ignoring physical reality. I seem to have to go through the physical, through the body. It's quite appalling, really.

I spend my time studying this. I begin to understand the care with which I have to work with all the elements. I never realized how meticulous I have to be in organizing material reality. Sometimes it feels like orchestrating a high mass.

When I was little, I thought the priest in my mother's church was very good at it. At the right time, in the right way, I hope I will be thrust into the sacred.

Amanda told Lance and myself, "You're my kinfolk," in case we thought she'd come to Devil's Peak for her last weeks because she had no where else to go. She said this two months later just before she took a shower, put on the white lacy batiste nightgown she called her dream shroud and drank the potion that was going to relieve her permanently of the extreme physical pain which she only once complained was, "drastically altering the sublime quality of my days."

Suicide? Maybe. But as I see it, after she'd found her real life, she began losing it and there was nothing she could do about it. So, rather than abandoning what she'd gained, she sacrificed it. It is possible that the potion she drank had nothing to do with it; perhaps she simply laid down, opened her arms so her heart would be bare and gave herself up.

Amanda reminded me of my grandmother; eyes flaring before they died. Using up, devouring, discarding all the fuel she had depended on until that moment, flashing up in a great light and then retreating, imploding into herself, concentrating into a wondrous numinous density, invisible to most naked eyes, but sending signals to anyone who was willing to see in the dark.

Sometimes I wonder if Amanda and Shaena have met there, on the other side. If they have tea together and cluck and gossip about us. Did their dying rescue something we've discarded? Did Shaena's death bring Yiddish back alive somewhere on the other side, in a parallel universe, even a co-existent universe, of which we're not aware? Is death the vortex that tears us apart reducing every molecule to the erratic dance of elements or did they both survive the violent gyrations until they were spit out into another life they are forbidden from leaving? And are we prohibited from entering it too, except that sometimes the walls between the worlds crack open just enough for visitations? My grandmother on the other side, really on the other side, speaking Chaldean with Amanda and both of them knowing the real meaning and influence of the stars is not such a bizarre idea.

Amanda was cremated, Cardinal, as she had requested. Lance and I buried her ashes just under a yucca couple who had fallen among the sage brush and pale pink clumps of aster and darker four o'clocks which bloomed after unexpected autumn rains. "I want to remain with you," were the very last words Amanda said.

Chapter 23

Felice Noël. Confession, Cardinal. I always long for Christmas. Not because it's my birthday but because it is so close to the solstice, and the possibility exists that the sun will be reborn. From the moment the sun set yesterday, I felt uneasy as if I were uncertain about whether it would rise this morning. And when it did, would it be a new light? All evening I paced back and forth restlessly. Lance was driving in from "somewhere" Colorado so I didn't expect him until this morning. Finally, I jumped into my down clothes and tromped outside to the ziggurat.

Within a circle of *luminarios*, sand filled brown paper bags with votive candles burning inside, Lance was seated cross legged, waiting to surprise me. He began playing his flute as he heard the crunch of my steps and as it was almost midnight, he played us across into the new day.

There's a sound Lance imagines and he is spending his life trying to make that sound. He keeps his flute in his pocket and he always fingers it; at his lips or not, it's always in his mind. Last night he said that if he could make that sound, something extraordinary would happen.

"What?" I asked.

He shook his head frustrated that he had neither words nor sound to speak of that either.

We felt strangely alone. Amanda should have been with us. I was wearing one of her blouses under my jacket and that absurd necklace with an amber sun that she had been wearing when she and I first spoke to each other.

"What shall I do, Amanda?" I asked. She's still so present in her absence.

Amanda didn't say a word. Just before the stars disappeared in the dawn, I admitted to Lance how close I am to considering a permanent leave from The Mountain. "I have no way to express my love anymore. There is no love for the stars at The Mountain even if there is the Law. There is a fierce desire to know what stars are, but there is no heart. But if I leave The Mountain I may be left without a language at all for my love."

For Christmas, Lance gave me a vial of stars. "These are the stars," he said spilling fine meteor dust to which he had added sparkles from the crafts store on to the palm of my hand. "An attempt to return a bit of yourself to yourself," he had written on the card. It was the perfect gift for a cloudy night.

Ancient astronomers spent their lives watching the sky, thirsty for the vision of each and every body of light, for the regular and irregular turning and returning, for the steady burning and the terrifying appearances and disappearances, and when they saw a sign, the star calling them, they set out. They believed that events in the heavens and events on earth were conjunct and so it was foolish to separate above from below as interactions between spheres are multiple and complex. Even Newton couldn't calculate the precise effect of gravity—the way bodies pull toward each other—because the orbits of any one planet depend on the combined motion of all the planets. Today we call this problem "the many body problem," as if we weren't talking about mysteries. We haven't been able to calculate the stellar and planetary interactions either as exactitude requires that we take *all* the stars into account.

My friends have been trying to fix the date of Christ's birth by reconstructing the ancient skies with computers and accurate ephemeris in order to identify the unusual stellar phenomena that the Magi, the Babylonian star gazers, took for a sign and followed. They're not trying to identify the moment when divinity entered the world, just what might have [mis]led the ancients. Kepler, who was "a bit of a mystic," wrote, "I do not doubt but that God would have condescended to cater to the credulity of the Chaldeans." Most of my colleagues argue for June 17, 2 BCE, when there was a brilliant conjunction of Jupiter and Venus (or Marduk and Ishtar as the Magi would have called them.) But Kepler argued that the Star of Bethlehem was the conjunction of Saturn and Jupiter that occurred on September 15, 7 BCE. The fifteenth century Jewish statesman, astronomer, astrologer, Don Isaac Abarbanel, argued that this same conjunction, this same Star of Bethlehem had announced the birth of Moses and would occur again with the coming of the Messiah.

Do *you* ever wonder if the light from *the* conjunction was truly more than light and the star more than a sign? Maybe the light which everyone saw actually entered a child who was shaped by it. Maybe those that saw that star and followed its light were star struck themselves and able to see what they might not have seen otherwise. Perhaps light is the counterpart of angels, the messengers or bearers of something we do not understand. Some deeper knowledge, or divinity, traveling in the light fields of stars, falling down upon us, while we, in our continual obstinacy, shine little mechanical lights back into the night so that the descending light is neutralized or obscured.

Why are we so sure that the stars don't affect us? We don't know what happens when light penetrates our bodies except that people in the far north go mad during the dark months. How can we assume the planets, let's say, don't affect us when great bodies bend space about them, hold each other in place, and influence us profoundly. Our own Jupiter is continually slinging meteors around our perimeter while comets sweep past our atmosphere causing shivers in every electron in the proximity of the wing of their energy and light.

I don't know what the Babylonians knew. Keynes called Newton "the last of the magicians, the last of the Babylonians." I feel affinity with Newton since I was born on his birthday, am also interested in gravity and in light and maybe I've also gone mad. Somehow with all he explored, he didn't abandon God. I'll tell you what intrigues me; after the crucifixion you can still imagine the possibility of the divine. But that *is* the mystery, you say.

Good night, dear Cardinal. Lance and I are taking this week off. These days always feel to me like a week between the worlds. Here I am, Cardinal, talking like Amanda. Perhaps she is answering me after all. When the new year comes, there is something I will tell you.

Chapter 24

January 1, 1990

Your Eminence, I can't put this off any longer. This afternoon I sit at my desk and look out at the snow beneath the junipers. The light bouncing off the snow is so blinding I can only look at it for short intervals. When I turn away, colors dance in the air before my eyes. Or if I close my eyes, I see turquoise and blue figures floating down a field of unimaginable orange. Dear Cardinal, Jean-Marie Lustiger, Your Eminence, do you remember that I agreed to write about Peter Schmidt today?

It is the new year. Lance played us across the border from the old year to this one. One of the demigods, Tammuz or Orpheus, played a flute of lapis lazuli in order to resurrect the dead. I can't blame the resurrection of the dead into my life on him but I can imagine the abhorrence and revulsion that Lazarus inspired as he came toward the living streaming with the taint of death, mushrooms and tubers dragging behind him. When you come back from *that* place, there's no way to escape the miasma. We never come in clean, not from birth and certainly not from death.

My own birth wasn't clean. Maybe no one's is. Maybe that is what you, Sir, mean by original sin. That we are all related, that everyone is, in one way or another, an incarnation of someone who came before and, therefore, we are all tainted as the one who came before us is inside us and shapes us from within. Some cords seemingly cut and others not. Peter Schmidt is my tether, a version of original sin, of which I was born ignorant if not innocent. And Peter, how did he come to be Peter?

Peter Schmidt appeared in my bed. In the beginning, he had no identifiable clothes on but he wasn't overtly naked and, simultaneously, he was in uniform, so that I couldn't help knowing who he was. It was like a dream where someone is undressed and dressed at the same time. There was a man in my bed or near by bed or in the room. A man I didn't know. He appeared under circumstances which I couldn't comprehend, but I understood his meaning and assumed we were speaking a common language.

Perhaps I appeared to him with the same suddenness. He was surprised, or rather horrified, in the same way as myself for similar, if distinct reasons. I only know what I saw. I can't trust what he said about his experience either in the beginning or at the end. As close as we were—and that closeness was horrible— we were still separated by an enormity which no time can heal, history. I am grateful for the inability to heal this—this collision of two stars which were hovering about each other.

When one star is drawn into the other, it is torn apart in the process. The pull is so powerful it disintegrates the one being pulled in the other. We think we know what happens at the horizon of a black hole, but what *is* really happening?

I had been ill. I had had a flu. I was not asleep when Peter Schmidt appeared. I had been in a hypnagogic state between sleeping and waking brought on by fever. I was sufficiently weakened to be somewhat battered, distracted and unable to imagine restoring order to my life. The flu brought with it a high temperature, pain in the joints, and exhaustion. These symptoms served to emphasize the hopelessness I was feeling and provided an aperture of defeat through which it was possible for unexpected fate to enter. The illness reinforced my growing distaste for my old way of life.

It wasn't long after Amanda's death. I had just consciously begun facing the seriousness of my attraction to solitude and its consequences for my career. I was facing the possibility I would not want to, or worse, would be unable to, resume my past activities even though they offered among other *minor* inducements: security in the world, financial support, prestige, accomplishment, success and recognized purpose. On the one hand, I was facing everything which had been meaningful, had engaged my curiosity and had seemed to be of some use and, on the other hand, I was facing what had killed Amanda. After some time alone, I admitted to myself that I had not been above wanting to make a very, very small contribution to the world. Pure science is what had originally engaged me, and pure science, pure knowledge of the stars, uncontaminated by theory or application, seemed potentially to be a contribution. I didn't know what to do.

I felt I had made the right decision the previous June to take a partial leave from The Mountain. I was living alone, exactly as I needed to. It was difficult, often boring, mostly confusing, but I was working hard studying many things I hadn't thought about before although I was not understanding anything yet. I was observing. I was reading, doing research but I couldn't make any sense of it; it all contradicted everything I had ever known.

Sometimes when I wondered who Shaena had been, I wondered who Amanda Cartwright had been. Then I would get up and, as if I were racing through octaves, would run my fingers across the books Amanda had left to me that were now alongside my grandmother's journals. Sometimes I was afraid that merely touching their bindings would affect me, that knowledge encoded in the light held in the molecules of the ink and paper would leap out into my fingers and I would not be able to protect myself against it. I had begun reading far outside my field on subjects which I had once categorized as the occult—and that with a shudder. Ancient history, anthropology, astrology, mythology, psychology, these subjects had never been in my library. There were even a few books on women's studies that Amanda had pointedly advised me to read.

"Don't be afraid. Twenty years ago you had to be someone's assistant to get to do research on Big Eye and now they let you use the same bathroom as the guys. You don't have to live in drag anymore if you want to do astronomy."

"Do you still want to do astronomy?" she had asked then.

I hadn't answered because I felt so much dismay.

These books weren't as disconcerting to me as the few books I found myself drawn to which had been forbidden. A few books with different perspectives on religion and spiritual matters and also a Bible which I had never glanced through before. The more I learned, the more alone I felt. The universe was indeed vast and the center didn't hold.

If I were on The Mountain, I could go next door and ask one of my colleagues to look at the data with me. Between the two of us, we might sort it out. That's how it always happened. That's how Marteen Schmidt figured out quasars and red shifts. He'd met Greenstein in the hallway, they had a chat, passed a few questions back and forth, scratched their heads, remembered some chance conversations with others, searched their files for some forgotten data, and there it was—the beginning of the universe spreading out before them from billions of years ago. But there wasn't anyone I could consult about this data that I was beginning to gather.

That afternoon I had been surprised when I wouldn't get dressed and rendezvous with a colleague whom I had planned to visit for weeks. Then I realized I hadn't finished the paper whose deadline I had already missed, hadn't written the monthly checks so they would arrive in time, hadn't done research to make an informed and adult decision about one car or another, couldn't (wouldn't?) acknowledge, within a graceful period of time, a gracious note from a colleague regarding an article I'd written. Then I was feverish and didn't know if it was to blame for my mental dishabille or whether my state had brought on a illness. But one way or another, I was dead to the world. That is when Peter Schmidt appeared.

This is how I wrote about it initially in my journal:

There is a man in my bed. It's the middle of the night. I'm writing about this as a way of calming myself down. If I write in my journal as he stands here, I can assume this isn't happening. I've had a fever. This is probably a hallucination. Nothing to be worried about.

He laughs. No. He smirks. He's German. That's not important. What is important? I don't know. I don't know what's going on. I just keep writing. It makes me feel as if I'm sane. Obviously, I'm not sane. But would an insane person write in her journal to record her insanity? I don't think so. I see: I'm writing in my journal so that I can alter the circumstances. I think I'm mad. I know I'm mad. The man is a Nazi.

How do I know? I don't know. I just know. He's laughing.

Who am I writing to? Who's going to read this? A doctor who will be trying to make a diagnosis? Or the cops who will want to know how this guy got in?

Ok, Doc, here's the scoop. All the doors and windows were closed. I mean locked. And they're still locked. And no, I didn't get up out of bed to open the door and then close it again. And no one knocked. Get it?

This is what's going on. There's a Nazi in my bed.

Do I know this man? Are you kidding? Do I look like the kind of woman who hangs out with Nazis? I'm innocent. I had nothing to do with this.

Do you know what I do for a living? I look at the stars. I'm not involved in anything. Why would I open the door to a stranger?

Is he a stranger? What do you think? I don't know him.

Okay. I do know him. I know the man. I have never seen him before. But I recognize the cackle. Yeah, I heard it before. Yeah, on The Mountain. He interrupted my lecture a few months ago. No, I didn't tell anyone or do anything. I didn't want to alarm the audience. So, now he's back. So maybe I was trying to escape him by coming here.

I think he is myself.

My eyes were light-sensitive from the fever and hurt. I closed them, focused very deliberately in my imagination on the (hopefully) blank wall across from my bed and then opened them determinedly.

He was still there.

I started writing again wanting a second chance. But when he laughed again, Cardinal, I threw the journal and pen on to the floor. I had been trying to neutralize the event, to normalize the inconceivable.

Time is supposed to be an impenetrable world.

I felt dizzy. I had nothing to hold on to. Even science fiction has a logic to it. There was no logic here. Yes, he had died. Yes, he was here.

Use your training, I said to myself. Just track this, record the data. Be objective. I picked up the journal again. As I go back now over these terrible notes and memories, I cannot tell whether this was the first sighting, or whether I had seen him before and not registered his presence. What I do know is that I entered a flux state wherein the past and the future and the present flowed in and out of each other in no predictable or comprehensible pattern.

What are you thinking, Cardinal? Do you believe me? Did I tell you enough? Or do you want to see for yourself? Do you find the scene disturbing? The Jewish woman meets the Nazi. A Jewish woman meets *her* Nazi.

You think I'm crazy, don't you? Crazy to write to you and then *crazier* to tell you all of this.

Or does it fascinate you? Maybe I didn't tell you enough. Maybe I should have gone into more detail so you know everything about that first moment? What happens next when I realize who he is and who we are to each other. Then do you want to know what happens between us, what we discover? Why it is that he and I have found each other *again*—so to speak? Maybe you want me to forgive him?

What *we* discover? When *we* have found each other? When *we* have found each other. *We.* Do you agree there's a *we* acting in this?

Is there a *we* acting in this relationship between you and me? Are we also a *we*?

Or are you saying you want me to take responsibility? Do you want me to acknowledge that I had some part in this? That I was searching for something, that I reached out for this experience? That I was not only the victim of this assault, this uninvited intrusion, but that I had, for my own purposes, invited this, agreed, acquiesced, and so I am implicated in it? You want me to agree that I am not innocent of this repetition, on a personal level, of what he was already perpetrated against the world. Is that what you want?

He appeared in my bed. And then, in retrospect, I saw him everywhere. Maybe in researching the past for earlier signs of him, for warnings, I unwittingly created them to accord with the present. It is not a original idea that we create the past as painstakingly as we create the future. It is not unusual to think that past and future spiral out of the present in their opposite directions and that the present, is therefore, the consistent and continuous point of origin, the permanent center of the universe.

I had awakened in the middle of the night and Peter was there. He appeared and I couldn't wake up from the knowledge of him and then I woke up and he was still there or I fell asleep and he was there too, or the dreams were his, or ours. I couldn't escape him. He was inside me, in the cells it seemed, and once recognized, always known, always had been there.

Chapter 25

I didn't tell anyone about Peter because I didn't know how to speak about it. He had spoken to me in the lecture room, he said, didn't I remember? He had never left me, didn't I know that? How stupid was I? Yes, in retrospect, I realized I had seen him before but without seeing him. Sometimes I had heard a voice. At other times, I was only aware of the presence of something I could not identify. Or maybe I hadn't seen him before but time slipped past me and then I had.

I had only pretended to forget the voice as if, as it turned out, I could pretend anything to Peter. The voice had a life of its own, independent of me. I vaguely began to understand that my parents were not afraid to speak of the past, they were unwilling. It was not that they couldn't bear the memory or were too frail or callous to confront reality, they were refusing to be in relationship to it. A courageous and futile stand.

He lay back on the bed, leaning against the pillows, leering. I'd just changed the linens, had wanted white sheets and pillowcases, a white cover for the comforter, everything white on the bed. That morning, before knowing I was ill, I had made up the bed completely even though I wouldn't get dressed. Even the mattress cover was new and white. I couldn't tell if he was sprawled out on the bed with his boots on or if he was naked under the bed clothes. It must have been both because every time he moved, I found myself wondering if I had enough bleach to wash out the mark of his boots.

Finally, I asked him, "What the hell is your name?"

"Peter," he said. "Peter Schmidt."

A long time passed. "Don't you want to know my name?"

"Stupid. I've already called your name. But from now on you'll be nameless," he said. "You will always be nameless," he said with scorn.

I rehearsed speeches to him. Of course, as they were in my mind, and as he was somehow also in my mind, it is possible they were not rehearsals, but were communicated to him directly in words, in thoughts or in twitches. That's everyone's dream, isn't it, that every feeling, every word, every idea can be communicated directly without diffusion to someone else. But that dream in which everything can be understood co-exists with another dream that it will be impossible for anyone to ever know anything we are thinking, that it will be impossible to read our minds, that not even torture will elicit any revelation from us. Then there's the nightmare, that everything we think is heard by another. Then there is another possibility. These weren't my speeches in my mind; they were his invention, were ideas he had planted there.

"I hate her. If I were to discover that I also love her I would be someone else. Who I am is my hate. Perhaps I also love her, but you must understand that I've lost the capacity to love. It can happen to anyone, of that you must be sure. It happened to me. To us. That is, to the Germans. But, maybe I do mean, it happened to us, to Daniella and myself."

I put these words in his mouth, to soften reality or alter it, but I didn't get away with it. Whenever I found myself trying to think his thoughts, I heard my own voice. These words were my understanding of how he would explain it. But he would not explain it. If he had explained it or anything else, he would have been, would be, someone else. No matter how much I wanted him to be someone else, he remained himself.

Maybe that is why I stopped bathing every day. Why I threw the deodorant against the bathroom door. Why I stopped changing my panties each morning. Within a short time my house was in the same disorder as my mind. I pulled everything off the shelves, left papers on the floors, forgot to eat, would put nothing away.

I began wearing the same pair of sheer nylon stockings under my jeans and hung them, unwashed, in the bathroom each night until they were ripped to shreds. I held nothing back. I stayed in my robe for days. I didn't change the sheets. I slept in the nude, on my back, like a wolf.

Lance, who knew nothing, was intrigued and then possessed. His passion knew no limits. We made love at high noon, in the earth, upon rocks, in the mud of the drying creek. I swallowed his sperm or wiped it on my face. My desire increased, whipped to a frenzy by the knowledge there was someone else, always there, entranced, riveted, watching.

For days I lived without groceries, then stormed through the nearby towns looking for motorcycle boots. When I found them, I indulged a recurring compulsion to polish them. His compulsion. They were heavy, plain, black leather boots reaching straight up to my knees with a narrow strap across the instep. I examined them to be certain that no scratches existed on their surface, that no mud had attached itself to them.

According to my father, his mother, Hannah Stanebruch, had polished her dining room table with great passion. She had scoffed at the trend in furniture-making to create reproductions, wide expansive refectory tables which appeared to be nicked and darkened by years of use. My grandmother wanted everything, no matter its age, to shine as if it were brand new. Everyone remarked, Aram said, that her house was so clean you could eat off the floor.

Our own, that is, Rosa's, ebony piano was polished every Friday with sabbatical devotion near to the hand polishing of Big Eye's mirror for two years. I knew a great deal about polishing myself. Every bit as much as Peter knew, if not more. Despite what he saw and had been led to believe about me or us. Despite what he wanted to believe.

I told myself he was in my mind. Then I saw him among the cottonwoods leaning against the trees, watching me, grinning. I pretended he was only ogling me, not stalking me. I recognized him and I didn't recognize him.

Peter Schmidt is a handsome man. He wears American clothes, blue jeans, newly washed, starched, ironed. He wears jeans as if they are leather pants. American attire but decidedly unAmerican. A heavy gold chain about his boots. The shirt that should be under his leather vest is missing. No, it's not that way. Not that stereotype—too easy. He is wearing a plaid shirt. Boots, hat, toothpick, vest. He wears a black leather belt with facetted brass studs which he polishes every day with lanolin and beeswax. It shines the way black shines so that despite the sheen, I see through the gold to the black beneath. No, he is wearing his old uniform. No, he wearing his prison clothes.

It's not unheard of that a woman like myself becomes fascinated by a man who stalks her. After living near Devil's Peak for some months, I knew almost everyone even though I was a hermit myself. A new man was attractive. His boots were shined. He didn't seem like a vagrant. He was fit.

Still, a mist hovered about him. Gas. Poison gas. From the beginning, I felt tainted. And if he touched me, he wasn't restored to innocence.

It was not the mist of his own death, per se. It wasn't Lazarus I was afraid of. There was a kind of death or hell he had experienced. As if death hadn't been able to abide him either. Because of the death and hell he himself had perpetrated, it had spewed him back to us—to me.

I saw him in the cottonwoods, then elsewhere. I would convince myself he was imaginary and there he was walking down the road. I would rebuke myself sternly, "Get yourself together," and mine would be the only face in the mirror and then he would be there too, jeering. I became afraid to look for him in my house or on the land and searched in public places to be reassured by others. Perhaps they saw him too. Perhaps he was not my imagination. Perhaps he was real, contemporary, ordinary, most commonly vicious and diabolical, only playing with me.

I saw Peter in a restaurant last week. When I was walking the few miles home from the post office yesterday, I noticed a male figure again by the creek, standing under a cottonwood. He was watching me. I think it was Peter.

I enter a restaurant. He is drinking a beer. I am drinking a beer. The only restaurant in town is a German restaurant. He is eating sauerbraten. I am eating sauerbraten. I am eating knockwurst. Is that why he is eating knockwurst?

I come into the restaurant the next day. Thankfully, it is empty and I order a meal. Afterwards in the middle of my meal, he enters but doesn't see me because

I have my face hidden in a newspaper. I go outside to the ladies room which is probably also the owner's bathroom as she lives at the back of the house. He leaves.

Why don't I ask the woman who owns the restaurant about him as we talk about the erratic weather, tourists and the local Priory? I can't. Not only because she is German like Peter but because the situation disorients me so. And that's why I didn't ask anyone else, not the grocery clerk or the auto mechanic. I'm too private a person. I have to rely on my own resources.

I try to construct a memory where I see him engaged in an activity independent of me. Where he is speaking to someone I don't know and I pass by and we do not connect in any way with each other. I try to make him into one of the homeless. I place him sprawling—even if he would never sprawl—asleep against lugs of peaches, pears and apricots, against the pale plywood boxes with the carefully printed labels in primary colors on glossy paper, gleaming oranges, yellows and blue, everything round and ripe, the apricots resembling the sun. But he is not there; the boxes remain a still life. I try to imagine him driving down the highway, oblivious to everything but the road or the glint of sun which makes macadam shimmer dangerously at noon, or the drawl of a country western singer on the car radio, "Failed love . . ." but I can't.

When I saw Peter dominate a room with his pressed stance, I looked for places where curves inadvertently blurred angles, where his chest plumped slightly over his breast bone, or his abdomen puffed out with his breath or where the rotundity of his genitals bulged ever so slightly against the zipper, where a crease was not distinct enough, where a line or angle was not exact; and I wanted to make the necessary corrections. I felt inspired to plane him smooth, to polish him, to run him through a mangler, those large pressing machines so popular in the late forties when women began running their households with the ecstatic efficiency they'd developed in the wartime factories.

It was not cruelty, you understand. I wasn't enticed to flatten him out. I was being drawn, without the ability to resist, into his need. For I could feel—against my will—the pleasure that he felt in the exactness of his body and the exactness he assumed, therefore, of his nature. Coming into the field of his intensity, the contained frenzy of his will to perfection, I was pulled down inexorably into the vortex of his passion, into his life.

Nausea overtakes me even now as I write this to you, Cardinal. Nausea is an inexact emotion. Nausea is sloppy and chaotic. And whatever is sloppy and chaotic can betray you by giving you away.

"Have you ever been lovers with a German man?" Peter asked.

Naturally, he would ask that.

I thought of the men I had had as lovers. There was never a German man. "Also," I said smugly, "there was never a man in my bed who went to war."

"So, you've been pretending I didn't exist. You've been pretending you didn't have an inkling of a thought about me."

"I once had a colleague who was born in Germany. His father went to the front in World War I when he was six. His mother didn't know how to raise a child. She gave him colored beads, crayons, paints, but nothing else. He was six at the time. She barely spoke to him or she pressed him to her body day and night while she wept. She never taught him how to tie his shoes. His shirts unraveled, she never noticed. For days, then weeks, then months at a time, she sent him to live in the country, then she brought him home and wouldn't let him out of her sight. In the country everyone was worried about the war and food and left him on his own. His schooling, whatever little of it there was, was always interrupted. Perhaps his mother had had to work to make money to support them, he didn't know. She didn't say and those who took care of him, they didn't say either. No one said much about her, or anything to him. He lived intermittently with her, then without her altogether for several years. Then she came to be with him again. She looked ravished. Not ravishing, as she had once looked to him. Ravished. All in all, he never had a father or a mother. When his father returned, when the family was united, the father rarely spoke either, except about the war. He beat his son quite often, sometimes only when the boy started to cry. That's what my friend told me about his life."

"How do you know me so well?" Peter asked. When he spoke again, his tone was snide. "What did you do with your colleague? Did you try to heal him? Did you think there was a cure for such things? What about yourself?" he asked me.

"How can I ever heal myself if you're my wound?"

"Oh, don't feel so sorry for yourself, No Name. Look at me closely. Look at the blond, straight hair falling diagonally across my forehead. I was thirty-eight when I died. We were all blond even when we weren't. We all had blue eyes even when we didn't. Hitler's blue eyes were brown. The acne scars under my cheekbones make them more prominent, don't they. I'm five feet ten. Am I tall enough, imposing enough to fulfill your stereotype? Do you want to know how I died? Will my death thrill you? Do you hope I was hanged from the gallows in Auschwitz with Commandante Rudolph Hoess? Do you hope I shit in my pants as the rope squeezed everything out of me?

"Lung cancer. I drowned in my own fluids. On September 1, 1946. The day after the Nuremberg trials began. I smoked too much. We all smoked. And the air around me was thick and oily with smoke those last years of my life."

Cardinal, he spoke about his death the way any man speaks about his death, with fear and awe. As if his life had mattered. As if, even now, he didn't want to have lost it. The way he had not been able to imagine those others had felt about their lives. The way he had not been able to imagine that they had had lives even though they would have deaths.

"I'm dreaming," Peter said, "the dream before my death. I was dying and I didn't. A dream kept inserting itself between me and my death. It takes a long time to die. Longer than you think, No Name. I couldn't concentrate on dying. I couldn't resist the fascination of the dream.

"What was the dream?"

"This was the dream."

"This?"

"This pissy, self-congratulatory, narcissistic life of yours. You took my dying from me, bitch."

When he touched me for the first time, I was startled by his fingers. It was not only that they were tentative, it was not only the fear and hate they transmitted, but that they were, as I finally understood, unavoidably tender. At this time, he couldn't injure me without inflicting a wound upon himself, now he couldn't kill me without taking his own life.

Peter Schmidt probed me. He touched me here and there. He examined me with the regard of a man who had been trained to scrutinize others. With the regard of a blind man who had suddenly been given sight and with a physician's clinical proficiency, both intrigued and detached.

"Your powers of investigation, No Name, do you think they come from me?"

"I don't see how they can."

"There's a lot you don't see, No Name. Let me look through your eyes. Let me see what you see."

I closed my eyes then, but it was too late. He was already seeing through them. I opened them. Maybe he looked away.

"Mengele would have loved your eyes, No Name. How he would envy me. I can see what they see without having to excise them.

"Don't blink, No Name. Don't flinch. We took so many eyes, No Name. Twins and Gypsy children and those with one blue eye and one brown one, they all gave us their eyes so we would learn how to see better. Isn't that what you want, No Name, that I should see better?"

Yes, it was what I wanted. That he would see. That whatever I saw, he would see. Whatever I saw in my mind, he would see in his mind. But whatever he saw or had seen, I was beginning to see as well.

"I see it all."

"I see it all."

"It's not the way I want it."

"Well, it certainly is not the way *I* want it."

"This is not my will."

"This is certainly not *my* will."

"I'm condemned to hell."
"I'm condemned to. . . ."
"I can't bear the sight of you."
"I can't bear. . . ."
"You're not a human being."
"You're not a hu. . . ."
"You make me ill."
"You make. . . . "
"You're a contagion."
"No. You'. . . ."
"I should wipe you out."
". . . ."

He laughed, Cardinal.

At first I saw him only intermittently and then I began to see him whenever I went outside. I became terrified of the light. It glanced off him. He was standing in intense sunlight at high noon of an unseasonably warm day and the light stopped short around him. As the afternoon advanced, a darker area formed about his body, what someone who knows about such things might have called a dark aura.

He was leaning against one of *los alamos*, standing in the shadow of the tree, in the dark side. And his shadow, which my grandmother, Shaena, claimed was a sign of the soul, merged with the tree and I could not tell the two apart or, maybe, his shadow was missing.

No, he had a shadow. He had been assigned by the gestapo to spend the war assisting the doctors at a death camp. Risking his life, he had climbed out of the little window of the guardhouse onto its small roof and stood there in the setting sun, watching his shadow stretch across the yard as if he were pointing out the hour, as if, in playing his demoniacally divine violin, he dissected the last minutes of day, his hand holding the bow moving up and down, slicing away, with the precision of the knife approaching evening. And below him, vermin riddled bodies walked through his shadow, and felt the cold weight of his darkness descend upon them. And for that moment passing through, they lost their shadows as well.

"Stay with this, No Name. You want to erase me now, don't you? To crush me? To smash me? Are you beginning to understand how it was?"

Cardinal, I'm sorry for the thoughts that besiege me. I think of erasing much of what I'm putting down, but that would be erasing evidence. Maybe you need to read everything to understand what happened. How do I know that we aren't all involved in this? If he sought me out and I wasn't innocent, maybe you aren't innocent either. Who inhabits you? I'm sorry. Once more.

Notes from the flux, Cardinal. I want to write: Peter walks into the room. But I force myself to write it differently. Peter walked into the room. I inspect him inspected him—as if I am / was the General. A green thread is / was unraveling from the buttonhole parallel to his shirt pockets. I thought of getting a manicure scissors so I could cut it exactly.

When did this happen? I didn't date my journal. I remember sitting down to write and asking myself to put a date at the top of the paper, but I couldn't. Then I remember asking myself to keep a bound journal and in each writing on loose-leaf paper, confusing the papers, entering them in a haphazard manner.

Peter would like to take the scissors from my hands. He would like to cut the thread himself; I can feel the pleasure he experiences as he presses the blades against the thread which he pulls tautly. He will be precise.

My vision is as small as his. I can see nothing beyond the figure of the man standing before me. Then nothing beyond the thread and the scissors. Then nothing beyond the sharp little silver blades. Then nothing beyond the snip.

I want him to be exact. I want that for him.

I am pulled into the task at hand, into the need which is crisp and sharp. I am pulled deeper and deeper into it. I am pressed against the sides of his need. The deeper I am pulled in the harder I am pressed against the sides of his need, the smaller I become.

The pressure increases. It increases and it begins to spin. Everything acts against everything else. The pressure increases, I am sucked down, I am pressed down, I am compacted. I become smaller and smaller. I withdraw even smaller into myself. I am so small, I do not exist. I am smaller than a point, smaller than the smallest, most dismal point in creation. The heat, the swirl, the compression, implosion is beyond what is conceivable. I am completely annihilated.

I don't remember, Cardinal, what happened then. Maybe I had a blackout. I had a few during this time. More than one world entered me; I entered more than one world. Having escaped from the illusion of the density of the one, there were no boundaries against the others. They all flowed in and out of each other.

There was something in me, in the core that was no core, at the center of me that had no center. It was a kind of magnet or attractor: A Great Attractor, a Strange Attractor. It drew the worlds through me. I had no power to resist.

Yes, I repeated to myself, I am going mad. I have gone mad. As if stating it, rescinded it. Or to be in agreement with the opinions I imagined others would hold if they could observe me. The reassurance of consensus. Of facts.

Because my colleagues would have seen that after Peter's appearance, I had stopped showering in the morning. Or that I showered several times a day and it was never sufficient. Or that I wept uncontrollably or was unable to weep. That ideas spurted from me like meteor showers. That I wrote incessantly. Or sat for hours in a corner without moving. That I saw things other people didn't see or that I didn't see what was obvious to anyone. That I ate voraciously and then didn't eat for days. That the sun tortured me and I walked outside without a head covering until I almost fainted. That I answered every letter as soon as it came or that I didn't pay my bills or answer a single letter or phone call. That I shook. That I was cold as steel and unmoving. That I heard voices. That I was suddenly deaf. That I couldn't find any meaning anywhere. That I couldn't go on. That suddenly everything had meaning. That one thing was related to another thing. That there were signs and omens. That I sometimes had a feeling of grace, of a divine finger descending through the curtains of clouds and illuminating my life. That the world was luminous. Worse, it was numinous. All of that.

I was terrified. I didn't care. For weeks, I didn't know what was happening to me. For months. Then I knew everything. I agreed that something had to be broken down. That even as I had no body, still the body had to be broken. I was made penetrable or I was made to know that I was penetrable. For if anything new was to enter me, I must not be armored against it. I couldn't allow Peter to be inside of me alone. Also I was bombarded by an incalculable energy that broke me into pieces but the energy released reconstituted me immediately. I had had to be smashed, as powerfully as if I had been in a cyclotron. Destruction and recreation in the same instant. In physics it is called particle reactions. In the books I was reading, they call this transformation.

And over all this were shadows. As if it were always solstice, early morning or late afternoon, as if it were never the equinox, never high noon. One thing became another. One being became another. And everything had its shade. The electron partnered with the positron. Particles had antiparticles. If there was matter, there was anti-matter, undiscovered, waiting to spring. There was light and there was also the dark, joined together.

In retrospect, Cardinal, it seems plausible that he was, as he said, with me constantly since the lecture some months before. That without realizing it, I had come to know him the way you know nothing at first and then suddenly know something and it seems as if you've known it forever. A life lived without a beloved seems inconceivable after the appearance of the beloved. Don't misunderstand: Peter Schmidt is not the beloved, but when one speaks about *the other* one often is compelled to speak about him in the language with which one also speaks about the beloved. Because of the tie between the two. Sometimes the tie is a wedding ring and sometimes it's a noose. Lance tells me that memories which have been suppressed and then surface are never really eradicated. Even if one's common understanding refuses to accept the reality of an event, Lance says that once the memory returns, it returns for all time and one cannot imagine that one forgot.

And, Cardinal, even as I was trying so hard to objectify him, he was telling me that I would fail no matter how hard I worked, no matter how diligent I was. He said he knew about such things because he had come to this experience before I did. But you know, Cardinal, I don't think that was true. We had to come to each other at the same time. Though we had been carried by different mothers we became Siamese twins at birth or was it at death?

"I never imagined evil in my life. Never." I told this to Lance in an attempt at confidentiality. "In my entire life, I never believed in the existence of evil. But one day, I felt something and I was afraid of it. And I called it evil."

"What are you talking about?" he asked. "I don't know what you're talking about."

"I can't tell you more about it than this," I persisted. He thought I wasn't able to express it better, the way it was hard for him to speak to anyone about music. I protected myself by letting him understand my dilemma in this way.

"Anyway that's not the point. The specifics aren't the point. The point is...." I was angry with him. I needed to think out one thing and he was curious about something else. "The point is the moment that I conceived of something as evil, evil suddenly existed. Don't you get it?"

"No. It was either evil or it wasn't evil, no matter whether you recognized it that way or not. Something exists or it doesn't."

"I'm not sure. I thought of it as evil and then I could feel its evil and I was afraid. I felt it inside of me. Do you see? Do you understand? Then there was evil inside of me. I know it was there. I felt it."

"Ssh. Let me hold you," Lance said as we dropped into sleep.

I dreamed of a Blind Museum. I didn't know if it was a museum of the blind or for the blind or simply a museum where no one could see. When one entered it, all the light went out. The lights in things went out. They withdrew their light. It was odd to see it, to watch the light being sucked in, diminished. Dark stains, rough outlines, racks, holes in the air appeared where the light had been. The rooms became increasingly dim and, worse, shabby.

A man stood in the middle of the museum. He was not blind. He watched as everyone entered and then as they crossed over the threshold, he began to orchestrate the dark. I watched him from a corner, hoping that he wouldn't find me, because if he did, I would not be able to preserve the privilege of my vision. I was noticing that he paced the darkening differently for each person, but no one was omitted from the ordeal. No matter what they did, no matter how they prepared, adjusted their eyes, put on their dark glasses, desperately wrapped their eyes in blindfolds, the darkness came up and enveloped them completely. Finally each one of them understood. The darkness wasn't in them, wasn't in their perception. The darkness was in things because the light had been withdrawn. Then he engaged in the last act, his final cruelty. It was his dramatic crescendo. He sucked all the light that was in them into a point, a point of a point; and then, as they watched knowing it was the very last thing they would see, he cut that very last point of light out of them completely.

"I have bad dreams," I said to Lance. "Very bad dreams. So bad I can't tell you about them."

His concern mixed with respect for my understanding of the situation.

"I can't speak about them. And I've already said more than I can say." I divulged only this much to him despite his obvious presumption there was more to my disturbance than dreams. While he acted as if he trusted my judgment, he was noticeably alarmed. I couldn't reassure him. He knew I was in jeopardy from forces I could not control that were drawing me into their orbit, and he was helpless before them. He saw that I was in despair.

I said nothing more to him. He watched me, mutely. I relied upon his watchfulness, trusting, or rather hoping, as prisoners must, that the fact of a witness offered a modicum of protection, meant that there were limits that the jailer will not cross.

Chapter 26

Peter Schmidt appeared in my house at Devil's Peak in November of 1988. He lived there with me for months. Peter Schmidt had been born in Erfurt, Germany on November 17, 1908. In 1934, he was twenty-six years old, Cardinal. He believed he should have been a doctor with an advanced specialty by then but his schooling was interrupted so many times because of World War I, and the recovery from the war, and the general dissolution which surrounded Germany, that he hadn't accomplished it.

This, Cardinal, is what he told me or let me know. He lived in Germany and Germany lived in him and there was no difference between one and the other. What Germany suffered he suffered. One country. One body. His first years were shredded by the world war which raged inside of him. When it was over, no side of him had won and he was left with nothing. By his own account, he was shattered, poverty stricken, greedy, vindictive and despairing. It was not that he was aimless so much that the parts of himself—the violinist, the doctor, the artist, the soldier, pointed in different directions and, as he couldn't subdue any of them, he was paralyzed. Therefore when the great, glorious black shining boots marched in . . . he joined them.

One morning he kept me awake by telling me a dream, insisting this time that I write it down word for word as if it were mine. I began to write:

> 1934. Peter is required to keep the radio on at all times. He is required to place the radio. . . .

He began ranting. His words crashed wildly in my head. As if one world was colliding with another. "Don't be so stupid," he screamed. "Write it the way I tell you to write it. Begin again. 1934. *I* am required . . ."

> 1934. I am required to keep the radio on at all times. I am required to place the radio exactly in the center of the room. I am required to measure the distance from the walls to the center of the room each day and realign the radio in the morning precisely at eight a.m. in case it shifted during the night. I have to realign everything in the event the street vibrated when a truck or tank drove down it. In case a squadron marched by. In case a stupid mob of unionists trampled through the street. In case the wind came up. Anything can cause the ground to shift. Anything can cause deviation especially on the second floor where I live. Traffic on the staircase can cause trouble. The man upstairs is always late and

pounds down the stairs when he runs to work. The woman who lives downstairs practices opera when she is alone. Her voice causes the dust to whirl and the windows to crack. The neighbors have dogs and cats who storm through the hallways. Deviation is inevitable. I have to protect myself from it.

There is a list posted on my door which I can not decipher. It catalogues all the conditions under which a radio might shift from its central position. The radio has to be exactly centered in order for me to receive the signal. The signal sounds an alarm if it is not received. The alarm, I am assured, will blot out everything. The alarm will even annihilate a violin. So to protect anything I don't want destroyed, I have to remove it from the proximity of the radio which can reach everywhere. To be certain, I have to obliterate it from my consciousness.

My task is to stand as if I am an empty cylinder and wait for the signal. When the signal comes, I am to salute. I don't know how they will know if I salute.

I don't know what the signal is to be. I will have to recognize the signal. I stand before the radio waiting for the signal. I practice saluting in my mind. I know that my salute will have to be perfect.

I wait. I face the radio. I hear the trains chugging into the Bahnhoeffer. I am afraid they are misaligning the radio and interfering with the signal.

Maybe the signal will not come from the radio. Maybe the signal will come from elsewhere. I think perhaps the signal has come. There is a high pitched shriek barely audible under the rumble of the trains.

I raise my arm in my mind even though it is against regulations to raise one's arm prematurely. I pretend I am reaching out to play an invisible bow. Then I forget the bow and the arm is raised in my mind.

Now I raise my arm and not in my mind alone. The angle is perfect. I can see my fingernails, but barely, over the bone of my wrist. Everything perfectly aligned; arm, wrist, hand, knuckles, joints, fingers, nails. I love the alignment of my arm. It is beautiful. I can hold this salute forever. Forever.

But my hand continues to move. I am holding my hand straight and stiff but it is moving. My hand is rotating, the thumb is raising up to the ceiling. The movement of my thumb is creating static on the radio. With every motion of my hand, the radio squawks. But my hand will not desist. Be still! It does not obey me. My hand is completely rotated. The palm is facing the sky which has entered through the ceiling. The fingers bend upward. It is horrible. It is the hand of a beggar.

The dream stayed with me as if it were mine. That's what he had wanted. First his dream would become mine, then his life. That way, I would disappear.

Writing in the journal helped. It sometimes created a certain distance in the way my grandmother's journal had a certain distance in it because she was writing both for the sake of maintaining her own sanity *and* so that I would remember her. Whereas for my father, the writing of the journal in a language deliberately remote was, in fact, a code, a means to keep a reality which would not stay close, close, an attempt to solidify a noxious vapor, to re-form the poison gas into transportable crystals. I needed the distance so that I could contemplate what was happening. My father needed to bring everything closer or else, he knew, everything would evaporate and he would remember nothing.

The man in my bed lived his life from beginning to end and then he died. Nevertheless, he is here now. I find the fact of his body as disturbing as he finds mine. I never thought about the past much and now I discover we have a common history. From now on, he assures me, we can never think of ourselves without thinking of the other.

Quantum objects influence each other, remain correlated without any intermediary connection. Are Peter and I linked for all time to come? If there is anything that can break this connection, he will find it. I will look myself, but I am not as clever as he. I do not know who is more determined to be free of the other, Peter or I.

If he had managed to exterminate my people, I would not exist. But, he failed, and here I am. Here we are. As closely linked as it is possible to be.

Nothing that I can think of can set us free. Perhaps this grotesque reliance upon each other for our identities is a force stronger than the logic of time and the finality of death. Whoever reads this someday, explain this if you can; he and I are both here now.

This Nazi, Cardinal. A dead man. Myself.

I asked him why he had initiated this. He sneered. He would have killed me, if he could have, of that we can be sure. He was familiar with death. He observed it each night from his perch in the watchtower at Birkenau on the south side of the Camp overlooking the crematorium. You can imagine the perspective he gained from that bird's-eye-view; he saw the Camp in whatever direction he looked.

I would like to be able to say that he came into my room, looked at me with scorn and said, "I want to kill you," and succeeded. But, poor Peter Schmidt could not kill me it seems without nullifying his former existence. He could not alter his future without also altering his past. And he had loved his life, at least the fact of it. Even in retrospect, he was not willing to sacrifice it, to disappear it, altogether. He was sentimental about his own life. Look what he had already sacrificed in order to maintain it as long as he had.

Would I have liked to kill him? Is it permissible for a woman to kill a man who forces his way into her house without asking questions? Under such circumstances, not killing the assailant is suspect. But we didn't kill. I, who for some perverse reason, despite history, am still sworn to not killing, didn't kill. Anyway you can't kill the past. It doesn't die. It is eternal.

Maybe I am as culpable as he. What, Cardinal, am I to think of myself? Aren't there enough instances of pain so that one needn't go out seeking more, let alone, manifesting them? Why would I search it out? Why bring it in from another time when one's own past, surely, is sufficient? Why bend back time? Why draw this extraneous bit of psychic matter through from one realm to another? Hasn't it done enough damage already? But wasn't this *my* past?

What did he do in the Camps? What did he do? Do you want to know, Cardinal? I wanted to know. I, who had refused to think about the Camps, who had not said the word "Camps" in my life, suddenly, I had to know.

"What did you do there?"
"I played my violin."
"Where?"
"There."
"Where?"
"In the Camps."
"What Camps?"
"The Concentration Camps, stupid. The Death Camps. The *Konzentration Zenter*, idiot."
"Which one?"
"Birkenau."
"Where?"
"Auschwitz. Auschwitz-Birkenau. You are not only stupid, you are ignorant. Morally ignorant."
"Where in Birkenau?"
"In the watchtower. I asked for extra duty in the watchtower and I played my violin there."
"You weren't a doctor then?"
"I was a doctor. Not as fully trained as I had hoped, but close enough."
"Had you wanted to be the doctor in the Camps?"
"No. There I didn't want to be a doctor, but I was a doctor, so to speak. That is the uniform they gave me to wear. An SS hat with a white stripe. Being a doctor in the camps didn't take much expertise. There was nothing you could do there except keep things clean. And that was impossible."

Why did he request to relieve one of the lower officers of this duty which only his rank allowed him to negotiate? Was he granted this favor so he could keep his boots clean? Intermittently he was granted eight hours out of the mud and blood. Above. Watching. But what? Not the birds. There were no longer any birds in this area. The stench kept them away. The stench and the smoke. How did he pass the time when the smoke blended with night? He played his violin.

"It was beautiful to play the violin and watch the sky, No Name. Who would refuse such beauty? Without it, one was. . . . How can I put it so you will understand? Anyone would kill for such beauty."

I turned to him in a rage one night when I couldn't sleep again because he, as usual, was torturing me with something he remembered, and asked him, "Do you intend to keep speaking about this when I have spent my entire life assuming the past didn't exist for me? I don't want to listen to you without end, I wasn't there you know."
"I was," he said.

Cardinal, I heard these words in my own head: "I was there and that place was myself. After awhile there was no way to distinguish one from the other."

An electron jumping between one orbit and other is, for less than a nanosecond, here. Neither in the one orbit nor in the other, nor in between. Then it is elsewhere.
My parents had assured me that I had been born out of nothingness, a different kind of immaculate conception, free of the taint of the other side where that history still resided. I had understood the Immaculate Conception to mean that the one born would not be contaminated by what had happened before and that the birth heralded a time when everything might be immaculate for everyone. Somehow I had hoped that was true and universal. It had taken me forty years to learn that my parents had lied with the hope that lies would become truths. There had been no immaculate conceptions, certainly not in this century. I had been birthed into history with a vengeance. I would never have chosen it. History had chosen me, the way history chooses everyone; no one escapes.

Chapter 27

No one escapes, Cardinal. Dark pulls us in; light penetrates us. One things eats another but first that other ate. No one is immaculate. Nothing is pristine. No one is separate from anyone else. Peter Schmidt invades my life and I invade yours. I try to imagine the expression of your face as you continue to read this letter. In an interview you gave after you'd become Cardinal, you spoke of cherishing the privacy of your life and still I beg you to let me tell you this story knowing the consequences, that we will never again be entirely separate from one another.

I think I should observe the niceties, make conversation as if we have all the time in the world to become friends, as if I could invite you to sit down at my table and I could offer you fruit. There you are walking down the road from the pear orchard at the Priory along the road bordering the creek stopping to sit on a boulder or a stump as others have before you. When you get to the crossroads, you will turn east leaving the creek where the road begins to ascend. Some miles from here, you will be high enough to ski, or you could climb Devil's Peak, but at this moment you have to cross the high desert, the border where sycamore and cottonwoods yield to sage and yucca, and then you will ascend again to a tangle of scrub and small trees.

I can see you coming toward me next spring from that far rise, walking slowly down the hill, disappearing in the hollow and then appearing again and climbing up the next miles toward me. When you turn the bend you will be able to see me waiting for you and I will come down the dirt path with a glass of water in hand and invite you to rest under the trees by the wild flowers, the beds of columbine, jack-in-the-pulpit, monk's hood, Jacob's ladder, sweet four o'clock, pasques, red cardinal flowers and honesty; I planted them for you or for their names.

Now there are only patches of snow on the ground. The back room of my cabin is narrow and dug into the hill, so that the windows running the full length of the room are set three feet up from the dirt floor, but on the outside they rest on the hill itself. One can see the mountain rising behind and the foliage that hides my ziggurat and the sky. If you lie down on the ground, it is very cool here even in summer, cool as a catacomb where, in the last war, so many were buried but also saved. From this vantage point, I do not always believe in the end of the world.

I want the world to rest for a week while we sit without speaking and watch the clouds roil across the hill tops. "Something always comes of silence," Lance says.

"Why?" I ask him.

"Silence is a glue," he says, "it mends the separation between worlds."

I have never kneeled to speak to someone in a Confessional. Is Confession the outpouring of a story that must be told? Can it be the review of the thing seen and the action taken, a baring and a bearing of the heart or the required transmission of a great secret which has been imparted to one without invitation or consent? And does it sometimes happen that taking great care and travail one seeks out the particular one—the only one—to whom the Confession must be made?

I am gratified that you have read this far. I accept this as a covenant between us. A relationship established between the priest and the woman. Perhaps it is not inappropriate to ask the Church to act as mediator between a Jewish woman and a Nazi. An opportunity, for the Church to redeem itself. *N'est pas?*

When I did once ask my grandmother—"Exactly what is the *H* word?"—she said, "Hell, Dani, darling, is to be enlightened and not redeemed."

There's something else I want to know: I want to know whether the priest who is listening to confessions, just listens or whether he—you—are sometimes willing to risk something yourself, as Virgil did, to go to hell with the petitioner?

Aram came to see me without calling first. When I saw him coming up the road, I was momentarily disoriented, afraid it might be a colleague, or that Peter, having fully manifested, was striding up to my front door. But it was my father who was checking up on me, coming upon me unawares, to see what my condition really was. I had been here about nine months but I hadn't ever told him how disheartened I was about my professional life. I looked quickly around my cabin. This week I had kept things in relative order except for dishes in the sink and papers on the floor. It looked like the house of a busy person; he would not be alarmed.

I should have recognized Aram's characteristic limp immediately, but I was thrown because he seemed shorter and slightly bent as he leaned into the hill while climbing it. Instead of coming to the door, he seated himself against the boulders behind my house like a man who had swallowed a stone. It was early in the day and when I came out and sat down opposite him as we had always done for each other in the past so that this time my shadow fell across his face so that he could look in the direction of the sun without needing to shield his eyes. As a child, when I'd heard stories of cats attached to stones so they would drown, or men whose feet were set in cement before they were thrown into the sea, I always imagined the stone was within them, that something inside was turning to rock, weighing them down, pulling them to the bottom of the sea. It was such a weight that Aram carried.

"I'm all right, Dad," I told him quietly and sternly. I almost never called him Dad, just as I almost never called Rosa, Mother, and never ever called her Mom. Now I was afraid that calling him Dad would make him worry all the more. Obviously I had done it, unthinkingly, to comfort myself.

"I'm all right, Aram, really I am."

"Well, you're still here," he murmured.

"Life is very hard," Aram spoke like a tired man. In the past, his passions had always overcome circumstances but now it seemed reality was getting the upper hand. Except for Amanda, I had almost never had to comfort anyone but myself. In a moment, I realized that my father had become a stranger to me. Aging had done it.

"I have my own life to bear," Aram continued, "and everything that comes with it. The past that is. But you, you have your life and everything that comes with it, including mine. Do you see?"

"I thought I came into the world clean as a whistle. That's what you always told me."

"I wish that were true, Dani."

"Your mother doesn't know I am here," he continued. "I didn't want to upset her."

"Where does Rosa think you are?"

"Out saving the trees. Anywhere, everywhere."

"Do you give her the slip often?"

"Never."

I scrutinized him. He was not lying.

"Are you worried about me? I tell you I'm really okay no matter how it looks. I don't mind being here. I haven't run away really. I actually prefer it. That's a surprise, but it's true." I was not lying. Only I was not telling him everything. We were speaking as we always had, in fragments.

Nothing I said reassured him. The stone did not dissolve. If anything, the weight was increasing because he was sagging down onto it. I could feel the insistent attraction from the center of density.

"Oh," I suddenly brightened with an insight. It was simpler than I had thought. It was actually rather sweet and touching what was upsetting him so. He was a father after all. His concerns were classic and conventional. "Look, I know you're officially retired and don't have the means to support me. And, of course, you're worried. But the truth is, I'm okay financially. I'm still on the payroll at The Mountain; I haven't retired completely. And if I weren't, Lance would certainly help. He would support me. He's offered more than once."

"A musician?"

So I was right. Instead of being irritated, I was rather touched by his concern.

"Well, actually, yes, even as a musician. He's very good, you know." I considered the next sentence before I said it, wanting to phrase it according to his values. "He's very well respected. Perhaps even renowned. Anyway, he's much in demand."

"I know."

"And very generous."

"It's obvious."

"And then there's Shaena's little endowment."

"It isn't much."

"No. But it's just enough. She planned it that way."

"Yes, I remember."

"Then why are you so worried about me?"

Now he looked me in the eye. Had that ever happened before? I could see the way his eyes penetrated me in order to see me absolutely as I was. I decided to let him in. I would keep nothing from him. I would let down my guard to him. It was, I was aware, a gift. It was not what I had expected to give to my father, but I thought he had a right. He had been an exceptional father. I opened myself wide to him.

And then I saw it, what I had not expected to see when I was completely undefended. Naked. That was the word for it. The only word. After I was naked with my father, I saw that he was naked too. But completely naked. Completely.

I must have gasped or flinched, done something to recede from him because sunlight struck him on his face. He didn't flinch. It was if he were a blind man, who could no longer see the sun. I had been completely mistaken from the beginning. Maybe he had never looked into my eyes to see if I were open or closed. Maybe he had come to me naked.

The blind carry a terrible nakedness. On the one hand, they can't see. On the other hand, they experience the extent of their own visibility. Because they can't see, they can hide nothing. Their blindness is written in their eyes; they are thus fully exposed.

Aram's nakedness was deliberate. He had splayed himself open.

"Trees can't protect each other, you know," he began. "In the beginning, if the seed doesn't fall too far from the furthest branch, the seedling grows up in the shade of the parent tree. Still, if it is too close it will not have the space, sunlight and nutrients it needs and if it is too far away, it won't have what little protection is possible. In the rain forest so little light penetrates the dense foliage, each seed travels far away from those parent trees which cast too much shade. The point is, the parent tree has no will to exercise on behalf of the seedling. From the moment the seed drops, it is essentially on its own."

"Did you really want to protect me? Did you think that would be a good thing?" I didn't mean to sound incredulous.

"I worked very hard at it."

"I don't think I noticed."

"Exactly. I am very good at what I do."

I thought he was joking, but there was no humor in his expression.

"Let us imagine, Daniella, that the tree gave the seedling shelter, or whatever it was possible to give and the little tree grew. Still if a fire came, the large tree could not protect the little one. At some point, they have an equality in their grief."

"Are we at that point?" I asked fearfully.

"We are at that point."

"What do you mean?"

"I can't contain my grief from you."

Out of his leather knapsack, he took that same black and white notebook from which he had once read to me. It was the book he had kept at the end of the war.

"I want to tell you something about the war."

"You did once read to me from this book," I said tentatively, alarmed now that he might have forgotten, that he had aged even more than I had thought.

"Yes, it looks like it is the same book, but it isn't. It's from a later time."

"I thought you never kept another journal."

He looked at me exasperated. "I want to read it to you; it is also about the war."

Why now? I wanted to ask him. Why now when I knew far more about the war than I ever wanted to know? Why now when I was living with the war every day? Why now when I was unable to live with Lance, the man I loved, and was living—completely against my will—with the intruder Peter Schmidt?

But I couldn't speak of this to Aram. Anyway, before I might even have begun to formulate words, Aram was describing the situation:

> "Immediately after the war was over, we saw that the Austrian oaks were being destroyed by a serious blight. You might not think this was a military issue, but everything was a military issue then. The Russians had a German prisoner whom they suspected of war crimes—he was also a leading expert on oaks. My commanding officer wanted to tell me his entire story, but I wouldn't listen. I didn't want to know. Everyone insisted this man was the only one who knew what to do about the oaks. I couldn't argue with them; I had tried everything I knew to no avail. So the Americans wanted him released so he could work on the tree problem . . ."

I didn't expect my father's voice to break as it had sounded to me as if he was giving me a report. "I think I'd just better read this to you," he picked up the book. He read to me in a shaking voice:

> "The dilemma has been taken out of my hands. The C.O. has decided for me without asking me. Of course he knows I am Jewish, it's part of the record. I do not have to make the decision. Such decisions are not made by people like myself. The Nazi will be liberated to our side without my consent, without my having to decide. And I will have to work with him without having to agree. The Russians will get something in exchange. Something very much to their liking. Of course, when the Nazi comes, he will not be a prisoner anymore. In effect, this clears his name. No one will ask what he did any longer. Like the rest of those who are escaping trials, he will take a new name. And begin again, as they say. There is nothing I can do about it. Mercifully, I am relieved from knowing what I would have done.
>
> "The C.O. says the man will arrive in a week. He says this with a big smile and shakes my hand heartily. He says that I have a week to get myself ready to do another round with the oaks. Only this time, I must work for the prisoner. The C.O. gives me the week off. He says, 'Go to Paris.' The C.O. laughs a scratchy laugh and I think of the dry thistles in New Mexico.

"They have freed the man. They have persuaded the Russians to release him. They must have made the Russians a fine offer for the Russians are not known to be conciliatory. What will the Russians get in return? How many mass murderers? Of what quality? How many *neutral* scientists will they get in exchange for this one that we supposedly need?

"I have a week to practice. To get my accent just right: 'Mr. ü, I am so pleased that you have come to cure the oak trees.

"'Herr Stürmfuhrer, thank you for coming to save the oak trees.

"'My dear Dr. Stürmfuhrer, how can I tell you what a relief and honor it is that we can work together to save the oak trees. As you have no doubt heard, there is a terrible blight. Nothing and no one can alleviate it. Until we heard that you were still alive, we thought all was lost. But what good fortune. You have survived and can take up your work again.'"

Aram's shaking voice faltered and sputtered. He was reading so quietly, I could barely make out the words. I moved to sit beside him so I could read the familiar, neat writing along with him. The sun fell fully on both of us.

"My German is no good. My accent is terrible. In effect, the Nazi will save the forests. That is what I was assured when I had to admit I couldn't do it; and I can't do it. That's the rotten luck. I can't. I don't know how. I don't have the expertise. I swear, I will never again allow myself to be so ill prepared. My ignorance is criminal.

"From next week on, everything I know will be contaminated by what I learn from him. The oaks, however, they will survive. The C.O. promises this. As if the C.O., the United Command or the Russians know anything about blight.

"I was walking out of the room. I had already saluted and turned my back when he called me back, using my first name, dropping rank.

"'You understand, Aram, the oaks will survive, otherwise we wouldn't be going through all this.'"

"Did they?" I asked when he had finished reading and slammed the book shut.

"They did. They survived that blight."

"And?" I asked him.

"And they survived. And he survived. And I survived. And you survived. And we survived. And they survived. And he survived."

I moved back to face him. The sun was burning the back of my head. I reached into my pocket for some pins to fix my hair in a bun on the top of my head, feeling the shape of it, a torus, tucking in the strands. Although I felt the fierceness of the sun, I didn't want to change positions because I was aware that he would not shift his position to remove himself from the blinding glare of sun. For all I knew, he would let himself go blind staring into the light.

"And? It's almost forty years later. Why did I come to see you? I'm not senile, Daniella. The past is returning. It is definitely returning. Look it's here." He took a crumpled ball of paper out of his pocket and began to smooth it out on his thigh very slowly and deliberately. "And so you see." He held up the letter briefly and then folded it and put it away again.

"Someone wants to put him on trial. Someone has stated that he must stand trial, that he was extradited and pardoned unjustly. This tree doctor would like me to testify for him. Maybe no one else who was involved in this is alive but him and me. After all, I'm seventy-five, and you know what happens to records of such transactions; they often disappear. The Nazi would like me to testify that he, Herr Dr. Stürmfuhrer, is a kind and compassionate man. He would like me to say that he was a good scientist. That he would never harm anyone. By nature a benefactor. He would like me to testify on his behalf that he saved the trees and such a man would do no harm."

"Will you go, Aram?"

"What can I say? The truth? That he was a damned good tree doctor and he saved the groves after the war? That I learned much of what I know about trees from him? That my expertise is based in large part on his knowledge?

"For all I know, Daniella, he learned what he did experimenting on trees. I never asked him about his training. I never asked him anything. Maybe he induced diseases into trees to experiment with different treatments or to follow the progress of a disease. That's not unheard of. It's common practice. What shall I say? I am one of the students of the 'Mengele of Trees.'

"It's all absurd because the trees didn't last long anyway, Dani. All the trees are going. Either they're dying from pollution or they're being cut down."

Then Aram faced me as if I were the interrogator and looked directly into my eyes. "Do you understand?" his voice was bitter as a cold wind. And then he sang tunelessly, a chorus by Leonard Cohen, which made him seem even more daft.

Everybody knows the war is over,
Everybody knows the good guys lost
Everybody knows . . .

"Do you understand?"

"Yes, Dad, I do understand."

"Do you understand that he did save the trees, that he worked hard at it, and that I am not going to say anything on his behalf?"

I nodded.

"I'm sorry," he said, "I'm so sorry that you understand. I tried to save you from this." Unexpectedly, he took me in his arms and held me as if I were crying.

Chapter 28

At the core of this galaxy is a dark force, dark matter, something invisible, inexplicable, mysterious, pulling everything toward and around it. A black hole is a place where a star has gone out. It is place where light which has burned for billions of years is extinguished. But it is not so simple. After it goes out, it becomes a dark power bending light and everything it can attract into its own darkness, pulls it apart, shatters it, destroys it. Light can't enter a black hole and remain itself. From the point of view of the black hole, light is something to be undone.

Peter was coming closer to me, whispering, pulling me in. I tried to resist him

"Of course, No Name, you think I must be the black hole. My black hole to your pristine white hole. What do you imagine I think?"

"I think that you were drawn to me, Peter, because we survived."

"Guess again."

What remains of the black hole is its hunger and its hunger is eternal. Perhaps there is nothing eternal in the universe but this hunger of the black hole. Some say over billions of years it will evaporate and disappear but others believe it will remain until the end time and then the universe itself will disappear into this hunger. At the last moment, the black hole will eat eternity. Will it be satisfied, Cardinal? I want to say 'Ask Peter.' but I know what he would retort.

"I need to know you, Peter."

"Need? What does that mean, No Name? Why do you want to be so intimate with me? Shall I take it as a compliment or a sign of your weakness."

"I will know what you know, Peter."

"*Will*? Ah, yes, you are showing your true colors, No Name. It doesn't take long to break your kind down. Knowledge is power, is that it? You want it and you will have it. The triumph of your will, No Name."

"That's not what I mean."

"Isn't it? Don't you mean you want to be in my shoes? Correction, you want to be in my boots. You know no boundaries."

After my father left that evening, I took my pillow and went outside where my heavy duty sleeping bag was spread out over a futon, weighed down against the wind with a few rocks. I crawled inside and lay down on my back. I could see Mira coming and going, waxing and waning, halfway between Mars and Jupiter, not far from Aldebaran. Further away, I spied Algol, the prankster demon star called Lilith by the Hebrews. Algol is a variable star, blazing at second magnitude for about 56 hours and then within five hours dimming to third magnitude and then blazing again. A dark companion circling the brighter star periodically cuts off its light. But, Cardinal, the great bright star would have diminished, even burned out, billions of years ago, if it didn't pull the smaller star into its orbit and cannibalize its light. The light feeds on the dark—how well you must know this Your Eminence—and then the dark eclipses the light. Once locked into the same orbit they move in tandem, revolving around and around and around each other. The darker one not completely destroyed and the now more massive blue one, dependent on the other for its life's breath.

It doesn't have to be a star, Cardinal, which locks another star into position. Sometimes a black hole captures a star which then circles that hole helplessly, unable to escape, unable to prevent itself from being devoured, its fire exiting in a powerful stream into the mouth of the other.

Nothing, Cardinal, is innocent because there is nothing that has not been altered, entered, and transformed. And in this process, the smallest particle is, forever, linked to any other particle with which it once connected. After Peter definitively arrived, it seemed to me that the stars were flashing chaotic messages in a disorderly code. In the presence of Peter, I no longer loved the stars. I forced myself to lay outside while Peter was jabbering, but I was quickly chilled and wanting to be inside. It seemed stupid to spend so much time outside in the dark.

Take off your clothes, No Name. It's not as cold as you think. This can hardly be called a winter compared with Germany or Poland. You can't imagine how much cold the body can take. Try it, you'll see. You can turn the hose on and wet yourself down and then lie out here. We did some experiments—really, you are hardier than you suspect. I thought you liked rigor, No Name. Don't you want to know how we did it?

I got up and went inside the house. First I sat in the kitchen because it is a simple room with a bright light over the table, then I felt his presence, a shadow without a shadow and went to the bedroom which was filled with dank anxiety and so I paced from one room to the other but without being able to escape him. Wherever I was, he was as well. But not Peter alone, Peter and the tail of his history, twitching.

Didn't I want to know how he did it? Didn't I want to know how he did it?

I began to write in my journal. Then I stopped and did all the dishes. Then I made the bed even though it was night time. I took a shower. Hot water. I put everything in order. Then I began to write in my journal again.

I began to write in order to blot out my curiosity. Didn't I want to know how he did it? Not so much to record things as to have a place to escape to hoping he couldn't follow me there, hoping it was private, hoping I could escape the question.

I answered him, "No, I don't want to know how you did it"

He hadn't disappeared under a wet cloth and Ajax scouring powder. "It's useful information, No Name, it could save people's lives."

"No, I don't want to know how you did it."

"Don't you want to know how to survive it? How long you can bear it? How long you will endure?"

"No, I don't want to know."

"You're lying, No Name. You're lying. It's so like you to lie. What do you want then? Do you want me to know something? Are you writing to me in your journal? I thought you wanted me to leave, why are you holding on to me?"

Yes, on the one hand, I had wanted him to flee, but something in me wanted to hold him with words.

Peter, you come to me the way dense bodies, stellar masses fall into each other, or one star embraces another, the way a star can be drawn inexorably toward and then into the other, or one star descends on the other, like a lover cleaves to his beloved, as if one part of the self must be reconciled with the other, no matter how much repulsion exists at their core or other forces attempt to pull them apart.

"How charming that is, No Name. But do you think it means anything? This Wagnerian rhetoric you love so much?"

Not that he would leave on any account. He made that patently clear. As far as he was concerned, he had just as much right as I had to this territory. He, like everyone else, had wanted a life. It had been taken from him. History had sucked it up. "That's the breaks", we say when we are talking about others. But he still wanted it. And it seemed he'd gotten it. Not a whole life, not a life that was entirely his, not a life he loved, rather a life he hated, but a part of life anyway.

I tried to find a place safe from him. A place where he could not intrude. Ironically, I thought it might be where he blended into me, where he became me and so disappeared himself. So I looked for ways to understand a progression from Schmidt to Blue. If you believe in cause and effect, time, learning from your mistakes and learning to bend space time through the force of your own mass or the vertiginous spin of insistence, then such a transformation is plausible, in this life as well as the past. I thought it made sense for him to have wanted—to want—to be me. Why not? I'm gifted and healthy. Educated. Respected. Professional. I don't kill. And I am alive.

I heard his voice whispering to me:

"Are we are so very different, No Name? Do you have all the virtues that I long for and did I come here to get them for myself? Do I want to be you so we can live happily ever after, me with my angel and you with your devil, God rewarding me after all?"

But I drowned him out. There was something else I had to say and I wasn't going to let him stop me. I'm Jewish. That's why you want to be with me. I'm Jewish.

Yes, I was the perfect way of getting clean, making amends. Redemption. Salvation. That's what he could get out of it. If one believes in time and the pristine progression from past to future, he got salvation and I, the innocent, had no responsibility for what happened. Another bonus: He would fall into innocence. What a good deal this was for him.

"No Name, your house is a pig sty. You are living in swill. Your research stinks. Filth is in your nature and you have the audacity to claim it is mine."

Once I got to this place, I heard his derisive laughter or maybe I even came upon the contradiction on my own.

For this theory to work, for me to remain innocent, time had to exist in an inviolable straight line. This theory also meant that such invasions could be matters of will. His will. The triumph of the will. It seemed like a dead end.

I tried thinking in another direction. Thinking was all I had. If I could find a solution to the problem. . . then I could do something. What? Remove him. If I learned how he got in, I could get him out. That was my first thought.

Imagine, I told myself, imagine that Peter is a particle. A particle caught up in a cyclotron, bombarded by an overwhelming force. One might predict any of several consequences, but one cannot predict which one will occur. It is not a matter of cause and effect. There is no linear relationship. There is no necessity to it. That's what my colleagues say.

I sat down with a pencil and a yellow lined pad, 8½" x 14" . There were no other papers on my desk. I sharpened the pencil in the electric pencil sharpener. I sharpened another pencil and another. I checked the erasers to be certain that they hadn't hardened, didn't smudge. I poured myself a cup of black tea. I added milk to it. I put Shaena Baena's European tea cozy, a doll with a Polish porcelain face and a quilted skirt, over the Wedgewood tea pot I had also inherited from my grandmother. I set down the first equation as if I were a school girl.

What force hit Peter Schmidt? What particle at what velocity? This intrigued me. If I could discover the nature of the impact I would be able to eliminate shame. There is no shame when a proton and a negative pion collide and transform into a neutron. There is no shame in the neutron; it has no charge. Its existence is a consequence of the collision, of the external influence.

I might be the stable proton, the one which would remain itself forever, unless it is shattered during a collision course with something else. Protons, electrons and photons are stable and then another force comes along, shatters them. It was not my fault. Peter was the pion. . . .

Or Peter was the proton. Then he was shattered. The neutron appeared. Then, it destabilized. Moi.

But there was another difficulty. I was no longer able to think in terms of stable particles. There is nothing stable and unchanging. There is no way to avoid collisions. One thing is always changing into another, dynamic systems, energy. Was Peter Schmidt always a possibility? A probability? Was there no way to stabilize safely without the possibility of his appearance? No way to protect the neutron from destabilizing into the proton, or the proton from transforming into the neutron?

There was a relationship here, a dynamic constant transformation of one particle to another. If I denied it, I denied my profession. I would be standing with those who said the earth didn't move around the sun, who said the earth was the unmoving center of the universe.

I can't abide this, I thought. Then Galileo was whispering in my ear. I had never understood his heresy so completely. He was whispering the voice of a demon lover. "Nevertheless, it moves," he was saying.

Formulas can proceed in two directions. The proton moving toward the neutron, let's say, is the same as the neutron moving toward the proton. It is not limited to one direction. Time is not a factor, because it isn't stable, isn't fixed, doesn't exist in one place. All of time exists in one place, the future and the past co-existing in one plane, as ever-present as space, as North and South. Time, is, therefore, immaterial. Time doesn't pass out of existence. Though the Big Bang theory solves the paradox of an effect without a cause by postulating an origin in which neither space nor time exist, I couldn't dispose of Peter Schmidt in this manner. In this universe, he and I existed. So Time was immaterial; it couldn't save me. I was trying to deal with matter but I knew I was not dealing with matter.

I came upon two certainties. In one dimension or another, Peter and I existed. This dimension was a supercollider. Who had constructed this supercollider?

In such a dimension the proton is inevitably bombarded. I understood this. And then there is a neutron. It is not stable. It can disintegrate spontaneously; its disintegration is built into it. A mathematician wouldn't put it this way, but I put it this way for the moment. The proton is implicit in the disintegration of the neutron.

Who is Peter Schmidt and what is his. . . ? That isn't the right question. Who is Peter Schmidt and what is my relationship to him? What dynamic are we involved in? Which is which? Who is who?

If one particle is ever part of a dynamic with another particle, no matter how different they are, they are always in relationship. The dynamic is what is given, absolute and inescapable. There is fallout, of course, from all of this. There are consequences, but I could not even begin to consider them. I was considering these two particles, their nature and their relationship to each other.

There were explanations for a star burning out and becoming a black hole. They had to do with weight, size, density. But they didn't explain anything here. There was more to it. There was more to understand beside the formula which could predict when the critical mass would descend into terminal darkness. It was not something my colleagues could discuss. And it was not something I had any preparation to investigate. I only had mathematics, physics and astronomy to rely on and they told me nothing.

It was night time when I looked up from the yellow pad. The evidence was overwhelming. I could check it out with a computer but that wasn't necessary. It wouldn't challenge my conclusions; it would only confirm them and I didn't want confirmations. It was night time of the same night or perhaps it was the next night. I had no way to know. I had disconnected my phone machine and turned off the ring of the telephone so if anyone had called to speak to me or leave a message which would have enlightened me as to the day it was, I would not have received it.

Someone else, for their piece of the puzzle, may have been given exile, or running for her life, crippling illness, or a sojourn in a POW camp, or the first glimpse of a very, very, remote quasar, or the calculations which make a black hole irrefutable, or the demand he listen to a distraught stranger who thinks she is inhabited by a dybbuk of a very particular kind. I got Peter Schmidt.

There was a significant and inevitable relationship between Peter Schmidt and myself. Or between myself and Peter Schmidt. And it was my task to discover its nature. That was my conclusion and for this, mathematics would not serve me.

I could have insisted that this had nothing to do with me but I didn't want to rely on accidents anymore than Kepler did or Einstein who said, "God does not play dice." And, although some of my colleagues believe both men were misguided, I had to find the necessity of Peter Schmidt and our intrinsic relationship to each other.

Cardinal, this is my confession: My calculations confirmed that I had been Peter. Somehow I had lived his life.

Lived it without knowing it. "Those who don't learn from history, are doomed to repeat it." I knew that much. The next step seemed clear to me: I would have to relive it. I would go back. I would go back to where my father had been. I would go to where Peter had been. I would stand under the shadow he cast. I would see it as he saw it. He would see to that. I would see it as I would see it. I would have to bring my entire will to this. And he would see it then.

I thought I knew how to do it. I knew how to arrange it. I knew where to go. A few months earlier I wouldn't have known a single name or place but now, somehow, I knew many of them. I knew everything, I thought, except why my father had chosen this time to visit me.

Did he know, my father? He didn't know.

Did he know, my father? He knew.

"You don't know everything, No Name," Peter shrieked in my ear.

"I know enough," I said holding on to that idea desperately. I know everything I need to know, I told myself, except how to tell Lance.

The next morning I booked tickets to Europe for the spring of '89. Eastern Europe: Germany. Austria. Poland. Wherever Peter Schmidt had been. When Lance saw the itinerary I had been concealing, he threw up his hands. I stared unblinking at him as I had never looked at him before. And I used whatever I thought I saw in his eyes for my own purposes. Anger? I could meet the anger. Resistance? I could meet that. Defiance? That too.

"Eastern Europe? And a scenic tour of the Camps?" he asked.

"That's right." I answered.

"It's a stupid thing to do. Especially in your state. Why are you doing it?"

"I have to know. I have to see what happened. Everything changed then. Don't you see, everything changed. And if I had been alive then, I would have been a part of it. I would have done it too.

"Why don't you go to Japan? If you want to know what happened. If you want to know the consequences of what you might have helped to create if you had been alive."

"This came first."

"No, it didn't. It came at the same time. The ideas were in the air at the same time. They may even have created each other. Annihilation co-created."

I said nothing.

"It is because of your father, isn't it? Because of what he told you. Because he's going nuts, do you have to go with him?"

I still said nothing. He returned my gaze equally, matching defiance with defiance while reaching into his wallet for a credit card. "Let's do the tour in concert," he snapped as he stomped out of the room. I nodded.

"I'm a grown-up now, Shaena Baena," I heard myself whisper.

Then I put Bach on the tape recorder. Thank God for Bach, I thought but what I really meant was: Thank God for Lance.

IV

The Ordeal

Chapter 29

Dear Cardinal:

"Take good care of her," my father instructed Lance as we left. Rosa hadn't come to the airport, of course. She hadn't been so angry and disappointed in me since I'd decided to study astronomy. What I didn't know is that she'd given Lance money to buy me the most extravagant bottle of perfume he could find in the duty free airport shop on the way home. Also she had given him a few things to tuck into his suitcase for me; a few tapes of her playing the piano for the trips in the rented car; also Stevie Wonder, *InnerVisions*—sometimes Rosa had a sense of humor. A flowered flannel nightgown and a new green silk robe, as my old one was shabby even by her standards, and finally several pairs of wildly patterned socks so that I would have warm and silly things to wear when we came back to the hotel from our dreary rounds. There were enough to give some away as gifts, but I wouldn't have thought of such a thing.

"Why is she going?" she had asked Aram when we were on the phone in a three-way conversation, she and he in separate rooms. Then before he could fully respond, she slammed down the phone in the middle of his explanation about Eastern European astronomers, so I never heard his entire answer.

It was as if there were three of us traveling together in the airplane. Lance on one side and Peter on the other where, in actuality an American business man was seated. He and I chatted intermittently after I correctly guessed he had done a tour of duty in Vietnam. I like looking at the stars from 40,000 feet, but after a few hours the weather changed and we could see nothing through the clouds.

The vet indicated he often traveled to Germany.

"Some people tell me Berlin is still the heart of darkness," I said.

"Oh no," he answered, "it's a wonderful city. Very lively. Very lively. Go to the zoo. The shops are elegant. I come to Berlin several times a year and I'm always sorry to leave."

"And the Wall?" Lance asked.

"Berlin's a green and golden oasis in the middle of the desert. Are you sorry to reach water if you're crossing the desert? Well, you're never sorry to disembark in West Berlin."

I tried to see it through Peter's eyes, as someone who had never flown in a plane, crowded into a narrow seat, leg room insufficient for him, the surrounding language alien. Someone seated in the "No Smoking" section, prohibited from smoking. As if I were he, I ogled the magazines advertising German cameras, furs, leather goods, Bavarian china. German cameras had always been good. Peter had had a Leica.

His grandmother had had Rosenthal china and gave it to his mother and once his father threw a plate and hit his mother in the forehead with it. "The china," she screeched involuntarily trying to catch the dinner plate before it crashed to the floor. Then she was on the ground trying to gather the pieces together. When his father left the room, Peter had sneaked out from behind the painted screen and helped her until every sliver was rescued. "You glue it together, Peter, you're so good with your hands."

"Don't worry, Peter. Your father only loses his temper because of the war. Go fix the plate and watch out for him until he gets his temper back. Don't practice your violin now. Put your paints away. Go for a walk after you fix the plate but don't let him see the plate. Hide it under your bed."

I couldn't listen to music or watch the movie as Peter's taste overwhelmed, sour in my mouth but persistent. He hated jazz, the black sound—too raw and he or I didn't want to hear Viennese waltzes, or Bach, Beethoven or Wagner. One of us put our hands over my ears.

Memories flooded me. Leni Reisenthal's documentary had opened with Hitler landing in a plane. The spring weather was glorious. He was greeted by round faced children in the crowd, smiling, round, golden sweet, innocent cherubs waving flags. Peter wasn't a child when he saw the film, he was a man. That is how his mother had spoken of him for years: "My little man." The private plane had descended and a small man emerged from inside. The crowd cheered. Sunshine then. Now this. The weather wasn't promising. We were landing in Berlin in freezing rain.

My head was heavy. I felt heavy handed, heavy hearted. I remembered JFK's words, *"Ich bin ein Berliner."*

"Not I. I come from Erfurt."

"Erfurt?"

"Yes, Erfurt. Pay attention. When you go to Buchenwald, there won't be rooms in Weimar. You'll stay in Erfurt, across from the train station which took me to Berlin and then to Poland. We're going to take a train to Poland. We're going to Erfurt because you want to see Buchenwald and the place where I was born. Isn't that it? Do I have it right? You want to see Buchenwald. Is that's what you call entertainment? Or do you want me to see Buchenwald? Are you doing this for me? Do you want me to sightsee through your eyes, *Fraulein* No Name, or would you like me to be your guide?"

Then his presence left me. I wrapped myself in the plane's blanket and listened to oldies, Nat King Cole. Peter didn't reappear. It was as if this were all an hallucination. At one point, I felt Lance tucking his blanket around my feet. When the plane began its slow descent, we made our agreements; Lance proposed to take care of me and I contended it wasn't possible.

"It's possible," he insisted, "and I will. I don't understand your intention, but I know enough German to negotiate taxi rides, follow directions to the autobahn, buy gasoline, talk to hotel clerks and order dinner. As for my Polish, it will work as well as yours."

"And, if . . ."

"And, if. . . . There aren't any 'ifs.' You're perfectly safe with me—though obviously it's not true the other way around."

"But if . . ."

"If I can't protect you . . . If. . . ? It won't be that I won't; but if can't, I can't. What I can do, I'll do. And for the rest . . . I won't leave you, Daniella."

"Why are you coming with me? What do you get out of this, Lance?"

"Don't I tell you all the time that your body is my oasis in a sometimes bleak desert?"

I think the vet overheard Lance because he was smirking a little bit. "Take good care of her—if you can." His voice was friendly as he leaned toward Lance while taking his hand luggage from the overhead compartments. "She's a tough one. You'll probably have to wrestle her to the ground if you want to have a good time." He put a cap on his head, tipped it toward me with a wink, wrapped himself in a yellow plaid muffler and disappeared into one of the empty seats in front so he could be out the door first. I thought I could feel the cold and snow entering my body even as the flight attendant gave us weather information again: 32°F, wind and sleet. Lance took my hand the moment we disembarked the plane and wouldn't let go.

"All the trees are dying over there because of the smog," the blond, middle aged, West German concierge noted as she served us breakfast before we crossed over to East Berlin. Dressed in a basic black dress under a hand painted silk kimono, and wearing real pearl earrings and necklace from her late husband, "real pearls, not cultured" she said rolling the strand back and forth between manicured fingers. Having fallen on hard times, she was presiding in the dining room of what had been her apartment and was now her midtown bed and breakfast accommodations fashionably located within the art gallery she also owned. She was serving us thin slices of black bread, and thinner slices of cheese, ham and salami from a narrow silver platter.

"The communists are remarkable," Lance had answered her a little impatiently. "They not only have the skill to keep their population from going over the wall, they manage to keep the air molecules from crossing over as well. Or is the environmental feat West German engineering?" I was amazed by his audacity that he had somehow couched as jest.

"Nevertheless, the trees are dying there," she repeated with smiling assurance. "You'll see."

"And not here in West Berlin?"

"No, not here. Of course not. Didn't you see the park yesterday? Isn't it green? Aren't the animals happy in the zoo? Germans have always been wonderful gardeners." Her pride was unmistakable as she surveyed our breakfast table to make sure that we had everything we might possible want. We went over the instructions for crossing the Wall for the third time. The taxi to the train. The train to the last stop. Then we would follow everyone into the tunnel, down stairs through several hallways all clearly marked with arrows and instructions, past a series of guards and turnstiles, showing documents, exchanging money, until we would walk out on the other side.

"Can you carry all your luggage?" she was momentarily concerned.

"We can," Lance assured her.

"Good. It will take about an hour or two by train," she said, "if you take a taxi across Checkpoint Charlie it could take you forever."

That afternoon in East Berlin a morose taxi driver gave us *the* tour pointing out the limits we couldn't cross without a special visa which would come with our rental car. As if to spite the concierge, tulips were just opening in the garden at Brecht's old house in East Berlin and *Unter der Linden* was lined with blossoming almond trees. When I was a little girl, Aram had read Kazantzakis to me, particularly the rhapsodies on almond blossoms which I believed grew only in the brilliant sunlight of the Mediterranean, but here they were in the cold and slush of Germany. Still, it was difficult to breathe in East Berlin though it had not been difficult in West Berlin as if, in reality, the gray stone wall topped with sentry stations and barbed wire did somehow contain the rotten air. Against Lance's protestations, I opened the windows of the elegant East German hotel where all western tourists were housed and the infamous yellow fog entered the room.

After dinner, we retreated to our room and pored over maps and papers. "The Rhine is dead," Lance was muttering from behind the newspaper he was trying to decipher. "That concierge is a seeress. She wasn't wrong about the pollution and she was right about the trees. They are dying, everywhere in Europe. It is just that everywhere is everywhere, not only the Eastern Bloc."

"I'll tell Aram."

Lance folded the newspaper and put it on the floor by the side of the wastebasket.

"That German your father worked with after the war . . . that German is not going to save these trees even if he is alive."

"Well, of course, he's alive. Otherwise . . ."

"Otherwise what? Otherwise we wouldn't be here? We haven't come here because of your father, Daniella. And we haven't come here because of trees. The itinerary you've put together does not, it seems to me, take us to the mass graves of trees."

"You don't see the graves of trees, Lance. They disappear less obviously than people. There's only an empty space alongside a farm or pasture or under a building or a parking lot."

"I know, Daniella. I'm a veteran of shopping malls. But that's not why we came here. Do you want to tell me why we came?"

"Aram says his old Nazi reforested a few areas under Speer's direction before the end of the war and that he saved the groves after the war. So, of course, it puzzled Aram that he was arrested now, what with acid rain and smog and soil pollutants and everything beginning to go. And of course Aram can't come . . ."

"Daniella, don't take me for an idiot." Lance had just folded his gray slacks over the back of his chair and was holding the skirt I had just dropped, smoothing it out, then lifting it in his hand and shaking it at me as if it were evidence. "Do you want to tell me why we're here?"

"No."

"Will you tell me?"

"No."

"Could you tell me if you wanted to?"

"No," I was almost shouting.

"Do you lack the words or the understanding?"

"I don't know."

"Are you prohibited from telling me?"

"I don't know."

"Does your father know?"

"No."

"So, of course, Rosa doesn't know either."

"No."

"Let's go to bed then. Tomorrow is the first of too many terrible days until we go home."

I was looking out the window at an empty street as Lance closed it and then the drapes. He had my nightgown in his hand; my robe was across the foot of the bed. I looked around the room; there was nothing left to do so I called room service and ordered two brandies and *linden torte*.

"I'm going to read to you," I said. "I brought something you'll like. It's science fiction. By Orson Scott Card." He nodded. "And it's about music. A galactic *meistersinger* who's trained to sing stories so that the listeners remember everything and are healed. But that's not the only feat—it's about the quality of his voice." I could see that Lance was pleased. "I need to do something, Lance, to return the favors you do for me."

He had gotten my hairbrush from my purse.

"Are you going to brush my hair?"

"While you read."

"Who's that for? You or me?"

"Guess, Daniella."

"Me."

"You're wrong."

Chapter 30

The first, gray dreary morning on the other side of The Wall, we took our rental car and drove to Ravensbruck, the special camp that had been set up for women and children. Lance practiced his flute before we left and then tucked a wooden recorder into his pocket, "For emergencies," he said. I was trying to develop the habit of ritual, keeping a journal and holding a little blue medicine bundle that Amanda had left to me with a wry note: "If it ever occurs to you this might be useful, you'll be okay. Carry it with you and think of me." I didn't know if the last sentence was a wish or instructions, but I took the book with me to be safe.

"This is my journal," I said sternly to Peter. "Keep out."

"Are you going to pretend this never happened?" he retorted and I recorded his words directly ending the sanctity of the book on the spot. Ritual, sanctity, Ravensbruck . . . how was it possible they invoked each other?

It wasn't as difficult as I had expected to find our route. It was marked with little white signs in black and red letters that trace the route of the *Todesmarch*, the death march of those who remaining alive in the Camps toward the end of the war were forced to embark often without shoes, always hungry, in the bitter cold and snow, pushed forward from one camp to another, by guards, soldiers and dogs so that the almost triumphant allied armies wouldn't find them. But even without the signs, it seemed to me I knew where to go when we had to make a turn or take another road. It wasn't as unfamiliar as I'd expected for someone who'd never been to Europe.

We came to a triangle of land, no more than fifteen feet on each side, where the road split into two; one went toward Ravensbruck and the other toward Sachsenhausen. I wanted to photograph the sign in the center of it that by its placement invited us to stop rather than move on.

APRIL 1945.
DER HAFTLINGE DES KZ-SACHSENHAUSEN OBER 6000
WURDEN AUF DESEM MARSCH DURCH DIE
SS ERMORDET.
IHR VERMACTNTNIS LEBT IN UNSEREN TATEN FORT.

Peter was silent. I thought he had been here before. If he hadn't, I wouldn't be here. The triangular memorial was so unexpected, I almost thought Peter had arranged it for me alone. Lance parked the car in front of a brick apartment house as I went out to the miniature park. An elderly woman was leaning, arms folded, on the wooden sill of an open window. Her lined round, weary face was utterly impassive as was the face of the eight year old girl beside her. In the States, I would have waved but she was so ungiving, I stiffened accordingly and then it was as if we had both stuck our heads in tattered cardboard figures—she the German and I the American—and we were both imprisoned in the moment. Maybe she had been watching from that window for forty-four years since the German army or the occupation forces or the *Todesmarch* itself had gone by. Judging by the lines on her face and the lips sinking in defeat, she would have been about twenty-one then.

It's rude to stare, so I spun away toward the sign on the monument when a young boy of ten or twelve, angelic in his appearance, gleaming, appeared out of nowhere with a troupe of other boys behind him and accosted me, sneering in a stream of German whose intent I understood perfectly but I wasn't going to relinquish the photographer anymore than I was going to ignore the *H* word ever again now that I had brought myself to the source of it. I managed to take the picture, though surrounded breast height by the jeering circle of boys. Holding the camera up above my head away from the grasp of the leader, I was backing up to the car, in effect dragging the circle of boys with me, but spying a great shot, the unruly grass around the small monument and the equally unruly circle about me, I swerved to take the boy's picture against the sign as he was reaching out toward me with a beatific leer on his face. Not satisfied with this triumph I took his picture again, as we were driving away and caught his small hand raised in an obscene gesture. A wave of rage from nowhere I could recognize inundated me completely as I imagined the worst about these boys who might have been like any other boys—and about the woman who had remained impassive and the little girl who already knew how to stare through events.

Lance, whistling a little tune, bent over his map, was oblivious.

"The little shit gave me the finger." I was shaking. My feet were steady but from the knees up I was trembling.

"Boys," Lance exclaimed barely interrupting his song. "I'm sure I did similar things when I was a young boy. It doesn't mean anything."

That young blond boy by the Todesmarch sign, Cardinal, marked my descent. At first sight, his face was sweet, the way a twelve year old boy is still sweet, the man in him foreshadowed but not yet formed and the possibilities of who he will become are endless. His lips were very red, strawberry red and juicy and his cheeks were burnished ruddy from the wind. White wool fleece on the collar of his denim jacket framed his face. The boy was living his life. He had a life, after all. Just as Peter Schmidt had had a life. A real life with a mother and father, home, sausage, animals, sunshine, needs, desire, ambition, hope, despair, even music. In other words, an ordinary life.

And I had decided I had a right to enter his life, familiarize myself with it, get so used to it, it would feel like my skin. That's what Peter did. He got used to it, it became familiar and comprehensible; it was his skin and so he wore it, nurtured it and then he tried to preserve it just like I was trying to preserve mine. So, Cardinal, from the beginning, Peter wasn't that different from myself. And then this brat came along and I lost all sense of resemblance. I couldn't have been that boy, I decided, and smelled the bad breath of my own arrogance. I started again. I started with feet. We both had feet. We both walked. Still, I wanted to smack the kid.

My dear Daniella. How very self-righteous you are. That impoverished woman leaning out the window of her poor apartment, with her poor, do you hear, do you understand poor, granddaughter, she is my witness. You drive up into a little village with your rented car burning so much petrol she can't even imagine where it comes from under the earth. You get out in your black down coat, goose down, no doubt, imported from towns such as this, no doubt, holding your expensive Japanese camera, with an extra lens thrown smartly over your shoulder, and you take a picture, right there, in front of everyone, of a little sign in a tiny park right in front of her window, without saying, "hello, may I, *bitte*, I hope I'm not embarrassing you. . . ." No, you take a picture of what you consider their shame and then you want to be treated well. She looks out the window each day and sees that sign. Why didn't you just pull her out of the window and stick her nose into it? You look at her without smiling, without any courtesy, you glower at the boys as if they're going to burn you alive and then you are distressed when one of them gives you the finger? That Japanese tourist who ran up to you and took your picture straight on while you were striding alongside the Plaza in Santa Fe, you remember him to this day. You wanted to pulverize his camera with your handbag. Oh, you thought, now I understand why taking someone's photo without permission is stealing their soul. So what were you photographing in that little triangle of a park, the directions to Disneyland?

That, Cardinal, was the first rite of my initiation. Then we arrived at Ravensbruck; I want you to understand: Ravensbruck is beautiful. Do you understand? It *is* beautiful.

It was like taking a Sunday drive in the country, speeding past trees and thickets beginning to green with April spring growth, glancing down the straight lanes neatly angling from the highway, lined with fruit trees in bloom. Pastoral sweetness and calm. Meadows, pastures, farms, villages ending in small circular islands of trees. The dark German woods I had read about were gone, culled then tamed. Instead, trees were planted in formal and orderly rows. We sped by miles and miles of pines with chevrons cut into them for the pitch.

Aram had taught me how to hide in the woods so that not even the animals would know I was there and I had been good at it. I could do it again if I needed to, but not in these woods.

"If we had to hide, Lance, we couldn't. There aren't enough trees. I don't know how we would survive."

I hadn't expected, Cardinal, that his eyes would fill with tears before he could answer me. "I'm sorry," I said, putting my hand on his arm. He took my hand and held it until there was a place to pull over and then we strolled through the spring grass to moss covered boulders facing a green valley.

"This is what I know, Daniella," he said. "When I play a piece of music each note disappears immediately. I can extend a note but its beginning is gone even as it hovers in the air. I can't hold onto the note. The past claims it and I can't retrieve it. Even a tape recording can't recapture the note from the past. The past is over there." He pointed behind me. "You can't hold on to it. It's gone. It's okay to want to know what happened then. It's good to read history as long as you can tell the difference between then and now. If I tried to hold on to any note, music would disappear."

As we left Berlin farther and farther behind, the road narrowed, then we turned up a road that divided at a bronze memorial; we went right, toward the lake. How peaceful it was. Ducks came up to the log hidden among the reeds. Almond trees were in bloom here as well. A black branch covered with blossoms jutted out upon the perfect circle of still water, laced in haze. The gray of the sky blended with the blue gray of the water and the haze curved like a scarf in the wind, tying it all together. Arriving thus, we were led to expect only peace. If we hadn't looked too closely at the statues at the entrance, glossing the emaciated figures with the mantle of heroism, the metal figures planted barefoot in the last of the winter snow might have been mistaken for the old ones inviting us in. If we didn't know where we were going, we might have seen only the trees along the road and the little path from the parking lot leading down to the lake; it was so lovely, I wanted to walk along the mirror edge staring down into the reeds, and it was very hard to hold back the words that came naturally to my lips in the face of such perfect beauty: "Thank God, we're here."

Within a few minutes, we came to the tastefully designed varnished wooden signs by the parking lot which point visitors in different directions, to the toilettes, to buy film, to the crematorium. I was wearing my black boots and was aware that my steps rang loudly on the walkways of concrete and brown brick set in a mosaic of meanders.

We had arrived mid-afternoon. A single tour bus parked in the lot opened its doors with a bellow of air as some teenagers approached at a gallop. Further down, teenage girls were running through barrack-like buildings examining the so called dormitories. There was a crush of children at the entrance to the museum and then several young boys burst out through the door in an explosion of French and we stepped back out of the way as they ran exuberantly down the long sidewalks along the carefully clipped lawn. They were awhirr like a covey of quail. Then they disappeared with the girls into the bus, amidst sounds of jostling, rattling of candy wrappers, the smack of purses against thighs, of hats being swiped and slapped, of laughter. The bus started and we were the only visitors in the camp.

I was relieved that Lance and I were here by ourselves. I was afraid of simple things. A cigarette, for example. I was afraid to see smoke.

"It is so clean. It hadn't been that clean. I wasn't here but once, but from my experience I know how it was. It was exactly as it was where I had been. They had
a lake here; we had a pond at Birkenau. It would have been enjoyable to walk
here along the edge of the water lapping up to the bank with such regular little
waves. The architecture has symmetry. Ravensbruck has become its own ideal.
A giant sculpture. A monument.

"You go in and out of the gate. No one stops you. No one asks you for identification. The Reds live here as if they belong here. I would have liked to see a few
racing skiffs, a team heaving together against the wind, the muscles pulling. It's
a healthy thing to do. But what do the Russians know about health?

"They live in our quarters but have they learned anything from us? You walk
innocently into their barracks, The SS insignia over the door means nothing
to you. They don't even ask you to leave until Lance tries reciting his few words
of German to the fat one in the kiosk who looks like a baker and barks back
in Russian.

"The lake is clean. It looks new. That's the way water is. This one has been restored. Someone cares about something. No one throws rubbish into the water.
Remove the women and everything gets clean. I know what this place looked
liked then, *Hausfrau*. It looked like filth. It stank. Not as much as Auschwitz,
but it had its stink. That's why we smoked. The cigarette smoke temporarily
entertained our nostrils.

"Having fun, No Name?"

I didn't know how to begin. I wanted to see everything, then I recoiled from the
notion of the museum and distant past. Light traveling for light years, is it simply
that, a moving picture or the real thing? The irritable Russian guard cursing me for
straying into his barracks was closer to the truth; I was glad I had aroused him as I
was grateful for the sounds of ammunition exploding in the distance. This was East
Germany and dangerous for Americans—good. I wanted to know it as it was. Did
I want to get a cup of coffee and go inside where it was warm and look at the mural
sized photographs depicting starving women and children? I could have stayed home
with a few books of award winning pictures. I could have taken them out into the
snow and examined them from there.

I wanted to see things through Peter's blue eyes. Everything glazed with ice blue,
cold, heavenly clarity. But who was seeing it? Him? That's absurd. What him? I was
seeing it. Me. Daniella Stonebrook Blue. That's the one who was seeing it.

"I no sooner tried to imagine what it was like to be a body shoved into an oven,
then in the next second, I was looking at the body through his eyes which were
mine then, watching it being shoved in. The stench and the horror are simultane-
ous and interchangeable. This isn't going to end. Tomorrow there will be another
body and the next day another, and I will never get away. I will be shoving bodies,

one after another, day after day. The bodies are unending, one cannot, will not get to the bottom of them. They keep reproducing themselves like mice in a cage.

"Even here, the women manage to get pregnant, though it is against the regulations, the laws of nature, against reason, against God; stupidly, they get pregnant. They make more of themselves and then they secretly suckle the little rat baby bodies from their dirty teats when they have no food themselves. I will be here forever smelling the stench of bodies burning, seeing the mud, the dirt, the shit, being knee deep in it, eyes and senses offended, wishing I were dead, anything to be out of here. But there is no escape from it. A curse. God's curse. It won't end. I can't get close to them or I will throw myself in on top of them and be done with it."

I was seated on the immaculate stone floor in front of one of two adjacent ovens. I chose the large black wood or coal stove that might heat large buildings in such winters, and sat down before it cross-legged. I don't know if I saw the fire in the oven, or the bodies, or anything but the empty space behind the open iron door. I tried to sit still. My mind leaped like drops of oil and water on a red hot skillet. This was the moment when Gretel had to push the witch in.

I tried to sit there but I couldn't. I willed myself to sit there. I threatened myself with guns, whips, torture. Imagine, you have no clothes on, I said, imagine you have to stand barefoot in the snow, imagine they'll throw you in the fire if you flinch. I couldn't obey my mind, "I'll kill, first," I thought, and ran out looking for somewhere to hide from myself, retreating into a narrow corridor between two stone buildings. Though it had been cordoned off, I crawled under the rope and ran to the end pressing myself against the icy brick wall so I wouldn't be seen by anyone passing by. This was no place to hide; if anything it was a trap.

"I am right behind you, Daniella. Wherever you go, I go with you."

There in the distance was the lake, a little path circling it winding through the birch trees, but I was restrained from going out to it. My real world ended here. I stood facing the back wall and when I extended my arms, I could touch the two other walls.

"Exactly the correct posture, but you're making it too easy. It's too easy to shoot you. Stop pretending you're not afraid, or cold or hungry. I like your kind. You're easy. You don't move and so you're quickly over with. Didn't you read the sign when you went in? This is the place, Daniella, where they shot the women and children. So now it's a comfort to you, is it? But don't pretend it looked like this. When you shoot people, even classy women like you in shiny boots and goose down coats, you see them piss and shit, bleed, thrash and scream.

"Yes, I also like the way this is now. Soil sometimes gets out of line but not here. Frost has packed it tight. It is exact. This is the way we always wanted it to look.

"All you do is raise the gun. You raise the gun and you see if you can do it
quickly. It's easier on everyone. You want them to have a quick clean death and
you hope to be the one to give it to them."

I can imagine wanting to get a good, clean shot, Cardinal. I can imagine that it's
not different than trying to get the telescope exactly in focus. Sometimes things
happen, the tracking mechanism is off and it doesn't lock into the star it's following.
One gets frustrated in those moments. You only have so much time before the sun
comes up or the fog rolls in, only so much time to do the photographing before the
moon rises, or the smog returns or planes fly through your line of sight or visitors
arrive. So you want a clean shot at it. You have a task to do and you want to get it
right. Efficiency. Freedom.

I had brought seeds with me. Pine seeds from the holy mountain. I could have asked
Aram what would thrive here, but I didn't. I brought these seeds because I was
determined that they would grow because I wanted it so. I bent down in the space
between the two walls and planted them in a row right down the very middle of the
narrow corridor, deluding myself that they would get a little bit of sun. Nothing
could grow here. I planted them anyway and regretted I hadn't learned how to force
them into bloom.

That was our first day. We returned in time for dinner. The air still stunk in East
Berlin. When we got back to the room, I lay down on the bed thinking about the
little seeds, willing them to grow. Then I got up and opened the window, smog be
damned. Leaning out, I saw a double line of soldiers marching up the street and behind
them a little gray haired woman carrying her supper in a shopping bag, oblivious to
their presence; and behind her another double file of soldiers. After several blasts
of stinking wind, Lance closed the window and I took a shower and let the water
fill up the tub. When the hot water ran out, I soaked and afterwards showered once
more until the water ran out.

"Why are you so afraid? Trying to keep your hands clean? No one gets to stay
innocent, Daniella. That's what we found out. The only thing we hadn't known
is how damned filthy death is. There's a point when you start getting pulled in,
pulled down, Daniella, when there is no escape. When nothing, no thing, can
pull you out. You'll see."

Chapter 31

Inevitably, Schmidt had been right. As we were leaving the hotel, we were informed that there were no rooms for us in Weimar, the home of Bach and Goethe, though my travel agent had wired the Elephant Hotel—the only place we would be allowed to stay—sufficiently in advance. We were booked instead in a hotel across from the railroad station in Erfurt, the city where they had manufactured the ovens. The walls were covered with burgundy velvet flocking matching the melodramatic drapes that weighed against the dingy windows. If you pulled the curtains, the outside world was completely obscured as it must be in such rooms designed for whores and diplomats. Our suite, they said at the desk, was the only accommodation available. And the most expensive. We were paying through the teeth.

We spent two days in Buchenwald. After the first day, I cried through dinner in the hotel restaurant though we did not have a private table. Just after we were served the soup, another couple was seated with us as is the custom, then another man, so we were five altogether, a sixth could have been seated with us as well. The couple was about seventy years old, ten years younger than Peter. Old enough. They were very polite. They said nothing while I cried. Made a little bit of small talk between themselves. Once they asked me to pass the butter and once they asked for the salt. The other man was a bit over thirty and blond. At first, I thought he was the couple's middle aged son who had arrived late, but he didn't speak to them except to ask them to pass the bread which was closer to us. Out of what would be courtesy in the States, I looked up at him to establish contact, but once I met his eye, I realized I had violated the etiquette of pretending that we didn't exist. He grimaced and his eyes went blank and I did him the courtesy of looking away.

After dinner, Lance and I wandered up and down the streets looking unsuccessfully for a place other than the hotel to have a drink. The few open restaurants were so filled with smoke, we couldn't see across the room. People were shouting to each other with either mirth or desperation and so we continued to walk. Waiting alongside us to cross the street, an adolescent boy reached toward me and took a silver amulet, a *hamsa*, the mideastern hand against the evil eye that Amanda had insisted I wear after she died, into his remarkably gentle but audacious hand. "*Auslander?*" he asked.

"*Auslanders*, Lance answered for me and continued in conversation with the boy to answer numerous questions in his careful and limited German. I could see in the boy's eyes that Americans were strange animals, intriguing and slightly fearsome; while once again I saw the kind of boy Peter Schmidt might have been.

Whether the boy wanted to know more about us or whether he wanted to reveal himself, he invited us to see his house, and when Lance declined, he indicated how we could walk to it at another time if we wished and then he took my hand and shook it once as if he were banging a gavel, cocked his fingers to his forehead in what was not quite a salute, smiled at Lance and crossed the street. As soon as he turned the corner and disappeared, I was drawn in his wake, and insisted that we follow him to the house but staying out of sight.

Orderly rows of tulips filled the very small garden alongside the stairs to the first floor of the little red brick house. In the otherwise somber block of houses, this garden was an explosion of color, a private park in the midst of houses constructed to be blockades against the elements. We would have certainly stopped to enjoy it if we had come upon it while strolling through the city, anyone would.

Maybe Peter Schmidt had lived there, I thought. Lance hoped I was refreshing myself, as he was, by breathing in this small patch of beauty, but I stood there until I knew how it felt to walk past the tulips and climb those stairs in the body of a young boy in the middle of a war and how it felt to forget those stairs and live elsewhere. Except for the flowers, it was an ordinary house, rendered more ordinary by the regime of wild color, fluted and fringed petals, black centers in fiery orange blooms, pale mauve within white, tightly curled red blooms, yellow tulips just opening bordering rows of mysterious indigo on one side and black tulips, not yet open on the other, all self-contained as tulips are but riotous together and so restrained by a fence of black iron stakes that marched toward a gate with a padlock on it. It was not impossible to imagine living an ordinary life in this house. But a young boy could not conceive of an ordinary life. A young boy wanted a destiny. I understood that perfectly. Though I was not ambitious in the usual sense, I had always assumed I had a destiny. I had been so certain my life would matter, to myself at the very least, I had never thought about it and had never acted otherwise.

The boy had been watching us. He opened the door and tripped down the stairs, red tulip in hand, which he presented to me with a wordless flourish, tipping it toward me so that I couldn't miss its starry golden center, looked at Lance with a kind of camaraderie one would not expect from a twelve year old boy, said a few incomprehensible words and bowing his head slightly before he could accept my flustered thanks, ran up the stairs and closed the door behind him.

"What did he say, Lance?"

"I think he said he was proud that he could show us how beautiful Erfurt is. Or he said I should be proud to bring such a beautiful woman to Erfurt."

"No, really. What did he say?"

"He said Erfurt is so very beautiful because the people have always loved flowers."

"No, really."

"Daniella, I have no idea. I recognized 'Erfurt,' 'beautiful' and 'flowers.' Put it together yourself."

I couldn't and when I leaned toward myself for a translation from Peter Schmidt, he had absconded and I was left walking down the street holding this foolish red tulip looking like a common thief.

Buchenwald is up on a mountain. The name means "birch woods." The area was the pride of Weimar. The Nazis had intended to name the concentration camp, Ettersberg, but that name figured so prominently in Goethe's work, they named it Buchenwald for the birch trees. Outside the Museum, a stump of a tree is enclosed behind a small iron chain fence. Called the Goethe tree, it is alleged to have been his favorite resting place before it was cut down.

It was raining at Buchenwald. A constant, cold winter rain though it was already April.

Lance went directly to the museum, wanting to know who, where, when, what and got lost in the photo murals which first showed the entire history of World War II and then documented the suffering and heroic deeds of the communist leaders. I walked through more quickly than he, attracted to a dark section of the museum displaying straw-filled wooden bunks, where sometimes as many as a dozen people had slept together. You're not supposed to stop for too long because the line gets long and then people wait outside in the cold until they can enter, but this was real, a real bunk and real straw and a hundred people shuffling along behind me. I was so tired I wanted to lie down there.

Peter had returned to his territory; now he was amused. "Take off your coat first. And your shoes. Or go roll in the mud outside and then rub up against each other."

His sneering tones inside my head, an attack of tinnitus. "You're still a tourist," he said. "Wait."

The last room marking the entry of the Red Army into Germany was festooned with red bunting. The color was shocking; I had been imagining the camps in black and white. The red impelled me out the back door into the freezing drizzle where a group of Gypsies had congregated, alternately laughing and weeping, and a German man in a camel's hair great coat with a standing collar was leaning back, one knee braced against the wall. Not knowing where to go, I returned to the entrance at the opposite end of the Camp and started to walk through the entire Camp systematically.

Long rectangles of small jagged stones mark the sites of the barracks. Enough stones for each person who had been housed there. There were enough stones for everyone who has ever died just like there are enough remaining stars to go out for every tree that will be cut down and maybe even enough dark matter for the universe to reverse itself and squeeze back down toward a single point, annihilating everything in its path. I sat down in the site of the Jewish barracks and started counting the stones the way I had counted stars. I cleared a little space and gathered the rocks into piles of ten and then gathered those into piles of one hundred. Maybe I had simply thought I had been living a normal life. By the time I got to five hundred, I had to blow on my fingers to get them to move. At one thousand, I couldn't flex them anymore.

What the hell was a normal life? People gave me a wide berth but no one else seemed inclined to spend a great deal of time in any one spot. They looked at the rectangles. Sometimes they uttered a quick prayer or cursed and went inside.

After twelve hundred I couldn't sit there anymore, even though I wanted to stay to learn how it had been in February without shoes. I didn't have the guts and I didn't have the stamina. Now and again I thought I caught a glimpse of the man in the camel's hair coat on the perimeter of another rectangle but when I turned to catch Peter, there was no one there. Then I saw someone some distance away by the chain link fence and went toward him. He was walking up and down the rows and I got behind him doing the same, but when I got close enough, I saw I had been tailing a tall elderly man with remarkably straight posture wearing a dark overcoat and a dark blue beret. At each rectangle he stooped to read the sign on the ground that told him which of the razed barracks had been there and walked around it before he went onto the next and bent down again. The way he walked, I concluded he had been an inmate there. Neither the cold nor rain affected him. He examined every inch of the camp as I kept a discrete distance, pretending to be involved in my own grief. At one point, when I realized that he was weeping, I put down my camera. It was only then I realized how deliberately I had been stalking him.

Embarrassed, I made my way back to a stone building called "the bunker" where special prisoners, the select, the important, suffered the most notorious agonies before their almost certain death, and seated myself on the stone floor at the far end of the narrow corridor between the cells so it was as if I were behind a telescope looking out into a rectangle of unknown territory. You don't just take a picture of the sky and hope to see something. You have to set an exposure time. Maybe you set it for a half-hour, or an hour, or four hours, and wait for the light to accumulate. Of course the longer you set it for, the more can go wrong, the more that can enter it that doesn't belong to it. You can't just point a telescope and camera at the sky and say "Okay, everything out of my way." Things seep in. Light from other places.

I was aiming my camera at a roll of barbed wire just outside the door when the straight-backed man stepped into the frame, and without thinking, I clicked the shutter before I could thrust the camera behind my back. I had wanted to meet his eyes with mine. But the iron gates of the gate-house say *Jedem Das Seine*: Each to his own. The old man was caught. That was the last photograph I took of strangers on that trip and when I developed the film after I came home, I was haunted by two strangers staring up at me, the young boy in the triangle and the old man against the barbed wire.

Since the bed incident, Peter had been silent. I began to hope I was imagining him; I preferred to think of myself as mad rather than possessed as I sat down in a corner behind one of the ovens by the stairs that led down to the medical experimentation rooms. Early on, people wandered in and out, bringing floral wreaths, holly branches, ribbons which they hung on the ovens. Then as it got late and quiet and I was sure that no one else would come in, I allowed grief to overtake me.

"Stop feeling sorry for yourself, No Name. We've all had to bear our share of grief. I felt grief, a universe of grief. So, what was I to do? Be crushed by it? After all, I didn't invite the grief in. It came to me in a blow. You square your shoulders. You stand straighter. That's what you do. You don't complain and you don't whine and you don't beg.

"Why do you turn away, No Name? You pretend to read character in that old man's face, in his posture and tears. You make him into something honorable in your *Weltanschauung*. A partisan, right? *Your* hero. And the other rats who betrayed the state, they were like him you imagine. All of them were like him. Noble. Bluebloods. Right? None of them were vermin? You think their shit didn't stink? So what was the stench then?

"If you had been here you would not have survived. The camps were not endurable. Fire is a purifier so we burned whatever we could. We always hoped we'd come to the end of it quickly. Afterwards, the ashes got into your pores and the lines of your hands until it irritated the skin. It was difficult, if not impossible to wash off, because these ashes were so greasy. Even if you washed your hands, the towels were full of them, and then you rubbed the ashes back onto yourself when you were drying your hands. Ashes in the groin, in your shit, in your hair. Little flakes of ashes as you pissed. The smell of urine, your own, mixing with the smell of ashes, and the faint aureola of grease around each light.

"The world is dead. It died in World War I. Believe me I know some things you don't know. World War II? Only an aftermath. Our duet. You took up with your experiments where we left off. How do know but maybe we were the guinea pigs. You needed an enemy and we volunteered. You wanted to see how hard you could push someone, how much physical punishment you could inflict, how much hunger we could endure before we were permanently altered—you remember Lysenko—or we fought back.

"Some little colleague of yours wants to know if rats have moral inclinations. He allows them to eat only a certain amount of food and punishes them if they don't leave anything over. They're hungry and jump up on their hind legs and beg but he is adamant. Morality is restraint if he demands restraint. One day he stops punishing them. They eat. Rats have no moral fiber, he says. The government pays him to do this. You think we did unthinkable experiments, maybe the unthinkable experimentation was enacted on us.

"Don't pride yourself, yet, No Name, on being free of taint. You and I are children of the *zeitgeist*. The kind of things I did, you would never do, of course. Not you, with your cool long look at the stars. Your mother's friends weren't exactly thinking of bombs, were they, when they looked at the stars? And afterwards they didn't want to have anything to do with our scientists did they? And your colleagues wouldn't do anyone any harm, would they? You wouldn't subject anyone who was unfit to any experiment. You would never suggest anyone might be dispensable. You wouldn't feed plutonium to the demented, would you ? You use rats; we used rats. Rats are not like people but you think they're close enough for the experiment to be valid. That's how you think about it; that's how we thought about it. Not people, but close enough. It was the best we could do. You wouldn't experiment on yourself or your own species even if it were more accurate, why would we? We were just as civilized as you claim to be.

"Are you getting cold here in Buchenwald? Your fingers seem to have turned white. Are you wondering how long they can stay white before you'll lose them? That's the kind of question we needed to answer. It's a legitimate question. We tried to find out. Someone freezes and we revive her and she freezes again and we revive her until we can't revive her again. It doesn't matter, I told you before, freezing is a good and kind death. Your good doctors are grateful for our information.

"I've always been curious about cold. I liked it in the guard tower in Birkenau because it was so very cold, particularly at night. I wanted to know how cold it had to get before I couldn't finger the strings of my violin. And in the beginning, but not later, you could see the stars. Maybe it was because of the cold, that we burned everything we could. If you had been there, you would have warmed us."

I got up and rubbed my hands together. Even though I was wearing gloves and had stuffed them in the pockets of my down coat, they were very painful. His words made everything colder and I didn't know how to be rid of him any more than those who had died in that room. There was only a little bit of light coming in from a high window, and it was getting dark. I didn't know what time it was because I had deliberately left my watch at the hotel.

But I walked to the door very slowly because it was also hard to leave. That may surprise you. I'd come all that way. I knew it was time to leave, but I was afraid I might have missed something. I didn't know what was required of me.

Iron is iron. It's made in the stars. Those ovens existed. I didn't invent them. I know that. What happened in them, I hadn't initiated. But what if I hadn't yet paid proper respect?

Soon I felt as if I would die if I didn't see Lance within the next few minutes. My hands were so cold, I needed his hands to warm them. My grandmother would blow on my fingers to warm them, then she would blow into the gloves and blow a third time after she tucked my fingers into the breath warmed wool gloves. I tried to do the same but I couldn't warm myself.

The iron door handle was colder than sin. I don't know why I removed my gloves to open the door. For a second the iron seemed so cold, I was afraid my hand would freeze on to it and not come free. But it wasn't my hand that didn't move. It was the door. I thought the door was frozen shut and I tugged at it, but it was locked. And the other door, the one downstairs which led toward the rooms of medical experimentation where they had taken out this organ or sewn that one shut or that injected illness, that was locked too. It must have been after five. I was locked in.

I started shouting: "Let me out, Peter. Let me out, Peter. Let me out, Peter," until my throat burned and my voice disappeared.

I don't know how long I banged on the door because I never stopped banging but flung myself against it again and again until it was opened by a matron with Lance standing behind her. He seemed surprised to see me. "Why didn't you shout?" he asked.

"Didn't you hear me? I thought I would die." I could barely speak now. The Camp was closed. Lance had roused the woman from the row houses where children were playing in the last light of day. The matron hadn't believed him that anyone could have been left inside.

"We check so carefully," she was perplexed, "and our security system never fails. How could anyone escape our notice?" I gave her one of the pair of socks that Rosa had sent along. They were black and white with patterns of fish.

That night I couldn't sleep. I lay awake all night in the velvet room listening to the trains coming into the station and leaving. I was remembering a young woman I had seen that morning saying good-bye to her young man. He kissed her. His eyes lit up, then closed. She smiled. He pulled her toward him. She continued to smile. Then something happened. You could see the smile freeze and her almost indiscernible retreat from him. Her eyes filled with tears and she turned away. Then he touched her again and she moved toward him, eager again. I could feel her belief. It was palpable. If she loved him enough, he wouldn't go. If he loved her enough, the world would let him stay. I saw it happening before me; the disintegration of magic and the construction of the rational world.

The station was crowded day and night. The sky gray, day and night. The air so full of cigarette smoke, it permeated our room. I got out of the bed quietly so as not to awaken Lance and sat in the living room on the overstuffed sofa, drinking brandy which I had found behind the leaded glass doors in the mahogany cabinet where there were also a few porcelain figures, two rosy children embracing on a park bench, a ballerina with gold ballet slippers on point, a spotted dog, cheerful and alert. The paintings were equally cheerful, a still life of fruit and a bouquet of flowers, mostly tulips, like those I'd seen growing in the small tidy garden in front of Peter's old house.

Not every star, Cardinal, becomes a black hole. Not every light which goes out becomes a dark maw. Only certain stars, of a certain size or magnitude, of a certain density, not the smallest and not the largest. Only those within a certain range turn themselves outside in. I was never interested, particularly, in black holes, but questions about density and its increase have engaged me. Questions about implosion and reduction, about how and when matter retreats into itself, draws itself together, or draws so deeply into itself there is no reversal possible. I am interested in the increase in density and in the later consequences, the inability to release the light it has consumed. Despite my interest, I cannot formulate the questions I have yet. And without questions, there is no science.

I sat still for hours. And then I stretched out on the sofa. Though I've never smoked in my life, I opened a pack of cigarettes which was also provided, along with chocolates and crackers and nuts. I could have paté if I wanted; I could have caviar. A split of champagne. I smoked a cigarette. I lay down on the floor. I smoked another cigarette. I hunkered down against the wall, between the breakfront and the window. I crouched in the corner. I put my head on the window sill and felt it vibrate as the trains left the station. I pressed myself against the wall. The matches said "Erfurt." I put my head on my knees. I put my hands over my head. I picked up my head. I put my hands over my eyes. I looked around the room through my spread fingers. There, across from me, was the coat closet. I stood up to turn out all the lights then I went down on all fours again and crawled over to the closet. I opened it. The light went on. I removed the luggage stand and pushed our clothes to the side. I sat down on the floor of the closet and quietly pulled the door closed. The light went out. I crawled behind our coats and Lance's pants and pulled them together to hide me. I closed my eyes, I wondered how long it would take Peter to find me when he came for me.

After some time, I fell asleep and dreamed.

I dreamed that I was seated before a furnace. Because it was so cold, I built a small fire in it to keep me warm. The furnace was very large, it was the size of a room, or a building or even a city. I moved closer to the door of the furnace and looked inside. The light of the small fire illuminated the ancient walls of pale brick. Light was shining on them from another source. When the cold became unbearable, I climbed into the furnace where I found myself in an ancient city. In the distance, lions and goats, smoky with ashes and burning with embers leaped about a building which was an endless series of stone stairs, hand cut and set in place. The stairs began at my feet and receded infinitely. When I began the ascent, a man's cold shadow fell upon me. I recognized its shape and was afraid but not so afraid that I resisted the compulsion to climb the stairs which led toward the sky. Then I saw another figure coming across the top of the building from the stairs on the other side. As first I thought it was a lion walking upright and a kind of goatish terror shook my body until I realized the man descending the stairs was smiling benevolently, his hands extended to take mine. I recognized the hands even before he said, "Do not be afraid, I am your twin." As I reached out to him, the earth shook and he and everything else disappeared into a haze of yellow clay. There I was again seated in front of the cold furnace as a wind blasted through the room and the iron door clanged shut.

It was not Peter but Lance who opened the closet door in the very early morning. Without saying a word, he lifted me out and returned me to bed for a few hours, wrapping his body around mine to take out the chill, he said, of the cell in Buchenwald. When I awakened finally, he was improvising bird calls and wind sounds from another world without cities or armies. Love songs. Mating calls. He played until I was dressed and packed and then we had breakfast and drove toward East Berlin.

Chapter 32

We revisited Buchenwald again on the way back to East Berlin. There was something I wanted to see that I hadn't seen. Something I hadn't done that I wanted to do. It was simply seeing if I could walk in the gate and walk out again.

I managed it, walking out through the gate, then down the path alongside a magnificent chestnut tree, then past the locked house where the Kochs had lived; Ilse, the Bitch and Karl, the Commandant, who the books say had a bad marriage. He, poor dear, screamed when the SS came to get him but was convicted anyway of stealing 200,000 marks from the Nazis and so was shot and burned in the crematorium at Buchenwald in April 1945 just days before the Americans liberated the Camp and the Germans surrendered. After the Kochs, you pass the movie house and the shop selling snacks and souvenirs and you're free.

Lance was waiting for me near the parking lot holding a small bouquet of wild flowers. Well, of course, I cried—what do you think, Cardinal?—and took off a glove so that I could hold it in my bare hand despite the cold rain which had begun to feel mean-spirited. "I have never seen wild violets before," he said.

Later that afternoon we were back in East Berlin with a few hours to kill before the train left for Poland, so we drove around aimlessly through immaculate streets with half-destroyed buildings that had not been repaired since World War II. And though the rubble caused by the allied bombings had been removed over six years, the imprint of the war remained on the careful stacks of salvaged bricks and stones that might some day be used for reconstruction and in the dust still rising up into the air from the explosions as if nothing had settled in forty-two years.

"Your version of the Big Bang." Peter's voice immediately dispelled whatever sympathy I was feeling.

"Wrong, your version. No stars come from this," I shifted the blame back to him rapidly but without being able to relinquish doom.

Do you think about the Big Bang, Cardinal, or do you think about Apocalypse? One of your colleagues, Cardinal, a portly Belgian cleric, George Lemaitre, conceived of the Big Bang in the '20s and then Pope Pius XII accepted it in 1951 with one proviso that no one ask what happened *before* the Big Bang. So what about the end, Cardinal? What about contraction, what about matter drawing in on itself so violently that it squeezes out everything—space, motion, light, until nothing exists but itself, a single point, absolute density.

How long will the end take? We can estimate it, but we can't be sure. Some say the universe will last 82 billion years from beginning to end. If we accept that theory, we have between 21 and 30 billion years to go until the universe stops expanding and the stars are called back toward each other. Why am I worried then about the end of time, you ask? What difference does it make if there are 30 billion years remaining instead of thirty-five billion? Why does that thought of the universe ending seem to be another good reason not to return to The Mountain?

Because the end is here. Because they can never repair Berlin. Because the war blasted us through to an other side, but not the one my parents anticipated. Because everything is different here on this other side than it was before the war, before I was born. That is how Peter Schmidt got to me; the living and the dead are now on the same side.

How do you kill time in East Berlin? Window-shopping is hardly what you do in East Germany and it wasn't quite what I had in mind. We returned our rented car and settled down on overstuffed chairs and velour settees amidst mahogany and cherry wood tables in the elegant, old world lobby of the hotel reserved for foreigners. We had a drink there and then we ate and then we had another drink. Then we read the foreign papers, and had another drink and cups of coffee, moving from the lobby to the restaurant to the bar overlooking the lobby as if each site were an event that might hold our interest. Lance unfolded his lanky legs across the couches and reeled them in again under the weight of tables laid with heavy silver carefully aligned on embossed linen and then extended them upstairs in the bar where bored and excited travelers gathered here in this restricted part of the world. We didn't chat with anyone. One didn't. What might one say that would be sufficiently neutral before someone who might be hoping to escape or an agent of the secret police who might be tracking her or us? We were, after all, behind the Wall that no one then could imagine coming down.

The European papers said there were about to be elections in Poland and they thought Solidarity might win but there was no sign of any such movement here. I was afraid even to hope for a Central Europe. Hope was treason according to the State. It betrayed those living here; it must inevitably be smashed.

I must have looked at Lance for succor, because he stood up suddenly in the bar, his head coming very close to the low ceiling and said, "Let's go," pulling me from my seat. We were down the stairs and outside and he had hailed a taxi before I had my coat on. We only had a short time before we had to go to the station for the train to Warsaw from East Germany, but it was enough, he said.

Dark streets. Because it was raining. Because of the air. Because of the time of day. Because it was April and winter. Because of something in the atmosphere.

The taxi drove alongside the Wall and then turned into the city and let us out in the rain before the Vorderasiatisches Museum which houses a major collection of Greek and Mideastern antiquities. Inside it was almost as dark as on the streets. No bright track lights illuminating geometric shapes painted in primary colors, mounted on dazzling white walls. Technology did not shine here. The dim lights were absorbed into the stone walls and the bodies of the dense crowds sprawling over the Altar of Zeus which had been shipped to the museum from Pergamum in Turkey after German archaeologists had excavated it. At the entrance to the ancient temple area it had once said, "In the name of the gods, Death may not enter here," but still we moved as in a fog of ghosts.

Lance cautioned me that closing time was at five and turned me loose so I ran through the rooms like someone pursued, wanted to scan it all before it was time to leave, until, at almost the last moment, my eye was caught by light, a flash of blue as of sky unfurling in a telescope, the shock of storm clouds parting to reveal day break. Something of heaven. I kept running toward it, but with eyes almost closed and cast down so I would be surprised, hoping that the flashes of yellow and white I'd glimpsed against the blue would be stars. I grabbed back toward the empty air for Lance's hand and then went on without him toward the blue.

Blue calling me as only blue can call. That exact blue that means the end of day or the beginning of night, that holds stars or rushes toward them, a blue threshold between light and the darkness. I never stopped running down the long corridor, running like a blind woman might run, reading the walls through my skin, nose out to blue, mouth open for its freshness, then quiet enough to hear blue, ceasing breathing, so I would not miss the first glimmer to appear at the horizon, for Venus to announce the morning or the evening sky.

I came to the edge of it and stopped short. I sensed a portal that opened into blue but I couldn't cross it. I wanted to go across; I put my hands out and walked forward. I felt nothing in front of me, that is, there was no metal, wood, stone or plaster. Open your eyes, I demanded, but they didn't open. You're ridiculous, I said to eyes that remained closed, to hands that were braced protectively in front of me, and to feet that had stopped moving. My senses told me, this is the end of the road. Then don't be stupid, I said, this must be the beginning, and tried to fling myself across the threshold but only fell down, what with carrying a purse and shoulder bag, coat and gloves, all flinging every which way. Stubbornly keeping my eyes closed, I had to fumble about until I found them all and piled them neatly on the floor, removing my sweater, wanting to be cold, and laying it alongside and then thinking twice about standing up, remained on my knees facing what felt both like emptiness and wall. A wall with as much will as I had, with more than enough refusal to match my desire. Then I was shuffled back, only a few inches, but enough to acknowledge the rebuff of a force field and be shaken by it.

This was the very first time in my life that I prayed, though I didn't know how or why. Eyes still closed, I invoked Amanda and my grandmother, pleading that they intercede with whatever was on the other side and allow me to pass across.

Scenes of dreams I had had of places I hadn't recognized returned to me, the dream of the night before, dreams where everything was built of dusty yellow brick, clay crumbling and smearing on my hands, tawny landscapes the color of lions and wheat sheaves, of mustard pollen and light honey. And in the background sometimes something blue, possibly a pool of water, but more likely a mirage or the sky momentarily brushed clean by a yellow wind, or tiled vaulted roofs and a glazed blue wall that stretched along a yellow river to infinity.

"Let me through," I begged, and not knowing what would come of it, I took a determined breath simultaneously opening my eyes, and stepped through the gate of my dreams. The room was entirely blue. Walls blue, arches blue, ceiling blue. Blue glazed brick emblazoned with deities in their animal forms, dragons and lions and bulls in gold and white. Gold on blue and white on blue and white gold on blue as if the sky reproduced itself, the constellations reappearing as they floated across the infinity of heaven.

Here was Draco the Dragon who had been once pre-eminent in the sky when encompassing the pole star as Marduk and before that as Tiamat, Chaos herself, the Mother of all things, at least according to Amanda. I ran my hands over her scaly body, part viper, part feline, part bird of prey, part scorpion, looking for the halo of dark matter, the unidentified shroud that contains her fuzzy light. Next was Taurus, the great golden bull and finally Leo, the winged lion with a diamond eye and Regulus as his heart whom I had dreamed frequently without knowing what I was dreaming.

I could not take my hands off the wall. I traced the figures again and again as if I were touching the stars finally and their animal light was entering me through my fingers.

A small sign in a corner indicated I had passed through the Gate of Ishtar. So I was in Babylon. For years thieves had been robbing the city and here I was in the presence of a final and most startling theft. The wall of Ishtar itself. That ruin. Here. Whatever had not been pulverized by time and grave robbers had been disassembled brick by brick, stacked, numbered, packed, shipped here to East Berlin and reassembled.

We are in Babylon, I said to myself not knowing who *we* were or much about Babylon except that I knew at the end of this Processional Way—*Aibur-shabu*, "the enemy shall never pass" was its name—I would have come to the greatest ziggurat of them all. The tower of Babel, Cardinal was also the foremost observatory of the stars.

Babylon was a beginning, Cardinal, where the magi, those Chaldeans, those astronomer-astrologers that the Old Testament rails against had watched the stars with unprecedented devotion, seeing light everywhere, seeing gods in the constellations and the spirit of light passing down into them as destiny. Babylon is where it had begun. The Babylonians had not distinguished between knowing the stars and their configurations, measuring the orbits of the planets, discovering the cycles of Venus, calculating the lunar and planetary ephemerides years into the future, regulating the calendar, studying equinoxes, solstices and eclipses, *and* discerning the influence of these stellar bodies. And by some grace, I had found myself in this silent blue oasis in the middle of darkness. A brief blue interlude within the fetid industrial air of the poisoned city of East Berlin.

These had been the people of the stars. I was of their lineage even though they had conquered the Jews and brought them to Babylon, including someone whose name I bear. Daniel, the great magician, who had visions and understood dreams, had been here. He had been a captive and lived his life of exile here. Both slave and minister, he had walked down this very processional. He had looked at the stars from this place. He had touched this wall. He had survived the lions' den and he had touched this lion. His hand on my hand through the fold of years. The same Daniel directed the Magi to follow the star that rose over Bethlehem indicating new light.

I had come through the arch of the blue gate, blue as the sky, with its gods, with its dragons and bulls of gold and white and was walking along the blue processional wall with its lions, gold and white as stars. There was no one else in this vast room that was, unlike the others, gleaming with the colors of light: gold of marigolds, white of lilies, blue of approaching light, blue of twilight and dusk.

Babylon was a point. A moment of light. Its rays like roads from the temple of the astronomer priests glanced off in different directions of space time: astronomy, astrology, cuneiform, writing, mathematics, diaspora, captivity, slavery, Talmud, Daniel, the Christ Child, Berlin and the Bomb.

There was something I had dreamed—I was in the dream again—but I couldn't remember what it had been. I was in the womb of the dream. I looked up at the shining blue, yellow and white. It was as though the vaulted ceiling had opened in a great tomb and the light of the stars had fallen in to resurrect the dead.

I began at one end and looked toward the other end of the room where the ziggurat would have been. Everything I had known about stars dimmed before this light that was invisible to me. What I had suspected when I left The Mountain became clearer, but not in words. I had been taken in by impostors. I had climbed the wrong mountain, I had aligned myself with the wrong powers, I had joined an elite and then I had bowed down to, had worshipped, the wrong gods.

I walked slowly and solemnly along the entire length of the blue wall past the dragons, bulls and lions, as if I were walking to the Ziggurat. When I came to the end, I counted to thirty-six repetitively, imagining that I was climbing the hundreds of stairs up the eight towers until I kneeled at the very top, where only the priests of the stars went, and with my eyes closed again, I raised my head to the ceiling. And I prayed again. First in gratitude that I had passed through and then that the intelligence of the ancient sky would be imprinted onto my mind.

Let's meet in Babylon, Cardinal. Let's go there together and watch the astronomer-priest climb the stairs to the summit so he can study the stars. He was the most honored one. After him came the ones who did the calculations and after them, the scribes who wrote it all down. Let us be with him there because shortly after this moment, he divided in two and the astronomer went his way and the priest went the other way and we see where that has led.

Chapter 33

The guards came through the museum like dogs flushing a rabbit onto the field, as if somewhere behind them were horses and men with guns and so the visitors poured into the lobby, stumbling over each other to get through the doors into the rainy night. Closing time. Lance, who had installed himself in a niche between the postcard counter and the entry wall, reached out and plucked me from the crowd, holding me against him until the surge diminished and then we sauntered onto the street, jumped into a taxi, sped by the hotel for our luggage and made our way to the station. We still had to get on the train.

Now, Cardinal, there is something I must explain to you. When circumstances get the best of you and you begin orbiting toward and then around a black hole, you must be careful to maintain the angle of the descending spiral, accelerating exactly, keeping control of yourself, aware always of your distance and speed, so as not to be pulled in. If you get caught in the orbit, if you lose your own power of acceleration, break down and have no ability to back up or to thrust forward into another orbit, you will float as if in free space in a smaller and smaller orbit, going faster and faster, until you circle down, hopelessly, crushed, reduced to a speck of ash, as you are drawn into the center, the dark place of no return.

Without your own opposing momentum, you will disappear across the singularity of the horizon line and from the point of view of an observer, you will no longer exist and nothing of you will remain, or for all we know, nothing will have ever existed.

It was night. We settled into our little compartment, confused and agitated. As we exited East Berlin, convoys of Soviet tanks were aligned in rows on flat beds along the rails. Conductors walked back and forth through the hall demanding tickets and passports in brusque and metallic voices. There was no food on the train, only warm beer, and not much of that according to the porter who, after complex negotiations, sold Lance four bottles, which was to be our ration for the night. In the berth above our heads, our suitcases creaked against each other as we huddled against the rough, red, stained upholstery that could have been fifty years old.

"Put your head in my lap and sleep for awhile," Lance suggested.

"I wouldn't dare sleep. Not from this point on. I'm not going to sleep again."

"I'm here. There's nothing to worry about. If I leave the compartment, I'll wake you first. Really, there's nothing to worry about."

"Nothing to worry about. That's true for you, Lance. Easy for you," I said. "There's no risk for you. It wasn't your family they put on the train."

"That's done," he said.

"Yes, done, indeed." I pulled away from him until he was at one end of the seat looking out the window and I was at the other, my head against the cold glass. "It's easy for you to say, it's done."

The glass was so very cold it took an effort to keep my head against it, but it was very satisfying to steel myself against any discomfort.

"We don't have the same name, Lance Decan. On my passport, my name reads Daniella Stonebrook Blue." I considered each word quite carefully, needing to make myself plain, the way one does with strangers. "And our clothing is not intermixed in our luggage. All my things are in my cases and your things are folded very carefully in yours. Except for our itinerary there is no reason for anyone to assume we know each other. Yes, Lance, of course I put my address, Devils Peak, not our Mountain address, on my passport; I didn't want to implicate you in any way. I will expect the same consideration from you, if the tables are turned. I wouldn't think you would want to take me down with you. Would you? No, I don't think so."

He was looking at me as if he didn't understand the drift of my conversation at all. Why didn't he understand? It was perfectly evident what had happened. We had visited three death camps since we'd been in Germany. Lance's brows tightened in a mixture of perplexity and anger.

"It's very simple, Lance. If they come for me, we don't have to acknowledge that we are partners. We never got married. Intermarriage pollutes the race. Who says that? Everyone. My people say it. They have always said it. From the beginning. The Nazis learned it from us.

"'We promise not to give our daughters in marriage to the people around us or take their daughters for our sons. We promise. . . .' I read it, Lance, I saw it, in Erfurt. When I couldn't sleep, I read the Book. Isn't that why it's there? Isn't that what you're supposed to do? It said promise, so I promised. I promise you, Lance, I promise your mother, your father, your grandmother, your grandfather, your everyone . . . I won't contaminate them, I promise."

The words burst out of me like artillery fire. The guns of the tanks swung in our direction. One tank, two tanks, four tanks, eight tanks, ten. . . .

"You don't think I'm a . . . you think I'm an American. Yes, well, you're an American even though your family comes from . . . but, you must realize, that I am not an American. But, you're right, I must pretend I'm an American. So if they stop us, I'll say, we're both American and we're on a business trip, trade representatives, considering making an investment in the new Poland—as soon as it's established—next week. American entrepreneurs. We'll say we want to be in Poland at the right moment to take advantage of the political changes we expect to occur."

"Don't be absurd, Daniella. You're a scientist and I play the flute."

"Yes, my passport says I'm an astronomer. It doesn't matter. There's an observatory in Krakow, not far from Auschwitz. It's really simple, Lance. You don't have to be ensnared in my life."

"It's over, Daniella," Lance repeated, a little white rage slipping out in a bit of foam between his clenched teeth.

The train picked up speed. We were going very fast, very fast, fast enough and with enough torque to hit another dimension—the past. We were losing time and history was gaining on us. I could smell it rising from the grind of steel against steel, our speed increasing and the wheels clanging beneath us, the cars swaying in the momentum and the dark.

"Before your parents died, they didn't really tell you anything about your grandparents, did they Lance? How do you know what's in your blood? Isn't that what they said about blood? Doesn't it tell? Yes, blood tells. They said so. Your great-grandparents came from Frankfurt, didn't they? They were pure. We don't want to pollute them, do we? Maybe we'll look for their neighborhood on our return so we can see where you came from. After we spend this month visiting the other death camps, seeing the sections my people lived in, then we'll go to a nice neighborhood in West Germany and see where you come from. You have the perfect background and a clean profile. Yes, I do have red hair and green eyes, but you know, a lot of Jewish women had red hair. You can tell, can't you, that I'm not Aryan. Anyway, the conductor knows. I could tell by the way he looked at me and how long it took him to peruse my passport while he barely glanced at yours. And if I pretend otherwise, they can get a blood test, can't they? Why would you want to get mixed up with me if there is going to be trouble? You can always get off the train. You can go back home. But I can't. You can, but I can't. You can . . ."

"Stop it!" Lance grabbed my wrists and pinned me down, when we heard a crash behind our heads as if something had fallen against the wall in the compartment next to ours.

Then we heard a woman's voice. Another bang and her voice again. Then we heard a man's voice, murmuring, and then shouting. The voices and thrashing mixed. They were making love, tossing about in the bed, mixing endearments with cries and little shrieks.

"I am with you. I am your partner." Lance was looking intently into my eyes, emphasizing each syllable.

But I was listening intently to the noises from the next room. The two of them were rolling around the bed and every moment or so one or the other crashed against the wall and groaned. Once or twice her voice elevated but we didn't understand a word.

Lance took his little soprano recorder from his pocket, but then she cried out again and he put it away before I could tear it out of his hand. Her cries penetrated us both though we didn't know what the words or cries meant. The sounds of a body crashing against the wall increased. Now it was definitely a body, not two bodies, crashing. Love can be violent. . . . The woman cried out and the man yelled back. Or he yelled and she cried out in answer. Who could tell? And then the thrashing again, sharp impact, slaps perhaps.

We didn't know what to do. I pressed my head against the wall trying to discern the nature of the cries. Trouble or pleasure? We sat there listening to the sounds, immobilized voyeurs. We said nothing, did nothing until our paralysis was unbearable.

We have to do something, I was thinking. I could see that Lance thought the same. If there were blows, they were increasing. I was pretending it was pleasure. Every time there was a cry, I hoped it was the final pleasure and blessed the silence. But then there was another crash and another cry. It went on interminably. "You know German, your grandparents . . ." I said.

"Only a few words," he said already up and buttoning his shirt, "but they're speaking Polish."

"They're not speaking." I answered.

There was a particularly piercing cry from the woman. Lance darted out of our compartment. I followed him. Four or five men were standing confusedly before the door. When they saw us, they shuffled uneasily, except for a thin, tall, blond man who was leaning against the wall, smiling superciliously. The type of man who pretends that he can take care of everything perfectly, if everyone else would simply leave it to him.

"What shall we do? What are you going to do?" I asked desperately. None of them spoke English. They were more embarrassed by my appearance. "Do something!" I demanded and they stepped away so that Lance could break through to bang on the door. Just then an officer appeared in the aisle asking for passports. The men gesticulated to the door, the blond man smirked at me, then turned on his heel and disappeared while the officer knocked perfunctorily, used a master key and entered.

The woman had been beaten. The officer insisted the two of them leave their room and stand in the corridor. The woman and the man stood there, as instructed, shivering before the open window. He only had pants on. She was trying to disappear into a faded salamander rayon robe, graying strings poked through the unwinding maroon tassels of the belt. Wind mixed with rain blew her hair off her face and formed a veneer of small droplets on her cheeks and forehead. Her makeup had run in black lines down her cheek toward the flimsy robe she had quickly donned. The man had his arm around her. He was kissing her tenderly on her face and stroking her hair back, whispering to her in Polish. I wanted to stay in the corridor to protect her, but I couldn't. I didn't watch them for long. Watching, even to protect her, seemed impolite, intrusive.

"I know this train, No Name. Lance is sleeping and won't be bothered if you raise the shade and look out the window. What do you see now? How many tanks did you count, No Name? They intrigued you. You did count them the way everyone counts something; the numbers of stars, and the number of bodies in a box car or the number of living carcasses walking toward the crematorium.

"I rode in a tank once and hated it. That's why I liked the guard tower at

Auschwitz and paid a guard in cigarettes and whiskey to let me take his duty some nights. I liked being in the open air.

"Well, No Name, did you enjoy this evening? You had a ringside view, didn't you, of what it was like to be what you call a good German. How long were you eavesdropping on the couple next door? Did it turn you on? Why didn't you save that little girl before she got beat up? Were you afraid of making a scene? Of being laughed at? You don't know the language. That's a lame excuse, lamer than any of the ones I heard people give. It's not like your life would have been on the line for knocking on the door. Or even knocking on the wall when she was smashed against it. And your honorable Lance's little flute, did he expect it to cover the sound? A little Bach tune to modulate the Wagnerian rhythm of drums, cymbals and blows from the other compartment?

"Or did you think it wasn't worth it to interfere. That's how they are, gentiles. Gentiles are like that, they get drunk, they beat their wives, they're stupid, they live those kind of lives. I know what you felt, No Name. You felt horror and the horror made you numb. You felt nausea and so you took a bite of cheese and a cracker, left over from your elegant hotel lunch, and washed it down with a warm beer. I also ate well when I could. I also told myself it was useful for me to remain alive.

"I took this train and then another train and then I was in Auschwitz. I was almost a doctor at the time. Almost. And I was an officer. These were very compact roles. The train was crowded. And the rails were crowded with trains. And then behind us or before us were other trains with other passengers who weren't seated quite as comfortably together. They were crowded in. Several times a woman gave birth in one of those cars where no one could move it was packed so tightly. If they were packed in tightly enough, they would ultimately hold each other up; that was the theory. Maybe it was kindness. Like the kindness you extended to the woman in the next cell, not to intrude on her privacy. By the time I was on the train, my heart was already squeezed into a ball.

"Are you following me, No Name? Good. A heart squeezed into a ball. It glows red hot. Hotter and hotter. And if it gets squeezed tighter, which it undeniably will, it will get smaller, glow hotter, get smaller, and before it disappears, it will pull everything surrounding it in its direction, will pull everything in to itself and then put out the lights. You are following me, aren't you, No Name? Of course you are. You wouldn't be here if you weren't following me. What is it, Daniella, about my heart which draws you so close to me now?"

Let me catch my breath, Cardinal. It was then and this is now but then and now converge, science says, they are not separate, past and future, we do not distinguish them. But let's pretend we can separate them, let's wait for them to separate themselves out like salt precipitating out of a solution. Let's talk about other things. About space, let's say. Space is empty and still not empty. The stars and the galaxies aren't fleeing from each other, rather space itself is expanding and carrying them along. That's the first thing.

This is the second: Space curves around matter. Space which is emptiness, also curves, or better said, is curved. It is curved by matter. Matter of a certain density exerts an influence on space and curves it, bends it around itself. It pulls space toward it, wraps space about it. Matter does that. Sometimes we say that light bends as it moves through a field, but really it is space that is bent and light, traveling through it, well, it takes the shape of the bent space.

Matter. That is, place. Place, therefore, is a force. This train. The camps. Forces. These places twist everything down around them.

Do you understand? Astronomers, physicists, when we talk about these things, we don't understand. Only to say that place, pulls, bends everything to it, even what is unseen, even what is empty.

Something else, Cardinal. Sometimes matter shines, radiates, but sometimes it does not. The universe may be darker than we think. It may be full of cold, dark matter. Ninety percent of it. This may be its nature. Cold, dark matter which doesn't radiate, doesn't shine, doesn't give off any light, unless, we can speculate, it is compressed into a point. I once thought the universe is shaped by light, but it isn't. Most of what is out there is dark and pulling on us; the denser the matter the more the space around is shaped by its presence.

I tried to crowd against Lance or pull him toward me, almost on to me. No sounds came from the two people in the next compartment. No one walked the train corridors. I heard only the continuous metallic drone of the train wheels against the rails. I didn't want to sleep alone in a berth and told Lance I was afraid. But when he turned in his sleep, I slipped under him so that I would know what it felt like to be crushed by a body. Under his weight, I begin to withdraw, to recede, to pull in. Under him, I curled up into a ball and my spirit contracted accordingly.

Does it matter any more, Cardinal, if a single individual lives or dies, is born or erased? When you count each one of the stars on a photographic plate and give each one a name—that is a number—it is because you want to have a record of that star, and not, necessarily, that you care about the star particularly. Sometimes, on closer examination, you discover that the star you are staring at is not a star really but rather a galaxy or a quasar. Then you may warm to it temporarily, give it another name that is another number and set it aside to investigate later. If it is a galaxy you try to go inside it with your telescopes and cameras, to measure it, to count the number of stars, to see their particular configurations, movements and relationships to each other, to note their color and, thereby, their age. You make precise records of each individual point of light, but not because you care about that point of light particularly, or believe it is speaking with you about the ways it sees itself, but because you want information to support your theories and their applications. And if the light goes out, you note that as well, when and where and how. But you do not think about the light itself. You just do the job.

"Because it's a job, No Name?"
"Perhaps."
"Because otherwise someone else will do it?"
"Perhaps."
"Because this way has superseded all others ways, made them obsolete, disrespected, irrelevant?"
"Perhaps."
"Because what you might learn another way has no currency in the society at large and at small."
"I don't know another way. My colleagues say, they like it better this way. It's not as cold. They like the comfortable quarters and the clear dials and luminescent screens and how far they can see."
"Don't you mind the cold?"
"Not very much. I find it invigorating, Peter."
"Only because you don't know what cold is. If you had stood all night in one of those guard towers then you would know what cold is."
"I don't think I would have had to be in a guard tower to know about the cold."
"You don't know anything yet about how it was, so don't speak about what you haven't known."
"Are you telling me not to speak?"
"Yes, No Name, I am telling you to *sveig.*"

Fevered dream images tortured me on that train ride. In some, I was counting the stars endlessly and hopelessly. Despite the floodlights, the night remained the night. And the little yellow stars lost their luminosity as they flowed through the gates and entered the narrow place. They passed, as the stars might pass, across the lens of a telescope, each flickering for a moment as it was given a number and then was sent on to oblivion. Sometimes one star called attention to itself and was, as it were, stopped in its path for the purpose of unusual observations. Maybe it gleamed more brightly than the others, or was erratic in its signal, or was a double star. Sometimes the color of a star like the color of someone's eyes was sufficiently intriguing to be selected for further study.

The train was arriving at a junction and a figure, a thin, tall, blond man, was counting the bodies of those who were able to move when they ordered us out of the cattle cars. At the last minute before the doors were opened, the yellow stars on our coats began to gleam with a light that should have blinded anyone who could still see.

That is the dream I remember from that train ride to Poland. The terrible dark in the car, the press of bodies against each other as the train lurched to a stop, and the yellow lights gleaming so fiercely, the walls dissolved in the light. Then I saw a man standing at the narrow place through which everyone would have to pass, counting, counting and counting. Sometimes I recognized the man but when I tried to remember who he was, I couldn't. Sometimes I was the man standing there endlessly counting, assigning a number to each yellow star as it passed across my vision.

Chapter 34

The train rattled on across the dark fields between stubborn rows of small brick houses fortressed against the constant din of the metal wheels along the metal rails. I put my head against Lance's shoulder and stared, unblinking, out the window. A tree swept by with its black bare branches grating against an aluminum sky. I hadn't seen stars for weeks.

Lance pulled me closer, and I folded into him, soft and dull as a rag doll. He wrapped himself about me, stroked my hair occasionally, kissed me on the forehead.

"What are you thinking now, Daniella?"

"It all feels so familiar, Lance."

"I don't know which is the worse torture, to be astonished by the unknown or the known."

"It's as if I remember, Lance."

"Maybe you overheard more between your parents than you realize. Otherwise why would we be here? Maybe you remember what your father saw."

"Will you sleep, Lance?"

"When you fall asleep. Or I'll sleep in Poland. You sleep now." He adjusted my weight against him; it made me feel like a child. Lance fell asleep immediately. Somewhere near the Polish border I fell into a stupor and it became Peter's night outright. A train. A dark tunnel of night. A stranger's voice that was becoming so familiar that, in the trance of the train wheels, I dreamed he was a friend.

"This is the train, Peter?"

"Yes, this is the train."

"This train goes to Poland?"

"Yes, it still goes to Poland."

"It left on time?"

"It always leaves on time."

"Do you remember Poland, Peter?"

"I remember Poland."

"I remember Poland, too."

"You remember, No Name, because I remember."

"No, my grandmother came from Poland and so I remember through her memory; she is in my cells. From the stories she told me about the cold."

"It was very cold."

"In the summer, Peter?"

212 %* The Other Hand

"There was no summer."

"Because the smoke blocked out the sun?"

"Yes."

"The fires blocked the sun the way light blocks the stars. Is that what you mean, Peter?"

"I don't mean anything. When will you understand?"

"I understand."

"You understand nothing, No Name."

I thought of waking Lance, but then I didn't. The metal wheels clacked hypnotically and I went down and down and down into the dark.

"I can't see any stars."

"Do you want this to be easy for you?"

"Don't for a second think this is easy for me, Peter."

"Think of how exceedingly unpleasant this is for me."

"Didn't you expect that you would be tortured after your death? Didn't you expect to be punished?"

"You are my punishment and my torture even if my life was already a punishment. If I expected anything, it was to have been to been redeemed. Isn't that what one gets from suffering?"

"From your suffering, Peter? How could suffering redeem you?"

"Why not? Is my suffering any less than yours?"

Metal against metal against metal against metal.

"And so, we are going back, No Name. You want me to see it through your eyes, No Name, through your very, very beautiful, oh so green eyes. How rare for a Jewess to have green eyes. How Mengele would have loved to study you, to see the relationship between your so very beautiful eyes and your very odd brain. You would have gotten special treatment, my dear. And that is what Jews want, isn't it, special treatment?

"I forget myself in your green eyes. Let me begin again. I have to see it through your eyes because they are the only eyes I have now. How amusing, No Name."

"This is unbearable, Peter."

"'This is unbearable, Peter.' Do you think I created the world, No Name and do you think I can fix it for you?

"What are you feeling, No Name? Are you feeling dread? Whose dread do you think you're feeling? Do you think its mine? Which dread then? The dread I felt on the way to Auschwitz the first time or the dread I'm feeling now as I return? Of which dread shall I relieve you?"

"Or is it your own dread of seeing with your own eyes and so you imagine I'm dragging you into this. One way or another, it's my fault, isn't it?

"Close your eyes, No Name. Go to sleep. Forget it all. Tomorrow you can be a tourist in Warsaw; it is a beautiful city now that it has been restored. Even in April, you can stroll across the plaza to sit outside of a restaurant at a little table under a red and green striped awning that says *Cinzano*. Sip an aperitif. Order caviar, yes, or smoked sturgeon, whichever you prefer. You don't want to be among tourists? Then sit on the banks of the Vistula and dream of the beautiful future."

Dear Cardinal, you know this train; it keeps going no matter what. It never gets derailed. It is never late. It never stops. We are on the train. Peter and I are on the train. Now you and I are on the train. Soon I would be in Warsaw. Soon I would walk along the river, just as Peter said. Soon I would be in Auschwitz, just as Peter said. Soon I would sleep at the Karmel. Soon I would sleep in the bed where you had slept. Soon we would be in the same bed.

Is this your dread about returning to Auschwitz? Or your dread returning there with me? I turn to you in order to blot out Peter's voice. I turn to you for comfort. Do you feel anything but the dread I feel? Whose dread is it, Cardinal?

Chapter 35

Dear Cardinal:

When I heard stirring in the train compartment next door, I tiptoed out without waking Lance, carrying a scarf, not something I'd bought to give away but one of the few things I'd bought for myself. Before we left California, I'd surprised myself by lingering over a counter of silk scarves because I was usually too preoccupied to bother with "such things." I had been in a hurry and I had stopped and I had been late for my appointment because I couldn't decide between a paisley pattern in magenta, plum and sapphire and a bold geometric design so ultimately I bought both. The paisley for Lance, I had thought and the dark green triangles, coral circles and white squares floating on a field of sea blue green for me.

Toward dawn, I was writing and rewriting a note in my mind and finally settled on something simple: "I'm sorry, I didn't act in time. I will act quickly next time. Consider me your comrade though we may never meet again." I signed it with my name and address, crossed out "comrade," inserted "friend" above it and sealed the envelope. The note was in English, of course, but I couldn't do better.

She was startled when she opened the door after my knock. I simply handed her the scarf and envelope hoping those elementary forms might be of some help to her. She spluttered something in Polish as I said "I don't speak Polish, I only speak English. I'm sorry." We smiled awkwardly at each other, both embarrassed, and she shut the door quickly having taken the scarf with the instinct even a woman has to catch a fast ball. Porters appeared like apparitions conjuring cardboard pyramids of orange juice, which I bought, two for her indicating that the porter deliver it, and two for Lance and myself. Then within minutes we were in Warsaw.

Looking behind me when we exited the platforms and entered the train station, I caught her eye and she set down the two suitcases she was carrying to wave tentatively to me while her lover continued marching forward, eyes focused directly in front of him as if any deviation would unbalance him, the rest of their worn luggage, and the order of things. What I wanted to do then was to set down my own luggage and run to her so we could weep on each other's shoulders. Instead, I smiled back, nodded, and continued walking. Her greeting relieved me as I'd been afraid that I had humiliated her again by giving her the scarf. I'd been clumsy; it wasn't only the language barrier. If I had been sincere in wanting to make amends, I would have put enough money into the envelope so she could get away; one more time my good intentions had gone awry. I hadn't had enough practice crossing into intimacy with women and wasn't there something intrinsically overbearing about a tall, broad boned, professional American woman standing in the doorway of someone else's small sleeping room extending a delicate silk scarf?

Lance didn't see it that way. "Two good deeds with one gesture," he teased, "You reached out to her in friendship and you gave away the right scarf."

There were no porters so we followed the crowd through the station, down a flight of stone stairs, through a long tunnel, its tiles yellowed with grime, then up some stairs again to the outside where, as it turned out, we were only a few blocks from our hotel.

An exceedingly large man with bandaged feet, which made him seem even more gargantuan, was begging near a red banner under a chalked red "A" for anarchists; so decidedly odd, he was an advertisement for them and they for him. I had never seen such a giant of a man, or such feet, or so much political graffiti or so much red bunting. We gave him an American dollar from the cache in a paper envelope we had prepared for such occasions and went on, though I regretted I had not given it entirely to the woman. Solidarity announced itself on every wall and post. Red was everywhere also; it jumped out from the gray dawn, it curled about lampposts, flapped in banners, stretched like tightropes across streets, flashed in traffic signals, blazed in lapel buttons, and paraded down the street in a pair of socks, a jacket here, a scarf there.

Our rooms were not going to be ready until noon so we transposed our East Berlin ritual to a morning routine, moving from the dimly lit lobby to the restaurant and back to the lobby and then back to the restaurant lingering over the now familiar Eastern European breakfast of sausages and cheeses. People bustled in and out of the hotel lobby stamping their feet and shaking the rain from themselves like dogs. Intermittently, Lance studied Polish the way he had studied German, welcoming any activity that might engage his newly acquired, "good morning," "thank you," "where is...?" "could you please...?" By the next morning, he would be greeting the hotel clerk, the waitress, and the beggars in their native language. This time I was one who stood up ready to run. Lance opened one eye: "Will you be okay? Don't tell any Polish jokes," and dozed again quite unselfconsciously in a very American sprawl over a yellow plaid couch while I pushed hard and impatiently against the revolving hotel door into the drizzly streets.

For so shabby a street, the boulevard was exceptionally wide, a business-like street, efficient and functional. Several blocks from the hotel, the Soviets had erected a monstrous edifice, a Stalinist monument of the postwar period that could have been designed by the Nazis. It was a wall of a building; an impenetrable monolith of brick. I looked for my beggar and the antidote of his gigantic bandaged feet.

"Ah, the romance of poverty, No Name. Why didn't you bring your camera, so that you could capture the misery of a failed country? Color photos so the red can inspire your colleagues at home to calculate the red shift to see how quickly this country is streaking away from everything else in the universe."

I quickly lost interest in the buildings and the shop fronts. Faces captured me. Everyone looked like my grandmother. Even the young people. I could see how they would look when they were older. They walked quickly but I managed to catch each face, then age it before I let it go. The skinny young men intrigued me. Blue jeans and sweaters, occasional ear studs, facsimiles of New York, London and Paris.

"You like those faces, don't you? You like the little caps the men wear. You like the particularities of the lines on their faces and their darting eyes. I can hear your thoughts, No Name. A relief, you say, from the stolid German faces you found so oppressive. What is it you like so much in Poland?

"You find the men attractive? Lively? Do you like that one? How about the young boy coming toward you with the torn sweater? Or that one with the leather jacket? Tough but intelligent. Or that one with the scar across his cheekbone? What do you think got him? A bullet? A knife? A club? Oh look, he's eyeing you. Maybe he knows you. Maybe he wants you. Or that one, maybe he hates you."

A young man shifted away as we approached each other. Had I spoken aloud? Or was he merely unnerved by my close scrutiny, by the momentary fearful widening of my eyes?

This is how it begins, Cardinal. Someone stalks you. It takes a long time until you are aware of him. Then when you're certain it is happening, you begin to watch out for him. You begin to look for him because you are more comfortable knowing where he is. Soon you are as focused on him as he as on you. After awhile, you don't dare take your eyes off him. You don't walk out of a door or into a room without looking for him. Soon you have eyes for him only. He has entered your consciousness completely; there is a way in which the two of you are never apart.

One young man after another walked by quickly. There was no end of men twenty and thirty years old who glanced sideways at my red hair which I had decided not to contain with a scarf. Lance said it wasn't the color which was so startling as the abundance of it. I had thought of getting it cut, of taming it for the journey, but at the last minute I didn't.

I played with ventriloquism, placing Peter's voice in each young man walking toward me. It was a dangerous game, as it wasn't my voice I was projecting but Peter's sneering voice coming at me from all directions. I walked in the din of it, shifting my weight quickly, flinching, avoiding first this one's eyes then that one's. As it got closer to noon, or as the neighborhood changed, the crowd thickened, women rushing to shops, men hurrying to lunch counters and a man in a dark coat brushed against me as he jostled his way forward through a small opening behind me. I didn't mean to gasp, his weight was on my shoulder only briefly, but my fear was enough to make him reel around and grab my arm. He said something, "Excuse me," I suppose, and steadied me while reading my face and understanding something, invited me to coffee in awkward English without either of us slowing our pace, so that instantly I was commandeered by his hand on my arm, first pulling at me, then directing me through the crowd.

"No, please," I stopped, "Peter," and pulled away from him. He wouldn't let go of my arm, jabbered at me in Polish now, repeating, "Peter," first smiling, then tugging at me playfully, repeating, "Peter" with amusement, then tightening his grip insistently until I had to wrest myself out of his grasp, and when I turned and started running back toward the hotel, he stood still in the street gesticulating like a man who had been robbed, berating me with a flood of Polish words whose specific meaning escaped me but not their intent.

"You've been running," Lance sprang up to his feet when I came into the lobby.

"I was suddenly so tired I thought I'd better run or I would fall down asleep on the sidewalk."

"They've just readied our room. I was trying to decide whether to wait for you or bring up the rest of the luggage. You get the other key and I'll get the other bags." He pushed my hair back from my forehead. "You do look exhausted. We have a room overlooking the river." He picked up two small bags in one hand and a large suitcase in the other hand and gently nuzzled me toward the desk. "Mmm, rain," he murmured, wetting his cheeks against my hair. "Your hair is on fire with rain," he whispered as we walked to the elevator, "it's burning my lips."

"Ssh," I whispered turning toward him and catching his lips against mine as the grinning elevator operator took the luggage from Lance's hands.

When we entered the room, I started to cry. "Guess what?" he said, "I met a lovely man who speaks English quite well. He taught me a few words so now I can make love to you in Polish, my darling."

I continued to cry. "Cry all you want," he held me tightly. "I cried myself, Daniella, when I first got to the room. It is so neat and comfortable, as if the worlds we are revisiting never existed here nor anywhere."

Chapter 36

"I have to sleep, Lance."

"Sleep until dinner time," he said, "then we'll find a meal somewhere, take a walk along the river, and come back to sleep again. By tomorrow you'll have recovered."

"What will you do?"

"I'll read or study Polish until you're sound asleep then I'll practice. Don't worry about me. I'm holding up better than you are. I've got my flute but it's been so damned cloudy, you don't have your stars."

Though it was afternoon, I put on a nightgown, brushed my teeth, washed my face, and lay down spread eagle across one of the beds.

It was becoming impossible to be with Lance and avoid Peter at the same time. I thought sleep would relieve the situation, because Peter began counter conversations when Lance was speaking to me and when I lay down, Peter continued to whisper. When I was dreaming, he entered my dreams. In one dream, I was fascinated by a great golden lion. Within seconds, I heard the report of a rifle. The lion was dead. Peter stepped out from behind an acacia wearing boots, khaki shorts and a hunting helmet. The uniform of the German hunter in Africa. "Your prize, Madam," he snickered. "Shall we send it to a museum?

"Not your prize? But, Madam, if not for you, it wouldn't be dead."

One dream burned feverishly into the next. The young boy who had given me the tulip kept changing into the boy who had razzed me in the park. Polite tones turned into abuse but when I responded angrily, he became kind and looked at me with remorse. Sometimes his tulip was a flower, then a red rude tongue, sometimes it was artillery fire. Finally, I leaped toward the boy whomever he was, and began to smack whichever face presented itself to me. First one, slap, and then another, slap, and then the first again or the other or both, blows following upon blows, as the faces presented themselves, leering now, daunting, and I hit them again, though I was exhausted and wanted to stop, but couldn't because when the face appeared, I had to strike.

I woke up but caught myself before I opened my eyes. By the feeling of light in the room, the intensification of gray, it was about 4 o'clock. Lance was playing "Afternoon of a Faun." I pretended to be asleep and invited the plaintive tones to act as an antidote to the dream; I couldn't believe I had been provoked to violence.

In the half-light of sleep, the music faded and Peter's voice eddied into my consciousness. He began to talk and I could not protect myself from him whether he was speaking in the hurt voice of a young man or in the sneering tones that had become so familiar and mercilessly unnerving.

"Smack my face? To correct me and set me straight? Is that it, No Name? With a swift blow you'll knock me back to the young, sweet innocent boy I once was, is that right? I was innocent, wasn't I? Everyone is born innocent, isn't that what you think? I was innocent and went sour in a country that was once innocent and went sour and you were born innocent and are still innocent born to a people that were born innocent and stayed innocent. Isn't that right?

"You're good and I'm bad, right? Evil doesn't exist but I caught it the way someone catches a flu, right? Or evil exists and I was born from it, it was my mother or my father, or evil exists and I consciously chose it, or evil exists and it overwhelmed me and your people suffered the consequences, is that right?

"Stop trembling. You don't want me to know how much power I have over you, do you? You're not being strategic. Oh, you're shaking because you hit that innocent boy. He was just a boy and you tried to beat the hell out of him and that upsets you.

"Do you want to know that little boy you abused? I'll tell you about him; then you can believe in him. Is that what you want?

"Here is he. Look close. Isn't he sweet? Do you see me?"

I thought I did. I thought I saw a hand painted tintype. Pink cheeks. Deep set blue eyes. A cloud of blond curls. Except for the sailor suit, I wouldn't have known if it was a girl or a boy.

"So very angelic, aren't I, in the blue sailor suit my mother bought me for the photograph session? Only it wasn't quite a suit at first, but a sailor blouse with a little navy blue pleated skirt to match the long blond curls she doted on. I was so sweet then. I was quite small and she only dressed me this way on special occasions and, of course, only when my father was away which was almost always after 1914 the year that I was six. My mother wanted to preserve my sweetness, she said. It was her God given duty and though she wouldn't admit it, she was relieved that my father was away at the war, secretly believing he was a bad influence. Most of the men were.

"Whenever my father was home, he was, naturally, out of place in the house my mother so carefully furnished to enhance innocence. He felt reproached by the little china figurines whose future he was either threatening or wasn't protecting well enough, or annoyed by the constant correction emanating from the embroidered homilies which she hung on the wall or stitched into pillows or wove into the tangle of antimacassars she had draped over the arms, backs and seats of chairs. We always had our asses on her good intentions.

"When father came to the door, mother darted around nervously, clearing a place for him, anticipating his slightest wish so that he didn't smash some favorite gewgaw as he swung his arms reaching for something he wanted or stretched out his restless legs into a tumble of toppling footstools, end tables and newspapers.

"One evening, I was crouched on the floor drawing, lost in an array of colors and paper, when he entered unexpectedly. Having settled into the only space large enough for my papers and my outstretched body, I was effectively blocking the path from the front door to the other rooms which were quite tiny and cramped with furniture. He had nowhere to maneuver because on both sides of the doorway were china closets where my mother kept her dinnerware trousseau which, with the petit point cushions, rosewood chairs and dining room table, she considered her great treasures. They confirmed her rank in the world and she, in return, protected them with the Kaiser's ferocity.

"He could have stopped and waited for me to gather my things and get out of the way, but he had already caught himself from stepping on me when he had opened the door, and my father was a soldier, trained to stop for nothing. Quickly assessing the situation, he stepped over me onto the papers, crushing a few pencils under his shoe, and in that same gesture, bent down to sweep me up onto my feet which he stomped upon so I couldn't get away. He had slapped me twice before I turned my cheek to the thrill of the blow, then forbade me to play with paints ever again and ordered my mother to cut my hair before she served me supper. When he let me go, I walked slowly to the bedroom the way I had seen my mother walk to their room after such a whack, only I didn't throw myself on the bed. Instead, I picked up a school book and huddled over it in my chair. When it was safe to move without inciting him, I crawled to the closet where I hid my violin behind my mother's fur coat and evening dresses, which she stored there as her clothes overflowed all the storage space in their bedroom. If he were to see it, he would step on it with great relish and there would be no replacement. My great uncle had made it and my father despised him.

"Do you feel pity, No Name? Of course, your mother must also have encouraged you to paint the world in rosy pastel colors. And where did it get you? You're here anyway, with me.

"Don't feel pity for me, No Name. It's misplaced. I understood my father when I was older and he was dead. I would come in from having spent the day walking in the rain, or climbing the nearby hills, and I would feel the same constriction of hot damp air as I opened the door in the room which never had the windows opened and I would find myself faint, all my blood vessels contracting from the smell of garlic and onions, pork, dumplings, wet laundry, furniture polish and piety. Then my dear mother would come at me, the perpetual smile fixed on her face, asking so very tactfully if I had found a job, stroking my hair back, just managing to stop herself from wetting her fingers with her tongue and wiping a smudge from my chin as she used to do when I was her babychild. Behind her were those framed adages she had embroidered in Gothic script and decorated with cross stitched little lambs and piglets that smiled at me sweetly from the walls. Bless Our Home.

"She was a good woman, yes? She meant well, yes? If only I had listened to her, yes? Would you have liked me then? Is that what you imagine I really want—is it, No Name, for you to like me? Shall I wait with a red tulip in my hand for you to come and visit me in my miserable cold apartment in Erfurt? And then what? Then you'll give me a smile and maybe a dollar or two from that precious envelope of yours and send me back to my mother's arms with a little tousle of my blond curls. And then when I'm grown you'll expect me to work hard, just as my mother expected it, so I can support her since my dead father didn't have a pension, and in my spare time I'll try to earn enough to make a dent in the national debt and contribute to the reparation payments which we owe because of my father's behavior, of course. And you'll think of me fondly and admire my industriousness.

"And the violin? 'Play it on weekends,' you advise me, after I've finished my studies. 'Play your violin dear,' you will think, or go for a nice walk in the country to refresh yourself, and try not to get too tired so you can go to work on Monday.

"Listen, bitch, when you're in the small room of a cramped apartment, No Name, and the little woman is hanging on your arm because she likes to be cozy, you have to slam her against the wall to keep from suffocating. Then she whines and cowers, and begs you to stop, but you know she likes it because she set you up; wasn't she the bitch who cornered you in the first place?"

I felt the slap and pulled back, but not far enough to avoid the next blow so I pushed away and hit back until the dream confused my blows with his blows and there were only hands and smarts, hands and blows.

Shaken out of my sleep, I cringed away from Lance who was holding both my shoulders. "Wake up, Daniella, you're having a nightmare." He had had to jostle me quite hard in order to awaken me from the dream which, he said, had set me moaning and tossing my head from one side to the other.

"What was I dreaming, Lance? Could you tell?"

And then I was asleep again.

I was on the train again. I was on the train again. I was going back to Germany. The train was going down faster and faster. It was being pulled into the center of the earth. I tried to wake up but I couldn't. And then I did wake up but I was still on the train which had picked up so much speed that the earth it sped past on its descent was as red hot as its metal sides. I was still asleep and woke up onto a train landing and picked up my suitcases, one in each hand, and then someone put a suitcase on one shoulder and another one on the other shoulder and before I could protest, he threw a harness over my head and I staggered under the weight of yet another valise, this one slapping against my back. When I woke up again I was walking on the street in East Germany and saw my college friend Alma walking toward me. I had forgotten that she had moved to East Berlin. She threw her arms about me and invited me home to have tea with her. I didn't want to go but she insisted. I suggested that we call Lance at the hotel and he would meet us at her house but she thought it would be most friendly if we had a little tête-a-tête, it had been so long since we had had anytime together. When I came to her house . . .

It was awful, Cardinal. Being asleep was awful and awakening was just as terrible. I kept my eyes tightly closed against the late afternoon light praying that I was home, that I would see blue sage when I opened my eyes, that I would see those very pale blue green leaves and the purple blossoms. What I saw out the window was Warsaw.

"I can't get up Lance, I'm exhausted." The words were spoken before I opened my eyes.

"You've just awakened." Lance was unable to disguise his disappointment. I'd also slept the entire afternoon the day before.

"I haven't recovered from not sleeping on the train. Anyway I dreamed again."

"Tell me your dream. I'll help you with it."

"Please don't help, it only makes it worse." Then, I relented. "It was snowing. I was so pleased. Snow, so late in April. The 20th. Hitler's birthday.

"Happy Birthday to you. Happy Birthday, to you. Happy Birthday, dear Hitler . . ." Trying to tell the dream, I was feeling quite mad.

"I can't remember, Daniella, do we go to Linz?" Lance interrupted. "It's shocking there is so little mention of the event except some small concern about pro-Nazi demonstrations in Linz where he was born.

"Yes, Lance, we'll be in Linz on the way to Matthausen. All too soon. But then we'll go to the Alps." Now I wanted to continue.

"It was the 20th and I met my old friend, Alma, on the street just after I exited the train station. I liked her in college but was too shy to pursue a friendship and so nothing came of it. Now she was living in East Berlin."

"Why didn't we visit her?"

"In the dream, Lance. In the dream, she had just married a German man, Peter." I stumbled on the name aware that it was the first time I had mentioned that name to Lance. "But her former boyfriend, whom I also knew, was living with them. She invited me to their house for tea.

"When I entered, I realized that the boyfriend and the husband had had an altercation and the young man was about to be punished. The husband asked me to discipline him since I am going to be living with them from now on. Alma looked pained, but shrugged and turned away. Her husband gave me two broken sticks. I was to shove up one up his ass and beat him with the other. I asked to speak to the young man alone. When I closed the bedroom door, I said, 'Listen, we know each from before and I want to be friends.' His face lit up.

"Peter," I stuttered again, "was hopeful. I stared into his eyes, but I don't feel pity. When he begged me for mercy, I said, 'I want you to act like a man.' He was crestfallen. I continued to speak to him as if he were a child needing toughening. Then I turned my back on him. As I walked into the next room, I was aware that this man had been tortured and would continue to be tortured and I would not say or do anything."

I paused desperate for Lance to do something, to say something.

He hesitated as he does before a concert so that the sound he made as he spoke would be exactly right, so that the breath and the note would fuse into a pure tone as he wanted to be one now with his voice. But, of course, the sounds that came out of his mouth in a hotel room in Warsaw could never be right. "My dear, dear Daniella, what, who is torturing you?"

"Don't say 'dear.' Don't say, 'dear, dear.' Don't patronize me." The slap of his hands against his thighs instead of my face had the ring of a defeated man.

"I'm not the dear one, Lance, I'm not the one being tortured. I did the torturing. I told him to shape up and take it like a man. I turned my back and walked away."

"How can someone so smart be so stupid. Daniella. You are torturing yourself. Alma, is your *soul* sister. You were once too shy to befriend her; now you get a second chance. She invites you home, but can't protect you, or herself it seems, and you blame yourself. The Berliner tortures the former boyfriend, the Daniella who doesn't care about her own suffering, they're all versions of self torture, sticking a bloody stick up your own ass. Let it go, Daniella and let's get out of here. We're going out."

"I don't understand."

"True, you don't understand. But I do understand and I'm not going to be a witness to you torturing yourself. That's not why you dragged me here."

"If you think I dragged you here, Lance Decan, then leave. Remember, you invited yourself along."

Lance could see the abyss before us. Seeing it didn't prevent it from yawning open. Didn't prevent me from running toward it and didn't prevent him from leaping into it himself and pulling me after him. There is something very attractive about the abyss. One is not alone there. Lance knew he could not, must not, stay out of it.

"I didn't do this to you." he said firmly and bitterly.

"And I didn't invent this." I answered. "Catastrophe is democratic. We all suffer the same end. No one is singled out for destruction or redemption, Lance. The universe will be crushed in a fist and everything with it, even your beloved, noble Johann Sebastian Bach."

"This isn't only yours, Daniella. This is not only about you. Not only about yours," he stammered out of frustration and anger. For once, he couldn't gauge my response and I wouldn't help him. "Dammit to hell. What do you want, Daniella?"

I couldn't answer him. Though I was sitting up, I closed my eyes. He was trying to sound reasonable. "Look, Daniella, it happened that some of us . . ."

"Which us?" I lashed out at him. "Which us? Your people? That us? Or are you trying to be part of my people? Do you imagine there is an *us* between us?" I wouldn't open my eyes.

He reached out to me. I knew what he wanted. He wanted to make an us. I pulled back.

"A fist closed around us once in this century and you say it is coming back again in another form—time, this time, the universe itself crunching down; let's be easy with each other, Daniella."

"What would you like?" my voice was sharp and bitter. "What shall *we* do? We we we we we. . . ." Neither of us could stop ourselves.

"Lance, shall we go out on the town tonight to that elegant restaurant your friend suggested? Shall the three of *us* drive around the city in a taxi before dinner to see the historical sites or the nice empty shops? Shall *we* drink vintage Hungarian wines? Shall *we* smoke a cigar with *our* brandy? Shall I put on the pretty dress I brought with me to delight you just in case *we* had such an opportunity to enjoy *our*selves? Shall *we* pretend that nothing happened to *us*. Shall *we* pretend . . ."

You couldn't say, Cardinal, that he struck me. That wouldn't be accurate. You couldn't say that his hand over my mouth was a violent act. You couldn't say that his hands on my shoulders pushing me down on the bed were violent against me. You couldn't even say that he wanted to silence me or that he hated me for hating us. Or that he was sick to death of the journey we had only just begun.

But you could say that there was violence between us. You could say that violence surrounded us and that we could not walk through it without being contaminated. You could say that there was no way to avoid it. The miasma of brutality and violence had slid through the floorboards and cracks of our relationship like a fog of poison gas.

The man, Cardinal, who had merely witnessed death every day from behind a little sealed window wasn't innocent. The man who watched until he was certain that every last person in the gas chamber had succumbed wasn't innocent. He wasn't innocent though he did nothing but watch evil. From the very first moment he saw it, from the very first sight of it, he was affected forever: he was the man who saw it, the man who was watching, who had been willing to watch, and then he became the man who watched it again. And again. And again. Until he could not be distinguished from it; until he could not remember that it was anything but routine. Until he accepted it as life and then, perhaps, even as right. He was not innocent.

There were some, like Commandante Hoess of Auschwitz, who admitted to being nauseated in the beginning, others who threw up violently the first time. As it happened, Zyklon-B was developed as an anti-nausea remedy for the soldiers who, standing alongside the mass graves and shooting so many people at one time, particularly women and children, were physically overwhelmed. Zyklon-B was ultimately more efficient and required fewer participants and witnesses, thereby sparing the soldiers their daily bouts with stomach upset. But even those who were nauseated, each of them succumbed gradually, the poison seeped into them whether or not they witnessed it or participated again. In the process of acclimating, whatever poison didn't seep into their bodies, seeped into their minds.

I had returned to Buchenwald in order to peer between the drawn lace curtains into the little house where Ilse Koch had lived. The woman who had lived in that house, had had prisoners flayed to make lamp shades from their skin. When I had returned, I had pressed my nose against the glass and though I couldn't see anything, I could feel something, an unquestionable presence, the unmistakable odor of evil.

My grandmother, like so many of her neighbors, had had a little figurine of three monkeys, one covering his eyes, the other covering his ears, and the third covering his mouth. See no evil, hear no evil, speak no evil. I liked the monkeys when I was young because I disappeared the world by closing my eyes, then miraculously reconstituted it through the voluntary effort of opening them again. Teaching me to read, my grandmother would point at each of the words on the metal base, and then laugh at the monkeys' wrong advice: "Just like a monkey not to want to know what's really going on," she would giggle, "Don't ever be a monkey, Dani." But was this tongue in cheek? Wasn't I being raised to be just such a monkey, Cardinal?

Peering into Ilse Koch's house, I had sensed evil and was afraid, really afraid. Not for my life. For something else. Maybe what people call their soul. In a single moment, my first conscious perception of evil coincided with a first conscious consideration of soul and I didn't know how to protect it.

Maybe Shaena was wrong in this one instance. Maybe it is right and proper not to see evil. Can evil exist without our conception, perception of it? If you don't believe in it. . . ? Not that one is oblivious to the occurrence of evil acts, but if you don't *believe* in evil itself, as an entity, an independent force in the universe, does it exist? What do the theologians say about this, Cardinal?

Heisenberg and Wheeler saw how directly we influence the universe, even create it by our observations and perceptions by the questions we ask, let alone the experiments we engage in. If one never believes in evil, then evil, at least for that one, is never substantiated.

As a scientist, I assume that knowledge protects me. The more knowledge the better. Aram and Rosa don't think that's true, they believe in innocence. Not in its existence, but in its necessity. And you, Cardinal? Do you *believe* in the Devil? Isn't that what the Inquisitors asked? You were damned if you did and damned if you didn't.

If, one day, you think about evil for the first time, if you recognize it where you never saw it before, if you name it, identify it, define it, do you, by those actions, bring it into being? Do you conjure it in that instance? If you think about it, point your finger at it, examine it—are you, by those gestures, unavoidably contaminated by it? For example, my colleagues speak of the radiant time before "matter *contaminated* the universe."

Nothing stops. Nothing is finite. Nothing is independent of everything else. Everything is a chain reaction. My mind reeled with numbers and formulas all pointing to doom.

We did take the day off. Lance insisted. After our fight, I was pliant, that is . . . subdued. We walked around the city, listlessly. We sat in the drizzle by the river. We ate in the hotel restaurant. Lance drank Polish mead after dinner. There was a Yiddish Theater, he suggested we attend. I was terrified and he desisted.

When we went to sleep, he took me in his arms. I did not resist but there was no spark in me either. He held me, that was all, and when he was fairly certain, judging by my less agitated breathing that I was asleep, he whispered to me that he loved me, that I was safe, that he would protect me because he loved me. He did this for hours. Years of practice, of playing music while I slept elsewhere, years of devotion, had inured Lance to fatigue. He was determined to care for me even if it meant that he had to do it at night, in stealth. And I heard every word. I had not been sleeping at all. Years of pretending to sleep while he played had prepared me to receive his love. I let it fill me, I bathed in it. But in the morning I was empty again. I had become a sieve, it had seeped out of me and, once again, I felt desperately alone.

"I apologize for being unable to go to dinner with your friend Marek, last night," I said upon awakening, finding myself on one side of the bed as far from his side as was possible, which meant that I had, after his long lullaby of loving, still willfully extricated myself from his arms. Because I never lied, it was obvious to both of us that this apology was a lie, and, therefore, in some way it wasn't.

"It doesn't matter at all," Lance also lied and, again, we both knew it. Lance tried to reach for me and I leaped away, aware that I was developing a taste for violence in lieu of his tenderness.

"This is arbitrary for you," I said getting out of bed and enjoying the sting of the very cold floor against my feet. "You can walk away from this, Lance. You could have walked out of this, if you had been here. I couldn't have walked away."

"Please, Daniella, not this again. I am here."

"Well, just remember that I didn't ask you to come. You decided to come on your own. And you can leave on your own. You have that freedom. *You* do."

"Not again, Daniella. Please. I don't have any more freedom than you have. Not as long as I am allied to you. So, don't start again."

But I was back in it again, repeating the same words I had taunted him with the morning before. "That's your choice. Your privilege, Lance. To make an alliance or not to make an alliance. To be with me or against me. I don't have that prerogative. You can choose. I can't choose."

I saw his eyes fill with tears. He was bewildered. I was glad. I had him. He didn't understand, Cardinal because he wasn't in my situation and that made me even angrier, even more certain there was a unbreachable chasm between us. And as that was the case, I needed to protect myself, to be certain he remained far away from me. Over there. On the other side. With them.

"No, Daniella. I wouldn't have been able to choose. I choose you and about that I have no choice. If I had been there, just as if you had been there, I would not have had any more freedom than you."

We were both speaking very slowly as if the other was a child. We were both trying to explain the basic laws of our worlds. Lance insisted we were living in the same world. I insisted we weren't.

"You get to choose, Lance. I don't get to choose. Do you understand?"

"I didn't choose you. You are a fact of life, of who I am."

He paused weighing it all, weighing each word, seeing if what he said were true, accepting the burden of having to disentangle himself from what might have been considered his lineage, even his own people. Unbearable. Unjust. Necessary. He repudiated them. He did. I was asking him to skin himself alive. He did it. Slowly, deliberately, with great care. But, also he was outraged with me because I was oblivious to his sacrifice.

"Do you understand? Answer me."

I couldn't. I was defeated and could say nothing. And so Lance couldn't stop himself from gripping my arm too tightly and forcing me to look into his eyes when I wanted to look away. He was determined to convince me that he was with me and also to communicate his . . . rage. He wanted to think it was only frustration, only pique. Pique, merely that. A small and petty word for what he hoped was only a small and petty irritation which gripped him and which he couldn't shake.

But it was rage. He couldn't deny it. Rage. He pulled his piccolo from the sleeve pocket of his kimono and stalked off into the bathroom, slammed the door and played his own discordant variations on a theme, shrieking crescendos disrupting a sublime order, again and again and again until he was calm.

Meanwhile, I sat in a torpor glancing at the maps we had accumulated, making disjointed notes in my journal, half listening to his shrill tones, more like blue jays squawking, until Lance came back into the room and I got dressed and we went out to the very famous Jewish Cemetery of Warsaw.

Later, Lance recalled that on the train we had known it would happen eventually, but that we had also hoped it wouldn't and hadn't known what shape it would take, the explosion between us, the inevitable repulsion and then distance and then distrust, from which we did not know how to recover.

Chapter 37

Sometimes I forget that I am writing a letter to you, Cardinal, that you exist, are another human being, not someone I have desperately conjured and that you know this suffering more than I can imagine. Because I forget that I am writing to you, I can't imagine what it must be like to read this letter. Do you want a break? Lance and I had breaks, so to speak. Taking the train was to be a break. Going to the Cemetery in Warsaw was a break from the round of Death Camps, because some of the dead had been there a long time, had lived full lives, had had a personal death and were buried properly with their families in attendance and the right prayers said. I want to be cremated, the way Amanda was so I can go right up, the way Edith Stein did. In the next life, I would like to be a star. But you know that by now.

The first saint I ever met, Cardinal, was the caretaker of that Jewish Cemetery in Warsaw. This gnome of a man was devoting his life to the care of both the more recent and the ancient graves exactly in the place where as a young man he had been hidden, first underground in the catacombs of the adjoining Catholic Church, then afterwards back in Jewish territory in the tomb of a Rabbi until he could be passed by the partisans to the farmhouse of a Catholic Polish peasant where he survived the war. Underground warrens still crisscross this area. He had scurried under the ground to safety while, just as I was standing there at this moment, Nazi soldiers had been waiting to blow off the head of any rodent that popped its head above ground. Moshe, the gnome, had only been thirteen when the Germans had come to the Warsaw Ghetto, but, as he put it, he was fully grown when they left.

Yes, Moshe had lived underground, even if no trace of this history remained in his eyes which did not avoid light or contact, nor in his face which was ruddy, nor in his spirit which survived whatever it had suffered. I shut my eyes against the brilliance of the cool, noon light and tried to imagine the dark that had protected him, the dark which my grandmother, Shaena, had enigmatically implied was different from the night sky when she was explaining that the wilder Polish Hassids had sent the young boys who seemed designated for mystical vision underground after their Bar Mitzvahs to study sacred texts, to stay there for years preparing themselves in the dark to be lights in the world. "It's like the stars," my grandmother had said, "you can't see them in the light of the sun and maybe they don't influence us, until the sun goes down. In order to see the light, Dani, darling, you will have to go to the dark. That's one of the secrets."

I remember my impatience with her: "Everyone knows you can't see the stars unless the sun goes down, grandmother." I was never too young to be insulted by anyone's assumption that I didn't know the simplest things, "And everyone knows that the moon and the light of cities makes it difficult to see the night sky. Everyone knows that if you want to see the stars, you go to the mountains when the moon is dark and you put red cellophane over your flashlight when you need light."

"Yes darling, everyone knows that, but almost no one knows what it means," Shaena responded kindly.

I liked the man immediately. I wished he had been my grandfather because I never knew my mother's father who had died just after Rosa was born. My mother, quite in character, never mentioned him, and Shaena, who wouldn't dwell on loss, never spoke about him either. I half listened to Moshe's words as he explained the process of restoring the cemetery which was his life's work and passion, comforted by the flow of his voice and the complex mixture of English and other languages, Yiddish, German, Polish; though I missed as much as I understood.

Moshe's children had left Poland as soon as they were grown. Almost all the children of the very, very few survivors of the Holocaust had left. They had wanted him to come with them, but he refused. He visited them only rarely. They implored him to come, but he had so much work to do, he said.

"I'll never finish this work," the Gnome was saying. "I am trying to restore all the graves. Not only the new ones, not only the ones from that time, but the older ones which were desecrated and those which fall in because of age. Then I restore the records so that anyone from anywhere can find his aunt Sophie who died in the Uprising or her great-grandfather who was buried here two hundred years ago."

Near his little office, the graves were already ordered in neat upstanding rows. It was Moshe's intent that those who had died many decades earlier would be remembered alongside those who had died during the War or in the Camps. We walked up and down the rows among graves that had been restored and that hadn't, past unmarked gravestones and others pock-marked by bullets fired, Moshe said, as the Jews from the ghetto ran across the Cemetery trying to get to safety. Ojciec Zaloman, Matka Bronia Zaloman, Zosia Zaloman, Fiszel Zaloman, Henia Zaloman had died in Treblinka in 1943. Sonia and Micha Neuman had been shot in the Cemetery. Atan Szpenman had been killed by Hitler's men on October 5, 1943. He had been twenty-two years old. Benjamin Flanctraich was killed in Treblinka in 1945. He had been fifty years old. Treblinka is a moonscape, rocks and boulders for each village, hamlet, town, city huddle against each other, broken monuments gouged out of the earth.

In the distance I saw a man leaning against one of the larger gravestones, then reclining against the statue of Janusz Korczak who could have escaped from the Warsaw Ghetto but instead accompanied his young, orphaned students into the Death Camp. When I looked in another direction, I saw him again, loitering among the trees where the old gravestones leaned against each other. A breeze came up, the leaves spread apart, and the sunlight glinted off his blond hair. Though I acted as if I didn't see him, I kept my eye on him; I had to be responsible.

The sky was clear blue, too newly born and the grass on the graves and between the gravestones was already a brilliant and terrible tender green. Long first shoots were pushing up from about the tumbled stones.

"My grandmother came here before she went to Canada," I interjected into an awkward pause in the conversation. "She's dead. She was interested in Esperanto."

Finally we came to the grave of L. L. Zamenhof. "The death of a common language." Moshe murmured without sentimentality. We admired the blue tile star with an "E" in the center of it set in a field of small multicolored stones. Nearby was a headstone with a perfect round hole where a bullet had entered and exited. My grandmother's death sped into this graveyard like a missile. I was standing in her footprints. She had stood exactly here when she had been a young woman just before she had left Warsaw for the new world.

"Zamenhof thought he'd found a way for everyone to speak to everyone else and it made him happy even when he died," she had told me just hours before her death. And then I remembered, which was exactly what she, on her death bed, had instructed me to do.

"You'll see, darling," she had said. "Then you'll have to stop, look up, and say 'Thank you.' And then also: 'I remember.' Remember, Dani, everything we've all forgotten."

"Thank you," I said to myself. "Thank you, Shaena, I remember."

Upon the headstone with the round eye that looked out into infinity, there were two standing lions of Judea holding a goblet between them. The bullet had removed half the date of death:

O45.

I went on reluctantly. It is difficult to tear oneself away from hope. It was a spring day so even the air smelled of hope. But I had to leave it; Moshe insisted. He took me by the hand and steadied me—but not too much—as I stumbled in the smooth bowl of green grass which, he was saying, had been hollowed out with the weight of the women and children killed there. One could assume, he said, even forty-five years later that every declivity, every smooth, circular, or semi-circular decline in the terrain indicated a mass grave. Every large hollow in the Polish woods indicated that dozens, scores, even hundreds of people had been stripped, shot, covered with quick-lime and hastily buried.

I looked at the size of the crater, its width and its depth and began calculating the size and velocity of a meteorite which could have created it, what possible effects, if any, it might have had on the surrounding area. It is speculated that the last ice age was caused by a meteor that had fallen into the sea off the coast of Mexico. Some people are concerned with global warming, but it is just as likely that the smoke screen of emissions between us and the sun could trigger another ice age. . . .

Moshe led me away from Lance to the exact center of the bowl, suggested I sit down there, then begged off to his office, taking Lance with him. "You sit here," he said.

"People sit here and pray," he continued. It was as if I simply did as I was told. I sat down, I meditated and then I was looking through the very center of the earth and beyond it. Little yellow stars, hundreds, maybe thousands of them, I couldn't count them quickly enough, each one on a coat were flowing down through the stones of the cemetery disappearing into the earth. The yellow stars had always seemed so very far away, I had not been able to grasp that they belonged to me. Now as I looked down into the blackness of the spring day and saw that they were not, as astronomers think, light years and light years away, but right here at my feet, my flesh and blood.

Particles manifest out of thin air, out of a vacuum. Virtual particles become real, become particles or anti-particles. What was not there is suddenly there. That is how the universe came to be. Latent energy precipitated into particles and everything follows from that.

Lance appeared over the bowl, with his wooden flute in hand, like some damned psychopomp. He motioned to me to follow him, turned on his heels and walked off in front of me. I couldn't refuse him either. I roused myself compliantly and followed behind along a path which meandered through a jungle of trees and very old gravestones, standing, toppled and overgrown. The sun behind us cast Lance in dark silhouette. I became aware of his tight, lanky body, its rigor and tensile strength. The movements which had once reminded me of birches, *bjove*, the one Polish word I remembered from those few Shaena Baena had taught me as a child, now resembled the gait of a procession of bones. Following Moshe's very careful directions, Lance was leading me to a set of irregular stone stairs which had been recently uncovered. A set of stairs, Your Eminence, leading down to a door leading into the catacombs, your territory, Cardinal.

Some unexpected instinct of respect caused me to cover my hair with the silk scarf that I had tied about my neck. Against the cold, I told myself, for the cold was welling up out of the earth which had, until that morning, been gripped by winter frost. Here, Cardinal, underneath the church we began a descent.

The dark? An American cigarette lighter served as a torch and my eyes from years of looking at the sky easily accommodated to very, very little light. A match can loom as bright as the sun. Too bright, in fact, obliterating everything in its light, so that eventually we relied on the bare dusting of daylight as it penetrated the twisted passageway from the entrance we had left ajar until we were really in the dark, walking with our hands against the clammy walls.

A sound as of wind or clearing spittle from his mouth. From behind him I couldn't hear what he was saying. The words, if they were words, sputtered in a series of crackles and Ss. Something as innocuous as "ssh, ssh," perhaps, but perhaps not, perhaps something else.

"Why do you speak to me in German?" I asked, understanding the meaning of the words but unable to identify the language.

Another hissing "ssh," insistent and brutal that seemed to repeat my question: "Why do I speak in German?" Then another "Ssh" even more insistent.

"Why?"

"It is prohibited. . . ." I couldn't make out his words.

"Did you get permission?"

There was no answer. I tried to catch up with him, but he was always a few steps ahead of me. When I tried to run forward, I tripped, but he did nothing to support me and so I used the wall to stabilize myself and continued. "Lance!" There was no answer.

"Lance, let's go back." No answer. "What are we doing here?" No answer. "Sssh." Again. And the hollow echo of his heels clanging against the stone floor.

"What's going on?" I whispered.

There was only an undertone, as of water rushing among stones in an underground river. I put meaning to the sound: "You'll see. You have to stay with me now."

"I'm free to leave."

"Neither of us is free." The floor and walls were stone. I knew that by the sound of his heels. "Neither is free to leave the other."

I don't know, Cardinal, if we spoke any of these words. I remember this exchange but also the absolute silence and our increasingly muted footsteps. And then his voice, or a voice, but inside me, I think.

"Of the four forces, which is stronger, Daniella, the one which draws the parts together or the one which repels them? What does it take for one of the forces to overcome the resistance of the other?"

"I want to go back . . ." and then I hesitated. I had wanted to say, "*Lance*, I want to go back," but I couldn't say his name. No name came. Before me was a back, a generic, indistinct but specific male back, its incontestable strength explicit in the tension of the cloth about the muscles. What was before me were shadows, this terror, and the entrance door far behind us closing suddenly in the wind so that with a crash, we were in absolute dark.

How do you know, Cardinal, when someone will turn on you? How do you know, even after a lifetime together, that you won't suddenly suffer a blow which comes out of the blue? That he won't leave you or beat you? That one or another fellow monk won't turn you in to save his skin? That the Pope won't turn against you? Or that your lover won't stab you in the heart with the butcher knife or pour gasoline on you and set it alight? Or open the door to the gestapo? Or become the "sondercommando" who, to save his own life for a few weeks, will thrust you and everyone you love, alive or dead, into an oven?

And who was he anyway? Who was this man who insisted on being with me, on following me, on watching me when I slept? Lance, he called himself, but how did I know? Maybe he was someone else. He and Peter Schmidt were equally tall. They were both blond. They were both musicians. They both followed me. So how were they different and how could I count on it?

We went along in the dark. I wanted to turn back but I was afraid to go in any direction. I was afraid to be with him, whoever he was and afraid to leave him. I was most afraid to turn my back. I didn't know what might arise from the tombs I stumbled against as we went down and down through narrow, black passageways.

We tottered down a long time. Once he reached back and jerked my hand after I staggered against something and heedlessly cried out. We inched our way. I had no sense of direction. Then we arrived somewhere and, whoever he was, pushed me against the wall.

"What is it?" I asked.

He put his hand on my mouth to silence me. I couldn't recognize the finger tips, whether the pads had been formed by pressure against the holes of Lance's flute or from pressing the strings of Peter's violin. I heard the scrape of stone against stone, muffled, rubbing, clanking. The man was lifting something. Then he was leaning it against the wall.

The man spoke. "I want you to know something. I want to show you something. But don't speak. Don't make a single sound, no matter what."

He pressed his hands over my eyes, closing the lids. His movements felt rough and agitated. He took my two hands in his and without another word maneuvered me into a small, cold and dark space, removed my fingers which were gripping the edge, and closed me inside a tomb, replacing the marble door.

Why did I obey? What an odd word! Obey! I heard a thump on the outside, the door moving even further into place, and the soft scrape of a body leaning against it. I could smell his weight.

I hadn't been vigilant enough. Peter had won after all. And through Lance. Why hadn't I been alert? The contagion had spread. Why hadn't I expected it when I knew it was inevitable from everything that I had seen? Decent people had succumbed. Had been overpowered one way or another. Peter had overtaken me and then he had overtaken Lance. It had taken relatively little coercion or exposure. Why was I surprised? Lance had a delicate nature and he had not been warned.

Madness, he might call it later. Of course that is what he would say. Madness, the universal excuse. What else? That he'd been possessed. Evil had gotten him. He had tried to resist, but he couldn't. He was sorry. He would confess to his psychiatrist. He would be consoled. He would tell his dreams. His psychiatrist would nod, would purse his lips, would make small, sympathetic, but not too forgiving sounds. It would go on for days or weeks or months or years. Then someone who still called himself Lance would emerge, feeling fine and thinking he still didn't know exactly what had come over him. He would set it aside. He would find another lover. She would be so very understanding. They would marry. He wanted to marry, to have children. He would take a steady job in an orchestra, plant a garden, live a normal life.

I came to. I woke up. I came out of my trance. And then I didn't care that he had told me to be silent, that he had said it was prohibited to be here. Had said, *Verboten*, had said, *Sveig, Verboten, Sveig, Toit*. Without realizing it, I had fallen under the trance of those words. They had repeated themselves like a dirge. I had almost gone under. I was almost fully asleep when something awakened me. Something from within. Something fierce and primal, coming from far, far away. Hate.

I began to push against the door. I pushed and pushed. I couldn't dislodge it. There was a stone against it. Or his body. It was immovable. I put my entire weight against it, pressing my head, shoulder, hip, thigh against it. Through the stone, I could hear a flute.

Had he been playing all along? Whistling in the dark? Music, C#, D, F#, or whispering to me, sounds, music, voice, sentences, shouts, whispers, beseechments, threats, C# an octave higher, and another note, higher still, prolonged. . . . I banged on the door. The whispering continued, or a man's authoritative voice: "Don't you understand? Ssh, Ssh."

My hands were scraped and the sounds of my fists against the rough stone were only dull thuds. The tomb was cold. I could smell death in every pore of the stone. The flute again and then his voice again, his lips against the stone now, in my ear.

"This is how it was, or might have been, Daniella. You are in the dark and I guard the darkness."

Then I screamed and pounded my feet against the marble, shouting, "Peter, let me out, I demand it, Peter, let me out or I'll kill you. I can kill you, you know, and I will. I *will* die and I *will* take you with me. That is certain." Again and again and again, until someone removed the door and pulled me into his arms.

And lit a match. It was Lance.

"Peter? Who is Peter? Is it the man you dreamed, Daniella? I didn't want to terrify you. I didn't do this to terrify you." The match burned his fingers as he groped in his pocket for the lighter, without letting me go, adjusted the height of flame so we could see, and then found a candle on a ledge, half burned down, and lit it. "This, Daniella was how it was or might have been and my life would have been risked to guard you. Do you understand yet?"

I wanted to ask, "Are you mad?" but I knew that he was. Even by that faint light, I could see it in his eyes, could feel it, only it wasn't the madness I had imagined. It was the madness of a man who was sleeping alone in a bed, a man who was not permitted to touch his lover, whose loved one had become a phantom, the madness of a man who was helpless, who watched his lover pulled away from him, pulled out of the bed, violated, out of the door, gone.

"The two of us are here together in the dark, Daniella." He was trying to steady his voice. "Not you alone, Daniella. Don't you understand? Two of us."

I didn't speak but it didn't matter because I was holding on to him so fiercely, he didn't need to hear my voice.

"And if I am not always in the same dark place as you are, if I am not forced to be in the same place, still I choose to be beside you. I insist. And if it happens that I can escape being in exactly the same dark place as has claimed you, then perhaps I can use my position in order to protect you. Do you understand? In order to protect you, not to hurt you, not to run from you, but to protect. If you have to hide, then I will be beside you, hiding you. Do you understand?

"It is how I've always been with you. A little outside, like a star which circles another star, not to devour it, but to offer it some of my light."

"Now, Lance, play to me," I whispered to my poor crazed lover, the man I had not ever before called my lover even to myself. My poor crazed lover and his lover equally crazed. And he played. "What if they hear us?" I asked.

"Who cares?" He played and I put my head in his lap. I was shivering but so was he and we couldn't tell if it was cold or fear or madness which shook us. I could hear each individual note in a way that I had never heard music before. Each individual note and its relationship to the one before and the one afterwards. Each note by itself as if each note were the entire song of a bird, the entire song it would sing in its lifetime and the notes which followed or preceded it, the songs of the other birds, the entire canon of bird songs offered to me as one song.

We came staggering out into the light, blinded momentarily by the sunshine. Lance closed the door behind us and we walked, hand in hand, along the graves. It was still shocking, but also reassuring, to have climbed back out into a cemetery. I had to lean against a tree to gather my strength. We were looking at each other shyly when a small brown sparrow alighted between us, or fell actually, at our feet. Its proximity was unexpected and caused me some alarm. I couldn't imagine why it trusted us to come so close. Despite the training I had received from my father, it was Lance that first noticed that it was blind. Most probably, its eyes had been pecked out by other birds. Soundlessly, Lance bent down and raised it up toward the tree. It rested in his hand only for a moment and then took off, awkwardly but ably, finding its way by unseen radar to a higher branch and hid itself under the leaves.

Chapter 38

Lance's new friend, Marek, was a young man with romantic inclinations, who once again invited us to dinner in Warsaw. Once again I found the idea unbearable and offered, as sincerely as I could, to spend the evening by myself until I saw Lance's face cloud over and realized he was also in hell and I couldn't refuse. Marek had assured Lance that the new Warsaw was as charming as any city in Europe and Lance needed to be charmed. The evening was not as difficult as I had anticipated. Marek was not unwilling to talk about current or past politics, was even willing to speak about the war. Actually, it was as if he had been waiting to meet us so that he could speak about the occupation to those who wanted to know about the nightmare time. But he was, himself, somewhat like the city where the use of new bricks to reconstruct the old buildings created a plaza that was strikingly fashionable, a little too modern, a little too overt in its display of inviting shops and smart restaurants with flowering patios where tourists sat with many newspaper-wrapped bundles at their feet. His own renovated history just a little too bright and perky.

The next afternoon, when the sunlight fell in a brilliant stripe upon the bed in our hotel room and called us down upon it into each other's arms, Lance whispered "*Ich hub dir lieb, mein tierinke.*" As I tensed, I realized I was mistaken again, and that it was not German he was speaking. "I am learning Yiddish from Marek," Lance smiled as he unbuttoned my blouse, gently, one button at a time so as not to frighten me, so as to ask permission, so as to comfort me as he did so, folding me closer to him with each opening, so I would be safe and believe that he was taking me into his hands for my own sake, though also for his.

"His mother was a Partisan," he continued with certain fingers undoing the single button at my waist band. "She hid leaflets and messages in his diapers." He was removing my skirt carefully, rolling down my black tights. "You might say he was a Partisan himself, because she was risking his life as well as her own when she placed him upon the contraband in his stroller and pushed him to a meeting with her contact from the Ghetto." Then he covered my nakedness with the sheet and his very large, gentle hands.

"I love you, my dear one. I love you in a thousand different languages."

"How old do you think Marek is?" I asked.

"About thirty, I would guess, maybe thirty-five. Maybe forty. Why do you ask?"

"Because he wasn't born then. If he was in a stroller during those years, he would have to be at least forty-six."

"Then he simply looks young. Why would he lie to me?"

"Marek is asking you to forgive him, Lance," I said later when I saw how adamantly Lance repeated Marek's story as if unable to grasp my repudiation.

"For what? Maybe your math is off, Daniella."

"It's simple arithmetic, Lance."

"Einstein couldn't do simple arithmetic."

"I'm not Einstein, unfortunately."

After we spent the evening together, we both kept in touch with Marek. He would come to the hotel when he was in the neighborhood, often bringing us gifts: books about the Ghetto once, another time a white hand-woven cloth and then, towards the end, a pair of amber earrings that were like drops of honey for me. He guided us through the market places and translated the political speeches in the squares and the posters which were proliferating each day.

He had been very happy in our company and was not quick enough to wipe away his tears before I saw them when we were saying good-bye.

"I remember the last day in school when I saw my Jewish friends. We were told they were being transferred to another school and then I never saw them again."

"You were too young, Marek," I said as gently as I could, trying to imitate Lance's extraordinary delicacy.

"I learned Yiddish from them," he was undaunted by my objections, persisting with a charming stubbornness.

"I doubt they spoke Yiddish. Their parents maybe, if they weren't dead, but I doubt they spoke it except perhaps in the home."

"No," he insisted. "They spoke Yiddish, some of them, among themselves, and later, also among themselves, to defy the Nazis."

"You're not old enough, Marek."

"We're all very old, here, Daniella. The Poles are very old. We've gone through so much, you can't imagine how it's aged us. *Gloibst mir nisht*? Don't you believe me?"

"You could be talking Bengali, Marek, I have no way of verifying that you're speaking Yiddish."

"She doesn't believe that we're comrades, does she Lance? You surprise me, Daniella. You're a scientist. In this country, despite everything, the scientists have always found a way to talk to the world." He was taking on the mannerisms of Soviet Bloc scientists at international meetings. There was always an initial formality which resembled shyness and dissolved into ease. Behind this, like a wall hidden by shrubbery, lay another distinct formality, more cultural. Over time and vodka this eased into such exuberance it denied the existences of boundaries altogether and the physical laws of the universe were called into question, until, inevitably, we encountered another higher, fully fortified, electrified impassable barrier, the border between dimensions, clearly political. A wall so absolute it had become transparent. And that was it, except in the most exceptional cases which I had only heard about but had never experienced,

238 ❈ *The Other Hand*

when the camaraderie of work overcame all obstacles and that wall dissolved also into alliance with all its attendant dangers and confusions on both sides. I had never had the occasion to go that far.

The three of us knew that this would be our only meeting unless, by some miracle we couldn't imagine, he came to the U.S. During our very last moments together, Marek pressed a folded piece of paper into my palm and closed my hand over it so that I wouldn't open it in his presence. When we returned to the hotel, I saw it was a hand drawn map of Lublin, with the names of a few restaurants and careful directions to the ancient Jewish cemetery marked on it and a note.

"You will not be able to find this without a map," he wrote. "The Cemetery Zydowski is locked. You will climb over the broken wall—here. He had marked the spot with a "✡"

"You said your grandmother was born in Lublin. You will want to see the streets where she lived," the note continued. There was another hand drawn map with the names of the streets penciled in. "These are the streets you will want to see." He guided us with an arrow up one street and down another so that we would walk all of them. "First you will go up hill and then down hill. You can watch the sunset from here." There was another star. "You will find your grandmother's spirit here, I am sure," he had circled an area which included the cemetery, "if she has decided to return."

On the back, he had sketched his self portrait, the intense eyes contradicted the oversized smile. Underneath he wrote, "You are right, Daniella. We like to take more credit for helping during the war. Yes, I was not yet born in the war. Yes, now I tell you the truth. My mother was a little girl then. *She* pushed her doll carriage to the Ghetto. In *her* doll blanket were messages. This is *true* ! ! ! *My* grandmother, *she* was the Partisan, *she* told me. I am studying Yiddish from the oldest man in the Warsaw Synagogue. *Ich vil dir bedim gehdenken.* I will remember you both.

"Please remember me always as your friend, Marek Kulowcywk."

Chapter 39

March 1, 1989
Dear Cardinal:

Two particles collide and transform. This will not be their only collision. They will collide and transform and collide and transform for the course of eternity—that is the existence of the universe—carrying the memory of their meetings as they re-encounter each other in new forms again and again. Writing to you has become my life.

I started writing to you because I wanted to end the story by putting it on a page and sending it off as far away as possible. I live at the edge of the high desert. Land-locked. Send it away. Across the ocean. But it isn't getting away from me, only you are being brought into it as well.

I am writing to you, Cardinal, from Devil's Peak but really I am writing to you from Poland. These days this cold, normally as light as a vision of stars, has become the cold of the weight of dark matter pulling all of one's warmth into itself like a furnace built in a world of anti-matter where everything is not as it is here. When I was in Europe, I didn't know what was coming, but this time I know.

The night sky is dark instead of being filled with light because most of the stars are so far away their light isn't reaching us. Also some stars have already gone out and nothing more of them is forthcoming even though their light bathed us once and is continuing to some more distant place in the universe, arriving elsewhere. Sometimes the light of a dead star will first appear in our sky in the form of its birth and we will not know the difference.

Darkness may not be merely the absence of light. Perhaps dark matter is transmitting its darkness to us. Perhaps the blackness of the night is a radio broadcast from dark matter. The light and the dark then, emissaries like the Magi, are the past, coming toward us, landing here, entering into us.

There must be consequences from this. We can not remain the same. We can not claim to be immaculate.

And what of the past, then? Is it altered in the process of insinuating itself into its future, by having arrived finally at this destination?

Lance and I began to live in the graves. Yes, there were hotel rooms and restaurants, and gas stations where we waited on long lines to fuel our little Italian rented car for which we had been allowed to purchase enough coupons to get us where we wanted to go, but not further. But our lives were in the cemeteries that we visited one after another, and what happened outside the graves began to seem peripheral just in the way that cemeteries in our countries lie outside our daily activities.

I had been looking toward Lublin because my grandmother had been born there. I had thought I might rest there, in her arms, eating cookies and drinking tea. She would explain it all. How it had been, how it would be again. But Lublin didn't smell of her or taste of her and like everywhere else we visited, I didn't want to be there.

I developed the habit of clinging to anonymous things. Entering a hotel room, I silently repeated, "bed, chair, dresser, closet." To reassure myself, I touched everything, opened every bureau, counted the drawers, the knobs, the contents. It was remarkably comforting to count the hangers in the closet, the towels and wash cloths. If they were white, I said "white." I said "two bath towels, green; two hand towels, green; one shower mat, green with black stripes; two water glasses; three pillows; two extra blankets, yellow, blue; one luggage rack," as if I were telling the beads of a rosary. If I were really upset, I heard myself saying, "one luggage rack, five long straps, four short straps. Slap, slap, slap."

After the tedious process of checking into the hotel, hanging up a few clothes, and itemizing the furniture, I bolted to the park across the street. Walking down the little paths, I was relieved by the spring green but then I had to return to the room because I found myself stumbling over trees and plants, unable to remember their names. I couldn't stop the litany; two women, one yellow scarf, two pair of black shoes, one brown purse, three trees, one pine, two green benches, one ice cream wrapper, one drooping calla lily, one garbage can. . . . I cleared my mind with an effort of will like inhaling a draught of ammonia only to feel myself falling again into the fixation of counting.

There was a woman in a hospital room across from my grandmother who kept shouting: "Help me. Help me. One, two, three, four. Help me. Help me. One, two, three, four." The Nazis kept impeccable records of goods confiscated, people arrested, delivered to Camps, disposed of. So many shoes, so many fur coats, so many watches, so many eye glasses, so many gold teeth. That's how they made a world. Past, present, future, statistics, predictions. Room numbers, birth dates, magic numbers, serial numbers, lucky numbers, blue identification numbers tattooed on arms. One two one two one two one two.

Back in the room, the numbers increased and I had to go out again. Lance remained behind reading a book. I walked through the park frantically tracing and retracing a figure eight of paths until they became familiar. Then I faced due North and quieted myself by standing still. Shadows extended as the sun went down. For a while, I could tell the time, then blackness.

Maybe nothing is faster than the speed of dark. Torrents of particles pass through us virtually undetected. SN1987 explodes and neutrinos stream toward us, piercing our bodies, the earth, moving on, leaving no trace. Or black holes pull on us, shaping our orbits, keeping us in check, sometimes eating us up. The dark matter problem, my colleagues call it.

Dark matter is the ultimate mystery; ninety percent of the universe is invisible to us. Astrophysicists who predicted we would know everything by the end of the century, have received a reprieve through the discovery of dark matter. Axions, photinos, cosmions, gravitinos, brown dwarfs; which of these chimera account for the weight of things? Fifteen years, they forecast, and we will understand it all. Twenty at the most. Longer seems inconceivable. Mystery is something to be dispatched quickly by a science which insists on the known world. What we can't know is exiled and lives beyond the pale. The known world is small but secure. Very few live in both worlds.

My grandmother's death was a final luminescence while Peter Schmidt's reentry, his disturbing reincarnation, was the fluorescence of dark. I have not escaped dualism, dividing the world into good and bad, valorizing one way of being over another. I also seek the comfort of daylight, the relief of stars, approve the necessity of sunlight and deplore what will not reveal itself to me. Did I expect sunlight and warmth in Lublin just because my grandmother had been born there?

The peasant woman in the black dress and sweater bending over at the base of the hill was picking dandelion leaves and her faded gray striped apron was full of green leaves and yellow flowers. The light striking the blossoms bounced up illuminating her face leaving a faint yellow glow the way a buttercup held under the chin of a little girl may cast a circle of light—an essential proof, my grandmother taught me when I was small—of the existence of a secret lover. Both Lance and I tried to get directions from her to the Cemetery Zydowski but, even though we showed her our map, spoke loudly and softly, used charade signals and hand motions, we failed to communicate what we wanted until she hailed an old toothless man, and in a torrent of incomprehensible Polish, put us in his hands. We attempted to speak to him, to show him the paper, but she interrupted with another long jet of Polish and waved us on so insistently, we understood we were to be silent and follow him obediently.

A long narrow road, dirt and stone, wound below the torso of the hill following its inclinations. On the other side of the road where it was flatter, we saw occasional old stone houses, the kind my grandmother's mother might have inhabited. Along the hill itself, there were remnants of the truss of an ancient wall. Cables, field stones and dark ochre bricks were deeply embedded in the earth in some areas and bulging away under the pressure of the collapsing earth in others. Along the top we could make out lines of barbed wire contoured to the hills' sagging curves.

The man without teeth smiled at us, encouragingly, but, when out of sight of the old woman, we offered him the map once again, he spooked and pushed it away. Again we were asked to understand that he was to lead, we were to follow, though he was not opposed to communicating with Lance in German, but it was not about where we were going.

The man was complaining about World War II. He had been twenty—judging by the number of times he flashed his callused fingers—when the Germans came. He had fought one winter against the Germans. He put an invisible rifle to his shoulder and trudged through knee deep snow, sleeping many nights in ice caves. His infant son had died. After the war, he had another but he continues to worry about him, to this day.

I expected the story to go on, but we had arrived at the top of a hill where he deposited us very ceremoniously at the door of a Church after knocking loudly at the heavy wooden door. When the prelate appeared in his long black robes, the man spoke to him with the same passion as the dandelion lady, and was, it seemed, equally convincing, for the prelate nodded and bid us wait. As I gave the man some dollars, he took my hand and traced a star of David on my palm and closed my fingers of it.

"Zydowsky?"

He laughed displaying gums mostly. But it was a hearty laugh nevertheless without even a twitch of his hand to hide the emptiness of his mouth. And shook his head again and again as if the shaking would bring on more laughter. Then extended palms facing down, he wiped the air with his hands moving back and forth tenderly along the line of his hips by which I understood that the Zydowskies had been finished, and if he had been Jewish, he would have been finished too, and so crossed himself and nodded with relief.

"Zydowsky," I said, pointing to myself, formally giving such information for the first time in my life. He jumped away as if he hadn't known. Was he afraid of being in the proximity of someone Jewish or protecting himself from the taint of the returning dead. He crossed himself again and scurried away.

In the meantime, the priest had donned a heavy gray sweater which didn't quite cover his belly and was unraveling at the elbow and, pulling a dark hat down about his ears, set out the front door, motioning us to follow. At no point did he allow us to catch up with him, but carefully preserved several feet distance between us. Within a few minutes we were indeed outside a gate that led to the ancient Jewish cemetery. Before we had our bearings, the priest extended his arm in a gesture that was unmistakable; he offered us the cemetery as he pressed a key into my hand. It was rightfully ours, he had only been its caretaker. Then he bowed to us courteously and, like the old man, similarly scurried away.

When he was out of sight, we turned to read the sign written in Polish and in Yiddish or Hebrew. It clearly indicated that we had arrived within the hours that the cemetery was open, but it was locked. Confused but eager, I ceremoniously tried the key in the lock; it didn't fit, it didn't come close. A hasty examination of the lock showed that it had not been open in months, perhaps years.

"He must have known." I was shocked.

"He knew." Lance agreed.

We took out the map and saw that we could follow Marek's instructions, by making our way back along the hill, counting the trees and the broken walls, until we found an outcropping where a brace of bricks had shifted under the pressure so as to form stairs, and the barbed wire was loosened so that it was accessible. After a cautious glance in all directions, Lance mounted the stones and hoisted himself to the top and put out his hand to me. I didn't take it.

After the hill had been sliced shear to create the road, the earth had been contained in wire and then contained once again by bricks which by now had fallen away here and there, creating precarious footholds. I leaned against the earth, my face and body pressed into it for leverage, and stepped up to the first ledge, feeling my gray flannel skirt—my mother's, the one my mother had worn for so many years at the piano—fall back to the top of my thigh, as my knee bent to the climb. I grabbed at roots, as I brought my other foot up until they were parallel and slid my right knee up to the next foothold and brought my left foot up to meet it, grabbing at whatever I could along the way, everything except Lance's outstretched and empty hand which extended like a dead branch.

When I got to the top, and bent under the barbed wire which I did allow Lance to hold up so I could crawl under, my right side had the stain of damp cold earth, a dark swath from my hair to my boots. I stood up and surveyed the area; the cemetery occupied the entire knoll.

Lance was preoccupied, having dropped some canisters of film he'd shot earlier. He was searching all his pockets again and again and then the area we had just climbed. It was gone. Lance was going back toward the car to look for the film.

"Give me an hour," I said.

He was startled. I could see apprehension in his face. Nevertheless, he agreed.

"I'll return in an hour."

"Stay away for the hour whether you find the film or you don't."

"Okay."

"Don't come back early."

"I won't."

"But don't be late either, " I added in panic.

He was observing me carefully. I wished I could reassure him, or explain but I couldn't. The priest had given me the cemetery. I wanted it.

Meanwhile, I was already investigating the empty bowl of earth just before me. Looking toward a small grove of trees, my eye was grabbed by the leg of a doll embedded upside down at the far edge. It was a porcelain pink, common both to dolls when I was a girl and the girdles and waist length brassieres Shaena Bluestein used to wear. But, it wasn't a doll when I got closer to it, having been careful to walk around the circumference without being pulled in, only some pieces of molded plastic. I slipped through another barrier of old, mangled wires and crossed the long, soft, new spring grass to the old graves.

It wasn't long before I came upon the first toppled gravestone, surrounded by high grass. I could not read the Hebrew but there were two crowned lions of Judah on hind legs facing each other, a wine goblet etched between them. It said 189. . . . The fourth number had been shot out.

I followed the old gravestones, fallen and scattered about my path like dead kids, and continued to the top of the hill. Then, finding that I was level with the upper street and could see across into the buildings, and therefore could myself be seen, I slipped down the hill in another direction. I was weaving between stones, some of which were still standing, but all of which were pock-marked with bullets, when I found a shelter under a tree where the pelvic bone of a goat, chalky with weather, had been slipped like a wedding ring onto a green limb.

I ran my fingers along its milky surface, rubbing the powder into my pores when I heard the rustle of silence behind me and swung around. Peter Schmidt was standing there laughing.

"Where are my horns, Peter, is that what you're wondering?"

"You're skirt is stained. You sidled up here on your hands and knees just like a . . ."

"Like an animal. I bet your mother didn't nurse you, did she?"

"I outgrew it, but I meant like a snake." He smirked. "You sent Lance away?"

His voice intrigued me. Like his body, there was darkness in it, negative space. Here he was, the man who had been following me through Europe; the man who had lurked in the doorways, or passed me on the street in Warsaw, or slunk out of the corridor of the train, or had sneered at me in Buchenwald. My past. My self. I wanted to see him better. I felt myself drawn closer. It was incomprehensible. I stepped closer. I wanted to touch him and see what he felt like. Curiosity, tenderness, lust, inquisition? Science or sexuality? Which?

"How much closer do you want to get, No Name?"

Sexuality, Cardinal—I must tell this—is irresistible magnetism, millions of years of evolution enacting the only drama there is: Continuity within flux, the paradox of shifting identities within the constancy of the species, the cellular necessity of the other, the graver dangers of narcissism and inbreeding. I was seized by a spasm of attraction followed by revulsion as I drew myself back violently from the brink. Death and carnage forbid the instinct; he was dead; he had committed murder with the hope of genocide. He would still have liked to kill this one who got away and yet he couldn't help himself either, he hadn't been able to resist the centrifuge that had cast us together and now he was also pulling on me.

I reeled in, that is, away, but didn't know what direction was safe, where in and out were, where he was, I was, where we were already joined and where we might separate. Fear of falling, snakes and the dark are imprinted on the infant's brain before birth. He could feel my fear but he could feel the pull as well. I didn't have the subterfuge that every other person has—the ability to dissemble, to disguise a split second of sordid inclination. He was outside now, but still inside of me. He knew everything. Could read and relish each flicker. And what he didn't know from within he knew through the laser-like telepathy of the dead.

I quickly saw we were two different people despite everything because he was managing to observe me from the sanctuary of his guard tower. From his perch, he detected each twitch of deception. Poised as if there were no shadows in the very center of the yard of his mind, the slightest movement on my part, let alone an involuntary leap, was noticeable. And despite my determination, as firm as any I attributed to the most tight-lipped and unyielding of his victims, a part of myself plotted escape *and* reconciliation. The male spider mates knowingly offering his head. The wildebeest admiring the taut movement of the lion approaching her, head down, ruff raised, the determined and insistent slouch, patient, precise, calculating, exact, hunger and desire so refined as to be pure magnetism, ineluctable fate—the wildebeeste's neck to the lion's mouth: socket, plug, fit.

I determined to turn off my cells one by one. I invoked a body of steel. Shining. A Brancusi sculpture. Bird in Flight. Movement unmoving. Utter stillness.

Peter's greatcoat was unbuttoned. His uniform was perfectly pressed. It was exact; it had beauty to it, the cold eros of perfection.

For a split second, I worried that I had ripped my tights and they were laddered by jagged runs from knee to ankle.

"Vanity, No Name? It doesn't become you. You'll never make a silk purse out of a sow's ear."

"What do you want, Peter?"

"Finally we're alone, No Name. Why don't you call your grandmother to protect you? Do you want me to find her for you? We found everyone. I even found you, didn't I? Or did you seek me out?"

"What brings you here? Isn't that more to the point? What do you want Peter?"

"What do I want, No Name? Once again you play innocent."

"You need me, Peter. I can live very well without you."

"Apparently that's not true, though you would like to believe it. Prey and predator? Which one are you, No Name? Don't answer. I know your preference. Your clothes are filthy but your hands are clean, isn't that right?

"I kill and you don't. That's the way you see it, right? You're good and I'm evil. Right? You're essential and I'm dispensable. What are you doing with me then? Who am I to you? Why did you seek me out, No Name?"

The only word that had come to me in all the hours I had already spent in the camps was "Why?"

"If one doesn't cull the herd, the animals run all over each other. They fight for a blade of grass. They foul their nest. They become ill. Lice appear. They gore each other to death. They kill for the females. They cross the species barrier and mongrelize. They eat their young. Sometimes they cannibalize each other. One species begins to dominate. It takes over the habitat. Other species go extinct or degenerate. Mutants appear. The land is quickly exhausted.

"In too small a space, the natural world becomes grotesque. Circumstances become such that someone has to make a decision to manage species and maintain the balance and sanity of nature. Isolate the offending species before it takes over everything. Sterilize them to prevent genetic contamination. Punish anyone who reproduces with them. Hunt so many, allow so many as prey, domesticate others for labor and production, protect others on preserves, select several for zoos. Place a few outstanding genetic prototypes in reserve. Designate some for research and experimentation. Breed a few for special studies. Dispose of the excess with maximum efficiency.

"You don't go through a herd of reindeer or a pack of wolves that must be eliminated interviewing the individuals about their preferences or ideas. That was one of our mistakes; they're so seductive with their alternatives and their tradeoffs. If you can't get all members of the species, you place a bounty on their heads. Keep them in control. Develop antibiotics and antivirals. Keep track of transformations and disguises otherwise you may not avoid a plague. Sometimes you see an exceptional specimen, green-eyed, robust, and you separate her from the herd in order to investigate her qualities, the illusion of her breasts, the fantasy of her cunt, the mirage of her mind, but ultimately she must be sacrificed for the good of the whole. We don't know how she re-produces, how she may enter into us. After such a contact, it's not easy to re-impose order. Sophisticated solutions are required. Sometimes you have to mobilize all your energy and intelligence to achieve your goals. If you aren't vigilant, the disease will break out, will wipe you out and everything that matters as well. Survival is a science as well as an art."

"It could happen to you, Peter. You could be culled."

"When the rats begin to organize themselves in armies, I'll worry."

"What do you want, Peter?"

"Oh, I forgot, you wouldn't interfere with anything. You never set a rat trap, did you? You never killed a fly. You never pulled weeds in your garden. You don't eat pigs. You never use antibiotics, disinfectants. You don't use insecticides. You don't approve of crop dusters. Your father taught you to leave everything alone. You never keep yourself apart. You don't take anything for yourself. You don't take anything that could be used by anyone else. You let everything be overrun, don't you? What's vermin, No Name? A species run amuck. First it's a pest, but then. . . ."

"What do I want, No Name? Why nothing more than to be at your service, madam! The past serving the future, isn't that part of your grand design?

"What do you want, No Name, isn't that more to the point?"

"I don't want anything from you Peter."

"To the contrary, No Name, you want everything. Explanations, reparations, restorations. Then you want self-examination and abject apologies. 'Down on your knees, Peter, see the light.'

"Then like everyone else, No Name, you want knowledge. You want to see into my mind. You want to dissect it. You want to see through my eyes. To know everything."

"To the contrary, Peter, I want you to see through mine."

"Yes, of course. You want to impose your view on the world. That's what we thought. And you're determined aren't you? Bravo!"

He stepped toward me. The man was wearing black leather gloves and pointing his second finger as if it were a pistol toward me and then over the hill a few miles toward the barracks of Maidanek.

He began to speak again.

"I want to make you an offering. I come bearing gifts: I bring you the dead. All this is yours."

"You've never brought anything else," I said, then waited. "Look at it from my point of view, Peter."

"You're not innocent, dear No Name."

"You, least of all."

"There are never degrees of innocence. You are or you're not innocent."

"But still, Peter, look at it from my point of view."

"And you, No Name, will you look at it from my point of view?"

"Without you, I never would have come."

"No. You wouldn't have come here without me."

"But then, Peter, you are here again as well because of me."

"Oh, do you want gratitude? Are you my salvation? From the beginning, No Name, you have been in my hands."

"Or you in mine, Peter."

The enigma, Cardinal. We were either similar or different. If we were alike ... bones, lungs, genitals, brain cells, blood vessels. . . .

And if we were different. . . . Matter and anti-matter. Wasn't I saying exactly what he had been saying all along, that we were different, that by nature we were different. . . . And then he had added that I, therefore, had to be eliminated to maintain that distinction before we annihilated each other. I hadn't—had I?—said that about him? Had I? Would I? Only in response to his saying it? Was that my rationale?

Was it possible we were completely different? Can any two human beings be completely different? Can we pride ourselves on that? Is it accurate? Did Peter think so? Did I? Was it true? I've asked these questions before. Or were we the same but living in parallel universes where everything is the same and also different? Were we mirror images of each other, present in parallel universes, spinning in different directions, torqued differently? The laws of probability permit these possibilities: The Inflationary Universe theory allows for a predominance of matter over anti-matter, superstring theory allows for a co-extensive universe of shadow matter.

Would I have done what he had done? Would I have done what he had done? Of course, I wouldn't have. Never. I never would have. Not what he had done, not what he had wanted to do from his perch there, away from it all, out of the shit and piss, in his illicit guard tower. His ziggurat. The place where he played God. You live. You die. You suffer. You bleed. You break. You starve. You go mad. No, I wouldn't have done such a thing. Not I. How could I? I was educated. I had good parents. I wasn't poor. I was taught ethics. But, he, of course, he wasn't . . . he had had . . . he had been . . . he wasn't . . . and God had deserted him, them, all of them, had turned His back, had said he, they were bad and had sent those others to prey on him, them, to suck his, their blood, and so, of course, he was angry and so he mounted his ziggurat to become God, to set it all right, like someone deciding they could create life and death. They could create another universe, eliminate what was inessential or destructive. Threatening and install what was beneficial, healthy, they could create beauty, heavenly music, a star, they could create a small star to play with, do you want the stars to play with? A star in a metal casing like a Brancusi sculpture, a star called a bomb.

"Your research, your curiosity, No Name, what does it lead to?"

I was turning cold, Cardinal. I recognized the chill as it took over my body and then my mind. It was not the first time I was overtaken by it. Now, in his presence, I entered it actively and with full consciousness. A survival mechanism I had first learned as a graduate student when I forced myself to stay up nights gathering data for a paper and became coldly focused, drew myself into a line, so thin and so sharp, it could cut paper. Nothing mattered but the work, completing the assigned task. Then afterwards, at different observatories and also on The Mountain, I would work night after night, like everyone else, precisely and steadily far beyond my capacity, unable to think of anything but the pressure of the deadline, the specifications of the task and what was required of me; I could feel myself narrow into such single-mindedness that laser light issued from my eyes. I willed it so.

Yes, I was afraid. I am afraid now. This afternoon. This moment of writing. So, I stop now because I can. I draw myself up, but not in the way I drew myself up then. I get up and face the window. I make tea. I go outside and water the flowers. I take off my shirt and let the spring sunlight warm me. It was winter this morning when I started writing and now it's spring here at Devil's Peak; I will it so.

I drew myself up and faced him. I found something very cold and defiant in me without which I knew I could not survive and I focused it at him though he overshadowed me with his mass and his great coat. He might kill me, of course, but my life was worth nothing if I cowered before him. So I stared at him. I dared him. I was meeting him, I told myself, on his own turf. Matching him, trying to match him, in order to survive, and feeling just the slightest twinge of nausea because he had led me here or I had led him.

I said I wouldn't go as far as he had. Wouldn't ever even conceive of going as far as he had. But I would go far. I would save my life.

At any cost?

Maybe. At the cost of his life? It was possible I was ready to go that far.

I stared at him. I had to know each feature of his face. I had to be certain that we operated under the same laws, that his kidneys were governed by the same laws as mine, that there was—had been—blood in his veins, that he had skin. I had to know this so I would know how to act.

A single particle sometimes acts as if it is two particles, sometimes appears like a particle sometimes appears like a wave. A particle sometimes acts in two distinct ways or as if it had dimension, extension, movement, far beyond its capabilities. We can't predict the behavior of the particle because of the action of the wave. It will never be where we expect it to be. Or it may be here and there. There is so much possibility and chaos. Schmidt and myself, Cardinal. In separate particular worlds, incommunicado for eternity, and then, without warning, within the wave, together are the wave, Cardinal. And yet I had believed myself to be a singular particle as if I always had been singular. Me. Myself. Myself alone. I. I. I. If this were true, I was safe. But physics, Cardinal, physics insists on the wave. Our commonality, Cardinal.

I had to be unerring. I had to find the precise boundary between us before I struck.

I continued to stare at his greatcoat. Cloth. Leather. Skin. Cotton. Wool. Cowhide. Brass. Metal. He shivered from the cold and refused to acknowledge it. Just as I did. And then he didn't shiver anymore. I could dissemble too.

I drew myself together. I found the borders and boundaries. I drew behind them. I became discrete. Concise. Decisive.

And then I caught myself. Peter was making me see it his way: Survival. Intent. Focus. Undauntedness. Fearlessness. Obedience. Perfection. Necessity. Ordeal. Distinction. Endurance. Separation. Objectivity. Purity. Potency. Aloofness. Impersonality. Rigor. Indefatigability. Stoicism. Indifference. Insensibility. Fixity. Determination. Power. Discipline. Will.

I had to pull myself away from him, had to differentiate myself, despite the scorn which would come from him. And also had to bear his contempt and make him see it my way if I could by setting up conditions he couldn't possibly avoid. And to do that, I had to find our differences. I had to separate from him. And in that very act. . . . As I did so, I was becoming him.

I was becoming him. Or I had been him all along. "Would you like to swing on a star. . . ?"

Then Lance appeared, trudging up the hill, not quite so taken by stones and grave markers as I had been—uninterested really—but concerned, as usual, and alert for the first glimpse of me. He was whistling. What was he whistling, Cardinal? He was whistling, *Peter's theme* from Peter and the Wolf. Do you believe it? It's true.

He smiled with relief when he saw me and continued walking toward me, hopeful that the straightforwardness of his stride, its resoluteness, would overwhelm me sufficiently to allow him to embrace me and, without wasting a motion, guide me back down the hill, through the barbed wire again, to our little car parked by the field of yellow dandelions so that he could drive me to the hotel and order a meal for me in Polish from the cranky waitress in the hotel dining room. And, hopefully, he could accomplish this without a word said about the cemetery, or the dead, or Jews or Nazis, or Poles, for that matter.

As if we were home. As if we were normal people who had gone for a drive in the country and were tired and returning home. As if nothing remarkable had happened that day. As if we were just enjoying solitude and also each other's company and finding simple pleasure in the sound of the other's voice, in hearing me say, "Please, honey, would you pass the salt?" Wanting nothing else. My voice once had music to it, I remembered. He missed it, I assumed. It had a harsh edge now and was sometimes flat, off key. But knowing him, he didn't let himself think about it.

He kept his eyes on me and tried to see me as I was. He saw that I was biting my lip. That my fists were clenched. That I didn't check my watch when I saw him approach. If I saw him approach. He could not be certain that I had registered his presence. He was tired of all of this. No, he hadn't found the film. He didn't care. To hell with it. He wanted to leave it all behind anyway. The sun was behind him. He watched his shadow creeping up toward me. It would be upon me before he was. He regretted this part of his approach. He knew how I had been suffering from the cold. He wanted the sun to be upon me.

Yes, he could have approached me in another way, but he also wanted to come right to me, and I was facing the sun. Trying to warm myself in it, rubbing my hands on my upper arms, trying to enhance my circulation. He would warm me. He was tired of this thin sun. He was tired of Poland. And everything else. He was resolute. He would tell me stories. He would make me laugh. He had once been good at that. We used to laugh together a great deal. Sometimes after we hadn't been together for a long time, I would relinquish the stars so we could stay up through the night. I would stay with him through the morning, talking, then laughing until I would plead with him to stop because my belly and ribs hurt from laughing. It didn't matter what he said then, anything would make me laugh. There had been exuberance in me. He was going to find it again. Even here. Even in Poland where the walls were so thin the people in the next room would have to join in our laughter.

I didn't know what was happening. It was suddenly so much colder. There had been a drop in temperature. Ten degrees, at least. Lance continued coming toward me. I must have looked confused. As if I didn't recognize him or had forgotten that he was returning. He didn't know if his plan would work. It looked doubtful. I assumed that he was seeing the sunlight upon me even though I was in the cold shade. Tomorrow we were going to Krakow. And from there to Auschwitz-Birkenau. I would need my strength. He would need his. I would need his too. What was left of it.

He walked toward me resolutely. His shadow was climbing toward my chest. In a moment, it would engulf me completely. He had to take me in his arms before the extreme cold overwhelmed me. He was determined and agile; he leaped and locked me in his arms as we faced a last instant of light. I must have looked as if I was going to say something.

"Don't say anything," he said, and then, inspired by his daring, grinned broadly.

I noticed that Peter Schmidt had disappeared.

I started to speak again. I wanted to ask Lance about the film. I wanted, finally, to tell him about Peter Schmidt. I had never told him anything about Peter. This was the time.

"There is something I have to tell you," I said earnestly.

"The hell with it," he answered me, beaming. "The hell with it."

He heard the rhythm of the phrase. And did a little jump to go along with it. A little jump and a fast shuffle. As if he were tap dancing. And then repeated it in the other direction. On his left foot. And started again with his right.

"Lance?"

"The hell with it," he chanted with his little dance.

"You're dancing on the graves." My exclamation sounded so absurd, I began to smile, even titter.

"The hell with it," he sang again. "To hell with it."

Chapter 40

The night before we left for Auschwitz, I dreamed:

> I saw a lion walking upright, like the lions carrying the holy goblet on the tombstone in Lublin. She was walking toward a dark cave, the stones dark as iron. When she reached the mouth of the cave, she turned and I saw the face of a woman with dark hair and deep set brown eyes that were absolutely fearless. I wondered how eyes so very dark could carry such diamond light. Then she turned from me, her brown hair falling down into a mane, and continued toward the mouth of the cave which had an iron door that she pulled open. Her den was in flames. Inside the flames I could make out the brilliant yellow and orange shadows of three other figures. The lion entered the flames and the four of them walked about inside. I heard her voice, like a night bird, singing, "Holy, holy, holy."

So that is how I met Edith Stein. Our intention had been to spend the day at Auschwitz, then drive to the village to find a hotel that could lodge Americans and then proceed to Birkenau the next day. But after a day at the Camp and the dream proceeding it, I couldn't imagine staying in a hotel. We had kept our room in Krakow so that no one would know we were deviating from our itinerary: I could make a plan. Lance had no idea what I was scheming when I asked him to circle Auschwitz so I could learn its extent from the outside. We drove around once and I spotted the Karmel Edith Stein I had been reading about. Then we circled again, we got out and walked to the gate and rang the bell. I knew that they didn't take visitors but we had made reservations to spend several nights at the Carmelite Convent in Dachau and Marek had written some generic letters of introduction for us in Polish which I had thought I might use with some astronomers in Krakow. Maybe I showed the gnarled woman who answered the door the letters, or maybe Lance played for her, or she saw that it was cold, raining and dark, that we didn't speak Polish and I was crying; something touched her and she invited us in and asked us to sit in a small ante-room and wait. Without saying another word, she returned to serve us bread and butter, sliced cheese and fruit, for which we were very grateful. Tea for me and coffee for Lance. The tea was very hot and I held the rounder, smaller tea cup in my two hands in order to warm them.

The Mother Superior appeared behind a grate with a young translator and several dictionaries. The translator did not really speak English. I had studied French briefly in high school and spoke it with my grandmother, Lance had some German, somehow we managed.

The Karmel was threatened, the Mother Superior informed us. The international Jewish community was protesting their residence in the supply house where the Nazis had stored poison gas, Zyklon B. They considered a Catholic sanctuary at Auschwitz, the slaughterhouse of the Jews, a sacrilege.

I could only reach my hand to Lance as I indicated that I was Jewish and he was not and would have taken the Nun's hand if we were not separated by the wall and the bars across the little window.

"Edith Stein?" I asked.

"Sr Teresia Benedicta á Cruce? She made of herself a holocaust."

"What does that mean?"

"It means she was a saint. She made her death into a holy offering."

I didn't understand and the Mother Superior felt my confusion. "Like Christ," she continued. We silently agreed to act as if our difficulty lay in not sharing a common language. She launched into a personal story; it was easier to make herself understood by talking about her own experience.

When she was a very young girl, the Nazis had searched her house for Jews one evening while her mother was away. She told the story as of Grace offered her, gave no other explanation. My inclination was to accept it as a gift. I was in need of kindness. She was not treating us in the manner of the priest in Lublin. Rather than assume she was being political, I preferred to imagine that this story was pivotal in her desire to pursue the devotions of the Carmelites, though she did indicate that she was at Auschwitz only because she had been born there.

"Visitors do not stay at this convent," she advised us and then paused. "But," she continued, "there is a room which is used for members of the church who come on official business." If we didn't mind waiting a little longer, she would have it made ready for us. And we could, if we wished, return the next evening if we wished a place to rest.

You know, don't you Cardinal, whose bed I slept in? As I think back on it, I like to think that it was pre-ordained that we stay there, that it was arranged so that your presence, even though washed out of the linens and swept out of the room, still remained in that little cell to give me strength.

We left the next morning with their blessings and went to Birkenau. The nuns invited us to come back and sleep at the convent again if we wished. But I already anticipated that after a second day in these two Camps, I would have to be alone. Looking at the stars is looking at the source of our life, is looking at our origins, at our birth. The light that reaches us is the past. Astronomers thrive on looking backwards. But Auschwitz-Birkenau is our death, is the end of everything, is the final destruction. Is the future. It's dark light just arrived at Capella, with the news; the final solution has begun.

After Auschwitz-Birkenau there is nothing but Auschwitz-Birkenau; it extends to infinity.

My parents did not understand cosmology. They thought that Auschwitz-Birkenau was the end of something and that I was born safe on the other side of it. They didn't know that it was a black hole, a star collapsed in on itself, devouring everything, a star from which nothing could escape. And I was born into its mouth. And since I was born so close to it, inevitably, I would be pulled into it, and being pulled in, would be pulled, inexorably, toward the past. I could never go far enough or fast enough to escape Peter Schmidt. And he, thrusting himself into a worm hole from the other side, still did not go far enough or fast enough to escape his future.

It was very cold that day I was at Birkenau. Lance and I walked around together and then he went to the car while I stayed behind. I wanted to go into every barrack. Down the road, in the middle of a field of yellow mustard, there was a new church built to serve the suburb which was growing around the Camp like a virulent weed. I had stopped at the field after we'd parked the car to pick the blossoms and eat them because my throat hurt terribly and I wanted to burn it into health. As I walked from the cars toward the gate again, the light was changing. The sky was darker. It was raining now. But the field kept burning with yellow flowers.

I realize now that this is hell. Forty-four years later this is still hell.

Even though I was very miserable, I hadn't known I was entering hell, only that I needed to be alone. I couldn't be with Lance and he couldn't be with me. I left him in the car. He said he was going to nap there. I don't remember what I said, maybe only that I was sick and cranky. We agreed to meet back at the car at the end of the day. Around five, just before the dark would begin to fall.

The light rain was more like a mist that came at one from all sides. The temperature hovered at the point where it could turn to snow, but it never did. So there was no disguise, no whitening of the landscape.

Auschwitz was just a very few kilometers away. Auschwitz and Birkenau were essentially the same camp. Birkenau was opened when Auschwitz wasn't sufficient for all the killing. Auschwitz is the great tourist attraction of Poland. There had been dozens of buses in the parking lot. People flock to it in the same proportion that people travel to American amusement parks. But Birkenau was deserted. During the course of the afternoon, two or three buses came and departed an hour later. A few cars. The visitors wandered through lost. There were none of the perky signs, no literature, no refreshment stands which turned the other camps and Auschwitz into museums. Of all the camps, this was the most deserted. No one came here unless they had a personal reason to be here.

There are two stars circling each other and one collapses into its own center and becomes a black hole and the gravitational pull, the tidal forces of that darkness, pull the living fires of the nearby star into it. Remember?

It had become clear how we were circling each other, how close Peter Schmidt had been coming to me or me to him, whichever it was. I was getting colder and colder as he approached. I think I had known all along what was going to happen; it was inevitable. And inevitable that it would happen here. In his territory. It was here he had played his forbidden violin.

I looked up to find his guard tower. They surrounded the camp, one every so many meters, but I knew if I were painstaking in my exploration I would find the one he had occupied. When I would draw close to it, its shadow would fit me exactly.

Maybe I always knew that I was going to confront Peter at Birkenau. Perhaps I always knew that I would have to see Peter fully at some time. Not as some wraith, not as some fantasy or hallucination, but as a living being, someone who had lived, done what he had done, seen what he had seen, and died. Perhaps I always knew that I would also have to enter him as he had entered me and that it wouldn't happen anywhere else. That the entire journey I had undertaken was leading me toward this inevitable and abhorrent ordeal.

I started out walking the perimeters. I walked from one end of the camp to the other, along the road, past the gates where the few cold visitors entered warily and exited hurriedly, bearing the same look on their faces, one of dreaded anticipation. As if one were going toward a giant rat waiting to spring out, its long teeth gleaming, its body plague ridden. Nevertheless one rushed forward.

I pretended it wasn't so very hard in the beginning. When I came to the place where the Camp backed onto houses, the way around suddenly disappeared and the ground was too muddy to cross over between the trees, so I turned back. There were some purple spring flowers, violets maybe, and some yellow ones growing in the furrows of the roots of the old trees. I thought of picking them but it was too cold to take my fists out of my pockets.

It took a long time to walk around the Camp to the other end also pressing into the suburb. I watched two men fishing in the cold May drizzle at a small pond at one end of the Camp. The pond was in a copse of trees some feet from the twisted metal and shattered bricks which had been the ovens. This, then, what we have come to, these "fishers of men."

Then I didn't know what to do with myself, so I entered a gate, not the main gate, but an auxiliary gate and began walking about in the camp. Once I passed a gate from which I could see our car and noticed that Lance wasn't in it. I looked about for him but he was nowhere in sight. The car was locked; he had the keys. I walked up one path and down the next one, methodically, so that over the next few hours, I traversed the entire area.

I overheard snatches of conversation from time to time. They were all the same.

Ordinary talk died here as had ordinary life. One fell into history and geography, pointing out the markers, saying this was the place where this happened and in this place, the other unspeakable things transpired.

I was very uncomfortable when I came face to face with any of the so very few visitors. Because we were so very few, I felt exposed. We knew why we were there. There was nothing to say to each other about it.

All the time, I walked up and down, my feet wet and freezing, counting the minutes and the hours as if a sentence had been imposed upon me and I couldn't exit until I had served my time. I was afraid that I would never get out because I had entered through the wrong gate and as no one knew I was there, no one would be able to liberate me and Peter and I would be there, together, as it had once been. After a few awkward encounters, "hello," or hand raised in acknowledgment, or shuffling out of the way, or nodding my head, carefully closing my eyes and opening them again, I learned to keep my head down when I passed others until I was able to feel that perhaps I wasn't seen myself, but then if I were visible I was concerned about troubling people by appearing beside them, crossing their path, again and again. A woman wearing a gray and black striped suit, the pattern so very close to the striped garments the inmates wore, stepped in front of me; I lost my balance and almost fell. She didn't notice.

I imagined Lance looking for me, tracking down a guard, and the two of them searching the area for me again, Lance alerted from the incident in Buchenwald to the ways in which I locked myself in, to the ways in which I disappeared. Then I came onto a tower that looked onto a yard and barracks I knew I was in the right place and that I was not alone.

"I preferred Birkenau. It was the dead end. I liked being in the watchtowers and looking out across the flat field. I felt free after the cramped brick buildings of Auschwitz. I couldn't bear the throngs of prisoners, the press of bodies, the stench of it.

"I wanted to be in the tower. I wanted it more than anything else. Too often I was condemned to be down there in the proximity of the mobs and I couldn't get away.

"I wanted to be at the end of everything.

"Come closer, No Name."

"Have you ever loved anything, Peter Schmidt? Did you love the violin, Peter Schmidt?"

"Yes, No Name, I loved it. And I hated it. And then, I felt nothing for it. I wanted to hear the sound purely, pure as a thought without a flicker of emotion. To hear sound for what it was before we contaminated it.

"Isn't that what you love about the stars, No Name, the fact that there is nothing, absolutely nothing, human about them? Sound is rarely as pure as light. We make noise but we don't shine. But sometimes a note on a violin has that purity.

As if the human hand had nothing to do with it. That's why I prefer strings to woodwinds or brass; they do not depend on breath.

"Come up here, No Name. It is not difficult to climb. No one will stop you. Come here and see this from my vantage point."

I refused him, Cardinal. He was in his place and I had to find my place which was somewhere down below. Now it was more difficult to walk, every step taken against resistance. I couldn't go where I had to go without him and he fought me every step of the way. Finally, I was walking alongside the barracks where the prisoners had been kept. Unlike the other camps, where only one or two *model* barracks were open to the public, most of these, unlocked, some doors unhinged, creaking open, were just as they had been. I entered one after another.

There was one I came to, which had a weathered sign on it indicating it had been a kind of infirmary. Peter had been here once; I could smell him. He had worked here. The huge wooden door was warped and hung slightly ajar so I could see inside. I entered and then, overwhelmed, left and continued walking. I had mud on my boots. It was getting colder. The rain was falling more heavily.

So I turned back to that barrack and went inside, Peter behind me somewhere, pulling back so it felt as if I were walking against a rip tide in space. The room was bisected by a concrete latrine. There were perhaps twenty holes on each side of the trough, some small enough for a very small child. And though it was so very cold, I could imagine the stink and the fact that there had been no water and that everyone there had been sick and also suffering with diarrhea. So I sat on that latrine and tried to pray, an audacious act. I didn't know if I could pray. And I didn't know if one could pray there. Would that be the most unforgivable sacrilege and desecration, or was it a holy act? I thought of those who had been there. Surely, they had not stopped praying to protect prayer from contamination. Or had they? Was that their last gift to God?

I looked up after some time. A prisoner is wary, her hearing improves, any slight shift in the environment, a mouse or a shadow, the drop of temperature, the breeze from a door or a window opening, anything can be dangerous and she needs to be prepared even for that which she draws toward her. I felt something or someone outside the barracks and wanted to compose myself, as a piece of music is composed, balanced from beginning to end. I saw nothing at first. And then I saw him. Not as I had seen him before. Not even as I thought I had seen him in the Jewish cemetery in Lublin. I saw him. There. In his flesh and blood.

When I saw Peter Schmidt standing there then in his shiny boots, I knew he was alive and that he had created this place and had brought me to it.

These are the facts. I was there and he was there. I thought I had come there of my own will and his incontrovertible presence proved that I had been wrong about that. I had been, not innocent but, *an* innocent, as I had been about so many things. Peter Schmidt had created this scenario—shall we say, once again—out of some compulsion, some longing, even he could not explain.

You know what he looked like. I had only known what he might look like from movies I had seen and the interminable and unbearable photographs I had been staring at since this obsession had overtaken me. The photos were accurate. The movies hadn't lied. From the outside, he looked exactly as shown. In truth, I hadn't really expected that. I had not been able to comprehend the reality of the image. I had not been able to imagine that anyone would seriously cultivate it. I, like some of the neo-fascists, had, it turned out, disbelieved in the entire event of the Holocaust.

But now he had appeared. Was present. I had to confront this reality. I had thought that science had broken my mind and I was used to incredulity, that is, I could handle it, could stay sane in the face of the impossible. And, I was wrong again. I was faced with two all too compatible truths: Peter was there and I was no longer sane.

We're almost at the end, Cardinal, if there is an end. We're almost at the point of no return when the universe will move over the threshold of gravity to infinite expansion, one galaxy departing from another in waves upon waves of red diminishing light until every star departs from every other star, until each particle streams off into its own emptiness. Or, on the other hand, the point where the forces of cohesion will call the drifting worlds back over the same blue journey of billions of years to the point of all beginnings. We don't know which way it will go. But let us stay together now, Cardinal until the forces of dissolution overwhelm us. For after all, Cardinal, hasn't this become our story? Yours, Peter's and mine.

When Peter came in wearing his shiny black boots, he had to step very carefully, not to soil them.

I could feel the action of his body in my body, Cardinal. Having been drawn back into his history, he stepped into it and strode up to the doorway with great pride in the strut, in the crease of the fabric of the uniform, in the slap of the leather against the earth. And then, having forgotten how muddy it was inside the barracks, adjusted suddenly, interrupted the last step so that it was smaller, so that it was more careful and, in correcting the balance, he tottered for a moment, needed to stop short.

And in that instant, you know that someone has seen you totter. And so you want to kill her. As simple as that: You want to kill someone who can barely stand herself because that person has seen you totter. Or you push her down into the shit, so that it is she, and not you, who is covered. And maybe you even step on her to keep your boots clean.

It is war time. There aren't many things to be had and you have a pair of black boots. Your father had a pair and that was because he was in the army. If he hadn't been in the army, he wouldn't have a pair of boots. And so you have to take care of these boots. You may never have another. And imagine, Cardinal, in trying to escape it, the Nazis were knee deep in it themselves. Knee deep in the blood, pus, piss, lice, smegma and excrement.

A woman in a coat. Her hair is red. Her eyes are green. Some say she is beautiful. Beautiful as the ones who, according to testimony, were so often killed last but with a little kindness, that is, a bullet directly into the heart or brain.

And she is extraordinarily independent. Even for an American woman, if you know what I mean. And until this moment, essentially fearless. Maybe defiant. Well, she was raised to walk in the woods alone and to sleep alone under the stars. An expert in the remote.

Then a man enters her absolute private domain. This is not the first time he had achieved this, but this time, more violently than ever—that is—at her insistence. He also wears a coat. Hers is lined with goose down, his is fine wool and belted at the waist. She is wearing boots. He is wearing boots. She has come to look rather fragile in her clothes particularly because of the delicate magenta silk scarf she wears about her neck. He is anything but fragile. He is armed. She is not. He holds a riding crop. She does not. She does, however, know how to ride bareback and he does not, he says.

He is standing and she is sitting. She does not get up when he enters as she would have were she in her office or in her home. If a friend or stranger had entered, she would have wanted to acknowledge the person. She does not want to acknowledge this person but then she quickly understands that his protocol insists on the inequality of their positions; she must not rise.

He stares at her. She does stare back. And she feels as if he is seeing through her. And indeed, she knows that he feels the same.

There is mud on her coat and a mud stain on her skirt which has been there from a previous day. On the other hand, his boots are muddied and she knows that the mud is fresh. His boots have been soiled by the muck at the entrance of the barracks. He looks at them surreptitiously and with distaste.

Yes, I stared at him and stared at him from my perch on the icy cold concrete latrine. And I knew as well as I had ever known anything about him, that he was alive and, also, that he was absolutely dependent upon my body. Without me, he was absolutely disembodied and so I had become his eyes. He saw what I saw. And he saw himself as I saw him. He could not escape my vision. Nor I his, Cardinal. He also felt it plainly. He could not see it otherwise. He could not look away. And so I had him.

Vertigo, Cardinal. Do you feel it? The way we were sliding between one world and another, banging into each other, becoming something else, returning to a former state. We were spinning between our separate realities, fusing and breaking apart, fusing and breaking apart.

I stared at him, not through the stupor of hunger, cold, exhaustion, disease and fear which had overcome those who were confined to that cold barrack, but in a torpor nevertheless, the torpor of one who was at the mercy of whatever fate awaited her and knew it, knew that she was the victim of that man who had entered the barracks and acted as if he could do anything he wanted.

How I longed for the stars. And he, how he longed for his tower and his violin.

But as I would not, could not, leave this place to which we were both condemned, we stayed there without hope, on that latrine, in the mud. And, Cardinal, I did begin to pray to God. Because I was so afraid. Because everything that I had experienced in the last few years, had, relentlessly, brought me to this.

Then I began to imagine unspeakable things. I don't think *imagine* is the right word. They were in my mind. Clear. I was coming to know the things he had thought and seen. I was coming to know the mind which was selecting, even then, this one or that, to be designated for this or that task or experimentation or death. And I knew everything which he had done and was capable of doing as I moved inside him and found nothing, no one, only a few atoms of self streaking away from each other at something approaching half the speed of light.

Timidly, but without looking timid, I probed him. I extended myself through the great coat and his uniform and his very muscular body. I was standing in his body. In his so very shiny black boots. When I stood inside him, I could feel nothing. As if boots and great coat were mounted on air or metal.

There was no earth in this man, no forest like the kind my father loved so much, no matter holding together the disparate pieces whirling with a fury so immense that their tendency to cleave to each other was overcome absolutely by the forces which blew them apart.

I hoped to recover my sanity by working to identify the metaphor as if I would know his secret if I could find the right formula to describe it. Was this the center of the black hole, the place where density, where mass had gone beyond what it could sustain and had collapsed in on itself and everyone or thing that could not maintain its own escape velocity was pulled over the gleaming cusp of its horizon, to be pulled apart, extinguished in the crucible of annihilation? Or was it the opposite, the failure of gravity to hold anything together, the stars, galaxies, the dreaded red shift, the entire universe expanding, splitting apart, an explosion rather than an implosion, an atomic bomb rather than a hydrogen bomb going off?

You can see that these thoughts were distractions, the riotous workings of a mind out of control. I was doing equations in my head. I was counting the buttons on his coat. I was reciting the table of the temperatures of the stars at each stage of development and decay. Then I fell back into his mind. I didn't know exactly how dangerous this moment was. After all, I had only read about it and seen photos and walked through the places it had been. I hadn't been there. And if you haven't been there you haven't been there.

I came to know something of what he was doing. He was looking at them, the ones he would condemn to death or select for work, and he was counting and choosing. I couldn't see them, of course, because he had never seen them even when we looked at them, but I could see how he was looking, I could feel it in the narrowing of my eyes.

Peter Schmidt was standing over me and I was seated—praying, now, and without inhibition—beneath him. He was standing in that place where he had lived out his life, having come again to the point of selecting someone. He had put his finger out to me, choosing me. There was no one there for him to choose but me because it was himself he was choosing, himself and his future.

He was selecting himself for this deadly game. And he could not stop now as he had not been able to stop himself then. He was being driven again to build the highest, hottest fire in the world in order to sacrifice himself in a blaze of cosmic proportions, offering up his own soul in an *auto da fe*. I felt his emptiness and wondered how I had been born from it.

"I offer you up to the flames, Daniella. Make of it a sacred holocaust."

Chapter 41

A breath, Cardinal, please.

Every so often when she thought I was asleep or occupied, my mother took off her glasses and placed them carefully atop her sheet music, got up from the piano, pulled the shades down, turned off the lights in the room, tied a scarf about her face to act as a blindfold, shut her eyes under the scarf and sat down again at the piano. Then placing one hand at the last bass notes and the other at the last treble she brought them together with a flood of sound and began to boogie. In the dark. Yes. Cardinal. Only in the dark. The music flying off her fingers like sparks.

She claimed it wasn't the same being born sighted. She said it wasn't the same with one's eyes merely closed. She said the blind, the ones who cannot see and have no hope of seeing, they hear what the eyes prevent us from hearing. In the most absolute dark she found she could lose herself completely in the music. She improvised, when she wouldn't otherwise, churning up the energy until she, herself, exploded like a supernova and set the minor scales on fire.

I spied upon her because I never knew whether the music was a way of being lost or finding herself. When I sat with her at the keyboard when I was very young, before she resigned herself to my obvious lack of talent, and we tried to play duets together or she wanted me to follow the score of a particular piece of music she was learning, or when she just plain wanted me to see improvisation right there, in the fingers, still I knew she wasn't there with me at the piano. She was at the piano but she was somewhere else. Gone.

I always knew when she was going to bring the wild home. For days before, her behavior changed. She was both agitated and distracted. I watched her through a crack in the door, yes, through a key hole, yes, with my ear against the wall, yes, crouching in the bushes, yes, on the roof with my head and shoulders extended down on to the glass, yes, from the basement, from the shadows in the outside foyer, yes, from the porch swing, and on one occasion from behind the couch, yes. I sat breathless, enchanted, and ecstatic. My mother. Crazed with the music. Bewitched. My mother. I wanted to shout with joy as I saw the woman who had conceived me.

Once I confronted her: "Have you always played with a blindfold on?" She was so shocked by my presence she flinched, stopped mid-note, and turned to me without hiding her pain at having been spied upon in her most private moment.

"No. Not always. A long time ago, before you were born, I could play with my eyes open."

"What happened?"

"What happened?" she asked as if the question were absurd. "My eyes were opened, that's what happened."

It has been a long time Cardinal since I have caught my breath. I'm in my cabin at Devil's Peak and Blind Willie Johnson is singing *Lord, I Just Can't Keep From Crying Sometime.*

Well, I just can't keep from crying sometime,
when my heart's full o' sorrow and my eyes full o' tears,
well I just can't keep from crying sometime.
Well, well.

There's madness here, Cardinal. Present tense. It happens again and again. It happened then and is happening again and again. Time from the future moves in fast against Peter, like a storm coming in. And the past is scudding up toward me in waves which recede and come forward breaking themselves on the present beach. He and I caught in this constant and unalterable present where we combat each other.

"Come closer, Peter, so I can see you better."

Chapter 42

Cardinal, no more pleasantries, we have to return to the barracks at Birkenau.

How does one become a holocaust? I am seated crosslegged on a latrine. Peter, who had entered me, has entered the room. At this moment, we are both the chosen ones, so I beckon to him with my finger the way he beckoned to the prisoners who were here once with his riding crop, or baton, or gun or with his gloved finger.

I can feel him tremble inside, can feel that impermissible shudder which he recognizes and refuses to recognize as fear or nausea. I know how to proceed because I feel everything he feels in my body. And yes, therefore, he feels himself, can not avoid feeling what he had avoided his entire life, because for reasons I can't explain, I am, in this moment, so defeated, I am willing to bear it all. He tries to put the feelings outside himself but he can't because I am keeping mine here, inside me, to the point of madness and he can't take them away from me. No matter how he tries, he cannot rid me of my fear, revulsion and panic, which I treasure now, as my weapons. We proceed, his history and experience, what he saw, co-existing with my nausea and vertigo. I move forward, driven, without knowing the outcome, without any sense of it. I draw him closer, navigating his body by remote control carefully toward me, through the mud, so that his boots, no matter how carefully he places them, slide into the mud, his pristine coat is spattered, and even the knees of his pants are spotted.

We are clear about certain things. He would like to exterminate me. He intends it. He can't pretend otherwise. He can't offer an unhappy childhood or obeying orders to erase that truth. This man standing before me would *like* to exterminate me. I have to take that in also. I can't afford to be sentimental or pretend to be invulnerable. People did die, millions of them.

I haven't eaten all day. It isn't much hunger but it is enough for him to recognize it. Peter is going to know everything I know because its his, like it or not, and I want him to know his world. It's my gift to him.

I take a breath and look him in the eyes. My green eyes, his blue eyes, lock. Then with the deliberation of a surgeon, I unbutton each button of my coat, and slowly, as if wielding a scalpel, remove it from one arm, then the other so that it falls down on to the ground.

I haven't been freezing for the duration of weeks or months but still the cold is hellish cold. Peter has been hungry and cold in his life, so it isn't unfamiliar, but it wasn't the good life he was after. Now he is suffering from the cold and it is suffering that was forbidden. He is suffering from it because I have no desire to pretend that I can bear this. I am fucking cold and this scene is unbearable and I have no intention of letting him turn away.

Peter would like nothing more than to exterminate me now. If he was half-hearted in earlier years or on automatic pilot, he is not half-hearted now. He would kill me if he can. His eros is in it. But poised though he may be for the opportunity, he can't do it. The laws of the universe which prevent it can not be circumvented. I'm afraid Peter may be up against God.

I don't bring him too close to me. I want him to see me as I am, hunkering down, my thighs and calves trembling from the strain, to be certain he has the entire pathetic picture in his mind and body at all times. I want to be certain he understands the entire situation and the rules of this competition.

"These are the rules Peter. We are naked now. Now you must tell me your story."

He knows he doesn't have to tell it aloud. It's only a courtesy, my request. For the circumstances which have brought us together are making our minds increasingly transparent to each other and there is nothing to prevent me from invading him completely and trampling over his memories. He can try to forget but he doesn't have the capacity and pretense won't work. Actually, my politeness is deliberate; I want him to know what I am doing. I relish it the way he relished performing experimental surgery without anesthesia and informing his *patients* what he was doing. I concentrate, as he concentrated on removing his victim's eyes, wrapping the two different colored eyes, one blue one brown, of the twins he had killed, and mailing them to Berlin. I have access to his most private life and I intend to use it.

Of course, there is a parity here. He has always had access to me. At this moment, I have nothing to protect except privacy itself and he shattered that months ago. I don't have more options than he does except those given to me by the accident, it appears, of my life: Shaena Baena got away.

He twitches every now and then but so minimally that only someone as attentive as myself would see it. I, on the other hand, have nothing to hide and so the grotesqueness of my position is flagrant. I am learning this method of observation from him, know how he also watched prisoners to see when they were cracking; Peter teaches me the signs. And I learn quickly. I see when he begins to feel us both simultaneously. As he feels himself for the first time, and feels me; two fears, two revulsions, two dreads, separate and equal. This is new to him. And by it, he is revealed both to me and to himself.

Theoretically, there is a way of passing through a black hole into another universe, but you must have enough velocity and must move with precision along a certain and unerring path. Now we begin to circle down toward that event horizon, passing out of space into time. The entire future of the universe crumbles. We will either be disintegrated or thrust out again into another world which may resemble this one but which will always be intrinsically other.

This passage is as perilous as the descent into hell. This is what my parents never told me.

Chapter 43

"Who are you, Peter Schmidt?"

I heard her impertinent question inside the body which was inside my great coat. I could have stopped her with a crack of my whip. I could have and I didn't. Having the option to choose, amused me; it always had. But then, I felt the question reverberating in each cell and this disturbed me greatly and distracted me.

Each cell wanted to answer for itself. The body is like the *volk*. If we are each to think of ourselves as distinct, if each cell is to think of itself as independent and not subordinated in function and loyalty to the greater need of the Body, what would happen to us? Or what would happen if any individual cell decided to strike out for itself?

She asked me and I decided to answer because otherwise she would interpret everything in her own confused and biased manner. She would find what she thought she was looking for in me, she would find something on her own but it would not be Peter Schmidt. She had no capacity to see me whatsoever because she had no ability to see me as separate from her and that, above anything else, is what is required.

Let's be objective. Yes, let's be scientific, as she claims to be. Let's look at her objectively. At first glance, she is cowering on that latrine, as well she should be. Look again. See the way she is leaning forward just slightly as if balancing herself, but in reality extending herself into spheres where she doesn't belong. Always wanting to touch, to reach out, to rectify her inherent imbalance. She slides this way and that. Her hand is clammy. I see it extend toward me. She would like to pull me in.

"There *is* something between us. It both separates and connects us."
"What is it?"
"Loathing."

She claims she has been trained to look at elements and to infer principles from them. This ability does not serve her in this case. I am not the elements just as I was not, ultimately, distinct from the *volk*. We were each the same and together we made a nation. The nation was the aggregate of ourselves. It was larger than we were and it was identical to us. Or rather we were identical to it. We were a small particle but identical to it.

There were some who were different. It was easy to see who they were. There was a system, most fit and some did not. We who belonged, fell through into the Reich like pegs through a hole. We fit. Exactly. Some didn't. And they undermined the perfect symmetry of it. When they were present, everything was askew.

We didn't know this in the beginning. In the beginning, I did not even think I was my father or that he was myself. I had thought we were different. This had been my great hope and torture. But as it turned out, we were exactly the same.

My mother raised me. I lived within her sphere like a rare bloom in a hot house surrounded by winter. I thought I was thriving there. In fact, I was wilting. But I didn't know this.

She raised me the way she thought my father would want me raised. He first left to fight in World War I and then he stayed in the army, the *volk's* army, the *Freicorps*, that protected us until Germany raised a real army again to fight for us in World War II. Sometimes I knew she was thinking about him when he was away on maneuvers or at the front, trying to imagine how he would wish her to respond to me. Then, unfailingly, she would gather me into her arms to shield me from some danger she suspected, including herself. In her mind, my father was a great benevolent stone wall which was extending itself around our city or the province or Germany itself and then when the War broke out the wall pressed its way further, extending our perimeters against our enemies so that we could be safe. When my mother was thinking about my father, she forgot the extent of her own fearfulness and thrust her arms around me protectively, pulling me into her soft and sweaty body.

I couldn't control Daniella's ability to work with the elements, all I could do was put it in a context for her. And why not? I insisted on control over my own material if I could no longer exercise any control over my own life. I had no desire to distort it. I wanted her to see it exactly as it was, as it had been. And to understand that it had nothing to do with her. That despite her malefic ability to draw me here to herself, she was still nothing and would remain nothing. I wasn't responsible for this. It was the world.

Daniella Stanebruch, I said. Stanebruch, not Stonebrook. Is she so naive as to think that she can change her name and get away with it? Does she want us to think she is an Aryan? Jew is written everywhere on her, even in her name. Let her wear the name then like a star.

Let me tell you a story, Stanebruch: It is called The Man and the Coat.

There comes a moment when a man puts on a coat and, is, in that moment, fully realized. Do not underestimate the power of the mantle. My mother would not have dressed me in such a coat, which is fortunate, for then, later, when I was ready, I would not have known what it means to have gained such a coat.

I was eleven years old, Daniella, when my father came home from the War. Most of the war, when my father was away, we spent in the country with my mother's family. We kept our apartment in Erfurt and, whenever my father was away, my mother rented it out to bring in some extra money. It was always an ordeal because we had to pack up all the lace, linens, porcelain, china, silver and pewter, and stack the boxes carefully in the only closet we had which could be locked so our things would not be damaged or stolen. My mother always asked for references from her tenants, but still she was afraid that her precious heirlooms would disappear.

My father hated the country and when we heard he was coming home we always moved back to the city so he wouldn't be discomfited and this meant, once again, unpacking my mother's treasures and arranging them on the mantles, the highly polished tables, the leaded glass cabinets. He never stayed home long. He was as restless in the city as he was in the country. There was nothing for him to do at home and he found farm work demeaning. He wasn't really trained for civilian work. He liked to solve problems and he liked to fight.

Once he came home on a short leave, too short for us to meet him in the city. I was ten. I remember it was after my birthday by the drifts of snow which were already outside the farmhouse. Winter was thick about us.

The wind was fierce when he arrived that afternoon and he had to wrestle the door open and fling himself through it. I hadn't seem him in a very long time and not expecting him—no one had told me why my grandparents had gone to visit a sister for a few days—I didn't quite recognize him and cried out in shock at the great force which wrenched the door open and blasted in. My mother and I were essentially city folk and we habitually kept the doors and windows closed and a fire going. She and I managed to live a cozy life.

Maybe he hadn't wanted to come home or see us. It had cost him considerable effort to make this visit, but he didn't mind effort, he minded that the effort was over. The heat from the fire hit him as fiercely as the icy air hit us.

"Close the door behind you, Heinrich," my mother squealed before she even greeted him. Then she reached for his coat but it was already too late.

"Why is the boy crying?" he demanded of her.

"You surprised him and so he was frightened."

"Frightened? Of his father?"

"Are you frightened of me, Peter?"

"Only startled, Papa," I managed to say. "It was the cold which startled me."

He looked at me puzzled. I don't know who or what he had expected. To recognize me, I think. But I must have looked like hundreds of equally frightened boys my age whose houses he had entered with similar force.

"The cold mustn't startle you, Peter. You and the cold must be friends, Peter. I'll show you." His voice was kind now, kind and large. He looked around and quickly found my jacket, gloves and a scarf. He put them on me with what felt like gentleness, tucking my shirt in my pants, tightening my belt, putting an arm in one sleeve and then the other arm in the other sleeve, and I found myself yielding to his affection. He asked me to extend my hands, which I did, and he held each one before he slipped the gloves on them, pushing at the web between the fingers so they fit snugly. His hand lingered on my hair as he put my cap on my head and I remember the sweetness of his kiss on my forehead. My father had come home. I leaned against his hips feeling the strength in him. He placed his large hand on my back and pulled me toward him, holding me there against the warmth and safety of his body and his great coat. Then with a whoop and a laugh, he opened the door again and shoved me out.

The door slammed and I heard him slide the bolt into place. It was late in the afternoon. Not quite dark but getting dark. This dark. I didn't know what to do so I made my way to a near window which was not blocked by bushes so that I could put my face against the glass.

He was waiting for me. "If you look in the house at the light and the fire you will quickly get even colder. Find another way," he said and drew the curtain closed.

With knowledge as sharp as the cold, I knew it would stay closed. Maybe he was right, I thought, but hopelessly. I walked away from the house, following in the snow trench he had made with his boots as he walked from the road to our house. I raised one foot high and then lowered it into his footstep and then raised the other as high as I could over and into the other, careful not to break the little snow dams between them and then walked along the road and made my own trail across the snow field which was thigh deep in some places toward our barn. When I reached it, I knew he was watching me and that I must not enter it. If I entered, I believed, he would come and find me and devise something even colder than what I was already suffering. I began to turn in my place, turning and turning and then stepping out a bit and turning again, treading down the snow in front of the barn. I walked round and round stomping it flat. I circled and circled as if it was wheat I was razing, the snow grasses bending down gracefully into the round. I went round and round, faster and faster. He was right, it was exhilarating. I began to sweat in my coat. I didn't call it dancing because I had never danced but it was something like dancing. Night fell. The snow began to freeze. It became smooth like glass. Slippery. I skated across it, running and sliding but then contained myself as I realized I was disturbing the perfect surface I was forming. I kneeled down on my hands and knees. The snow was cold on my legs but I no longer minded the cold. I began to polish the snow surface. I firmed it and smoothed it. I wanted it to be flawless. To achieve that, I would have polished it for years. I wanted it to reflect, perfectly, the stars which were appearing overhead. The stars in the snow shone upwards as the stars in the sky shone down. I fell in love with my mirror. It seemed to me I could see myself in it, that I was there, not in the faint shadow produced by starlight but in its exact reflection of who I was becoming through this process of smoothing and shaping.

I put my lips against it. I kissed it fervently. The skin on my lips were sticking to the ice but I kissed it again. I was overjoyed. Then I lay down on my back, my arms and legs outstretched and laughed and laughed, inviting the stars down into my immaculate body. I suppose that is how they found me. When I awakened I was in my bed and my labors covered by a new snow which my mother said had fallen during the early morning.

As I have said, I was eleven when my father came home from the war. He stayed long enough to instruct my mother properly as to my education, in case he would not return again. He spent a good portion of each day polishing the guns he had kept, wrapping them in oiled cloth, hiding them away as if he were not repeating what he had done the day before. He had so meticulously carved out a section of floor under which he stashed his weapons that the trap door was not in any way obvious though he took the precaution of covering it, also, with a rug.

When he was not cleaning his rifles, he agitated about my upbringing. Grateful for the attention he gave to my future, I quickly decided not to mention the violin which I had once when he was in a rage relegated to a hiding place nor that I had always expected to train as a musician. My father decided that I should attend a military academy or study to be a doctor. He believed his honor depended upon it. He asked me if I was reliable? I assured him I was.

Germany was in a morass, he said. He wanted to fight in the north. He wanted to live outdoors. Once he almost hit my mother. It was just before he left. She had broken a jar and the floor was still so sticky from her home made preserves, you could hear the strawberries squeak under his boots as he strode across the room. "This is a swamp," he shouted. Or maybe he said she was a swamp.

I looked at her and understood what he meant. We had been studying equatorial countries in school. I had fantasized a heat so intense that women would melt in it. I could see my mother's breasts sliding down her chest in long milky globules. I saw her hair dissolve into tendrils. I thought of taffy and molasses. Her feet turned into dark, glutinous roots. I looked down at the kitchen floor; it was a dark and rancid pool.

"Make sure this boy gets fresh air," my father shouted. "If he stays in here with you, he will surely get lung disease."

He knew he wouldn't return. And he was right. He died in a border skirmish but there was never any official acknowledgment of his death. The government acted as if he had never existed. I was fourteen when he died. He was lucky he died. Otherwise, he would have ended up in prison with Hitler and his buddies. We were suddenly poor. My father had been right. If I was going to think about being a violinist I might as well run off with the Gypsies.

It is not only that poverty is dreary, it is humiliating. Your crash came in 1929, but we had been in the mire for years. And, of course, your government like every other government was sticking our nose in it. My mother didn't see any of this. She was quite happy among her Dresden dolls and lace antimacassars. She had painted once but then had given it up, wanted me to paint instead. She started to collect sheep. Porcelain sheep. All the artists were painting skulls and blood, apocalypse in red and black, and my mother collected porcelain sheep.

I once dreamed my father was in the trenches with Georg Grosz. My father lay down and took off his pants and Grosz painted Berlin on his ass with the fine point of a bayonet dipped in blood and shit. Then a grenade came over and exploded the painting outward in lightning and the painting repeated itself and repeated itself as the corpses lined up. My father was the perfect canvas for Georg Grosz.

What do you want to know, Daniella? Did I become a doctor? Was I called Herr Doktor? Do I regret my life? I was in and out of the university and medical school for years. It wasn't only the lack of money which made life difficult. My mother got sick. She had diabetes. Sugar stockpiled in her. Then gangrene. Her body began to rot from the inside out. I tried to take care of her but I couldn't bear the stink. The tightly fastened windows were opaque with steam as if they had been fashioned from the thinnest sheets of human skin. My father had said all women are whores. Berlin was a whore. A whore full of whores. I nearly drowned there in its storehouses of syphilitic menstrual blood. I was glad when my mother died. I was free.

You, Daniella, put on your life, the way a woman puts on a dress. Underneath she is essentially the same no matter whether she is wearing a misshapen house dress or is trussed into a corset for the sake of an elegant black silk evening gown. Women think they can change their clothes according to their whims. They have only to go to a shop to become someone else.

You must understand, Daniella, when a man has a series of experiences, they shape him and he grows according to them. Then, at some point someone looks at him, and sees, "He is ready." Until that moment he has not dared to judge the extent of his accomplishment because he has been a man trying to see himself through a periscope. From this angle, he is essentially blind.

In the beginning, his experiences are inchoate and he is not aware that he is being shaped because he can neither feel nor see the shape which is being created. Rather the opposite. He continues to feel himself as undefined, shapeless, lumpish because nothing that he experiences within has a corollary or function without. And vice-versa. Nothing which comes from without seems to duplicate itself within. Thus he is disconnected from cause and effect.

For example, pain doesn't seem directly purposeful. He cannot understand what he is to do with it. Still he realizes he is being exposed to it. There must be a purpose. If he is intelligent, he contemplates this. He holds the pain within himself until he can understand its purpose. He does not try to move away from it; he tries to endure it, to sustain it. After a while, he realizes it is not to have another effect. It is itself.

How, he wonders, would one teach someone who is blind? He imagines himself as blind. When the whip strikes, he thinks, I know it is a whip. What, then, don't I know about it? He feels what happens to his flesh. The whip is sharp but his flesh swells and oozes. His flesh becomes the exact opposite of the whip.

He realizes he only superficially knows what a whip is. There is a deeper form of knowledge. He is to imitate it. Ah. Pain from a whip feels like a whip. He has come to understand this. He then learns how to become the whip. He is whip-like inside. He smarts and he burns. He is alert for the whip is alert. He is fast because the whip is fast. He is cutting because the whip is cutting.

He comes to understand that he must not be different from the world outside. He is being shaped into an image of the world. It will take a long time, too long, he realizes, if he doesn't accelerate the process by trying to meet it.

He feels the whip. And he moves toward it. The whip is the gift of knowledge from the outside upon him and he moves to imitate it within himself. He whips from within. This is not anger or sadism. He is simply following the teaching, he is shaping from the inside what is being shaped from the outside. Soon the two whips meet. They merge. In that moment, he disappears. He has become the whip. Success.

Now he knows how to proceed. He does this with each lesson. He carves away, he burns off, he shaves, he slices, he compresses, he cuts off until the alteration is perfect, he has shaped himself into an exact image of the world.

One day, someone looks at him. Within he may still feel like a shapeless mass looking for a form but the man who sees him sees what he has become. The man takes a coat and puts it upon his shoulder. It fits. He has become the one who fits the coat.

He is not transformed by putting on the coat. He is materialized. The coat is his skin or it is his skeleton. It is both sign and symbol. It is his protection and his badge. He has spent years trying to gain this coat without knowing where he was going but when the coat fits, he understands the process that he has undergone.

Your coat, Daniella, first you didn't earn it, secondly you borrowed it, thirdly it is only utilitarian, and fourth you have been foolish enough to take it off despite the cold. Your behavior is, from beginning to end, foolish and without purpose.

> "Yes, Peter, my behavior, is foolish. But it is not without purpose. Watch me. Yes, I have taken off my coat and now watch me as I take off my boots."

I said each word aloud, Cardinal, so he would hear it.

> "There, I have removed one boot. And now, I am removing the other. And now I am carefully rolling down these black nylon tights. Look, Peter, I am exposing this very white flesh. The flesh of a red haired woman. What do you see, Peter? Do you see the crease where my thighs meet my hips? Do you have a glimpse of black lace underpants? And through them can you glimpse a burn of damp and matted dark red curls?"

"Trust me, Peter, take off your coat."

Chapter 44

You, Daniella, want to return to the past because you want me dead. Let's stay in the present, then. In this little slit of time in which the two of us co-exist, this cozy little universe we have created in which only the two of us exist.

After we part, you will want a bath won't you. You imagine that you can wash me off your immaculately white body. You think it is that simple. A hausfrau's potion; soap and hot water.

You love the dead, don't you? You dig your fingers into the soil and bring the ashes up under your fingernails, rubbing the fragments of bone in the palm of your hand. And all the time, in your mind, you are humming Bach. Out of ashes, one can make soap.

I hear a flute. Do you hear it? Don't look up. Keep your eyes down. Where they belong. Don't look up. The smoke has covered the stars.

The flautist in the tower is skillful. From where he is perched, the platinum notes fly up directly without being soiled. He has found the tower to God.

You want me to say that I am mad. Or depraved.

You, Peter, want me to return to the past because you want me dead. Let's stay in the present, then. In this little slit of time in which the two of us co-exist, this cozy little universe we have created in which only the two of us exist.

After we part, you will want a bath, won't you? You imagine that you can wash me off your immaculately white body. You think it is that simple. A German potion; soap and hot water.

You love the dead, don't you? You dig your fingers into the soil and bring the ashes up under your fingernails, rubbing the fragments of bone in the palm of your hand. And all the time, in your mind, you are humming Bach. Out of ashes, one can make soap.

I hear a flute. Do you hear it? Don't look up. Keep your eyes down. Where they belong. Don't look up. The smoke has covered the stars.

The flautist in the tower is skillful. From where he is perched, the platinum notes fly up directly without being soiled. He has found the tower to God.

You want me to say that I am mad. Or depraved.

I know the words you want to use:
Disgust, nausea, repulsion, contempt,
horror. You say them again and again.
They create vertigo and then you're
drawn down into the vortex. You hold
them lovingly in your hand, you protect
them like a woman running from a firing
squad her entrails in hand. Sausages and
excrement.

You in your black leather boots crafted
so carefully at the heel so as to lift you
out of the cow flops and horse manure.

Yes it's true, each word is a blow. I
calculate where it falls. It macerates the
flesh. I want each word to spatter and
explode. It is what you deserve.

Your past has brought you here. Your
history. Your *volk*.

You feel the compulsion too, don't you.
You can't stop yourself. You repeat each
word. You pretend to turn away but you
echo each phrase. You take it in your
mouth. You smear yourself with it like
a child tarring her body with excrement
while thinking the other one is foul.

You persist. You curse, you batter, you
rage.

You want me to beg, to grovel, to plead
and to crawl.

And all this because you want me to see
you, need me to see you, as you are.

I know the words you want to use:
Disgust, nausea, repulsion, contempt,
horror. You say them again and again.
They create vertigo and then you're
drawn down into the vortex. You hold
them lovingly in your hand, you protect
them like a man running from a firing
squad his entrails in hand. Sausages and
excrement.

You in your black leather boots crafted
so carefully at the heel so as to lift you
out of the cow flops and horse manure.

Yes it's true, each word is a blow. I
calculate where it falls. It macerates the
flesh. I want each word to spatter and
explode. It is what you deserve.

Your past has brought you here. Your
history. Your *volk*.

You feel the compulsion too, don't you.
You can't stop yourself. You repeat each
word. You pretend to turn away but you
echo each phrase. You take it in your
mouth. You smear yourself with it like
a child tarring his body with excrement
while thinking the other one is foul.

You persist. You curse, you batter, you
rage.

You want me to beg, to grovel, to plead
and to crawl.

And all this because you want me to see
you, need me to see you, as you are.

Chapter 45

Why, Peter, have I taken off my boots and my stockings? Maybe it is to prove my ability to endure the cold. But you know what I can bear, you saw it from your perch every day, where Lance, even now, is making music for the birds which have returned. Look. They were not there for you.

Come closer, Peter. Oh, are you afraid? Don't fantasize that I am going to try to seduce you. I want you even closer than that.

You saw nothing from your perch in the tower. You saw without seeing. That's why you were there, isn't it, so that you could gaze up through the smoke and observe the eternal circling of the little yellow stars?

Here is a question for you, Peter: If you are so interested in the dark and immaculate sheen of your polished boots, why have you chosen to live in the shit and stink? Why did you bring me here so you could follow me down?

Yes, you know how the cold feels in your body, but now, come down here from your perch, to see how it feels in my body. This is what you were dying to know.

It stinks here, Peter. Even in the boxcars, the people were alarmed by the stench as they approached the Camp. Even from there, when they had been pressed against each other for days, living and dead, without water or toilets even from there, they could smell it as they approached the Camps.

Come closer. Take it into your nose. It's yours.

You've brought me here. If you didn't repeat yourself so very well I wouldn't have learned—what I have learned—that you are indeed yourself.

I remember when you first appeared in November 1987. How fitting that it was November. Was it on your birthday that you decided to relive your life? It has taken you a year and a half to drag me out of my former life, to shatter my career and my mind, and to bring me here to your place so that we can reenact it all again. So you can return from your heights to this place of mud and shit. Were you lonely for it? Is that why you want my body? You can't live without it, can you?

The commandants of the Camps were always family men. Without the women, they would not have survived. Oh, with very few exceptions—Frau Stangl, whose priest consoled her in the confessional and absolved her Paul of the crimes of Treblinka—the women were their blinders. They baked cookies, and planted flowers in the garden to camouflage the stench. You had no blinders, my dear Peter. How did you survive?

Oh, I begin to feel them—lice. Yes, they must also have lain dormant here waiting for our return. You know, Peter, you can't control lice with a whip or a barbed wire fence. If I have them, they are going to crawl on you. But that's what you need isn't it, to find your body alive, finally, by any means?

When you were speaking to me earlier and repeated my name, again and again "You must understand, Daniella"—I could feel myself shriveling simply from your tone which was so quiet and viciously tender. Is that how I now say your name, Peter? Do I also erase it as I utter it? Am I a good student?

You must understand, Peter, that I feel you in my body. I can remember. I can climb up into your perch and hear the orchestra and the forbidden wild and uncontainable impulses of the Killie Dillies, the Ghetto Swingers. Can you hear that rhythm, Peter? Boogie Woogie. My mother plays Boogie Woogie, Peter. It gets to you, doesn't it. It doesn't move out of the body easily, it stays in the bones. You can hear the rattle. It's skeleton music. Once it gets you, it stays inside. Listen to it without running, Peter. If my mother were here, she could play the keys of your spine.

Where are you running Peter? To your solo unaccompanied violin so you can tighten the strings grinding the peg into the hole tauter and tenser until you disappear in a high unbearable pitch? I can feel your frustration that sound travels so much more slowly than light and that you will never reach the stars on your violin.

So I call you closer. What makes me so brave is my understanding that we will both feel the whip if you use it. Now it is just a matter of endurance, mine and yours, and I believe, though I am a woman, that you have met your match. I can feel you tensing your body, making it steel. I do the opposite. I let it go slack. If I were to use the whip, I would meet steel; you will meet dark pools, oil and water.

Yes, hello, there is your rage. I can feel it. It is like a burning stone. Yes. When a star like our own begins to die, it still glows with intense heat as it becomes a white dwarf then a red dwarf until it is a black dwarf, an inert, cold lump of iron. You are going out, Peter. Even the stars go out.

Yes, there is your loathing. It enters me like poison and I can feel myself dissolve in it. What is it about me you hate? Let me see if I can experience it. This body, yes. Its smells, yes. And the hair, Grosz red, which is thick and clammy like blood. What would happen if you came close? You would feel the ooze. It would draw you down like Charybidis into its stinking center. Don't faint, Peter, your buddies would be humiliated. Stand erect against its gravitational urge.

Watch this, Peter. I am going to piss. Vertigo is the movement of the spheres. Everything spins Peter, everything. Women, they turn you around, they draw you down, don't they Peter, down into dissolution. Particles, planets, black holes spin, all of them. That is why they named the dissolution of the universe, black hole. "A black hole has no hair," John Wheeler said. Astronomers have to have humor to survive what they see. You don't have humor, Peter. Everyone has heard of Jewish humor, but Nazi humor is a contradiction in terms. But the humors, Peter, you know about them, don't you? Blood, phlegm, choler and melancholia or black bile.

Come closer, Peter, take off your pants. Just take off your pants and then squat next to me. We can piss together. You can smell the odor of uric acid rising up warmly into your nostrils. Did your mother keep cats in her hot house? Did it reek?

Are you afraid of losing control? How can you if I am in control? And if you join me, as we are indeed joined by some accident you devised with fate and time, how can you lose?

What I do, you do. What I feel, you feel. What I see, you see. I am pissing on your boots, Peter. I am so sorry; how clumsy of me. You'll have to take them off. And now your coat too. Finally, you'll be rid of that damn coat.

I'll tell you a secret, Peter. There were people, Hitler especially, who believed that people like myself have special powers and that Jews could enter into your very cells. During love making, Peter, did you ever make love or were you too afraid to enter a woman? An invisible and undetectable poison from our bodies enters into your blood stream and can never be filtered out. And then, Peter, you know what happens. The poison, it doesn't kill, it contaminates; It grows inside; It overtakes you; You are helpless to fight it; It begins to run through your veins.

It multiplies. It devours you until you become *IT*.

Any Jew, they said, could do that to you; you Peter, became me.

Come closer. Don't be afraid. You won't die. Look, we didn't die. I'm still alive.

Come even closer, Peter. That's right, even closer. Right inside me. Your body in my body. Your feet in my feet. Your belly in my belly. Your cock in my cunt. Your asshole in my asshole. Your heart in my heart. Your arms in my arms. Your hands in my hands. Your mouth in my mouth. Your eyes in my eyes. Now look!

We're going to move out of here now. Keep your eyes open! We're going to walk barefoot on the wet and icy ground. Feel it. My foot. Watch out! Your foot.

We don't walk too well, tethered as we are to each other. This shuffle of an old man must be humiliating to you. And here you are rounding grotesquely as you are bending to shape yourself to my body. And your belly so soft and distended now because it resembles mine and the shameful roundness of your hips. It's difficult. And your eyes darting, our eyes darting, here and there, fearful that the men in the tower who look so like towers themselves will see us and think we are a rat that wants to be shot.

Shame. You feel it now in your gut, don't you? It drags you down. You slow down. Shame makes you sluggish and clumsy. You want to disappear. You know anyone would want to kill someone as despicable as you have become simply because they could not tolerate your existence in their sight. Be careful, duck away from the view of the guard tower. You hear Lance playing don't you? Bach. Such sounds are not made for your ears; you muddy them.

Oh, I know you're hungry. I can feel it. You're hungry inside yourself and now you feel it. Yes, that growling in your belly, that roar, it's hunger. But, Peter, there is nothing to eat. Nothing but that piece of dung in the corner. Bend down. Yes, you, bend down, eat it. Down, on all fours. It will make you vomit? It better not, if you vomit it up, you'll only have to eat it again. It's for you.

Now, lick the ground with your tongue. Clean it with your lips. Cleanliness is your god, is it not? If we had only taken our boots, Peter, if we had not left them in the barracks, you could also clean them with your tongue.

Come on, Peter, let's cross the field. Slowly, as slowly as they walked because they were too weak to walk faster. The truncheon, there, on your back. It hurts when you're not steel, doesn't it? When you're broken already, it hurts.

But aren't you grateful? You have a body, now. You never had a body. You always wanted a body. You wanted to sing, Peter. No, not those drinking songs which weren't your songs anyway, but your own song, your own particular melody, your own harmony around a note, your own minor key.

And your heart, you wanted to feel a heart, didn't you? Don't be afraid. It will break, but it doesn't matter, hearts do that. It's an explosion like a star breaking open into the universe. It's over in an instant and then the light shines for billions of years.

And your eyes, you finally see where you are going. You finally see the light. Isn't this what the artist you might have been longed for? Light, color, incandescence, luminescence, radiation—stellar light piercing you through my eyes. Lets follow it, let's become one with it.

Don't be afraid, dear Peter. Come with me. No, not in that direction. This way. Toward the furnaces, Peter, just as you suggested. Aren't you cold? Let's get warm. Come, my dear, you know what happens to skin when it burns, how it smells when it crackles, when it melts. Let's burn, Peter. Let's walk into the furnace, Peter. Together.

We were all made in the furnace of stars, Peter. Come back home, my dear one.

Come.

✳ ✳ ✳

Then, Cardinal, there was a violent explosion. The heat was unbearable and the atom we had become was split apart in an eruption of heat and light. I found myself lying on the ground outside the barracks. I had been thrown hundreds of feet into a puddle of mud and melting ice.

Some yards before me, a shadow moved along the barbed wire of the Camp, a darkness in the shape of a man. It moved slowly and evenly but with the wariness of a man without shoes on icy ground. I couldn't move. I watched it slide along the walls of the barracks and then onto the wire again. It darkened the yellow fields of mustard and shrouded the puddles as it passed. It felt as if it took hours for it to make its way along the entire end of the Camp away from the furnaces. Then I saw it stop and hesitate. And then a wind came and began to lift it, a tornado lifting up off the ground, a dark wind in a swirl, swinging a few broken twigs, discarded papers, smears of cigarette butts into its vortex, rising up, and up the broken stairs of the tower which was now blackening and charred with the vertiginous shadow of a man. The storm passed into the tower. A silence fell everywhere, a silence which literally sucked the breath out of me. From the center of it, I heard the maddened shrieks of a violin. Then I thought: "Of course, he has put out his eyes."

Everything went black and I was somewhere in the blackness but without a center that I could call myself. I knew that I was there somewhere but he wasn't there anymore. He couldn't take it, I was thinking. After all that, he couldn't take it. I felt a little bit of glee. What was it that was so difficult for him? Seeing it the way I saw it? Isn't that what he had wanted? Hadn't he set it up? Or was it becoming what he had despised? Wasn't that inevitable? If he didn't know that would happen why had he set it up?

I couldn't see. I didn't know if I would ever see again and yet I felt victorious. I had survived and he hadn't. I had endured the ordeal and he hadn't. The tables were finally turned. Retribution. His tactic from beyond the grave had backfired. Justice had been done. Vindication. Triumph.

I opened my eyes to a greater blackness than I had ever imagined. Nausea overwhelmed me as I felt my skin peeled from me until nothing protected me from the vision that poured into my body. I had heard people speak of double vision and now I had it and could not shut my eyes to anything for every time I tried to look away my eyes opened even further into the dark.

Then I understood. Peter Schmidt had not wanted to come back. He had been happy when death had come for him. Then he had been whirled into my life, a particle spun helplessly through a supercollider. He had not asked for this. Peter's life flashed in front of me. I had never seen it when we had been so close to each other. I had never opened my eyes to it. I hadn't wanted to. No matter what I had claimed, I had refused. I tried to refuse again but this time I couldn't. I opened my eyes to the last year and a half. I saw it from his point of view. I saw it once again from hell. His hell. He had been one of those blond haired boys born into hell. His innocent face had deceived him just as mine had deceived me. Not knowing what else to do or how to do it, he had accepted what came to him and everyone he knew. Instead of paradise, he had gotten the charnel grounds. So be it. There had not been a single moment of beauty in his entire life. He would be strong. There had not been a single free moment. Maybe freedom wasn't important. He had not been given the grace or beauty of the stars. He would not complain. He wouldn't wish his life on anyone. He would not have children. His life in and of itself had no importance. His life belonged to the state. No matter what, he would not kill himself. Instead, he offered his life over. This was his fate. He would carry it with something he called dignity. That's what he had been told it meant to be a man. But sometimes, at the risk of his life, he climbed the stairs to a guard tower where for a moment in the cold and loneliness of the music he loved, he could be alone.

The entire spiral of history descended into the wretched soil like a sheet of flame. Simultaneously, he experienced his life which had no solace in it and also the second briefer life-time he unwillingly spent in mine through which he saw it all again with his eyes open; saw it once more exactly as I was seeing it. So that it was everywhere he looked and coming at him with the crushing speed of the universe turning in on itself. Until he was confronted by heat and intensity which this time, try as he might, he could not bear. It crushed him and then it pulverized him. And finally, grateful, I think, he was no more.

And I, Cardinal, I was no longer innocent. Even in such a moment, I knew that.

Lance found me on the ground. I would have frozen to death if he hadn't found me. I don't remember much except opening my eyes and seeing stars and then fainting again. Lance must have carried me to the car. He said lightning had struck a transformer and a tower went up in flames. He said my clothes were strewn everywhere. He threw out my mother's skirt, the stain would never come out of it. My coat was filthy and ripped in a few places. He couldn't find my boots. He took me to a little hotel, I don't know where, the first one he found outside of Auschwitz. He said he took off our clothes and wrapped us together in a feather quilt while the bath tub was filling with hot water. He said I awakened in the bath tub, that I turned to him without recognizing him and said something he didn't understand:

"Peter Schmidt is dead. May he rest in peace."

V

Return

Chapter 46

May 6, 1990
Dear Cardinal:

I haven't been myself. It's as if I've been living through a prolonged blackout. I didn't think it had been so long since I last wrote. I thought it was a few days. It seems it has been weeks.

Lance proposed that we cancel our trip and return home. Poor Lance. He was confined with an invalid in an unpleasant, dimly lit room in a small town in Poland where he could not speak the language and there was no amusement other than walking the dreary streets. His first thought was to return to Krakow immediately, but he quickly saw my condition and he was concerned that the ride in the cramped Italian Fiat might do me in altogether. Also he had managed to borrow [for a small fee] an electric blanket, which an American relative had brought to a neighbor of the woman who managed the small hotel he had found right outside of Auschwitz. With the help of a down comforter, it kept me warm. And, most importantly, he said later, he had found someone to mend my coat. I was not aware of time passing, but lay buried in the odd warmth of electricity and feathers or floated in a stupor in the hot baths with mineral salts, which Lance insisted I take several time a day.

Lance attended me as he would have someone in a coma. Hypothermia, was part of his diagnosis. So as soon as he had gotten the blankets and installed me in the room, he stripped us both naked and wrapped us together in the comforter, using his body warmth to resuscitate me.

After a few days, I was ready to travel. Lance decided we would go directly to Mittersill in the Austrian Alps where he had the name of an Inn that had been recommended for its privacy and graciousness; it was ideal, he been told, for rest and skiing.

On the way to the Alps, we stopped at a cafe at the outskirts of Vienna where a few tables were set up on a sunny patio on the far side from the road, just across from a lovely park which served as the front lawn of an old Church. Lance suggested that I sit facing the shrubbery at the far table closest to the grass while he went inside to order for us. I agreed because we were both starving and learned that I could steady myself if I held on to things with two hands or braced my elbows on the table and cupped the coffee mug in my palms as I like to do anyway to absorb its warmth. Lance was exquisitely sensitive to the situation and ordered sandwiches and French fries so that

I didn't have to use a fork or knife and be reminded of the fact that no matter what I did, I was suffering tremors which were sometimes moderate and sometimes extreme.

"I didn't mean to leave you alone in Birkenau," he said while we were having the meal. "If I had any idea, I would have stayed with you. I thought you wanted to be alone."

"I wouldn't call what I felt *wanting* exactly." I was trying to explain something to Lance until I saw the dismay on his face. "I had to be alone," I added quickly. "It was a long day. How did you spend it?"

"I couldn't wait in the car so I wandered up the road and came upon a church which, though unheated, was warmer than the outside. From afar, it looked very warm because it was in one of the brilliant fields of mustard and I imagined sunlight shining up out of the flowers. But I wasn't settled into a pew for a snooze for more than a few minutes when parishioners started arriving and within minutes they were observing a Mass."

He stopped speaking abruptly and looked at me hard. "You didn't have the other key to the car with you, did you, Daniella? I locked you out of the car, didn't I? I locked you out in the cold, didn't I?"

"I wouldn't have used the car. I had other work to do, Lance." It was a statement of fact; I was not trying to reassure him falsely.

He pulled his hand out from under mine as if my warmth were an assault to him. "But, I locked you out!"

"Maybe it was a gift." He looked incredulous. "A gift from God, Lance." Embarrassed now, I pressed him about his experience: "Did you stay in the Church, Lance?"

"No. I began dreading the moment at the end of the Mass when everyone holds hands and blesses everyone else and, as I'm not Catholic, the thought of it made me uncomfortable. It was best to leave before my sense of separateness had been interpreted as insult.

"You must have been driven mad by the sound of my flute." Lance continued, forlorn. "I don't know why I felt inclined to play. It was when all the buses and cars had left and I knew no one was there to be offended. I climbed up into one of the guard towers to survey the area. Then I had to play; it was the only offering I could think of making to the dead. There were so many birds, I played to them. From time to time, I thought I saw you and the music was my form of greeting."

"I was relieved by the music," I said. "But what was it you were playing? It was familiar to me but I couldn't place it. It's what you were playing in the little hotel outside of Auschwitz."

"This?" He whistled a few bars. "And this? And this?" He whistled one theme and then another. I knew it and I didn't.

"I was playing some themes from the Magic Flute. When I saw the birds, I assumed they wanted to hear Mozart. Sometimes I played Papageno . . ." by this time he had his flute in his hand and accompanied himself, "but mostly I played the hymns to Isis and Osiris, the forces of light conquering the forces of darkness, wisdom over chaos . . . you know. My prayers, I guess. I didn't know where you were, I didn't know, don't know really, why we were here, so I tried to accompany you as best I could. It was my way of playing the stars for you, bringing them into that little room—I didn't know if you would recover—the doctor was cautious—bringing them into that place. . . . I did my best. . . . but, I locked you out. . . ."

"It was exactly right. You were an instrument. . . . Please, believe me, Lance."

"Why didn't you come and get me before you were overwhelmed?"

"Despite all the fire in all the billions and billions of stars, the universe is exceedingly cold and there is nothing we can do to alter that situation."

"That's why humans stole fire from the gods, Daniella, so they could warm themselves by it."

"I didn't want to change anything. I am concerned about the way humans want to alter the universe. How many variables should we consider before we try to change the world? What's getting snuffed out for the greater good? My research, my curiosity, Lance, what has it led to?" I was wringing my hands. I told myself, silently, "You are wringing your hands, stop it," but I couldn't. Then I was tearing at my hair and told myself, "You are tearing your hair, stop it," but I couldn't.

Lance was looking at me intently, his blue eyes searching my eyes to see if he should be alarmed by the agitation in my voice which I could not control. Only weeks afterwards did he tell me that he did not know if I were still ill or if I had been permanently damaged by the blast, by hypothermia, or by the ordeal of the last weeks. "What's wrong?" he shouted. It was sufficient to bring me to.

"I think I'm shattered. But it's not a bad thing altogether. I only wish it had happened earlier or more gradually. Or better yet, had happened when I was alone at Devil's Peak and you wouldn't have to suffer it with me."

"I am rather relieved it's happening while I am with you because I don't think you are able to take care of yourself." He was smiling now, guardedly.

"I think this is something like what happened to Amanda when she quit working for the Observatory, but I didn't understand it at the time and didn't take care of her."

"It didn't seem as if she wanted to be cared for, she did withdraw quite dramatically from her former life."

"Yes, but she did come to Devil's Peak to be near me."

"Perhaps she came because she saw that you had left The Mountain."

"Have I?"

"Of course, you have."

"I was thinking I am on a sabbatical."

"Leaving was a done deal months ago."

"I didn't know."

"That's true. You couldn't face it."

"But now I'm shattered."

"Maybe now you're ready to put the pieces together in a new way."

"I don't want to learn about the stars anymore Lance. I want the stars to teach me." I waited for Lance to object, to laugh at me.

"That's what music is, Daniella."

"What?"

"The sound of light. That's it. When I play, I listen."

Someone I couldn't see opened the doors of the church from the inside. "I think I let her down."

"That's why, Daniella, I feel so bad that I let you down by leaving you alone in Birkenau."

"But I am alone."

"That isn't true."

"How do you know?"

"Because the waitress is walking toward us with exactly the kind of pastries you love and, unless she's clairvoyant, it must be because someone cares enough to know that you want that particular dark chocolate torte and another Viennese coffee with sugar and whipped cream."

There were no guests at the Inn in Mittersill. Lance asked for and received a room at the far end of the hall away from the stairs on the third floor guaranteeing absolute privacy. He thought I might want to cry again. I was continually surprised by the tears when they came, as they did, at odd times when Lance was away or I was in the shower or as he was reading to me or as I was dressing or as he was waxing the skis we rented or just when we were preparing to take off across the dazzling snow toward a green lake surrounded by a small grove of trees.

"Don't let tears freeze on your face," Lance shouted as he made his way toward me to wipe my eyes and nose, as if I were a child, with the tissues he had stored in his pocket so that I would not have to take off my gloves.

At night, Lance wrapped us up in sleeping bags and skins he had once again enterprisingly borrowed and we slept several nights like TB patients on the private balcony of our little room, breathing in the icy air and the emanations of stars. Each morning I felt restored by the energies of the night fires. You would think it was warmth I was seeking, but it wasn't; I relished the cold and the night.

"The stars are speaking to me again," I said one morning as Lance pulled me into his arms as the old red sun dawned at the edge of the valley. It was not what I intended to say. I had intended to tell him that I had dreamed about my father.

Aram and I were seated cross-legged facing each other on a minuscule traffic island formed of rubble from broken church steeples, stone hands and feet, plump and rounded, cracked and exploded faces of cherubs and gargoyles, bits of columns and balusters, broken walls and granite gorgon wings. He was wearing his army uniform, though I had never seen him in it, and I was wearing the padded, goose down uniform I donned when working on the telescope on The Mountain. I had a laser beam aimed at his eyes in order to keep his attention from wandering to the Porsche racing cars and occasional high speed German tanks which were whirling about us.

"Tell me, Mr. Stanebruch, was there a trial? Tell me the truth."

My father placed his left hand on the blasted eyes of a cherub and raised his right hand as if he were swearing. "Everything was such a hallucination."

"What about now?"

"The hallucination never ends, Your Honor."

"But is there a trial going on now, Mr. Stanebruch?"

"Yes, there is a trial now."

"Where?"

"Where? I can't answer that question, Your Honor. Everywhere. There is no center to the universe."

"Are you certain there is a trial going on now?"

"A trial? Yes. In the past. It is there and it will never end there."

"Do you know the man who is being tried?"

"It is hard to say. But, Your Honor, I can see some things clearly."

"What do you see, Mr. Stanebruch?"

"Well, now, Your honor, I see, that is I testify, that . . . well, your Honor, the Stormfueherer is dead."

"How do you know?"

"Because I heard his last words, Your Honor. When he died, he said, 'Tell them, Aram, tell them that at least I saved the trees.'"

I couldn't speak to Lance about the dream; I had wanted to tell him that my father had relieved me of the obligation to attend his trial. I also wanted him to know that I was taking responsibility for this ordeal but when I began a conversation with him, he stopped me abruptly. "We're both in this together," he said and walked away before I could protest.

When Lance was out, I wandered through the empty Inn trying all the doors. Some were unlocked. Each room was almost exactly alike, the bedspreads were made of the same floral print with huge pink and red roses on a gray background and the windows had the same hand-crocheted lace curtains. I entered each room and sat on the bed trying to imagine how it would be if it were my room and there were my things in the drawer and I had another name and spoke another language. Then I got up and smoothed the bed the way I had seen my grandmother, Shaena Baena do, not because it was rumpled but because she loved to run her hands over silky cloth.

One day when I felt stronger, I went down stairs and wandered through the foyer, the parlor, the ante-rooms, the large kitchen and dining room where we had been asked to make ourselves at home. In one of the rooms, I found books categorized according to languages, German, French, Italian and English. I was not surprised to find an English edition of my little yellow book among them and I opened it to the table of contents to find a hexagram which spoke to my situation. I remembered that Shaena Baena had taught me that eighteen was *Chai* in Hebrew and *Chai* meant life. I needed a little life: I read number eighteen: *Ku* / Work on What Has Been Spoiled [Decay].

> What has been spoiled through man's fault can be made good again through man's work.

I sat down on the edge of the bed and held the book firmly open with both hands. I felt fear as I read it but it was a different kind of fear that didn't make my fingers tremble.

> The conditions embody a demand for removal of the cause. We must not recoil from work and danger.... We must first know the causes of corruption before we do away with them. Then we must see to it that the new way is safely entered upon.

I wanted to go out for dinner. I took a shower and washed my hair. I put on the white angora sweater I had been saving for a special occasion. I used green eye shadow and tied the scarf Lance liked in my hair. He had once given me a necklace from China with lions of pale green jade alternating with lions of gold. I had never expected to wear it on this trip, had taken it only out of love for him. When he came in, I was smiling.

We were seated cozily in a booth in the restaurant looking out the window onto the river and the mountain. Lance ordered champagne. "There is something I have wanted to tell you for months, but I was saving it for the right time." He waited for me to understand how important this was and drew my attention toward him until we were looking into each other's eyes.

"When a Benedictine monk first discovered champagne, Dani, he called out to his brothers, 'Come quickly, we are drinking stars.'"

Chapter 47

Beyond this place where the Word is given and shared, we will find ourselves "outside"—not in communion with the world, but in a profound dissonance. Because who in the world outside will want to listen to the secret message which resounds in our night?

—Jean-Marie Cardinal Lustiger

Dear Cardinal Lustiger:

Please be with me this last time as we go to Dachau, you and I. It's our turn. When Lance and I were there last spring, it was within days of the forty-fourth anniversary of my father's arrival with the first forces of liberation on April 29, 1945. Come with me Jean-Marie Cardinal Lustiger, Your Eminence.

The prescribed time of mourning is almost over. It is only a matter of hours. This letter which I have been writing to you has been my version of saying Kaddish in my own language as Shaena Baena instructed me on her death bed. Please come with me, Aaron.

It would be easy to pretend that everything was completed at Birkenau. But I am no longer naive. We had, have, to go to Dachau. Because of my father, of course. To visit the place of his trial, sentencing and ordeal. What he was unable to escape seeing. To honor him and the life he attempted, afterwards, in the rubble.

Now I must return for myself. When I was at Dachau, something frightened me so, I stopped short of seeing it. Now I must return, I am asking you to go with me.

I waited a long time until I was ready to complete this letter but all this time I have been writing to you for the sake of this moment when we descend together into the very fire, the sacred furnace, the heart of a star, into that point where everything begins and ends, the universe, all life, ourselves. Time gathers itself in and explodes; all possible histories are drawn down into and exploded out of the gravity of this intersection. The brilliant glow of photons begins. Up and down do not exist in the universe. Descent can not be differentiated from elevation. All of space-time converges, diverges, all worlds drawn toward and away from each other like angels dancing on point.

From Munich, Cardinal, we'll drive to Dachau. When we get to a billboard advertising new suburban homes adjacent to the old SS headquarters that now house the secret police, we'll know we're there. At the other end of the Camp is the Karmel, the Convent of Holy Blood, *Heilig Blut*. The sisters have planted a garden on the site of the whorehouse for the SS officers. The chapel is erected where so many priests were tortured. The Star of David atop the Jewish memorial just beyond the North guard tower can be seen over the convent wall. Lance and I stayed here three nights.

We are at the Convent, Cardinal. Come in.

All day, each day, for three days, Lance and I walked through the Camp at Dachau. I saw it through my own eyes as I was free of Peter Schmidt's vision, but without him I would have seen nothing.

No one is innocent any longer. No one is born on the other side of a singularity. After the Concordat between Hitler and the Vatican which lasted throughout the war, it was said, "The bishops cannot fight where Rome concludes Peace."

In 1942, the Pope said, "We are unable to denounce publicly particular atrocities."

When Lance and I came in from the Camp at night, we passed through the gate in the high stone wall and entered the Chapel of Holy Blood where the Sisters with voices of angels, their faces radiant, were singing the Psalms. "For the Jewish dead," they said.

The first night at Dachau, I dreamed I was visiting a concentration camp. In the dream, there were places I was prohibited to go.

The second night, I awakened from a dream, strange sounds issuing from my mouth. Four words were on my lips in a foreign tongue. Holy words. Syllables which burned. *Vet- Shechinat Hashem Hagadol Be-emptzah*. The Holy Name is in the Center. There followed four other words and they were mute like ash.

The third night, I dreamed I held something triangular in my hand which very closely resembled the leather pouch of keys the Sisters had given us. Keys which opened the gate to the convent, the gate into the courtyard and the door to our room. Just before she died, Amanda Cartwright had given me a gift of a medicine bundle. It was a little blue suede pouch, as blue as the tiles of the Ishtar Gate. She had embroidered it herself. Triangular in shape, it was an exact duplicate of the leather key case which the sisters had given us. Not knowing where else to put it, I had slipped the key from the cemetery at Lublin into this pouch. It was unclear whether I was instructed to bury the blue pouch or the keys at the base of a tree in the courtyard of the convent.

In the dream, I understood that it was necessary to gather up holiness and bury it in the center, in the heart of this sanctuary. I was told that what rises up must descend. Prayers must be answered. A new path up and a new path down must be carved out.

On the last day at the Camps, I was seated in front of a furnace that was removed from the all the others, so I was alone. I was meditating. The oven door was open. From behind me the light of the afternoon sun entered and illuminated the bricks which began to gleam in tones of russet, gold and black. The bricks blazed as if they were the walls of a city illuminated by the setting sun. I had lit a candle before the furnace and the very white flame of the candle blended with the ruddy rays of sunlight, each illuminating each other. For a split second, the light blinded me and it was beautiful. I remembered with a shudder what Richard Grossinger had written in his book, *The Night Sky*, about the stars: "Our deepest fears may be evasions of beauty."

The bricks within the oven also blazed in this extraordinary light and I had to close my eyes. When I opened them, I saw that the bricks were darkened in a few places by charcoal markings—Hebrew letters. As if someone in a death agony had raised a hand to trace the last letters of flame upon the wall. As I stared at the writing, it was as if I were looking upon an ancient city inside the furnace and reading the writing on the wall there. I reached within the furnace and traced the letters on the old bricks, then copied the letters in the oven as best I could onto a piece of paper. In that moment, I knew, without any doubt, that the name of the city that lay at the tips of my fingers was Babylon.

Immediately I showed the letters I had copied to one of the sisters. She recognized them as the first letters of four words that are so familiar that she could find the passage for me in the Book of Daniel in the Old Testament. She said a disembodied hand had written the words on the wall of the banquet room of King Belshazzar of Babylon the son of Nebuchadnezzar and only Daniel who understood dreams and visions, only Daniel of all the king's magicians, astrologers, sorcerers, Chaldeans and astronomers, could interpret the text:
MENE MENE TEKEL UPHARSIN

These were four of the words of my dream. I said nothing to her.

This is something of what I know about Babylon. Everything converged in Babylon: The gods and the stars were one. Though Daniel, my namesake, was brought to Babylon as a slave by Nebuchadnezzar, he soon became the supreme adviser to the kings. Two ways of knowing converged in Daniel when he ascended the ziggurat each night; the way of God and the way of stars and maybe they are the same. King Darius the Mede who conquered Babylon ordered Daniel cast to the lions when Daniel disregarded his prohibition and kneeled to pray to his own God, but Daniel was not devoured. Earlier in Babylon, Daniel's three Jewish companions were thrown into a furnace and were not consumed. Shadrach, Meshach, and Abednego.

It was Nebuchadnezzar who built a processional way of blue tiles ornamented with 120 lions in glazed brick relief, gold and white upon a blue ground. In East Berlin, I went through this blue wall and found myself in a procession of lions, like those which come to me in my dreams, Your Eminence. Another world opened at my feet and I descended into it. The processional way ran through the massive Ishtar Gate along the street known in Babylonian as *Aibur-shabu*, "the enemy shall never pass," to the holy of holies, the Ziggurat where the priests studied the stars.

Astronomy began in Babylon. The Magi exited from Babylon when they were following the star. Daniel had instructed them, before he died, to watch for this star. He did not know how many generations they would have to wait. But Daniel could see that it was coming and they were to follow this star to the new light. What Daniel didn't know was how quickly some of those charged with carrying the light would put it out.

If I had been one of the astronomers of Babylon, I would have spent my life on the highest terrace of the Ziggurat watching the stars. I would have ascended the Ziggurat each night and I would not have distinguished the observations of science from the observations of prayer.

All life began in a star. Everything, the entire universe, began in those furnaces.

I sat for hours before the furnaces where the dead wearing little yellow stars had disappeared. There were those, Cardinal, like Edith Stein, who believed they were walking into their lives. The church says those who died in the furnaces were a holocaust. A sacred offering. Does the Church mean that these six million have become light? Do they redeem us? Is this the end then?

After Ravensbruck, I became a mathematician. I started counting the number of dead the way I used to count the stars in the Andromeda Galaxy. In Maidanek I sat in a mass grave, counting. There, 18,000 of our people were killed in one day. Paul Dirac said, "Find the mathematics first, and think what it means afterwards." I said, "Never again. However the Nazis came to be must never happen again."

Bruno said the universe was infinite. He said there were worlds within worlds. He would not recant before the Church. He said, "I await your sentence with less fear than you pass it. The time will come when you will see what I see."

The morning of the day we left Dachau, we were invited to an audience with one of the Sisters who speaks English. She asked us, "What have you seen?"

I didn't know how to begin. I said the names: Ravensbruck. Buchenwald. The Warsaw Ghetto. Treblinka. Sobibor. Maidanek. Matthausen. Auschwitz. Birkenau. Dachau. She repeated the names as if she were saying a rosary. Then the three of us said them together.

I said, "Sister, I must tell you my dreams. Last night, I dreamed I was to bury a triangular pouch, either your key case or the medicine bundle that I have been carrying since I arrived here, at the foot of a tree in the courtyard. The medicine bundle was given to me by my friend, Amanda, who died after teaching me that I didn't know anything at all about the stars. As I buried it, I was to say four words taught to me in a second dream: *Vet-Shechinat Hashem Hagadol Be-emptzah*. The Holy Name is in the Center."

Here are broken pieces of stars, Cardinal: A lavender triangle for the homosexuals. A red triangle for the political prisoners. A green triangle for the criminal prisoners. And the two yellow triangles that the Jews wore required to wear that form a six pointed star. Earth and heaven moving into each other in the manner of the union of the branches of the Cross.

The Sister asked me to show her the pouch. I tell you, Cardinal, I was afraid. After everything I had seen, I was still able to be afraid. But I am more afraid to tell you this. After all, you are a Cardinal or you may be Pope. Millions of witches were burned at the stake for less than this. Kepler's mother was tried as a witch. I have no idea what you are thinking. I do not want to endanger the Sisters, but I am compelled to tell the entire story.

I laid the medicine bundle on the table and next to it I placed the pouch of keys. The medicine bundle had a star embroidered on it. The Sister picked it up as if it were something precious, then she gave it back to me. I opened it. Inside there was a ball of lapis-lazuli. She said, "This is the sky, this is heaven." There was a crystal inside. In truth, Cardinal, I had not looked inside the pouch before. She said, "This is clarity. This is an eye." There was a gold heart. She said, "I know the heart." There was the tooth of a mountain lion whose territory is Devil's Peak. She said, "I know this fire." There was a six pointed gold star. The Sister said, "We know this star."

Last, I took out the key. "A priest in Lublin gave me this key to the Jewish cemetery," I said. She said, "As you are leaving, I will, if you wish, caretake these dead in the sanctuary of my heart." I couldn't speak. She took the key and put it on the key ring that hung at her belt. "This is your key because it belongs to your people," she added. "but, I will keep it until you return."

There is a point. It breaks apart. It explodes. Then it gathers itself again.

I give you these broken pieces. A furnace with a procession of little yellow stars. A bomb in the shape of a star.

My father would have happily put out his eyes when he saw the furnaces of Dachau if he had not had to attend those who were not consumed. My mother wished she had gone blind when she saw that star explode.

I think my grandmother has become a star. The gods lifted her up as they did in the old days and made her a permanent light. The laws articulated at the Observatory on The Mountain are not The Law.

Each night at Dachau, Lance and I made desperate love under a crucifix in one of the little monk beds.

A swastika was a wheel of life, was the eternal return, but now it is a broken cross. A hakenkrist.

Shortly after the new light was born, it expanded for centuries like a supernova devouring all the surrounding light before it also went out.

I went into the convent courtyard by myself in the very early morning. In the dream, a voice had said, "The light which rises up will come down; the light which comes down, rises." I didn't have a trowel, but I had spoon and I dug a hole under the tree with the spoon. It took a long time. I am afraid I didn't bury it deeply enough. I was afraid to find ashes in the earth. Now, I am afraid that something will uncover what I buried there.

The Sister asked, "Show me the place where you were instructed to bury this pouch, so I can pray there each day."

There are mysteries which we can not encompass. If we are fortunate they break our hearts.

In the beginning, a star. A point of light. An explosion. Take these broken pieces, Your Eminence. A mind exploding and traveling faster than light in all directions at once. We are the people of the star. A star appears and we follow it for we recognize the star from which we emerged. It is our origin. At the end, we are sent back into the furnace of stars.

When Shadrach, Meshach and Abednego, wouldn't worship his gods, Nebuchadnezzar, the Babylonian king had a furnace heated seven times hotter than usual and ordered the three men into it. The furnace was so hot that the flames of the fire killed the soldiers who took up Shadrach, Meshach and Abednego.

The Hydrogen bomb, the star exploded at Eniwetok with an energy of 10.4 million tons TNT equivalent, was a thousand times more violent than the little star my mother saw go out at Trinity.

Once there were so many dead in Auschwitz that the furnaces were ordered heated many times hotter than usual and then the crematorium itself caught fire.

Shadrach, Meshach and Abednego were in the furnace when there appeared a fourth. What does it mean to be thrown into the furnace and not be consumed?

There are furnaces from which no light can ever issue. The entire universe could die in such a furnace. Everything could be snuffed out.

At the furnace where I was seated, the light from the sun crossed the light of the candle. The beauty was more awful than I could bear. I wanted to faint away, but I had fainted away too many times arriving at this moment. I had to bear this light.

Some say we have come to an end of time. That a star rose and is setting. That we followed it and didn't follow it. That it was born and that it died. That it exploded and devoured us. That we learned the secret of its light and we made a bomb. That it is the fire that does not consume. That we follow the stars but we do not follow the stars.

The light from the stars does not appear in telescopes. When I and my colleagues ascend The Mountain, we do not know the god we serve.

In truth, Cardinal, I don't know the language of the stars. Not one of us knows that language any longer. When we try to translate the language of the stars into our own language, the wisdom of the stars go out.

At the foot of the tree, the Sister, Lance and myself, said prayers in three languages. I chanted the words I had not been able to remember after I dreamed them.

I walk outside, Cardinal. I climb the stairs behind this house. I spend the night with my eyes open like a priest on a ziggurat. When there is no moon, I see all the stars which can be seen with a naked eye. That is what I hope for, Cardinal: A naked eye. I have been working my entire life to reach this understanding.

Sometimes I am mad. But no more than anyone else.

I take a small telescope and look up at the sky. I look at Andromeda because it is the first world outside our world. I look at her gold and silver hair.

I want the answers to questions. I want to know what people thought when they first saw the stars. I want to know how they learned the stars were God. I want to know if they read the braille of light on their bodies.

At night, I lie naked under the sky and pray that I will be pierced with the light of stars. Teach me, I pray.

It is more than I can comprehend.

I want to say it all again: I walked past the lions and through a gate. It was the color of sky. The gate belonged to Ishtar, Lady of Stars. My name sake, Daniel, walked through that gate each day. He could tell dreams. He could see when others were blind.

The Germans stole this gate. They placed the gate and the processional wall within museum walls in a walled city from which it is impossible to see the stars. When you go through this gate now, you do not go through the gate.

There is another walled city in a German town called Dachau. When I went through that gate, I saw the handwriting on the wall.

There are furnaces which snuff out all the light and furnaces from which worlds are born. A supernova is a great light which eats the light and a black hole is a furnace which eats all the light.

It was from that place Babylon that they followed the star that appeared in the heavens. In that place, they calculated the cycles of the planet Ishtar, and they recognized that the stars were gods. They followed the star because they were following God.

When I was in Dachau, I saw Ishtar, the morning star, rise silver as a flute over the Star of David along the black stone walls of Dachau.

We must not put out the Light.

I have sinned. I engaged in research without considering the questions I was asking, without considering the uses which might be made of the knowledge. Without considering history.
   Forgive me, Father.

I thought I could separate myself from the world. I thought I could be objective. I thought I could learn the exact nature of a star. I thought I could learn to duplicate the process of light. I thought we could remake the world.

Forgive me Father.

I thought I had a right to be innocent. I thought I had a right to know anything and everything. I searched out the date your mother was sent into the mouth of the star.
   Forgive me, Father.

I was sitting before a furnace. Letters of flame appeared in the furnace. The handwriting on the wall. A disembodied hand. Words heard in a dream. A warning:

MENE MENE TEKEL UPH ARSIN
Our days are numbered. Our time is brought to an end.
We have been weighed on the scales and found wanting.
Our kingdom is divided and given away.

When I was broken beyond healing, I sat before a furnace. The light fell in such a way that the door became a temple and the beauty of it was unbearable. I tried to close my eyes but I had to read the handwriting on the wall.

The days of our reign are numbered. Our time is brought to an end.

I have gathered these fragments for you.

In the beginning, I hoped for something from you: Understanding. But as I wrote, I began to want to bring you something: Understanding.

The understanding we have is not sufficient.

We are weighed in the balance and found wanting.

Forgive us, Father.

Your Eminence, Kaddish is a prayer for peace which acknowledges and praises God. This praise, it is said, elevates the souls of the dead and helps all—the broken, the wise, the lost and the righteous—to ascend from one level to the next.

Come with me, Aaron. Let us mount the stairs of the ziggurat together as we did in the old days which we have both forgotten. I ask you, Cardinal, to join me. Please, Your Eminence, let us say Kaddish for our dead.

Yitgadal veyitkadash, shemei raba bealma divera chireutei, veyamlich malchutei bechayeichon uveyomeichon uvechayei dechol beit Yisrael, baagala uvizeman kariv, veimru: amein.

Yehei shemei raba mevarach lealam ulelalmei almaya.

Yitbarach veyishtabach, veyitpaar veyitromam veyitnasei, veyithadar veyitaleh vey-ithalal shemei dekudesha, berich hu, leeila min kol birechata veshirata, tushbechata venechemata, daarmiran bealma, veimeru: amein.

Yehei shelama raba min shemaya vechayim aleinu veal kol Yisrael veimeru: amein.

Oseh shalom bimeromav, hu yaaseh shalom aleinu veal kol Yisrael, veimeru: amein.

May the Great Name whose Desire gave birth
to the universe Resound through the Creation
Now.
May this Great Presence rule your life and
your day and all lives of our World.
And say Yes, Amen.

Throughout all Space, Bless, Bless this Great Name,
Throughout all Time.

Though we bless, we praise, beautify,
we offer up your name,
Name That is Holy, Blessed One,
still you remain beyond the reach of our praise, our song,
beyond the reach of all consolation. Beyond! Beyond!
And say, Yes, Amen.

Let God's Name give birth to Great Peace and Life
for us and all people.
And say, Yes, Amen.

The One who has given a universe of Peace
gives peace to us, to All that is Israel,
And say, Yes, Amen.*

---

* This version of the Kaddish was translated by poet Peter Levitt and Rabbi Don Singer. It was first used publicly at a ten day vigil by the Order of Peacemakers at Auschwitz, November 1996. on that occasion, the Nuns at Auschwitz joined in the saying of the Kaddish.

Biographical Note

Deena Metzger is a poet, novelist, essayist, storyteller, teacher, healer and medicine woman who has taught and counseled for over forty years. She is the author of many books, including most recently, *From Grief into Vision: A Council* (Hand to Hand, 2007); *Doors: A fiction for Jazz Horn* (Red Hen Press, 2005); *The Other Hand* (Red Hen Press, 2020); and T*ree: Essays and Pieces* (North Atlantic Books, 1997).